# Notorious

ALSO BY MICHELE MARTINEZ

**Most Wanted**
**The Finishing School**
**Cover-up**

# Notorious

## Michele Martinez

*wm*

WILLIAM MORROW

*An Imprint of* HarperCollins*Publishers*

NOTORIOUS. Copyright © 2008 by Michele Rebecca Martinez Campbell. All rights reserved. Printed in the United States of America. No part of this book may be used or reproduced in any manner whatsoever without written permission except in the case of brief quotations embodied in critical articles and reviews. For information address HarperCollins Publishers, 10 East 53rd Street, New York, NY 10022.

HarperCollins books may be purchased for educational, business, or sales promotional use. For information please write: Special Markets Department, HarperCollins Publishers, 10 East 53rd Street, New York, NY 10022.

FIRST EDITION

*Designed by Susan Walsh*

Library of Congress Cataloging-in-Publication Data has been applied for.

ISBN 978-0-06-089902-8

08 09 10 11 12   OV/RRD   10 9 8 7 6 5 4 3 2 1

*For Jack and Will,*
*who make my life beautiful*

# Acknowledgments

I could not have completed this book without the support and encouragement of some wonderful people.

I'm grateful to my husband and my kids for always being proud of me and never complaining about the time my work takes away from them.

I'm very lucky to have Meg Ruley as my agent. She and the great folks at Jane Rotrosen Agency are always there for me and do a huge amount to support my work. I'm also extremely fortunate in my editor, Carolyn Marino, and my publicist, Dee Dee DeBartlo, both of whom are superb at what they do and always believe in me and my work.

Hugs to my blog sisters at The Lipstick Chronicles (Nancy Martin, Harley Jane Kozak, Sarah Strohmeyer, Elaine Viets, and Kathy Reschini Sweeney) for being the best writer's support group a girl ever had.

# Notorious

# 1

The man Melanie Vargas was talking to would die violently in a matter of minutes. But in the here and now, he was so very alive as they debated the handling of a case that she couldn't have imagined it.

"You need to ask the judge to put off the trial," Lester Poe insisted. "The request has to come from the prosecution. If I ask, we might as well call a press conference right now and tell the world my client's ready to snitch."

They stood in the grand plaza outside the federal courthouse in New York City. It was an eighty-degree afternoon in March, and the unseasonable heat blazing down from the bright white sky added to Melanie's anxiety. She was a young prosecutor, respected in courthouse circles but unknown outside of them. Lester Poe was the most famous criminal lawyer in America and had been for thirty years. With his trademark shoulder-length white hair and craggy, handsome features, he was highly recognizable. Several people walking by had already turned to stare. Melanie didn't like talking about such a dangerous subject out in the open like this.

"Let's keep our voices down," she warned.

Lester was enough on edge himself to accede to her suggestion, taking papers from his briefcase with studied nonchalance, as if he was consulting with her about them. The mere fact that they were seen talking shouldn't arouse any suspicions. They were adversaries on a celebrated case, scheduled for trial in little more than a week's time. Nevertheless, it paid to be careful.

"You're right," Lester said in a low tone. "You may want Atari locked up, but other people want him dead."

Atari Briggs, Lester's client, was named for the video games his gangsta daddy had loved to play, and their magic had rubbed off on him. He'd worked every heroin spot in East New York and rained down murder and mayhem on his enemies, then retired at twenty and turned his street cred to gold in the recording studio. On the same day that Atari's sixth CD went triple platinum, DEA arrested him for a murder he'd ordered ten years earlier.

"What's your client got to tell me that's worth killing him over?" Melanie asked. "Does he plan to finger somebody else for the murder he's charged with?"

"If all I had for you was a lousy drug murder, honey, I wouldn't keep you from your tuna fish sandwich."

She smiled. "You take a pretty bleak view of my lunch situation."

"I know what the government pays you," he said, smiling back. "What I'm about to give you, you can take to the bank. My client can give up Gamal Abdullah."

"The terrorist?"

"Call him what you will, but we're not talking about some lowlife in a suicide vest. Abdullah's a major player internationally."

"I know exactly who he is. That's why I find it hard to believe that a rap artist has the goods on him. This isn't a ploy to throw me off my trial prep, is it, Lester?"

He looked genuinely hurt. "Darling, would I scam you?"

"You're smart enough to try, anyway."

"Maybe with somebody else, but never with you."

Lester's eyes lingered on her face. They were stormy gray under dark brows, and he was famous for mesmerizing juries with them.

"Okay, I'll bite," she said, all business. "What does your client want to tell me?"

"About six months ago, Gamal Abdullah used Atari's yacht to meet with some of the biggest drug kingpins in the United States."

"Meet about what?"

"A major supply agreement. Afghan heroin, to be exact, to the tune of a hundred million bucks a week, with the proceeds going straight back to Taliban-associated warlords in Afghanistan."

"Your client witnessed this meeting?"

"Not only witnessed, he filmed it. His boat has a state-of-the-art surveillance system. I haven't seen the DVD yet, but from what I understand, it's enough to persuade any jury. You'll get Abdullah dead to rights, along with just about every other major player in domestic narcotics in the whole damn country."

"Where's this DVD now?"

"In a safe place. We can get it for you, but in order to avoid arousing suspicion, that may take time."

"And I'm supposed to ask for the delay in the meantime, with no proof?"

"You don't trust me enough to do that?"

"You, I trust, but your client? Uh-uh."

"Maybe a showing of good faith would help. How about if I give you a significant lead for free, no strings attached? You can check it out and see if I'm being truthful. If you're satisfied, ask for the delay by the end of the week."

"All right."

"Here it is, then, straight from my client's mouth an hour ago. Gamal Abdullah moves in and out of Western Europe using various aliases. The current one is Sebastien Calais. As of a few days ago, he was in Spain, first in Madrid, then in a town in the south called Ronda, traveling under that name."

"That's it?"

"Yes."

"Okay, got it. I'll have it checked out right away."

"And, Melanie, secrecy is key here."

"I understand."

"No, you don't; you can't possibly understand the full implications," he said, his voice urgent. "I don't want to alarm you, but some very dangerous people would go to great lengths to prevent this cooperation from happening. And beyond that, I don't trust the phone lines in my office. I think they're bugged. That may sound crazy to somebody your age, but I was bugged in the sixties, in the South, when I was doing civil rights work. I know the signs."

"Lester, are you serious? What are you doing about it?"

"I'm taking care of it. I have a company coming in to sweep. The bug may have to do with something separate and apart from the Briggs case, but in any event, the point is, you and I *cannot* discuss this over the phone."

Lester was watching the park across the street as he spoke, his expression anxious.

"I promise," she said. On an impulse, she reached out and squeezed his hand. "Please, be careful."

He turned his gray eyes back on her. "That's very sweet. You know, I can think of something that would make me feel better."

She laughed. "Don't start."

"Why not? We had a great time when I took you out last summer, didn't we?"

"That was business. You were trying to recruit me. But now we're adversaries on a case. Seeing each other socially isn't—well, it's not a good idea."

"When the case is over, then. I'll take you to Daniel, get us a great table. We'll order the tasting menu and a bottle of Margaux."

Lester was a lot older than Melanie, but that didn't make him any less madly attractive. Her real problem with dating was that she was still hung up on the last guy. She had to get over Dan O'Reilly sooner or later. Why not sooner?

"When the case is over. It's a date," she said.

They said their good-byes, and Lester dashed across the street toward his silver Maserati. As she started back to the courthouse, Melanie noticed a man in a dark jacket walking his dog. The dog was sniffing a parking meter, but the man's eyes were on Lester, blazing with such intensity that it caught her attention. Melanie stopped to watch him.

Lester was at the door of his car now, pulling keys from the pocket of his charcoal-gray suit. As he lifted the key toward the lock, the man with the dog held up his cell phone and pointed it at the Maserati. Melanie had seen enough Homeland Security training videos to recognize the gesture for what it was. The hair on the back of her neck stood up.

"Hey!" she yelled, but the man didn't look up. He was focused on his phone, checking which button to push.

"Lester!" she shouted at the top of her lungs. "Get away from the car! Get away from the car!"

She ran toward him, screaming, and the force of the blast knocked her back off her feet.

## 2

The world erupted in fire and blood. Melanie's head hit the rough cement of the sidewalk, and she cried out in pain. All around her, pieces of flaming metal rained down. She was choking on thick smoke. She rolled over and threw her arms over her head, feeling the wetness there. She was bleeding, but the blood she saw all around wasn't her own. Lester! Lester was dead. She closed her eyes for what felt like a long time, not believing this was really happening, thinking she could wish it away if she tried hard. Sirens blared from every direction. Fire? Police?

The man with the dog! She needed to tell them about him.

Melanie struggled to her knees, dizzy and nauseous. She didn't know how much time had passed. Strong hands grabbed her under the arms and pulled her up.

"You need a doctor, miss?" the cop shouted over the din of sirens. Two enormous fire trucks had screeched to a stop mere feet from her. Men were jumping off, running and shouting, throwing things down off the truck.

Melanie fought to stay upright. Her legs were shaking so badly that her knees nearly buckled.

"It was a bomb!" she shouted, her voice shaking, too. "I saw the guy detonate it."

The cop was very young. His eyes widened at her words. "You're sure?"

"Absolutely. He detonated it with a cell phone."

"You see this man now? Look around. Look everywhere!"

Black smoke poured off the flaming wreck of the Maserati. Melanie's eyes were stinging and tearing from it. The fire extinguishers made a terrible hissing sound as they spurted out their foam.

She squinted, peering through the dense blanket of smoke. "I can't see!"

"Try!"

Melanie staggered down the block toward where the man had been. She turned first one way, then the other, ignoring the throbbing pain in her head. He wasn't there. She couldn't see him. He was gone, gone, gone.

"He's gone!" she cried, her voice a forlorn wail.

The cop whipped out a notepad. "Physical description?"

"Male," she said, trying to get her breathing under control. "Thirties. Medium-dark complexion. Middle Eastern or Hispanic. Dark hair, black jacket, slender build, maybe five eight, five nine. He had a dog on a leash. The dog was brown, medium sized. A mutt, it looked like. It was a prop. The dog was just a prop to make the guy blend in. I realize that now. I bet it didn't even belong to him."

Melanie put her hand to the back of her head. It came away red. She wanted to cry. Not for herself, she wanted to cry for Lester.

"Did you see the victims?" the cop asked, scribbling notes furiously. "Any idea how many people were near that car when it blew up?"

"One victim. Lester Poe, the lawyer. Do you know who he is?"

"No. Should I?"

This cop looked like a teenager, with big ears and baby fat. He was doing a fine job, but he seemed nervous. Her opposing counsel had just been assassinated in an important federal case. She needed to put her personal feelings aside and give some guidance to this rookie beat cop. She needed to take charge.

"Officer Ruiz," she said, reading his name tag. "I should have told you up front. I'm a federal prosecutor. What you see here is a federal crime. Mr. Poe was murdered because of a case he's working on. Take the description I gave you and put it out over the radio. Do it now. If you can grab this guy, you'll be a big hero with the FBI."

He looked at her for long enough to realize that she was telling the truth. "Will do. Yes, ma'am," he said, and ran back to his car.

The Atari Briggs case was big and splashy enough to warrant assigning the two top prosecutors in the Major Crimes Unit—Melanie, who was the deputy chief, and her boss, Susan Charlton, the chief. Susan was the first person Melanie called.

"Where are you?" Susan demanded, her voice riddled with anxiety. "We're all locked down in here. There was a bombing outside the courthouse."

"I know, I'm right there. I was in it! They blew up Lester's car. He's dead. Oh my God, he's dead!"

"Lester Poe?"

"He was hit! Assassinated. Call the FBI!"

"I just turned on the TV. I think I see you. Yes, it's definitely you. You're on New York One. It looks like—is that . . . Mel, is that blood on your clothes? Are you okay?"

There were a bunch of television news vans on the block already.

A camera pointed directly at her. She'd felt the bright light on her face but assumed it belonged to a fire truck.

Melanie turned her back on the camera and walked fast in the opposite direction. "I'm fine. Susan, did you hear what I said?"

"Somebody killed Lester."

"Yes. With a car bomb. I saw it happen. Lester and I were standing in front of the courthouse talking. He'd just told me that Atari Briggs wants to cooperate, that he has national security information, stuff I can't discuss over the phone. Then this man with a dog detonated the bomb. Right in front of my eyes. I tried to warn Lester, but it was too late!"

There was silence on the line.

"Susan, are you there?"

"Yeah, I just—I can't believe it. What does this mean for our trial?"

"Who cares about the trial? Lester Poe is dead, and I think they killed him to stop the cooperation!"

Thank God Melanie had pushed Lester for details. She already knew a lot. She prayed that it would be enough to work with, enough to pressure Atari Briggs to flip anyway. Lester Poe had died trying to bring that information to light.

"You said you saw the bomber?" Susan asked.

"I saw everything." Melanie's voice caught in her throat. "Susan, I saw Lester blown apart. I mean, chunks of him landed near me. I couldn't even tell what it was! Susan, I cared about him. He was—he was my friend." She started breathing hard again, hyperventilating almost.

"Okay, okay. Come back to the office, babe. Sam Estes keeps a bottle of bourbon in his desk. I'll have a shot waiting for you. It'll calm you down. And I'm calling the FBI right now. We can't leave this to the beat cops. I'll get a good crime scene team out there right away."

"Yes, good, do that. I'll stay here and wait for them to show."

"No! You come back here."

"Susan, no. I'm an eyewitness. I can do more here. The crime scene guys might need to interview me."

"I want you protected. You're not safe on the street."

The cops had cordoned off a large area around the blackened hulk of the Maserati. All the big firemen were blocking Melanie's view, but she could see that the smoke had stopped, and they were spreading sheets over the remains piled up in various places along the street.

"It's fine. The fire's out," Melanie said, choking back a gag.

"Mel, where's your head? You saw the bomber's face. If this was really an assassination, and you're an eyewitness, you're in danger."

3

Everybody needed to interview Melanie—the FBI, the NYPD, the DEA agents running the Atari Briggs drug murder case. Susan Charlton's corner office was crowded with cops and agents, all buzzing around talking on their Nextels, trying to catch leads. A car bombing in broad daylight in a key Manhattan location, possibly terrorism related—this was the biggest thing to come down the pike in years. Susan's phone was ringing off the hook with calls from the press, but the Front Office had ordered a total information blackout. Decisions about what explanation to put out to the public would be made at the highest levels, in consultation with the FBI, Homeland Security, and intelligence operatives. If it got out there that Gamal Abdullah was involved and that law enforcement knew it, he and his associates would be somewhere on the Afghan-Pakistan border by tomorrow. If they weren't already.

Melanie was doing her best to focus on her little piece of the puzzle and give detailed answers about what she'd witnessed, but her mind was still reeling in the aftermath. She couldn't believe that the glamorous, vital man she'd been talking to an hour ago was now in pieces in a body bag. Part of her wanted to be out there bearing witness and tracking the killer. She'd followed Susan's orders, however, and left before the crime scene team arrived. In the ladies' room, she applied pressure to the cut on the back of her head until the bleeding stopped. The cut was superficial. She'd already washed away the blood and downed some Advil, followed by the shot of bourbon that Susan pressed on her, but Melanie knew that an ugly black cloud of loss was waiting to pounce the second she was alone.

Melanie now sat in front of Susan's desk talking to a whippet-thin FBI guy with short gray hair—Group Supervisor Rick Lynch, head of the Joint Terrorism Task Force and condescending as hell. The Bureau was taking this very seriously. Lynch was a heavy hitter, not somebody who normally deigned to conduct witness interviews himself, but the name Gamal Abdullah had brought him running. Unfortunately, his interview skills were rusty enough that he was doing a good job of turning an ace federal prosecutor into a recalcitrant witness.

"I'm gonna ask you again," Lynch said, rubbing his eyes like Melanie was giving him a headache instead of the other way around. "What did the man in the dark jacket do after you and the victim moved away down the block?"

"I told you. I wasn't watching him then."

"Did he have the cell phone out at that point?"

"I don't know. Like I said before, the first time I noticed the cell phone was when he held it up and pointed it at the car. You keep asking me the same questions."

"You have an appointment or something?" Lynch snapped. "We're mobilizing a lot of men to work this investigation, moving them all over the world as you and I sit here, all on your say-so. I've got thirty men in New York alone looking for a man in a dark jacket with a brown dog. If what you saw was just some citizen holding up his phone to get better reception—"

"I know what I saw! That man was there for us. He waited until Lester got right up next to the car. Then he pushed a button, and boom, the car blew up. It wasn't a coincidence. It wasn't my imagination."

"You're saying this man was standing there waiting for you and neither of you noticed?"

"I know!" she wailed, on the verge of tears. "Incredibly, incredibly stupid. And Lester's dead because of it."

"Hey, hey, hey," Susan piped in. "This is not your fault, Melanie. It's the fault of the asshole with the bomb. We're gonna get him, and we're gonna make him pay. Rick, stop giving her a hard time, you hear me? This isn't some dope dealer you're interrogating. Mel is my deputy chief. If she says something, you take it as gospel or you get the fuck out of my office."

Susan Charlton was an Olympic silver medalist in backstroke. She was also one of the fiercest prosecutors in the U.S. Attorney's Office. A lot of the cops and agents called her "Miss Alternative Lifestyle" behind her back because she lived with a woman, but they respected her.

"I apologize," Lynch said meekly. "I get a little overenthusiastic sometimes."

Susan was on hold with the judge's chambers, the phone tucked against her shoulder. She was waiting to give a report. Her second line wouldn't shut up, and the constant shrill ringing set them all on edge. But updating the judge was more important than answering press calls. Judge Bernadette DeFelice, who was handling the Atari Briggs case, was a temperamental, controlling bitch who raised hell if she wasn't kept in the loop at all times. Melanie and Susan understood this well, because until a few months ago, Bernadette had been their boss.

"How long was the delay between when he held up the cell phone and when the car exploded?" Lynch asked.

"A few seconds at most."

"What did he do after the explosion?"

"Ran away, I guess. I don't know. I was knocked off my feet, and by the time I got up, he was gone."

"Based on his position the last time you saw him, which way do you think he went?"

"I'd be speculating."

"Speculation can at times be a useful investigative tool, Ms. Vargas."

"Okay, give me a street map of the area and I'll do my best to answer that."

Lynch nodded at a lackey, who ran off to do his bidding.

"You think you'd be able to pick this guy out of a mug-shot book?" Lynch asked.

"If he's in there, sure. Provided he's clean-shaven like he was today."

"What about describing him for a sketch artist?"

"Yes, certainly."

Lynch rubbed his jaw. "I find it interesting that this mope made no effort to conceal his face."

"That's not unusual in a terrorism case, is it? They were sending a message to Atari Briggs to keep his mouth shut. Why else would they blow up Lester in broad daylight right in front of a federal prosecutor? They don't care who sees them."

"Maybe."

Across the room at Susan's conference table, DEA Agent Papo West, the lead agent on the Briggs case, gave a startled grunt and held his phone away from his ear.

"They found the dog!"

"The dog I saw?" Melanie asked.

Papo looked upset. "A brown mutt, right? They found him in a Dumpster a block from the courthouse with his neck wrung."

"Why would somebody do that?" she cried.

"So we didn't find the dog wandering around, I guess, and realize he was a cover," Papo said. "At least now we know you were on the money, Melanie. The man you saw had to be the bomber."

# 4

When on the bench—which was the only place Melanie had seen her for months—the Honorable Bernadette DeFelice wore the somber black robes that were standard issue for federal judges. Looking at her in that setting, you could be forgiven for thinking she'd calmed down and changed her ways to better fill the distinguished shoes left by the Honorable Leland Cordell when he'd retired at age eighty-five. But beneath the robes, Bernadette was still the same royal terror she'd been as chief of Major Crimes. Her hair was still that bright unnatural red, her dark eyes still merciless, and her language still foul. If anything, power had gone to her head and made her more reckless than before.

"Who the hell do you think you are, Ms. Charlton, refusing to answer a direct question from an Article Three judge?"

Melanie and Susan had been waiting in the courtroom for Atari Briggs to arrive with his replacement lawyer when Bernadette summoned them to this meeting in her chambers. The meeting was unorthodox—what was called an "ex parte communication," because only one side was present. But that's what Bernadette had wanted, and she was the judge.

"You, Ms. Vargas," Bernadette exclaimed, turning on Melanie. "I can't get a straight answer out of you, either, after everything I've done for you? Ungrateful little—"

Normally, Melanie would've felt like a bug wriggling on the tip of a pin. But she'd just watched a man she cared about die. In light of that, Bernadette didn't seem so scary.

"You're not a prosecutor anymore, Your Honor. You're the one who taught us about security clearances and confidentiality and limiting information to need-to-know personnel."

"Oh, I'm not need-to-know?"

"How could you be? You don't work on the investigation."

Bernadette's face turned as red as her hair. "This trial, if I allow it to go forward, happens in my courtroom. The safety of the parties is on my conscience. No goddamn way am I risking bloodshed. You're going to tell me who blew up Lester Poe and you're going to tell me now, or you will sorely regret it, and that's a promise."

"Judge," Melanie said, "we want to give you the information you need to keep everybody safe, but this is a sensitive investigation. What we can tell you is, Mr. Poe was murdered. The explosion was not an accident. Based on what we know, there's a possibility Mr. Briggs is also a target, so we advise extra courtroom security."

"Do you live under a rock? Every newspaper and TV station in this town is reporting that Poe was killed by a car bomb. I know that already. I also know that an eyewitness saw the bomber, and that he was Middle Eastern."

Shit, it was out there about the bomber.

"What I want to know is why Islamic terrorists killed Lester Poe," Bernadette demanded.

"We don't know that that's what happened," Melanie insisted. "We're at a very preliminary stage in the investigation."

"Do I look like an idiot to you?" Bernadette said.

"No, ma'am."

"Do I look like a sap?"

"No."

"Then stop treating me like one. You tell me who killed Lester, or I am dismissing this indictment and sanctioning you ASAP."

"Susan, feel free to jump in here," Melanie said, but Susan gave an innocent look and a little shrug. She was a genius at keeping her mouth shut and her head down, which was why she never got in trouble with the judges. Somebody else took the drubbing. Melanie was designated whipping girl today, and she was in no mood for it.

Bernadette's eyes were boring in on Melanie. "Well?"

"I guess you'll just have to sanction me."

# 5

**G**ood work in there," Susan said as they made their way to the court-room.

Calling Bernadette's bluff had worked. She'd yelled a little more for good measure before kicking them out of her chambers. But Melanie and Susan knew their former boss well enough to see the noisy posturing for what it was: Bernadette backing down.

At the door to the courtroom, security was tight. Eight or ten U.S. marshals—a huge complement for one courtroom—were stationed there, checking IDs and doing random bag searches even though all the spectators had gone through a metal detector already when they entered the building. Inside, the benches were packed with reporters.

Melanie sat down between Susan and Papo at the government's table and scanned the crowd nervously. Back in the office, she'd changed out of her pantsuit into a skirt and sweater she kept in case she got called to court unexpectedly. The quick change had erased the evidence that she'd been at the scene of the crime, but it was still possible that she'd been seen and recognized. Susan was right. Melanie wouldn't feel safe until the bomber was caught.

The door behind the judge's bench banged open, and Melanie spotted the big hair and tight clothes of Tracey Montefiore, Judge DeFelice's courtroom clerk. Tracey flounced up to her desk beside the bench and dumped an armload of files, her face puckered like she'd just tasted something sour. The first time she'd met Bernadette's new employee, Melanie had thought, *You get the courtroom deputy you deserve.*

"I'm gonna go ask Little Miss Sunshine who Atari's new lawyer is," Susan said, getting to her feet.

Tracey greeted Susan with a barely civil nod, and the two conferred for several minutes until the red light on Tracey's special phone lit up, signaling that the judge was calling. The old-fashioned dial telephone rang directly through to the judge's desk. There was one just like it in every courtroom in the courthouse; they were affectionately known as "Bat phones."

"Well?" Melanie asked when Susan returned.

"Evan Diamond. We should have guessed. He was Lester's partner, after all."

Melanie had never met Diamond, but his loyalties were common knowledge. Diamond was a "cartel lawyer," the kind who took suitcases full of cash from the kingpins, who never let his clients cooperate with the feds. Melanie happened to know that little love had been lost between Lester and Diamond.

"They weren't truly partners," Melanie protested. "They just shared office space."

"Either way, we'll never talk to Atari now," Susan said.

# 6

When Atari Briggs walked through the door accompanied by his new lawyer, a discernible wave of emotion swept over the packed courtroom, traveling from back to front like a living being. Jaded reporters elbowed one another out of the way to catch a glimpse. Regular people gasped and shrieked and fanned themselves.

"Atari, Atari, over here!"

"He smiled at me."

"Yo, dawg, we behind you!"

"Strength, brother."

Melanie watched the crowd with a mixture of envy and dismay. Atari Briggs had evoked this reaction every time he'd come to court. He was every inch the superstar, with dazzling caramel skin and liquid eyes, a three-piece pin-striped suit, diamonds glittering on his fingers and in his ears, and no sign of fear. Yes, the evidence was strong, but at moments like this, Melanie wondered how she was supposed to find an impartial jury. Look at this crowd—they loved him. No, love was the wrong word. They worshipped and adored him. If this crowd felt that way, surely some prospective jurors would, too. And if the jury was biased, what incentive would Atari have to flip and give up Abdullah? From the looks of it, he couldn't lose.

"A-ta-ree, A-ta-ree, A-ta-ree!"

Briggs turned and drew his hand across his throat for silence. The chanting throng instantly shut up.

Evan Diamond strode over to the government's table. He was tall and slender in an expertly tailored suit, with the perfect amount of silver kissing the temples of his jet-black hair.

"Can you believe it?" Diamond exclaimed, swallowing up Susan's hand in both of his. "This crazy world we live in, huh? Who'd hurt a guy like Lester? He did so much good."

"We're in shock, too," Susan said. "Everybody in the U.S. Attorney's Office loved him."

"Greatest legal mind of his generation. Nobody else in his league—not even close."

"Whatever you need in terms of a delay, you can count on us to support you," Susan said.

Melanie watched Diamond, studying the shadows around his dark eyes as if she'd find answers there. She hadn't forgotten Lester's cryptic comment about the phones being tapped in his office. She'd never understood why a man as honorable as Lester had teamed up with a snake like Evan Diamond, even if they'd been partners in name only. Yet Diamond seemed genuinely shaken by his partner's death.

Diamond felt Melanie's glance and offered his hand. "Melanie Vargas, right?" he asked, gripping hers too hard.

"Mr. Diamond. I'm so sorry for your loss."

"Call me Evan, and it's everybody's loss. You for one lost a major fan. Les talked about you nonstop, so much that just the other day I had to remind him you were opposing counsel."

At Diamond's words, Melanie felt her throat closing up. "It was mutual," she said. "I, I'm—"

Words failed her for a moment, but feeling Susan's interested gaze on her, Melanie got it together.

"He was a wonderful man," she finished.

"That he was."

"Now that you have the case, I was hoping we could continue some conversations I had with Lester about your client."

Diamond looked alert. "Conversations? Really? Les never mentioned that."

The sound of a gavel crackled across the courtroom like a gunshot as Bernadette swept onto the bench, bright red lips and bright red hair glittering above the black robes.

Diamond squeezed Melanie's arm. "Talk soon, hon."

"All rise; parties please approach!" Tracey Montefiore called out.

The court reporter began typing furiously.

"Did I say too much?" Melanie whispered to Susan as they hurried to the government's podium.

"What do you mean?"

"Evan didn't know about the cooperation. Atari must not have mentioned it to him. Do you think he doesn't trust his new lawyer?"

Susan smiled. "Would you?"

"Ms. Vargas, stop yammering or this hearing is gonna end in sanctions," the judge snapped.

Evan Diamond stood at the defense podium waiting for his client to join him. Briggs took his time, sauntering up to the bench like he owned the courtroom. As he got closer, he turned to face the gallery and flashed a gang hand signal. The spectator benches erupted in applause and cheers.

The judge smacked her gavel. "Enough! Mr. Diamond, you'd better control your client or we're going to have a problem."

"Yes, ma'am."

The noise died down.

"You have my gratitude for appearing at short notice under these tragic circumstances. But don't push it. I run a tight ship. I called the parties to court because Mr. Briggs's previous attorney, Lester Poe, was killed two hours ago in front of this courthouse when his car exploded. The cause of the explosion is under investigation. Naturally, we are all terribly upset, but our responsibility is to this case. Today is Thursday, and the trial is scheduled to begin a week from this coming Monday. That date is not realistic given the change in circumstances. Mr. Diamond, I called this status conference to let you apply for a postponement, and to set a new schedule that will allow you adequate time to prepare."

Diamond drew himself up in a great show of offense. A murmur spread through the crowd.

"The defense doesn't want a postponement, Judge. Mr. Briggs is an innocent man. The government doesn't like my client's music. His frank treatment of life on the streets makes them look bad, so they're trying to silence him with a trumped-up case, plain and simple. We don't want to put the trial off. Not for a week or a day. Not for a single minute."

Cheers and whoops broke out in the courtroom. Bernadette pounded her gavel.

"Silence!" she shouted, glaring out at the gallery. "Did I hear right? Are you saying you're prepared to go to trial as scheduled, with no extension, ten days from now?"

"Not only prepared, we can't wait, Judge."

Atari Briggs turned to face the audience again, his beautiful eyes narrowed to slits. "We gonna beat this bullshit rap. Bring it on!"

The echoing roar came back from the bleachers. "Bring it on! Bring it on! Bring it on!"

Bernadette pounded her gavel to no avail. People in the audience were leaping to their feet, pumping their fists in the air.

"Bring it on! Bring it on!"

Briggs picked up the refrain along with the crowd. The chanting was getting louder by the minute.

The judge turned up the volume on her microphone. Her powerful voice rang out over the chanting. "Silence, silence!"

But the chanting continued.

"Marshals!" the judge shouted. "Clear the courtroom of anybody without a press pass, now."

Within seconds, the courtroom was swarming with uniforms. Minor scuffles broke out as the marshals hustled people toward the door.

Melanie drew closer to Susan. "What the hell is Diamond up to?" she whispered, the chants covering up her words. "Why doesn't he want more time?"

"Just look at this crowd. He's sure he'll win."

"He still needs to try the case, and he doesn't know the first thing about it. Maybe he has some ace up his sleeve."

Susan shrugged. As the last protesting spectator left, the marshals slammed the courtroom door and gave the judge the all-clear sign. Bernadette glared down at Diamond.

"Mr. Diamond, if you or your client ever pulls that kind of stunt in my courtroom again, I will disqualify you from this case so fast that your lips will still be moving when you land on your backside in the street. Do I make myself clear?"

"Yes, ma'am," Diamond said, but he looked quite satisfied with himself.

"Now, about the schedule," Bernadette said. "Most lawyers would require months to prepare for a trial this important. Why should I believe you can waltz in and do it on a week's notice?"

"My ability to prepare depends on the evidence I get from the prosecution. I'm a quick study if I have the material I need. If I can get the witness list and all witness statements by close of business today, I can swing it. Judge, my client wants to move forward and not have this hanging over his head."

"The witness list," Melanie whispered urgently. "Susan, that's his ace. He's planning to threaten our witnesses."

"Sounds reasonable," Bernadette was saying. "I like not having to move my calendar around. Can the government meet that request?" she asked.

"No! Close of business today is not possible, Judge," Melanie blurted.

"You're telling me three hours isn't enough time to type up a god-damn witness list?" Bernadette asked. "That is not an acceptable answer."

"A lawyer on this case was just murdered. The case is obviously more dangerous than anybody thought. We need time to make sure our witnesses are protected before we reveal their names."

"If anybody should be worried about safety, it's us, not them," Diamond said. "It was my colleague, my friend, my partner of many years who got blown up. For all I know I'm next. Maybe I need pro-tection, but the prosecution witnesses? Nobody's threatened them."

"Good point," the judge said, nodding. "It's Mr. Poe who was attacked, not the prosecution witnesses."

"That doesn't mean they're not in danger," Melanie insisted.

"If I knew anything about this investigation of yours, maybe I'd have the evidence to back up your claim. But I don't, do I? I'm grant-ing Mr. Diamond's request, but I'll give you an extra day. The gov-ernment has until close of business tomorrow, let's say six P.M. Friday, to turn over a witness list and statements. You have all day tomorrow to get your witnesses secured, Ms. Vargas. Adjourned!"

Bernadette pounded her gavel and strode off the bench.

# 7

"I can't believe you didn't back me up in there," Melanie exclaimed as they hurried back through the tunnel toward their office. "Now Evan Diamond gets our witness list."

"He's entitled to it anyway. She was never going to rule in our favor. All you did was piss her off and make us look bad."

"At least I tried. You rolled over, and now our witnesses could be in jeopardy."

"Oh, right, because Evan Diamond is planning to whack them? Please! Where do you come up with this stuff?"

They'd reached the elevator to their building and Susan pounded the call button.

"Why else would he ask for the list early?" Melanie demanded.

"Maybe he's yanking our chains. That's a specialty of his. Or maybe he actually wants to prepare. Did you consider that? I'd be more worried about that than about witness killings if I were you. The judge hates us. The public hates us. We're gonna lose if we don't get our act together and stop worrying about far-fetched—"

"How far-fetched can it be when Lester Poe was murdered this afternoon, Susan? Maybe you've forgotten. I have his blood on my suit back at the office if you need a reminder."

"Girls, don't fight," Papo said, looking alarmed beneath a nervous smile. "We're a team, remember?"

Melanie was on the verge of tears, the sound of the bomb still ringing in her ears. Susan scrutinized her with narrowed eyes.

"Was there something going on between you and Lester?"

"What?"

"Evan said Lester always talked about you. You two weren't—he was opposing counsel. You weren't involved with him, were you? I'm not asking because I'm mad. If you were involved with opposing counsel, you should disclose it or—"

"Of course I wasn't."

"Okay, good."

The elevator came and they all got on. Melanie glared at Susan.

"That was a low blow."

"I'm sorry. I didn't think so, but I had to ask. Truce, okay? We're both stressed out. We're ten days from trial, and I for one am starting to think we're gonna fall flat on our asses with the entire world watching."

To Susan, the only thing worse than losing a trial was losing a big, important trial with press attention. But Melanie had deeper concerns at the moment.

"I'm not so worried about whether we win or lose. I just don't want anybody else to die. Lester told me his office phones were tapped, and that we couldn't use them to discuss Atari's cooperation. He never came out and said it was Diamond doing the tapping, but don't you think that casts some suspicion on him?"

"No. They share office space. Those are Evan's phones, too. Why would he tap his own phones?"

"Maybe they have separate lines."

"Let's calm down and wait for the evidence before we start jumping to conclusions."

They'd reached the sixth floor, where Rick Lynch and his FBI team were waiting for Melanie in a conference room. The FBI had retrieved the videotape from a security camera near the Dumpster where the dead dog had been found, and they wanted Melanie to review it to see if she could spot the bomber.

Melanie flung the door open and marched in. The men waiting for her all leaped to their feet. Along with Lynch and his counterterrorism agents, a group of top brass from the U.S. Attorney's Office was there. Mark Sonschein, the chief of the Criminal Division, came over and gave Melanie a circumspect hug.

"You okay, kiddo?" he asked. Mark was Melanie's boss, and known for being humorless and intense, but he could be a solid friend.

"Hanging in," she said, extricating herself. "I'll feel better once I'm working on finding Lester Poe's killer."

"Uh, yeah, about that," Mark said. "You should know, I'm assigning a separate team to work the bombing investigation. You don't have time. You need to prepare for trial."

"A separate team? But I was there. I saw what happened."

"Another good reason to keep you away. You're an eyewitness. If you know too much about the investigation, your testimony will be tainted."

"I'm not sitting still for this, Mark."

"It's not your decision."

"You can't do this."

"I can. I am. And there's no reason for you to complain. The team is top-notch. Baker, Monahan, and Yee. They'll locate the bomber in short order, and you know they will. You have other responsibilities. Nobody else can take your place on the Briggs trial."

"But I have specialized knowledge about the bombing, too. Lester Poe told me things before he died that affect how the investigation should be conducted," Melanie said.

"That makes you a witness, not an investigator. Witnesses can be interviewed. Convey your information to Group Supervisor Lynch. He's standing right beside you."

Melanie was furious, but she could see that Mark had no intention of backing down. She decided not to waste her energy fighting a battle she couldn't win.

"Where's that surveillance tape?" she snapped.

"We've got it cued up right here," Lynch said. "But first, I should tell you that we have a report from our field forensics people supporting your account of what happened. They're quite certain we're looking at a VBIED."

"Translation?" Melanie asked.

"Vehicle-borne improvised explosive device. They believe it was attached to the underside of Poe's car using a magnet and exploded remotely, presumably by the gentleman you saw, the one with the dog. What's more, the field tests indicate the presence of a chemical taggant in the explosive residue that's identical to that found in residue from a nightclub bombing in Barcelona last year. If the lab confirms that, it's big news, because a cell linked to Gamal Abdullah pulled off the Barcelona bombing."

"If it all lays out like we're thinking, we'll be able to link the bombing of Poe's car directly to Abdullah," Mark added. "Which would be huge."

"Our top priority is to arrest the bomber and question him," Lynch said. "Thanks to your information, we stand a decent chance of doing that. I wanted to apologize for being short with you earlier today. Your information was accurate. You're our star witness. Now let's cue the tape."

He nodded at one of his agents.

"You'll see a man leading a dog into an alley. Let me know if you recognize him."

"Okay," Melanie said.

A grainy black-and-white image appeared on the TV screen,

showing the concrete wall of a building and the busy intersection beyond it. Within seconds, the man in the dark jacket whom Melanie had seen on the sidewalk walked into the frame, leading the brown dog on a leash. The camera had a good angle, clear enough that she could make out the man's sharp features, and see the dog wagging his tail. The dog had a shaggy coat and a friendly face. The pair walked far enough past the camera that they went out the opposite side of the frame. Several minutes later, the man passed by again—without the dog this time. He looked noticeably more rumpled, and he was wiping his hands on his pants.

Everybody turned to look at Melanie. She felt something wet on her cheeks. Tears for the poor damn dog? *Pull yourself together,* she thought. She wanted to get this asshole, and she couldn't do it if she was falling apart.

"That's him," she said.

# 8

Melanie Vargas had been born and raised in the Bushwick section of Brooklyn, a largely Puerto Rican neighborhood that—at least when she was growing up there—had its share of problems with crime. When she was thirteen, her father had been shot before her eyes during a robbery in his furniture store. He'd survived, but he'd been a changed man, and he'd left them shortly thereafter to start fresh in Puerto Rico, with a different wife and new children. That was one way to get over a trauma—cut and run and never look back. His absence from Melanie's life in the years since had marked her indelibly, and so, in that sense, had the long-ago crime. It was a big reason she did what she did for a living. But on nights like this, she wondered about her career choice. She'd made it out of Bushwick, which hadn't been easy. Why the hell was she risking everything she'd worked so hard for by putting herself smack in the line of fire?

To avenge the death of a man she'd cared about, that's why.

Agent Papo West had given Melanie a lift home, but she'd declined his offer to come inside and do a security sweep. She lived on the eighth floor of a doorman building and felt confident that nobody could get in without being noticed. Thankfully so, since her daughter was at home with the babysitter.

On the surface, all was serene in Melanie's apartment. But as she got out of her work clothes, she switched on the news, and every channel featured Lester's murder. The local network affiliates all had the surveillance tape from the alley by now. They were flashing the picture of the man in the dark jacket and asking the public for help in identifying him. Melanie felt her chest tighten and sank down on the edge of her bed. Would they find this guy? Was he out there gunning for her, or was he half a world away by now, on the lam? Wherever the bomber was, the bombing was here with her, and not only on the TV. She couldn't get the stench of blood and smoke out of her nose. That smell. She'd always remember the smell of Lester's death. Lester, her friend, her dear friend.

The babysitter called from the foyer, ready to leave, so Melanie hauled herself up to say good-bye. She emerged to the sound of her two-year-old, Maya, giggling as the nanny, Yolanda Fernandez, lifted her up for a hug and kiss.

Yolie was in her late forties, a mature woman, not a kid, and somebody who'd had a long career in child development. She had a graduate degree, and had worked as the director of a private nursery school in her native Venezuela. She'd come to the United States for the sake of her journalist husband, who'd fallen from favor with the government, but found that she couldn't get teaching work without going back to school, which she couldn't afford. So she was babysitting instead, pouring her substantial wisdom, expertise, and kindheartedness into taking care of Maya. Not only did Yolie—who had no kids of her own—adore Maya, but Maya loved Yolie back more than she'd ever loved any other babysitter.

It hadn't been easy to find a nanny as qualified as Yolie. When the last babysitter had had a child of her own and stopped working, Melanie was on the verge of a mini-breakdown, so convinced was she that she'd never get a trustworthy replacement. She'd even considered quitting her job, but two things stopped her. The first was doing the math. Steve, her ex, was responsible with the child support; still, Melanie couldn't afford her mortgage if she quit her job. Second—and this had been harder to face—she didn't want to quit. Maybe if she'd still been married, but as a divorced woman, Melanie found the thought of giving up her career too scary. Besides, she loved the work. So she'd sat Steve down and had a serious talk with him, and together they'd found more money in the budget for child care. Melanie ended up forking over a hefty fee to the best employment agency in town. She'd run through seven other candidates before Yolie walked in the door. With her calm, intelligent demeanor, her kind eyes, her grown-up, motherly looks, Yolie was the one. Melanie knew instantly. And if she didn't do housework, well, Melanie could live with dust bunnies so long as her daughter was in good hands.

"Bye-bye time!" Maya was squealing.

Yolie had established a hello and good-bye ritual that Maya loved, which made transition times a lot easier.

"Bye, Maya!" Yolanda cried, a big grin on her face.

"Bye, Yolie!"

"Bye, Mommy!" Yolie said.

"Bye, Yolie," Melanie replied.

But Melanie's heart wasn't in it, and Yolie was too observant not to notice.

"Are you okay?" she asked Melanie.

"Tough day at work. I'll be fine now that I'm with her."

Yolie scrutinized Melanie like she might decide not to leave Maya with her. "You sure? Because I can stay awhile. Andres is working on an article tonight anyway."

"Positive. I'm going to give her a bath. You go home and have a nice night."

A few minutes later, Maya was splashing in the water playing with her plastic doll. She was a perfect little doll herself—big brown eyes shining, chubby cheeks glistening—and she was the most important thing in Melanie's life. They had a deal. Melanie worked long hours, but when she got home, she belonged to Maya. Somehow, she found energy and cheerfulness to show to Maya, no matter what had happened at work that day. Unfortunately, today's events were presenting a bit of a challenge. Melanie sat on the closed toilet seat, calling on every ounce of concentration just to stop herself from staring off into space.

"Mama, see the baby."

"She's beautiful, just like you," Melanie said, injecting extra perkiness into her voice. Kids sensed from your tone if you were upset about something.

"Mama look, baby's swimming!"

"What a good swimmer she is. Mommy's going to get you swim lessons this summer, too. I bet you'll love it."

As Maya played in the water, Melanie's mind started wandering, and a sigh escaped before she could catch it.

"Mommy's sad?" Maya asked, looking up. She reached out with a wet hand, and Melanie leaned over so Maya could pat her cheek.

"Nope, I'm happy when I'm with you," Melanie said.

Reassured, Maya went back to her doll. But Melanie was fibbing. Of course she was sad. A few hours ago on the sidewalk, Lester Poe had been blown apart and Melanie's life had changed. She couldn't say for sure what she'd expected from that relationship, but she'd expected something. She recalled the dinner Lester had taken her to last summer. The restaurant was a sleek box carved from lavish materials. Copper floor. Teak walls. Snowy linen tablecloths laid with precious china and silver. And from every window, the lights of the city at their feet. She'd been nervous at first. Lester was famous, and besides, she wasn't quite sure what he wanted with her. Supposedly this was a recruiting dinner, but when they'd met—at a cocktail party for a political candidate who'd been under investigation—she'd felt the chemistry. She suspected that his interest in her was more than professional.

"So I read your résumé," Lester said as he filled her wineglass. "You know we both went to Harvard?"

"I did know. I looked you up in Martindale-Hubbell."

"I hated it there. I was such a nobody."

"I can't believe you were ever a nobody."

"Well, at first anyway. A poor Jewish kid from Brooklyn trying to keep up with the rich prep school boys. It toughened me up. Sink or swim, and I swam."

"It was still like that when I was there. Everybody else was so connected, and if you didn't fit in, too bad. People were *rich*. Me, I couldn't afford a sandwich in Harvard Square. I did dorm crew to pay my tuition."

"You cleaned toilets?"

"Yeah, didn't you? I thought all the scholarship kids did."

"Didn't need to. An uncle of mine was a bookie in Dorchester. I worked as a runner for him. It was very lucrative. Not to mention educational."

Melanie laughed in astonishment. "You just confessed a federal crime to me."

"Yes, but you can't touch me, darling. My uncle's dead and the statute ran a long time ago."

"You had that all figured out, didn't you?"

"Of course. Otherwise, I'd never confess to a barracuda like you."

"I'll take that as a compliment."

"I meant it as one."

A silence fell. Melanie glanced down at her food, feeling suddenly shy. The waiter came to clear their plates away.

"So, I take it from how very articulate you are in English that it's your first language?" Lester said after a moment.

"I'm a New Yorker, born and bred. My father was originally from Puerto Rico. He came here as a child, but I've barely ever been there."

"I'm disappointed," he said in a joking tone. "I love Spanish. I'm taking a conversation course at the Spanish Institute."

"Oh, I speak Spanish."

"You do? Say something for me."

"What?"

"In Spanish. Go ahead, let me hear you speak it. I can only imagine how much better it'll sound coming from your lips."

"*Tu me matas,*" Melanie said, laughing.

"*Tu me matas.* You kill me, right?"

"Yes, very good."

"*Tu me matas,*" he repeated. "I like that."

The waiter arrived with their next course: oyster tapioca in paper-thin china bowls topped with tiny grains of caviar that glistened like onyx. Melanie stole a glance at Lester as he listened to the waiter's description. He had an amazing face—strong, intelligent, noble even. She was surprising herself by feeling drawn to this man, by flirting with him. She was divorced, but she wasn't single. Should she tell Lester that she was involved with someone? But how presumptuous; this was supposed to be a business dinner. It just didn't feel like one.

"So, enlighten me. What's this dinner about, anyway?" she asked, after the waiter left.

"It's about your future. About whether you'll come to work for me."

"I already told you, I can't do that."

"I thought I could change your mind."

"Because you're so persuasive."

"I've been known to be. The fact is, it would be a great opportunity for you. The cases are fascinating, and the money's—" He waved his hand at the room. "Look around. I don't know about you, but growing up poor like I did, I care about coming to places like this. About nice vacations. The Caribbean in winter, the Hamptons in summer. Even if you're not a materialist, even if those things really don't matter to you, I think you'll find that freedom from worrying about money is a luxury in itself. You can't know how good it feels until you experience it."

"I'm not rich, but I'm not starving, either. Changing jobs, well—I wouldn't do it for money alone. I go to work every morning and I'm where I belong. Everywhere else, I'm an outsider. That feeling of belonging—I couldn't give it up."

"You'd belong working the defense side, too. It's the same work from a different angle. Representing the individual against the power of the state. David against Goliath. There's beauty in that."

"Beauty maybe, but no truth. All the clients are guilty."

"Most are. But some are guilty of less than what they're charged with. And a precious few are innocent."

"So that's what motivates you?" she asked. "The innocent few?"

Lester grinned. "Me? No. I just like to win."

She laughed. Their eyes held. She studied the lines around his, the snow white of his hair. They didn't make him any less attractive.

"Why me?" Melanie asked after a moment. "Why the full-court press to recruit me? I'm sure you have plenty of bright young lawyers beating down your door begging for work."

"I do, but —" He hesitated. "It's the chemistry. We met and we clicked. Honestly, I thought you were extraordinary. That's the only explanation I can offer."

"Thank you. I'm flattered, truly. But why didn't you just . . ." She hesitated.

"Ask you out?"

"Yes."

"I considered it."

"And?"

"I thought you'd turn me down. I didn't feel like hearing that I was too old." He looked her in the eye. "But now I think I'm ready to go there. If that's a problem for you, I'll understand. You can be honest."

There was a pause.

"I'm confused," Melanie said. "Are you asking me—"

Lester's words tumbled out in a rush, as if he'd been holding them back. "If you don't want to work for me, fine. I'd rather date you anyway. Would you go out with me, or am I too old for you? And if I am, please, tell me the truth."

He looked nervous as he waited for her reply.

"No, it's not that. I'm seeing somebody."

"Ah, the FBI agent," he said.

"You know about him?"

"Uh-huh. I have to confess, I asked around about you."

"You snooped on me?"

"'Snooped' is so pejorative. I investigated. Wouldn't you? We're neither of us careless people."

Melanie sat with that one for a moment.

"Are you angry?" Lester asked.

"No, actually, I'm sort of flattered. What did your investigation reveal?"

"That your life is complicated. Recently divorced, young child at home. And the FBI agent is seen as a rising star but also . . . difficult."

"Huh."

"Is it serious between you and him?"

"It was. We'd been talking about getting married, but we've hit a rocky patch. At the moment we're taking things one day at a time."

Lester went silent for a moment and seemed to contemplate the view. Then he smiled and gave Melanie's fingers a little squeeze. From that small gesture of resignation, she saw how much he liked her.

"I'll hope for your happiness, but if things don't work out, I want to be the first person you call. Now, tell me about the interesting cases you're working on."

In the dream, the noise was a siren and Melanie was screaming. She was back in the afternoon, back in the bombing. But from far away, she heard the telephone ringing in her bedroom, and knew that this time, the smoke and the flames were in her imagination.

The ringing was real. Melanie rolled over and fumbled in the darkness for the telephone. The clock on the bedside table said 3:20. It must be bad news. What else could it be, at this hour?

"Hello?"

There was a slight delay, a buzzing on the line.

"Melanie?"

The voice made her sit bolt upright in bed. Rough and sweet, with that unmistakable New York accent.

"Do you know what time it is?" she demanded.

"Sorry to wake you. Where I am now, it's hard to predict when I can get to a phone," Dan O'Reilly said.

The timing of the phone call wasn't what made Melanie angry. It was the fact that he'd called at all. She was doing well. She was moving on with her life. But hearing his voice was enough to set her back. Melanie had met Dan O'Reilly on a case and fallen hard for him, right in the midst of her painful split from her philandering ex-husband, Steve Hanson. She'd survived her divorce with flying colors, only to let Dan break her heart.

"What are you doing calling me? We're not speaking," Melanie said.

"You said that. I never agreed."

"Fine, I said it. That means I don't want you to call."

"I heard about that thing today, that you were there when it happened. I'm working with the guy who interviewed you. I can't say any more over this phone."

He must be assigned to Rick Lynch's squad, then. And the hissing and time delay on the line meant he was on a satellite phone. Dan was a third-generation New York City cop, the first in his family to go federal, and he worked terrorism now like everybody else in the Bureau these days. At a dire moment in their relationship, he'd accepted one of those if-I-tell-you-I'll-have-to-kill-you assignments overseas. He'd run away just like her father had, and as far as she was concerned, he shouldn't bother to come back.

"Are you okay?" Dan asked. "My friend said you looked a little shaken up. He said you looked good, though."

Melanie wanted to hang up, but she was having trouble gathering the willpower. Hearing Dan's voice after months of not talking to him was such a shock.

"That reminds me," Dan was saying, "guy I know, a different guy, said you put, like, blond highlights in your hair. I keep trying to imagine that. Melanie as a blonde."

There was a smile in his voice. She pictured the laugh lines around his blue eyes. What the hell are you doing, Melanie Vargas? Talking to Dan was about the stupidest thing she could do.

"I'm fine, and I'm going back to sleep."

"Wait! Please, you have a right to be mad. I've been out of touch. But that tip you passed along? It's looking good. I'm shipping out tomorrow to follow up on it. I'll be closer. I'll be able to call."

"I ended this relationship, remember? It's over. Do not call me. Understand?"

"But—"

She slammed the phone down.

# 9

The morning dawned too bright and sunny for Melanie's mood. It was hot again, so hot that the deejay on the radio dispensed dire climate predictions along with the traffic and weather reports while Melanie got dressed. She put on a summer-weight pantsuit with a tank top underneath, something she hadn't worn in months. The suit hung baggy on her slimmed-down frame. Melanie had lost twelve pounds since breaking up with Dan—an unanticipated benefit of her unchosen freedom. She got up an hour earlier each morning and ran on the new treadmill in the corner of her bedroom to keep the weight off. It made her feel like something in her life was under control.

On her way out the door, Melanie stopped in the kitchen, where Yolie was packing a picnic lunch so she and Maya could spend the morning in the park.

"Mommy, say bye-bye," Maya called from her booster seat. She was finishing her oatmeal, her hair already arranged by Yolie in ponytails with bows around them.

Melanie couldn't help smiling. "Bye, Maya!"

"Bye, Mommy!"

"Bye, Yolie!"

"Bye, Mommy!" Yolie said, smiling too.

At the office, things were far less cheery. Susan had called a team meeting for nine o'clock sharp. When Melanie walked into the chief's suite a few minutes early, she found Shekeya Jenkins seated at her old desk in the anteroom. Shekeya had been Bernadette DeFelice's secretary before Bernadette became a judge, back when she still ran Major Crimes with an iron fist. After Bernadette's departure, Shekeya herself had been promoted to paralegal. She was now assigned to help Melanie and Susan with the Briggs trial.

"I'm getting major déjà vu, seeing you sitting there," Melanie said.

"What, like Bernadette's inside instead of Susan? Please, that woman knows if she shows her ugly-ass face around here, blood is gonna spill."

Shekeya had undergone a major makeover since her promotion, wearing conservative business suits and returning her previously orange braids to their natural ebony color. But her tongue was as sharp as ever.

"Why, what's she done to you lately?" Melanie asked.

"I was here till eleven-thirty last night xeroxing witness statements because of her goddamn early discovery order, that's what. So do not expect sweet words from me this morning."

"Sweet words right now would make me barf."

Shekeya eyed Melanie with real concern. "I heard you were right there yesterday, when it happened. You okay?"

"Do I look okay?"

"No, you look like shit. But I mean that in the nicest way."

Melanie laughed.

"Here's some news that's not gonna help, so brace yourself," Shekeya said. "We got a new addition to the trial team. A recent hire. Jennifer Lamont."

"Why is that bad news? We can use an extra pair of hands."

"She's young and pretty and she was Judge Fox's law clerk. Need I say more?"

"That doesn't mean she slept with him, and it doesn't mean he got her the job here. You pay too much attention to gossip."

"And *you* live in a dreamworld."

"If she can read and write and doesn't have two heads, I want her on the case. You weren't in court yesterday. We need all the help we can get, or Atari is gonna walk."

"Don't tell me that."

Melanie poured herself a cup of coffee from the pot on the credenza and walked into Susan's office. A young woman seated at the conference table put down her own coffee with a start.

"Oh," Melanie said, startled, too. Could this be Jennifer? She glanced over her shoulder at the open door, wondering how far Shekeya's voice had carried.

"I was early, so I just came right in. Susan said it was okay. I'm Jennifer Lamont. I'm new. I just got assigned to the case," the young woman said. She had an unusual voice—soft and husky, with a Southern lilt.

"Melanie Vargas. Glad to have you aboard."

Melanie slid into a chair across from Jennifer. The girl was pretty enough, with long brown hair and a nice figure, but hardly looked like a femme fatale.

"I can't believe my good luck," Jennifer said. "Just entered on duty, and not only am I on the trial of the century, I'm working with the best lawyers in the office. I hope you won't mind if I ask a lot of questions, but I want to learn the ropes quickly, and everyone says you know what's what around here."

The comment pleased Melanie. "Sure. Ask me whatever you want."

"My first question is, what's this meeting about? I was told to report here, but not exactly why."

"There's news out of Washington relating to the bombing yester-day. Mark Sonschein is coming to brief us."

"Mark Sonschein? The chief of the Criminal Division?"

"Yes."

Jennifer's eyes widened. It *was* a lot to be meeting with the big boss your first week on the job.

"Don't worry, you're not expected to say anything," Melanie said, feeling protective of Jennifer already. "You're here to listen."

Jennifer smiled with relief. "Thanks."

What was Shekeya talking about? The kid was sweet.

Papo West came in with several DEA agents. They sat down, and Melanie introduced them to Jennifer. A moment later Shekeya entered pushing a cart loaded with three-ring binders. She cocked an eyebrow when she noticed Jennifer, but Melanie ignored her. Mark and Susan appeared in the doorway and conferred in hushed tones for a moment.

"Melanie," Mark called. "Can I talk to you for a second?"

"Sure."

"Out here, please," he said, jerking his head toward the ante-room.

Melanie passed Susan on her way out and shot her an inquiring look. Susan just nodded encouragingly. Susan's secretary, Vonice James, was now at her desk. Vonice was calm and polite, not salty like Shekeya, but not as proactive a worker, either. She glanced at them impassively, then turned away and resumed typing on her computer.

"Big news," Mark said in a hushed tone. "We think we found the bomber. You ready to look at a picture?"

"Of course."

Suddenly the full implications of having witnessed Lester's murder sank in. She'd have to testify. Point her finger at him in court. Get protection, most likely.

"Prepare yourself. It's not attractive," Mark said, opening a manila folder.

"He's dead?"

"Yes."

She didn't show her relief. This was good for her, but bad for the investigation. A critical participant in the crime was now beyond the reach of interrogation. Most likely, he'd been killed by his controllers in order to silence him.

Mark opened the folder. It was a color fax, the man's face in close-up, the top of his head blown off.

"It's him. Where'd they find him?"

"In a ditch right off the Northway in a little town called Champlain. The assumption is, he was heading for the Canadian border with a coconspirator. He let his guard down. Maybe even fell asleep. Woke up dead."

"Any witnesses?"

"Not yet."

"ID?"

"His pockets were stripped clean, but they left his fingers and his teeth. The M.E.'ll lift prints. Who knows, maybe we'll get something, but a lot of the terror guys don't show up in the system. They've been off in some training camp at the far end of the earth."

"This guy didn't act alone. He was a mope, a nobody. How do we find the masterminds if he's dead?"

"That's not your problem, Melanie. Your job is the trial. Speaking of which, people are waiting for us. Come on."

Melanie followed Mark back into the office and took her seat at the long table. The picture of the dead bomber stayed with her, bringing her some measure of comfort. He'd stood there watching them, lying in wait until the moment he could press the button that would take Lester's body apart. He deserved what he got. Hell, he deserved worse.

At the head of the table, Mark was glancing at some notes on his yellow legal pad. He looked grim and tired, but then he always did, the result of dark circles around his eyes and five o'clock shadow that Melanie had never seen him without. Both seemed noticeably worse this morning.

Mark cleared his throat. "Good morning, folks. Let's get started. What I'm about to say can't leave this room, understood?"

Everybody nodded.

"That's more than just a figure of speech. The press is going berserk with the bombing story. Every news program led with it last night. So far, none of them has the Gamal Abdullah angle, and we have to keep it that way. The second Abdullah knows we're looking for him, he'll disappear without a trace. If that information were to leak—well, let's just say you'd all come in for some pretty uncomfortable scrutiny from the Office of Professional Responsibility. Are we clear?"

Mark made stern eye contact with each of them in turn, then flipped a couple of pages ahead in his notes.

"The first piece of news, which is about to hit the airwaves any minute, is that the body of the car bomber was discovered at approximately six o'clock this morning in a ditch upstate, not far from the Canadian border."

A murmur went around the table.

"Cause of death appears to be multiple gunshot wounds to the back of the head," Mark continued. "The FBI is investigating. You'll be updated on a need-to-know basis only. I'm reminding you that I am your Chinese wall. All briefings about the bombing will come through me. You are the trial team. AUSAs Baker, Monahan, and Yee are the bombing team. You are not to speak to them. They are not to speak to you. You are not to speak to the FBI agents investigating the bombing, either, at least not without my permission. These precautions are being taken for a reason. The bombing team will be reviewing many of Lester Poe's files looking for leads. Poe's partner, Evan Diamond, is now your adversary on the Briggs trial. We need to avoid all allegations of impropriety, or our former colleague Judge DeFelice will be only too happy to nail us to the wall. Clear?"

Everybody nodded. A muscle twitched in Mark's cheek.

"Good. Now the update. The lab confirmed the field findings that the explosives used to kill Lester Poe were chemically identical to those employed last year in the Barcelona nightclub bombing. This strongly suggests that Abdullah found out about Briggs wanting to squeal on him, and assassinated Poe as a warning to Briggs. In your dealings with Diamond and Briggs, you should be alert for any insight into Poe's death. If you come up with something, bring it directly to me and I will put you in touch with the bombing investigators under appropriately controlled circumstances."

Mark took a sip of water. "Now, as for the Briggs trial, which is scheduled to begin a week from Monday, you may have noticed that your nice little drug murder case has morphed into a major terrorism investigation. Hate to break it to you, but this means it's no longer yours. All sorts of people have their claws into it, and I'm not talking just FBI and Homeland Security. I'm not even talking CIA or military. The president of the United States was briefed on the Poe bombing this morning."

Everybody exchanged nervous glances. It didn't matter how ambitious you were; scrutiny from that high up the food chain was not a good thing. It made the bosses crazy and magnified the slightest misstep into a monumental screwup.

"Here's the bottom line," Mark said. "I've been instructed that developing information leading to the capture of Gamal Abdullah is now the top priority, bigger than victory at trial. Therefore, we've been ordered to approach Atari Briggs and make whatever plea offer it takes to secure his help in capturing Abdullah."

A shocked silence descended on the room. Melanie was the first to break it.

"Mark, you heard what happened in court yesterday. Atari's hell-bent on going to trial. He'll turn us down flat."

"Why would he turn us down? Unless Susan's been misleading me for the past several months, your proof is strong. And like I said, you're authorized to make *any* offer it takes. If we have to agree to dismiss the case entirely, so be it."

Susan threw her pen down. "The man is guilty. He's a killer. And instead of going to jail he gets to—what—be on the cover of *GQ*? Please!"

"I'm not here to debate this. We have no choice in the matter. We're dealing with a directive from on high. We're being told to approach Diamond and get Briggs to cooperate. We have to do it. End of story."

"Right before trial, too," Susan said. "We'll look weak. He'll laugh in our faces."

"What should I do," Mark said, "refuse to obey a direct order from Washington?"

They stared at each other.

"All right," she said, sighing. "But don't expect me to be happy about it."

"I'm not happy, either, Susan."

"So who makes the contact with Evan?"

"Melanie discussed the cooperation with Poe," Mark said. "She's the logical choice to call Diamond. Not only does it seem more natural, but it keeps the approach low-key. If we send in somebody with a big title, like me or even you, Susan, we tip our hand about how hot we are to make a deal. I don't want to give this thing away for free if we don't have to. Ideally, we can get Briggs to plead to the charges."

Susan nodded. "Makes sense. We don't want to undermine our bargaining position. But are you up for this, Mel? The Briggs case is yours, too. You've been working on it every bit as long as I have. Are you comfortable making that kind of approach?"

"Seeing Atari walk would be disappointing," Melanie said. "But seeing the people behind the bombing walk would make me sick. Lester Poe died in front of me. I'm catching the ones responsible. Mark won't let me near the bombing investigation, so I'll do my part this way. I'll flip a scumbag like Atari Briggs and deal with a snake like Evan Diamond, if that's what it takes. I'm getting justice for Lester."

# 10

P oe & Diamond, PC, had an unusual location for a criminal defense firm. Rather than being downtown near the courts with all the other law offices, it occupied the first two floors of a lavish limestone mansion on a prestigious Upper East Side block. A young receptionist in a short skirt and trendy eyeglasses ushered Melanie into Diamond's office.

Diamond sprang to his feet and came out from behind the big mahogany desk to greet her. Melanie was struck by how handsome he was, how perfectly groomed and tailored. He didn't look like a lawyer so much as an actor who played one on TV.

"Melanie, welcome. Have a seat. Can I get you some coffee or soda or something?" Here on his home turf, his manner was surprisingly humble and down-to-earth, with a touch of Brooklyn in his accent that humanized him.

"No, thank you, I'm good."

"Nothing for now, Deb, thanks," he said to the receptionist, who backed out of the room and closed the door softly behind her. Diamond retreated behind the big desk, where he took a seat in a glossy leather chair.

"I was surprised to hear from you," he said. "I figured you'd be so busy trying to prove what a scumbag my client is that I wouldn't see you till opening statements." Diamond's smile was warm enough to take the bite out of his words.

Melanie forced a laugh. "Don't worry, I'm working on that."

"Of course you are. This case is a great opportunity for you. If you win, you can write your ticket. But tell me, to what do I owe the honor? It must be something important for you to schlep uptown this close to trial."

"Yeah, I'm surprised you're located here," Melanie said. "It's a spectacular building, but it's really off the beaten path for law firms, isn't it?"

The small talk was intended to buy her a moment to think. The importance of this meeting weighed so heavily on Melanie that she had butterflies.

"Les bought this building for a song thirty years ago," Diamond said. "It's worth ten million today. He lived upstairs. You should see the place. Gorgeous. Me, I commute in from Roslyn. I was downtown, like you say, but one of the big firms made an offer I couldn't match and took over the whole building. I lost my lease. Out of the kindness of his heart, Les took me on."

"So you're not actually partners?"

"We share expenses here for overhead, staff and the like. We joined the name on the letterhead. But we each have our own client base."

"I see."

"Now that he's gone, I'll be looking for space downtown again. Even if I wanted to stay, Brenda would sell the place out from under me. She needs the cash."

"Brenda?"

"Les's wife."

"Lester was *married*?" Melanie tried to picture his hands. There hadn't been any ring.

"Yeah, to Brenda Gould. She was that big fashion designer in the seventies. Maybe you're too young to remember."

"H-how can that be? I can't—I just can't believe it. Lester never mentioned being married. I never saw it in anything I read about him, either."

As Diamond watched Melanie, understanding dawned on his face. "You had something going with Les. That's why you wanted to see me."

"No."

"If he promised you anything—look, honey, I have no control over the disposition of his assets."

"No, you're wrong. Lester and I had a purely professional friendship. We were colleagues, nothing more. I'm just surprised he never mentioned a wife given how much we'd . . . chatted, that's all."

"It's a marriage in name only at this point. Maybe that's why. Brenda's not a well woman, and Les took care of her out of the goodness of his heart. There wasn't much romantic left there."

"Still."

Diamond shrugged. "So I hear you were there when it happened yesterday."

"Who told you that?"

"Grapevine."

Diamond's eyes were dark like her own and appeared trustworthy enough. But you didn't get a reputation as dangerous as his for no reason. This man might talk. Even with the bomber dead, Melanie decided she'd be wise to take herself out of the picture as a witness.

"I'd turned away right before it happened," she said. "I heard a big boom, and then there was smoke everywhere and I couldn't see a thing."

He nodded.

"We should get down to business," she said.

He glanced at his watch. "You have my complete attention."

"Right before the bombing, Lester and I discussed the possibility of a plea. He wanted me to ask the judge to postpone the trial so we could talk about it."

"Huh, really? That surprises me."

"Lester didn't mention this to you?"

"Didn't mention it. Didn't write it in the file, which I've carefully reviewed. And what's more, my client doesn't want to plead guilty. Not even close. Atari has fire in his belly. This is a lousy trumped-up rap, and he wants to beat it."

"Save the speeches for the jury, Evan. You and I both know the proof is solid."

"One tape and a few cooperators who're dirty as the day is long? If my guy doesn't walk with a case that shoddy, I deserve to be run out of town."

"If that's how you feel, I won't waste your time. Take your chances in court."

Melanie started to get up, but Diamond waved her back into her chair.

"Wait a minute, don't run off. I admit, you got me curious. What could you offer him that would make it worth it? You're bound by the mandatory minimum. The way I see it, on a drug murder, even with credit for the plea he'd still have to eat twenty years."

"Not if I write him a substantial assistance letter."

"Cooperation?"

"Yes."

"You'd cooperate Atari Briggs, the black devil who's corrupting the young people of America?"

"Oh, please. Be serious."

"I am serious. I'm shocked."

"If Atari is sincere about wanting to help, and his information is good enough, we'd be happy to work with him."

"Atari doesn't have any information. He's been clean for over a decade. Who's he supposed to give up, Jay Leno? He has no contacts in the drug business anymore."

"I'm confident Atari could give me people I'm interested in."

"You're basing this on what Les told you yesterday?"

"Yes."

"I'm all ears. Who'd he say Atari can finger that's so important?"

"Ask your client. Or better yet, let me ask him. Bring Atari in for a meeting and we'll talk to him about this together."

"I can't go to the client looking like an idiot, not knowing what my own partner discussed with the government. Do me a favor, Melanie. Tell me what Lester said."

If Melanie told Diamond that the name Gamal Abdullah had come up, would he keep that to himself, or would he sell Atari Briggs out? He was pushing pretty hard to get a name; suspiciously hard, and Mark had said the Abdullah angle was to remain a closely guarded secret. She couldn't take the risk.

"Like I said, ask him yourself."

"To go to him blind, not even knowing what you want out of him?" Diamond shook his head. "I don't think so. Cooperation isn't my thing anyway. I don't like rats, and I don't like representing them."

"So I've heard."

"Yeah, I know. As far as you people are concerned, representing a few narcotics defendants makes me the equivalent of Pablo Escobar. Let me tell you, honey, if you want to make a living in this business, it's either the kingpins or the white-collar guys, and frankly the kingpins are better people."

"I don't care who pays your bills, Evan. But if you're an honest lawyer, you'll take my proposal to your client. You don't have a choice."

"Of course I do. I represent him; I make the decisions about what's in his best interests."

"If you don't tell him about this, I'll have a duty to inform the judge."

"The judge? Your former boss, you mean. You two go girlfriend shopping together at lunchtime, or what?"

Melanie laughed. "You don't know Bernadette. She spanks us every chance she gets. But I can tell you, she won't tolerate you refusing to communicate a valid offer of cooperation to your client. That's the equivalent of turning down a Get-Out-of-Jail-Free card. I'll make sure she hears about it."

They stared at each other in silence. Melanie refused to look away. She needed him to understand that she was serious.

Diamond blinked first.

"You came all the way uptown to make this offer," he said. "I'd hate to see you leave empty-handed. I'll convey your proposal to Atari. He'll likely take it as a sign that your case is weak and you're panicking. But I could be wrong. If you lose this trial, you go home to your family at the end of the day. If Atari loses, he gets twenty to life."

# 11

In the vestibule outside Diamond's office, weak winter light filtered through the etched glass door, revealing a graceful staircase curving upward. Lester Poe had lived up there in a grand apartment. His wife—his widow—was probably at home right now.

Melanie couldn't explain why she'd been so shocked by the news that Lester was married. Her father had cheated on her mother. Her ex-husband had cheated on her. Then she'd fallen for somebody new, and he'd cheated, too—well, close enough, anyway. She attracted them somehow. She shouldn't let this one bother her; she'd barely known Lester. She looked at her watch. It was time to get back to the office.

Outside, she couldn't help noticing something she'd missed on the way in. There was a second buzzer under the one with the large brass plaque beside it proclaiming POE & DIAMOND in engraved letters. This one was unmarked. Presumably the only people who pressed it were those who knew to look for it.

Melanie's hand wavered, then reached out of its own accord.

"Who is it?" asked a woman's voice, low and cultured.

"Is this Brenda Gould?"

"Yes?"

"I'm Melanie Vargas. I'm an Assistant U.S. Attorney, from the federal prosecutor's office. I—I'd like to speak to you about your husband's death."

There was a pause. And then the heavy door that had swung closed behind her a moment before buzzed again. Melanie pushed it open and headed up the curving staircase.

At the third-floor landing, a woman waited. She was skeletally thin, with dark eyes that burned in a pale face and short salt-and-pepper hair, wearing black slacks and a mannish black sweater that was much too big for her. The woman looked ill and exhausted, yet the refined bones of her face were still beautiful.

"Ms. Gould, or do you prefer Mrs. Poe?" Melanie asked.

"It's Gould, but just Brenda is fine."

"Thank you for seeing me, Brenda. I'm Melanie."

"You're from the U.S. Attorney's Office?"

"Yes."

"I thought it was the FBI that was coming. Can I see some identification? Sorry to be such a stickler, but that's how Lester taught me."

As she handed Brenda Gould her credentials, Melanie chastised herself silently for giving in to curiosity. This wasn't about generating leads, and she knew it. She'd be stepping on the FBI's toes, taking a career risk over this stupid preoccupation with Lester. But it was too late to turn back. Brenda gave the creds back and motioned her inside.

"Come in. I have a few people here helping me with the funeral and shiva arrangements, but we can find a quiet spot."

They walked through enormous rooms full of good art and antique furniture until they came to an office at the back of the house that had obviously been Lester's. The walls were lined with floor-to-ceiling bookshelves served by the type of elegant rolling ladder you'd expect to find in some medieval scholar's library, or in the lair of an archvillain. Redwelds and law books were piled everywhere, toppling over, spilling papers. It was hard to believe in the midst of this glorious mess that Lester was dead, that he wouldn't walk in the next moment and pick up some book, find his place, and start reading. The room still smelled of his cologne.

Brenda moved a pile of papers from a sofa to a coffee table and they sat down.

"Lester had an office downstairs where he met clients," Brenda said, "but he did all his important work here. Sorry it's such a mess. Nobody was ever allowed in to clean."

"It's perfect. I can totally see him in it," Melanie said.

Brenda fixed intense dark eyes on Melanie's. "You knew my husband?"

"Oh, yes. I'm one of the prosecutors on the Atari Briggs case. I was there yesterday when it happened. We'd just been standing outside the courthouse talking about the case, and then he went to his car, and—then, then, well."

Melanie looked down at her hands, fighting for composure.

"My God, I had no idea. How awful."

Brenda squeezed Melanie's hand and passed her a box of Kleenex.

"I must be more upset than I realized," Melanie said. "I'm sorry. I came here to comfort you. To offer my sympathy, and to let you know that, having witnessed your husband's murder, I'm deeply committed to bringing the killers to justice." She thought about telling Brenda that the car bomber had been found dead, but she wasn't sure if it was public information yet.

"Thank you. It gives me great comfort to hear that," Brenda said. "Was there something you needed to ask me?"

Melanie was sorely tempted to find out what Brenda knew that might relate to the bombing. But interviewing her would be disobeying a direct order that she was to focus on the trial and leave the bombing investigation to others.

"Not exactly," Melanie said. "Didn't you say the FBI is coming to talk to you?"

"Yes, later this afternoon. They want Lester's files."

"They'll question you about his business dealings and other things that might help with the bombing."

"Yes, that's what the man said on the phone. So, if they're going to question me, why are you here?"

Melanie's cheeks burned. "This is more of a condolence call."

"Oh." Brenda studied Melanie's face for a long moment. "What exactly was your relationship with my husband?"

"We were adversaries on a case, that's all. Anything more would have been unethical. Besides, I didn't know he was married, but if I had—I mean, not that we were doing anything. We weren't."

"Don't feel compelled to lie on my account. This might sound strange, but if you were seeing him, well, it's not my business. Lester and I were married on and off for thirty-five years. The romantic part ended between us years ago."

"I'm not lying. I didn't even know him that well. It's just—I'm sorry, I'm finding it difficult to explain."

Brenda took a cigarette from a pack in the pocket and lit it, regarding Melanie with interest. "No need to explain. He was a very compelling man. You strike me as somebody he would have bothered to charm. He could be very charming when he wanted to."

"You said you were married on and off?"

"We were divorced for a long time in the eighties and nineties. I'll tell you the story if you like. It feels good to talk about him today."

Melanie knew she shouldn't. Not only was she wasting valuable work time, she was feeding her growing preoccupation with a dead man.

"Yes, I'd love to hear," she said.

"We met at Studio 54," Brenda said, dragging on her cigarette and exhaling a cloud of smoke. "That says it all, doesn't it? It was the late seventies, and my father, who was in the trimmings business—buttons, sequins, that sort of thing—had gotten me this marvelous job working for Halston. Well, my fashion friends were very fast. One night I was at Studio 54, absolutely strung out. Too many Quaaludes. I remember feeling faint, and the next thing I knew, I was in Lester's car and he was driving me to Jones Beach. In April, no less! I'd never met the man before in my life, but he took me and he kind of shook me around in that sea air and poured some coffee into me. We talked until the sun came up, and before I knew it I was sober as a judge and madly in love. He was incredibly handsome. Fantastic in bed. We were married a year later."

Tears leaked from Brenda's eyes and began to roll down her waxen cheeks. "Hand me that tissue box, would you?"

"What happened after that?" Melanie asked, riveted.

"A lot of things happened. Lester was involved in the civil rights movement, doing these very sexy cases, getting his picture in the paper. Women threw themselves at him. Me, I did as I pleased. I had a glamorous career. I traveled, I did lots of drugs, I had lots of lovers. It was fashionable back then to have an open marriage, and we were fashionable people. Then it ended. Things . . . came between us. It was me who left. That was in '86. We had a very friendly divorce. No children involved, and we both had our own money. I moved to Big Sur to follow this yogi I was obsessed with, and Lester went about his life. But everything went a little flat after that. I guess that's how it is, isn't it? There's a golden time, and then you're older and nothing is quite as fun anymore."

Brenda paused, wiping her eyes, stamping out her cigarette.

"The two of you got back together. How did that happen?" Melanie asked.

Brenda sighed. "That story is less pleasant. I fell on hard times. Lester and I had remained great friends, and he was good enough to bail me out."

"He didn't just bail you out. You actually got married again."

"Yes. I was having some, some . . . well, medical problems." She fiddled with the bangles on her thin wrist. "Oh, hell, I'm not ashamed to say it. It was drugs, okay, but I've been clean for years now. Lester had power of attorney. He was appointed my guardian for a while, but it turned out to be simpler to be legally married."

"And you lived here with him?"

"I have my own floor, the top floor. It's nice. Dormered windows and very delicate northern light. I do yoga. I do still lifes in pastel. I read some lovely books. Lester and I have dinner together sometimes." She drew a quick breath, like she'd felt a sudden pain. "Had dinner, I should say."

A moment passed. In the silence, Melanie heard the clock ticking on the mantel, marking the minutes as they passed. People were waiting for her. She had work to do. She should go.

"Thank you for sharing your memories," she said, getting to her feet. "I'll go now, and stop taking so much of your time."

Brenda stood up to walk Melanie to the door "Don't apologize. It's been wonderful to talk about him. It was really thoughtful of you to come by, especially since the circumstances are a little—unusual, I guess you could say."

"It was nothing. I was downstairs meeting with Evan Diamond anyway."

"Oh!" Brenda exclaimed, stopping short.

"Is something wrong?"

She frowned. "Watch out for him, you know."

"I know he doesn't have the most honorable reputation, but he's been fine with me so far."

"Evan's a good actor. He'll fool you into thinking he's your friend, but he was giving Lester a lot of trouble. I'll be sharing a few things with the FBI about that."

"Trouble in what way?" Melanie asked, remembering Lester's remark about problems in his office.

"Should I tell you? I thought you said to talk to the FBI."

Time was, Melanie wouldn't have been able to stop herself from pouncing on this tantalizing lead. But she'd matured as a prosecutor, and besides, she hadn't forgotten Mark Sonschein's warning earlier that day. If she got caught digging up dirt on opposing counsel, she could undermine the whole case against Atari Briggs. She managed to restrain herself.

"You're right. Better that you talk to them," she said.

"I'll do that, but you be careful. In fact, wait a minute. I'd like to give you something of Lester's before you go."

"Oh, no, I can't take anything of his. Really. Keep his things for yourself."

"I have three houses full of Lester's things, dear. This relates to his work. Somehow I think he'd want you to have it."

Brenda crossed to a beautiful desk that sat beneath tall windows and rummaged in its drawers. She came back and dropped a cold, shiny object into Melanie's hand.

"What's this?" Melanie asked.

"It's a Saint Jude's medal. The patron saint of lost causes. It was given to Lester by a client who was pardoned literally moments before his execution. They strapped him to the gurney, he handed Lester the medal, and the pardon came through. Lester kept it because he thought it brought him luck."

"I—I'm so touched. But—wait a minute, I really shouldn't accept this. It's too much for you to give me."

Melanie held it out, but Brenda pushed it back into her hands.

"Please, take it. Do it for me. Some might say I'm superstitious, but it's just that I've studied spirituality, and I know that certain objects hold powers we don't fully understand. I want Lester's murder solved, and this medal will help you do that. If you're dealing with Evan Diamond, trust me, you'll need it."

# 12

Melanie reported to Mark Sonschein as soon as she got back to the office and filled him in on her meeting. He thanked her and told her to call him the second Diamond contacted her with an answer. They'd all be waiting anxiously to hear whether Briggs would cooperate, but in the meantime they needed to act as if the trial were going forward. The amount of work Melanie needed to do to prepare made her quake in her high heels. As she strode down the hallway, Melanie found herself reaching into her pants pocket and closing her fingers around the Saint Jude's medal for luck.

Papo West was waiting for her in her office with an incarcerated defendant named Vashon Clark, the star witness in the Briggs trial. Papo and Vashon were chowing down on pepperoni pizza. Melanie dropped into her chair, her nose wrinkling as she caught a whiff of the grease-sodden box.

"Hungry? Grab a slice," Papo said, his mouth full.

"Thanks, but my stomach isn't great today."

"The new chick came by looking for you," he said. "She wouldn't eat, either. What's up with you women?"

"They watching their figures," Vashon said.

"You mean Jennifer?" Melanie asked. "What did she want?"

"Susan told her to sit in on witness prep."

"Oh, okay." Melanie picked up the phone and dialed the main switchboard. The operator told her Jennifer's phone wasn't hooked up yet, but that she'd track her down and tell her to report to Melanie's office.

Melanie hung up. "Hey, Vashon, watch the tomato sauce. If you drip all over your prison blues, people will figure out where you've been," she said. For his own safety, Vashon had been instructed to tell his cell mates that he was going to court on an appeal.

Vashon smiled. "Yeah, this ain't no baloney sandwich from marshals' lockup, right? They'll know y'all wining and dining me."

Papo had unlocked Vashon's handcuffs so he could eat. They were in violation of virtually every prisoner transport safety rule in existence. U.S. Marshal's Service protocol called for an incarcerated witness to be interrogated in a secure interview room rather than in the prosecutor's office, to be escorted by at least two federal agents rather than the case agent alone, and to be handcuffed except when in a locked holding cell or when appearing in court. But as Melanie well knew, there weren't enough conference rooms or federal agents to go around, and a well-fed witness was much easier to work with than a hungry one. For the sake of the trial, she ignored the technicalities and took comfort in the fact that Papo was twice Vashon's size, not to mention that Vashon was too eager to cooperate to try anything stupid.

Vashon Clark was a pudgy, baby-faced twenty-seven-year-old doing a life bid at FCI–Fort Dix for a string of drug-related homicides. With all that time on his hands, he'd gotten to stewing over the fact that he was the only one from his crew who hadn't turned state's evidence and bought himself a sentencing reduction, and he'd finally decided it was time to take the plunge. Trouble was, there was nobody left from the old gang to give up. They were all dead, in jail, or in Witness Protection. So Vashon had reached back in the memory banks and pulled out a hit that Atari Briggs had ordered him to commit back in the day, when Vashon worked for Atari at a heroin spot in East New York. Normally nobody would have been interested in a witness who started to sing so late in the game. Nobody would have believed him, either. But Atari Briggs's name commanded enough attention that DEA had heard him out and, fortunately for Vashon, discovered that he had hard evidence, not just gossip.

"We should get to work. You can eat and talk at the same time, right?" she asked Vashon.

"He can, but it ain't pretty," Papo said.

"I need to look at my computer anyway to work on his direct testimony," Melanie said, turning sideways and pulling up a document on her screen. It felt good to focus on the trial, to let drop the burden of Lester Poe's death for a while.

This was her third prep session with Vashon. In the first two, they'd covered the period from when he'd entered the drug trade at age nine after his mother's overdose death, to when he'd done his first murder at fifteen. They'd also reviewed the six homicides he'd committed that had nothing to do with Atari Briggs. They were now poised to get into the meat of Vashon's trial testimony—the year and a half he'd spent working for Briggs, complete with blood, guts, and pyrotechnics.

"Okay," Melanie began, "the last time we met, you told me how you were working those crack spots in Bushwick and you were getting caught up in the war between your crew and the Dominicans."

"Yeah, it was like, race war. I just want to do bidness but there was a lot of blood getting shed. I was looking for a change of scenery, you feel me? That's when Atari came looking for me."

Somebody knocked on the door.

"Yeah," Melanie called. Her fingers were flying over the keyboard, making notes on Vashon's testimony.

Jennifer Lamont poked her head in.

"Hey, Melanie, hope I'm not intruding. Susan said I should sit in on this so I can see how it's done."

Melanie didn't look up. "Sure, have a seat."

The small office only had two guest chairs. Papo stood to offer his, but Jennifer waved him down and went to perch against the credenza instead.

"Jennifer, this is Vashon Clark," Melanie said. "Vashon is our single most important witness. In 1998, Atari Briggs ordered him to kill an underling who was selling his own drugs at one of Briggs's heroin spots. We're just about to go over that testimony now. The call where Briggs orders the hit was caught on tape, so we have fantastic corroboration."

Jennifer nodded.

"Tell me how Atari first approached you," Melanie instructed Vashon.

"It wasn't him personally. He sent somebody. My spot on Troutman had just got stuck up by the Dominicans, and I run them gangstas off. Clipped two of 'em. After that, my name blew up huge on the street. Peoples talking as far away as Canarsie, saying I stood tall in the fight. So Atari sent over a scout and ask me to come work for him."

"Who did he send?"

"His boy Two-Ton Tyrone. Two-Ton roll up on me in a big black Jeep. I'm thinking I'm mad dead, 'cause this motherfucker for real. But then he step out with his hands in the air and say he ain't strapping. Said he heard good things and he come to recruit me. After that, I went to work for Atari, managing some spots in East New York."

"Did you deal with Atari directly?"

"Sometimes, but mostly I go through his lieutenants."

"You've said before that Atari had three lieutenants during the time you worked for him."

"That's right. Two-Ton, a guy named Vegas Bo, and the one they call Shake and Bake 'cause he like to kick the shit out of peoples and set 'em on fire."

"Do we have positive IDs on the three lieutenants?" Melanie asked Papo.

"Yes, ma'am. One moment." Papo reached down into a briefcase that sat beside his chair and pulled out a file. He riffled through it, picked out some mug shots, and slapped them down on Melanie's desk, then began reading from rap sheets printed out on bright yellow paper.

"Malik Sanderson, aka Shake and Bake," Papo read, "doing three lifes at Marion on twenty-three hour lockdown for multiple homicides with torture and lying in wait, plus distribution of heroin and cocaine base. Tyrone Clinton, aka Two-Ton, deceased from multiple bullet wounds at a stash house in Bed-Stuy in 2000. And—uh— Kevin Bonner, aka Vegas Bo, sentenced to sixty months for conspiracy to distribute heroin. Released in 2003 with five years supervision, which recently ended. Whereabouts currently unknown."

The funny thing was, of the three lieutenants, Shake and Bake looked the least frightening—slim and almost intellectual—whereas Two Ton had been humongous, and Vegas Bo had a cruel face, with tattoos down his neck and a scar on his cheek.

"We need to put together an organizational chart for the jury," Melanie said to Papo. "Give these mug shots to Shekeya Jenkins and have her send them over to the graphics people."

"Will do."

"Yo, Ms. Vargas, I know where Vegas Bo at now," Vashon said.

"Oh yeah, where's that?" Melanie asked.

"Vegas. Where else, right? I hear he dabbling in some dope. More than dabbling, actually. I hear he set up real nice with a serious source of supply. Kingpin level, I heard."

"Dope. You mean heroin?"

"Uh-huh."

"What source of supply?"

"I don't know. Something big, though. Peoples saying he hit the jackpot."

"Do you have an address?"

"I can find out. I need a phone call."

"We can arrange that. Monitored, though."

"Whatever."

"You think Bo might be interested in testifying?"

"What, I'm not good enough for you?" Vashon asked with mock hurt.

"You're good enough," Melanie said. "But the more the merrier."

No reason to tell a witness you were worried about losing the case. It could only make him nervous on the stand.

"Yeah, Bo might could testify. He got a beef with Atari."

"What's that?" Melanie asked.

"Atari get rich and famous and forget about him," Vashon said, laughing.

"Is that why you're testifying?"

"Me? Hell, no. I just want less time."

Great. The jury was gonna hate this guy's guts. But what could she do? He was her star witness, and he'd just given an honest answer. Without him, she wouldn't be able to get her smoking gun tape in evidence, and the case would fall apart. Besides, he was telling the truth. It was her job to make the jury see that.

"You said sometimes you dealt with Atari directly, right?" she asked.

"If I had sensitive bidness, I'd deal with Atari face-to-face."

"And that included the incident where he ordered the hit on your associate Little D?"

"First we met face-to-face and talk about the fact that Little D stealing. Then later, Atari call me over the phone and tell me to take Little D out."

"Let's start with the background. Who was Little D, and why did Atari want him dead?"

"Okay, Little D was my shorty from back in the day, from the block. His government name Damond Purcell. The boy was trouble. Always looking for a score, always playing fast and loose. I knew it, but I hired him anyway, because we was friends."

"You hired him?"

"Yes, ma'am. I was managing. If I want to put somebody on the payroll, I could do it."

"Is that why Atari held you responsible when Little D screwed up?"

"Exactly. A poor management decision on my part that come back to bite me."

"Explain what Little D did wrong."

"He was stealing Atari's customers. Selling his own drugs at the spot. It was obvious, 'cause we got long lines of customers but we wasn't moving no weight. Little D thought I wouldn't tell, but I had no choice, else Atari's gonna think it's me stealing."

"I'm going to bring that out in your direct testimony. It makes your role in the murder a little more palatable. No offense, but it's a tough sell to put a shooter on the stand against a guy who didn't touch the trigger, even if he ordered the hit. Especially here, because you killed your old friend."

"Even though I done it all Geneva Convention and shit? One to the head, real painless?"

"The jury may not appreciate that nuance, Vashon."

Vashon looked surprised.

"Okay, now for the tape," Melanie said. "I can't believe how lucky we were to find this."

She nodded at Papo, who cued up an old-fashioned celluloid tape. A decade earlier, when Vashon had spoken to Atari Briggs about killing Little D, wiretaps hadn't yet gone digital, and street drug dealers were still relatively careless about talking business over the telephone. Vashon had had the poor judgment to borrow a cell phone from a friend who was the target of a major DEA wiretap investigation. He'd carried the phone around for days, transacted business over it, then sweated bullets when his friend got arrested. Luckily for Vashon, the friend kept his mouth shut, so the feds never learned whose voice it was on that series of unidentified calls. Years later, when Vashon decided to cooperate, he remembered that the tapes existed and pointed Papo West in the right direction. They were gathering dust in the DEA evidence vault, a few months away from mandatory destruction.

Papo pushed play. Shrill beeps filled the room as the Vashon of ten years earlier, a mere seventeen years old, dialed up Atari Briggs on the borrowed cell phone, unaware he was being listened to.

"Yo," Atari answered.

Briggs was only a few years older than Vashon, but his voice carried a kingpin's authority.

"Yo, boss. Bo told me to get with you," Vashon said.

"You made any progress on that problem we discussed the other day?"

"I talk to the man. He just say ain't no thing."

"He denying it?"

"Yeah."

"Then we got to take care of it, son. Something like this go unpunished, my name worth shit in the street."

"You know, maybe I'm wrong about what I saw. Maybe I—"

"Don't you pussy out on me." Atari's voice was low and threatening. "You know what he done, and you know what you gotta do. We understand each other? Because if he don't pay with his life, somebody else will. I don't need to tell you that means you."

"A-ight. No worries. I take care of it for you, boss."

"Bo gonna give you a clean nine. When you're done, throw it in the river."

The line went dead.

Melanie shook her head in amazement. "'Pay with his life.' He tells you straight out to kill him. We have crime scene?" she asked Papo.

"It's all good," Papo said. "Vashon dropped Little D in the street in broad daylight less than an hour after this phone call. The cop who responded to the scene is still on the job, and I put in a notification for his testimony. We have photos showing Damond Purcell's body lying in a pool of blood, the autopsy report, the medical examiner who removed the bullets from the corpse, and the ballistics guy who'll say the bullets were fired from a Glock nine millimeter semiautomatic."

"The 'clean nine' Atari refers to on the tape," Melanie said.

"Yup. Plus, like you told me, I found a voice identification expert who can testify that it's Atari's voice on the other end of that phone call. Though honestly, I don't think we need him. Atari's got the most famous voice in America. Half the jury will recognize it with no help whatsoever."

"Let's not get lazy. We want to give the jury more to go on for the voice ID than Vashon's word."

"Whatever you say," Papo said, leaning back, twining his hands behind his head. "That tape is so good, I don't see how we can lose."

Melanie was tempted to point out the holes in their case, or at least the fact that half the population was crazy about their defendant, but she went easy. Why burst his bubble? It wouldn't last long in this environment anyway.

"Hand Vashon the phone and let's track down Vegas Bo," she said instead. "Sounds like he was right in the middle of the hit. An extra witness never hurt."

# 13

The Drayton Hotel in Soho was a favorite hideout of anorexic starlets, billionaire moguls, and supermodels with substance-abuse problems. It didn't surprise Evan Diamond a bit that his new client had chosen to shelter himself from the paparazzi there. It didn't surprise anybody else, either, and the place was swarming with reporters when Diamond pulled up in his midnight-blue Mercedes.

"Motherfucker," he said under his breath.

His redheaded driver, whose name was Alexei, caught Diamond's eye wordlessly in the rearview mirror. Alexei was a former client, and was possessed of many qualities that had proved useful to Diamond over the years. Chief among these was the fact that he almost never spoke.

"Go around the block, come back, and drop me in front," Diamond said in response to Alexei's inquiring look.

As they turned on to Prince Street, Diamond snapped open his briefcase and studied himself in the small mirror affixed to its inside cover. By the time they'd finished their circuit, he'd combed his hair, straightened his tie, and taken the shine off his nose with a compact he kept hidden in an inner compartment. He traveled with his own makeup for moments such as this, but he preferred to keep that fact private.

"Right here. Wait for me across the street."

Diamond sprang from the backseat and headed straight for the cameras. There were so many of them in front of the old terra-cotta building that they spilled off the sidewalk onto the pavement, blocking traffic but otherwise suiting Diamond's purpose to perfection. The government was gonna have some nice pictures to prove he'd gone and met with his client just like he'd promised.

"Hey, that's Atari's new lawyer!"

The flashbulbs were so thick that the effect was of a continual strobe light. He blinked but he didn't flinch.

"Mr. Diamond! Mr. Diamond, over here. Channel Seven News."

"New York One!"

"Mr. Diamond, Associated Press."

"What's Atari's defense?"

"Channel Nine. Who killed the lawyer?"

"*Rolling Stone*. Is it true Atari's working on a new CD about this experience?"

"Is he going to trial?"

"Have you gotten any death threats?"

Diamond stepped onto the sidewalk and held up his hands for silence. "I'd like to make a brief statement."

The shouting stopped, but the air was thick with braying car horns and the *pop-pop-pop* of the flashbulbs. Beneath his feet, the subway rumbled. The wind had picked up. It was whistling down from the north, carrying the sharp taste of cold. Diamond drew on all his skills to project his voice into the roar of the New York afternoon.

"My client, Mr. Briggs, is innocent. This is a vendetta by the government. Why? They don't like his message, so they attack his

legend. In doing so, they're willing to trample not only his civil liber-
ties, but yours. Today it's music they're censoring. Tomorrow it'll be
poetry or journalism or literature. We can't let them win. My partner
refused to allow it, and I'm here to pick up the fallen sword."

"Who killed Poe?" somebody shouted.

"I don't know, but I can tell you this much. Lester Poe was a great
lawyer and a great American."

Diamond let himself well up for the cameras. He rode the emotion for a dramatic moment, then swiped a knuckle at his eyes and
switched over to an expression of solemn determination.

"His murder was an attempt to prevent Atari Briggs from mount-
ing an aggressive defense. Lester Poe would not want us to falter for
one second in defense of the innocent. This is how I will pay my
respects to my partner. I will take Atari's story to the jury, and when
they hear it, they will walk him out of that courtroom a free man,
with his head held high and his name cleared! Bring it on!"

Diamond raised his fist in a black power salute. All hell broke
loose. He turned and strode into the lobby.

"Keep those bloodsuckers out on the street where they belong,"
he said, thrusting a hundred-dollar bill at the doorman.


Alone in the elevator, Diamond allowed himself a small smile.
When the elevator reached the penthouse and the doors slid
open, he found himself staring at two massive bodyguards, both
white. They appeared to be in their thirties, and they wore conservative business suits and neutral expressions. If not for the fact that
they were built like bouncers, he might have taken them for accoun-
tants or software engineers.

Diamond stepped off the elevator, and the bodyguard on the right
stopped him in his tracks with an iron fist against his chest.

"Your name, sir?"

"Evan Diamond. What do you think you're doing? I'm Atari's lawyer. He's expecting me."

"I'm going to have to ask you to step up against the wall and spread your arms and legs so I can check you for weapons."

"Are you fucking kidding me? The guy's my client."

"Nothing personal, sir. Routine precaution. We do this with everybody."

"I don't like another man touching me. What if I tell you where it is?"

"We can't take your word for it. We still need to pat you down."

Diamond rolled his eyes but turned and did as requested. In truth, he was no stranger to the pat-down. He did too many jail visits, and had too many clients with prices on their heads.

This bodyguard was swift and professional. Within a second, he'd come up with the .32-caliber revolver that Diamond wore strapped to his right ankle.

"I'll need to safeguard your weapon for the duration of your visit, sir."

"All right. But I want a receipt."

"I'm sorry, we're not equipped to do that. But I assure you there won't be any problem. This is the only weapon we have in custody at the moment."

"I better get it back. It has sentimental value."

"You will. Don't worry, sir. This way, please."

The bodyguard led Diamond to the large double door across the hall. He opened it with a card key and stepped aside to let Diamond enter. Light spilled from two walls of enormous windows into a spectacular corner living room, bouncing off gleaming hardwood floors and reflecting back on shimmering golden drapes. To his right was a small kitchen; to his left, a closed door that presumably led to a bedroom. The furniture was mod and groovy and mostly white, and the room was so clean and perfect—and empty—that it seemed impossible that any human had ever set foot in it.

"Mr. Briggs is occupied at the moment," the bodyguard said. "He asks that you please enjoy the refreshments he's provided, and he'll join you shortly."

The bodyguard retreated and closed the door behind him, and Diamond looked around for the source of the oniony smell he'd noticed when he entered. A tiered tray with a complete caviar service had been placed on a beautiful black lacquered dining table. Beside it stood a bottle of champagne in a bucket of ice. Diamond crossed to the table, keeping his eyes on the bedroom door. Behind it, a woman was moaning.

*Not bad,* he thought as he glanced down at the label on the champagne bottle. 'Ninety-two Dom Pérignon, and the caviar was Osetra, five ounces of the stuff. He sat down in a black leather chair and fixed himself a blini with all the trimmings.

Behind the closed bedroom door, things were getting rowdier. Jesus, the life this guy had, and what the fuck had he done to deserve it? Sold dope and wrote a few songs about it? Diamond had listened to enough of Atari's so-called music to have concluded that it was nothing more than a thug bitching and moaning about the hardships of the life while making a mint off it. He wouldn't mind watching the guy take a fall, but then he felt that way about most of his clients. At least with Atari, he could expect a big payday.

The girl behind the door was moaning like crazy, so Diamond got up and walked over to the window, which looked out onto Prince Street. He couldn't tell from this angle whether the reporters were still there. He picked up a clicker and turned on the flat-screen TV, flipping channels for a while. When he didn't find anything about himself or the case, he settled for a Knicks game on ESPN, ate some more caviar, and waited. He was just starting to get pissed off enough to think about walking out when the bedroom door opened.

The girl came out first. She was spectacular to look at—a leggy blonde with a perfect body and an angelic face who couldn't have been more than eighteen or nineteen, wearing the tiniest minidress. Atari followed close behind her. He hustled her toward the door, shoved a wad of cash into her hand, and pushed her out.

"Call me again sometime," she said.

"Yeah," he said, and closed the door in her face.

Atari came over to the table and shook Diamond's hand. He had a bodybuilder's physique, not overly tall, but powerful and thickly muscled, and his hands were strong. In exquisite pin-striped pajamas, his flawless skin gleaming with sweat, he was an amazing specimen, and Diamond saw the physical charisma that had made the man a star.

"Well, well, Atari," Diamond said. "You're looking very prosperous."

"Yo, sorry for the wait, son," Atari said. "A little tension relief. I been real stressed with everything going on."

"I don't blame you. That girl was something."

"You want some on the way out, say the word. I got a roomful of pussy on the fourth floor ready to party."

Diamond had learned the hard way not to accept offers like that from clients, especially clients with a known fondness for hidden cameras. He tapped his wedding band against the table and shook his head no.

"True to your woman?" Atari asked, eyebrow cocked. "That's a new one from you."

"It's been a long time since you and I worked together. Maybe I've changed."

Atari laughed, popping the champagne cork with practiced ease.

"I doubt that. Gangstas like you and me, we never change. But circumstances change, and I'm willing to truce if you are. Some a this?"

"Sure, what the hell. We'll truce, seal it with a drink."

They clinked glasses. Atari sat down across from him, and they took a minute to size each other up.

"A shame about Lester," Briggs said.

"Crying shame."

At the same moment they both broke out into big grins.

"I didn't body him," Atari said, shaking his head.

"That sounds like a confession to me, kid."

"Naw. Why I body my own lawyer? That's the man who protects me. But you? Wouldn't surprise me one bit if you were the guilty party."

"I've thought about it once or twice. That much I'll admit. But I'm innocent, too, on this one. I didn't kill him."

Atari laughed. "I'm glad to see you again, Diamond. You always were good for a laugh, and I never was happy with how Lester handled shit."

Diamond paused for a sip of champagne. "Lester could be pigheaded. It's no surprise that somebody took him out. Casualty of war."

"You should know."

There was a venomous pause.

"I thought we said truce," Diamond said, thinking about the holster strapped to his ankle, and how empty it felt.

Atari spread his hands in a gesture of conciliation. "You're right. Let bygones be bygones. Let the dead rest, and do our necessary business."

"Exactly."

They drank some champagne.

"You know, Atari," Diamond said, "if I'm gonna be in your corner, we need to take care of the damage to your reputation that's been done recently. I can't be associated with it."

"What's that supposed to mean?"

"I had an interesting visit from one of the U.S. Attorneys on the case this morning, Melanie Vargas. She seemed to think you wanted to cooperate with the government and make cases."

"Cases? Against who?"

"She wouldn't come right out and say, but I have some ideas. Perhaps a mutual friend of ours."

"Oh. Him. Look, that's bullshit. You know I ain't no rat, and you can tell him I said so," Atari said.

"I hope that's true. Because we've both seen what happens to guys who snitch, and it's not pretty."

"You *hope* it's true? Suck my dick, Diamond. You go back to that little prosecutor and tell her she better stop spreading rumors or she'll regret it. I ain't never ratted before in my life, and I never will. Besides, I got nothing to give up, since I'm innocent of all charges. Lester was lying to her."

"Why would Lester lie?"

Atari shrugged. "You know the man. Moves within moves."

Diamond nodded slowly, his eyes on his client's face. "True."

"Diamond, I know who you are and where you come from. I'm the same as you. I obey the code. This is all a big misunderstanding. So you go back and tell that to our friend, since I know he's the one pulling your strings, understand?"

"Atari, please, I work for you."

"Oh, right. Just like back in the day."

"What happened to trucing, baby?"

"You gonna take care of my problems the way you did back in the day, too? Because then maybe I would find it in my heart to forgive you."

"You know I am."

"Nice," Atari said, laughing. "Then I am truly blessed. You get me out of this, man, and the sky's the limit. Politics is next. I want my face on money. I can't have no felony conviction if I'm gonna get my face on money, can I?"

# 14

The afternoon was waning, the condolence calls were done, and Brenda Gould had thirty minutes before her next appointment. Alone in the apartment with her memories, she was trying not to hear the siren song coming from the liquor cabinet. She needed to stay sober to talk first to her lawyer, and then to the FBI. If they didn't believe her, they wouldn't take her side in the coming battle. To Brenda, Lester's death read like an early warning strike in what was sure to be a long and bitter war. The forces massing against her were not to be underestimated.

She'd pulled out the stack of old home movies. Funny, what you saved and what you discarded over the years. Inspired by the asceticism preached by her yogi, Brenda Gould had given away more than most people ever owned. Amazing clothes she'd worn in the seventies that would be worth a fortune as "vintage" now. Paintings and sculpture and avant-garde furniture. Virtually all of her jewelry, including the wedding and engagement bands from her first marriage to Lester. (That desperate second wedding hadn't stooped to anything as sentimental as rings or a white dress.) Material things weighed her down, yet she'd kept a pile of old movies that featured a person she'd hated with a passion and who had hated her; a person who'd ultimately succeeded in destroying her life. Not only had she kept the movies, she'd transferred them from film to video to DVD, carefully preserving them so they'd follow her into old age. Why?

The apartment had a media room fit for a Hollywood mogul. Brenda drew the blinds and flipped through the DVDs as if they were cards in a deck. She chose at random; the one she popped into the player was from 1980. As soon as the first frames flashed across the screen, she lost her battle with the bottle. No way could she look at this stuff without some moral support.

A few minutes later, Brenda sank into a leather armchair with a tumbler of Macallan in her hand. She'd left the bottle downstairs. Pouring more would therefore require a journey, though hardly one arduous enough to keep her away. Not with what she was about to watch.

Appearance and reality could be poles apart. As Brenda stared, wild-eyed, at film of herself from a long-ago summer day, her heart filled with bitterness. She was lounging in a chair beside the pool at the house in Sagaponack, holding the ever-present glass of wine, waving off the person holding the camera. Who'd been behind the lens? She and Lester and Philippe were all on the screen, so it wasn't any of them, but she couldn't remember. A long time ago, and she looked so young. Brenda's dark glasses obscured her face, so she couldn't read her own expression. Anybody watching the woman in the lounge chair would assume she was happy. The luxury of the surroundings, the glory of the day. It would take a real cancer, growing silently and out of sight, to wreck a life as charmed as hers had been. The camera panning to the grass court, catching the satisfying thwack of racket on ball as her husband and stepson played tennis, couldn't see such stealthy evil. The three of them looked the very picture of a happy, loving family.

The thought that the cancer might have been her own addictions briefly occurred to Brenda, but she pushed it away.

Before she knew it, she'd watched a lot of videos, and the bottle of Macallan sat empty beside her on the glass table. Here was Philippe washing the Jaguar, older now, nourishing his secret resentments, plotting against her. And the various women who'd wandered through their weekends, flirting openly with her husband in front of her like she was an irrelevant old hag. Why hadn't she left sooner? Why had she tortured herself in that way? Because it gave her a bitter satisfaction to keep tabs on Lester, to stand in his way and frustrate him, to outmaneuver whatever woman—or women—pretended to the throne that year.

Ah, yes, there was that one. Brenda couldn't even remember her name, that girl who'd been the cause of so much trouble. She'd been named for one of the virtues, but which one? Faith, maybe, or Hope. Not Chastity: Brenda would have remembered the irony if that had been the case. The camera had loved the girl, or somebody had, because there was a hell of a lot of footage of her from that summer. There she was sitting at the teak table, eating an ice-cream cone, sticking out a pink tongue coated with vanilla as Philippe gazed at her with adoration. And there she was in a tiny bikini, getting pushed into the swimming pool by Lester, the frank invitation evident in her every giggle and squeal.

The bottle was empty, but Brenda had her wits enough about her to realize that it was time to go. She'd agreed to meet Bob at that diner to escape the watchful eyes of Evan Diamond. Evan, who had his fingers in everything. But Brenda had figured out a bargain she could make with Mephistopheles. Evan on her side was better than Evan as an enemy, that much she was beginning to figure out.

Brenda grasped the arms of the chair and hauled herself up with both hands, not minding the darkness that came across her vision or the numbness that she felt cascading from her teeth to her toes. Old junkies didn't get high anymore; the best they could hope for was to feel blank. But as Brenda's eyes cleared, her hearing sharpened, too, and she became aware of . . . wait a minute, could it be? Footsteps in the hallway? When had they started? Could she be hallucinating on a few glasses of single malt? That must be it. All that muck in her system from years gone by, combined with some truly fine liquor.

But the steps were coming closer. Now it sounded like two people. Two men. She heard voices. But she wasn't imagining it. They were in her apartment.

# 15

Shekeya Jenkins wheeled the cart into the windowless conference room, righted a few binders that had toppled over, and turned to leave.

"Where are you going?" Jennifer Lamont asked, alarmed.

Shekeya put her hands on her hips. "It's after six and I was here half the night last night. I don't spend two nights in a row away from my kids. I'm going home."

"But Diamond hasn't shown up yet to get the discovery."

"He'll show eventually. You got to wait."

"Don't leave me here by myself. I've never done this before."

"What's to do? Make him sign the sheet before you give him the binders, that's all. You went to law school, right? I think you can handle that."

"What if he has questions?"

"Tell him to call Melanie or Susan. That's what I'd do."

Jennifer stood in the middle of the floor, looking helpless.

"Look, you can't screw this one up," Shekeya said, and despite the exasperated look on her face, her tone was not unkind. "The only screwing up you in danger of doing is pissing off the support staff, you feel me?"

"Yes."

"Good, then we understand each other. Have a nice night."

The door clicked closed behind Shekeya. Jennifer stood there for a moment, uncertain of what to do next. Her mouth was dry. She thought about making the trip to the vending machine for a Diet Coke, but she was afraid to leave the room. What if Evan Diamond came by while she was gone, and thought she'd left for the night? Not only would she get in trouble for not doing her job, she'd lose her chance to see him in the flesh.

That Diamond was a man to be both feared and admired Jennifer had believed for some time. About a year ago, he'd done a gun-running trial before the judge she was clerking for, and she'd watched him in action. He was handsome and quick, yes, but it was another quality entirely that attracted her attention. Diamond had power over people. He got them to do and say and agree to things that they shouldn't have done or said or agreed to, things in direct conflict with their own best interests. She didn't know how he achieved his ends, and she didn't care. To Jennifer, the power was compelling no matter how he came by it. She was a timid person—an unsuitable quality in a lawyer and one she despised in herself—who aspired to influence people. Influencing people was something Diamond did like nobody else.

Daydreaming about an unattainable man like Evan Diamond helped fill the gaping hole in Jennifer's love life. She hadn't had a steady boyfriend in years. Plenty of guys asked her out, but it was the same story every time. They seemed like Mr. Right, so she slept with them, but then they didn't call. So she'd call them, and they wouldn't call back. Then she'd call a few more times, and they'd leave a message telling her to stop calling. But she'd ignore it, and they'd decide she was a psycho. She saw the vicious cycle. She really did, but it was hard to stop. Therapy didn't help. The only thing therapists ever wanted to talk about was the ugly stuff that had happened when she was a kid, and Jennifer had absolutely no interest in dredging up all that crap.

The phone rang, and she jumped.

"Conference room."

"Is this Jennifer?"

"Yes."

"This is Al out front. I got a Mr. Diamond here for you."

"Oh, yes. Send him in."

"Send him in? No way, hon, you come get him. We don't let defense attorneys wander around unescorted. Didn't they tell you that?"

*Jerk,* she thought. "Fine. I'll be right out."

At the end of the hall, Jennifer opened the bulletproof door and poked her head out. Diamond was in the process of peeling the back off a visitor's pass and sticking it to his suit jacket. She drew a sharp breath. He was even more gorgeous than she remembered.

"Mr. Diamond?"

He glanced up at her and did a double take.

"Hey, Dixie. Look at you all grown up, with a big girl's job."

Jennifer blushed, worrying that the guard had heard, but he was on the phone.

"It's Jennifer," she said.

"I know. But I always dug that cute accent."

She smiled. "Come on, this way."

Diamond fell into step beside her.

"You remember me," Jennifer said.

"Of course I do. You were the best thing about Charlie Fox's courtroom. I'm just surprised that he let you leave."

"My year was up," she said.

"And you landed here? I had you figured for one of us."

"Maybe someday. I need trial experience first."

"Oh. A résumé maximizer. I like that."

"Résumé maximizer?" she asked.

"I have this theory that AUSAs can be divided into two categories. Résumé maximizers, who're looking to check off the trial experience box and move on. And true believers, who think they're on a mission from God. True believers are a pain in a defense lawyer's ass. Glad you're on board, Dixie. You can save me from Charlton and Vargas on this one."

Jennifer giggled. "Yeah, they're definitely in the true believer category."

"Talk about humorless. I like to have a good time at trial. Now that you're here, I can have some fun."

They passed the vending machine.

"Hold on a second," Diamond said. "I need a soda or something. I just drank some champagne with my client and it gave me the worst headache. Can I get you one?"

"Yes. I'd love a Diet Coke."

He fed a bill into the machine, and a can plunked out. He opened it and handed it to her, his fingers brushing hers.

"Thank you," she said, looking at him, remembering how she'd study his face during the trial, his voice and his gestures. Had he noticed her watching? Jennifer didn't take her hand away, and she held his gaze a few beats too long. There was no mistaking the hunger in her big green eyes. Surprise registered on Diamond's face, then curiosity.

He turned away and got himself a soda. Neither one of them spoke again until they were seated across from each other at the conference table, but by then the air between them was thick.

"So," she said, her voice husky and breathless, "I have the discovery binders all ready for you. The only thing you have to do is sign—"

He reached across the table and placed his hand on top of hers. His fingers were cold from the soda can. The words froze on her lips.

"Slow down," he said.

"Slow—slow down?" Her heart was hammering.

"It's been a crazy day, and I'm under a lot of pressure. Let me sit here and enjoy drinking this soda with you."

"Okay," she said. With great effort, she took her hand away, glancing at the closed door. She had no reason to think anybody would walk in. But if they did, she'd better not be seen holding hands with the defense lawyer.

"Remind me now, where exactly do you hail from, Dixie?"

Her new colleagues hadn't troubled to ask her the first thing about herself today. She'd felt so lonely and at sea. She looked up. Evan's eyes were the darkest brown. Black, really. So opaque that she couldn't see into them.

"Tennessee," she said. "But I hate my accent. I'd love to lose it but I can't seem to."

"No, don't say that," he said. "It's completely adorable."

The praise made her glow. She couldn't believe that she was alone in a room with him, or that he'd touched her. Any of it.

"You think so?" she asked.

"I do. But here's my question. You're a Yalie. College and law school, right?"

"I can't believe you remember that."

"Why wouldn't I?"

"I don't know. We only talked that one time. When you came by to drop off the jury instructions, remember, and I was alone in the judge's chambers?"

Something flickered in his eyes, and she realized how pathetic it sounded that she recalled the exact circumstances. But he wasn't put off. To the contrary.

"I listen when you talk to me," he said. "I always will."

"That's nice," she said, smiling.

"Tennessee to Yale. Big leap. How'd you swing that?"

"Just smart, I guess." She managed a flirtatious toss of her head, and he laughed. She was actually flirting with him, just like she'd fantasized about. But she felt all hot and prickly, like her body wasn't real, like any minute she'd wake up from the dream.

"Well, your parents must be very proud."

He'd put his finger right on her sore spot. Suddenly she was looking at the room through a haze.

"I'm an idiot," he said. "Here I'm so excited to run into you again, and the first thing I do is make you cry."

"I'm not crying," she said, blinking hard. "And it's not your fault. I've had a rough day. New job and all."

"I should know better. I come from one of the world's most dysfunctional families myself."

She laughed in shock. He'd gotten it exactly right.

"So what do you say we make a deal?" he said. "You let me take you out tonight. Anywhere you want. And I promise never to make you cry again."

But he'd overplayed his hand. Those words brought her to her senses. This was not a daydream. Her actions would have real-life consequences.

Jennifer sprang to her feet.

"Don't be silly," she said, and marched over to the cart. "You're married, and you're the defense lawyer." She took a deep breath. "There are twenty-three binders here. They're all labeled. You probably want to count them before you sign off that you received them. How are you planning to carry them?"

He came over to where she was standing. She wouldn't look at him.

"My car's right outside," he said, and his voice was gentle. "Can I borrow the cart to get the binders downstairs? I'll send it right back up in the elevator."

"Certainly."

He bent over and signed the acknowledgment form that was sitting on the table. His suit jacket was so precisely tailored that she could see the muscles of his back moving beneath the taut fabric. She wished that he would touch her again.

He turned to give the form to her. This time, their eyes met.

"I'm sorry. I didn't mean to offend you just now," he said. "But I felt such a powerful connection to you. The words popped right out of my mouth before I could stop 'em."

She looked away. She wanted to scream—*I felt it! I felt it, too!*

"It's okay," she said. "Don't apologize. Let's not mention it again, though."

She opened the door, and he maneuvered the cart through. He stopped and turned back to her.

"Good night. Be well," he said.

The concern in his voice seemed real. She smiled.

"Good night."

She closed the door quickly and sank, weak-kneed, into the nearest chair, where she proceeded to put her head down on her arms and relive every moment of their encounter. Only much later did she remember that she was supposed to have escorted him out.

# 16

Melanie was in the middle of a heart-to-heart with Agent Papo West when she looked up to see Evan Diamond lurking in the doorway of her office.

"Are you lost, Evan?" she joked, but this was no laughing matter. They'd been talking about the importance of locating Vegas Bo and convincing him to testify for the prosecution. If Diamond got hold of that information, he'd surely do his best to subvert her plan. She wondered how long he'd been standing there and how much he'd overheard.

"I was on my way out with the discovery binders, and I heard your voice," Diamond said. He glanced at Papo as if unsure whether to continue. "You're on my list of people to talk to, Melanie, about that thing you brought up in my office this morning."

"You can speak in front of Agent West. So, what's Atari's answer?"

"Just what I predicted. He has zero interest in cooperating with the government. I believe his exact words were, 'I ain't no rat.'"

"You told him we're negotiable on the plea terms?"

"I told him everything. This is how he feels. There isn't any point in speaking with him further."

"What brought about his change of heart?"

"It's no change of heart. Atari claims he never told Lester he wanted to cooperate. He says if Lester told you that, he was lying."

"Why would Lester lie about such a thing? I don't believe that."

Diamond shrugged. "Beats me. But that's what my client says."

*Yeah, because he's afraid of you,* Melanie thought.

"Too bad," she said.

"It is what it is."

"Why don't you let me speak to him? Maybe I could—"

"My client doesn't want to talk. What don't you understand about that? The discussion's over."

"I guess we're going to trial, then."

"That we are. See you at jury selection."

He turned to go.

"Wait a minute," Melanie said. "You need an escort. I'm surprised at our paralegal, giving you the run of the place."

"You worried I'll start boosting documents from your file cabinets?" he asked, smiling.

"It's policy. Nothing personal. Agent West will see you out."

While Papo was gone, Melanie left an annoyed message for Shekeya Jenkins reminding her of the office policy on defense lawyer visits. Then she called Mark Sonschein and delivered the bad news.

"What the hell is Atari thinking?" Mark said. "He's dead in the water with that wiretap tape. He should be falling all over himself to cooperate."

"Oh, please. Have you seen the papers? 'Attack on a Legend'? I want to barf. The press is totally on his side. The jury will be, too."

"That's always been true, but yesterday Atari was eager to cooperate. Why the sudden turnaround?"

"Why do you think? They murdered his lawyer. Atari's no fool. He got the message."

"You really think that's the reason?"

"Of course it is. That was their plan, and it worked. We need to find out who told Gamal Abdullah that Atari was about to snitch. Was there a leak somewhere? Is the Bureau investigating that? The answer to that question could turn this whole case upside down."

"Don't worry, the Bureau is exploring every angle. Leave it to them. You keep your nose clean."

"Are they looking at Diamond, or are they giving him wide berth because he's the defense lawyer?" Melanie pressed. "Diamond shared office space with Lester Poe. Who knows, maybe he overheard something about the cooperation. He's got a reputation for being untrustworthy."

"It's a big leap from untrustworthy to getting your partner killed."

"They weren't exactly partners, and besides, I'm not suggesting that Diamond had Lester killed, just that he might have leaked information. He's quite capable of that."

"As far as you're concerned, Diamond is opposing counsel, nothing more, Melanie. And you know I can't get specific with you about the bombing investigation."

"That is so stupid."

"Sticks and stones, kiddo."

"What's that supposed to mean? I should come over there and break your leg if I want information?"

"Very funny. Now get back to work. Convict Atari at trial, and maybe he'll come around."

Melanie hung up, frustrated, as Papo walked back into the room. She was glad to have him to vent to.

When Melanie first met Papo West, his scruffy redneck appearance made her think that he was some kind of slacker thug. At six four and two hundred and fifty pounds, with the long ponytail of a guy who spent his free time on a Harley, he was both intimidating and out of place in the buttoned-down atmosphere of a prosecutor's office. Melanie was accustomed to working with clean-cut agents who looked like feds, her former boyfriend Dan O'Reilly being a prime example of that animal. But Dan was FBI; DEA, the agency Papo worked for, had a higher tolerance for cowboys, especially when the look suited the job. Papo, it turned out, was a great undercover, a distinction few white men could claim. He played any role from pothead hydroponic farmer to proprietor of a meth lab to leader of a biker gang with utmost credibility. What surprised Melanie was that he was also a decent case agent, that he maintained the concentration necessary to run a big investigation or a complex trial. He was a solid guy and pleasant to work with in the bargain—father of two, married to an ER nurse. Of course, none of that made her want to run into him in a dark alley late at night. Melanie had few illusions about the guys she knew in law enforcement. Most of them lived on the knife's edge of violence, and you'd be wise not to cross them. Papo certainly fit that bill.

"What's the word?" Papo asked as he settled his bulk into her guest chair.

"Mark says we should keep our heads down and prepare for trial."

"And let that scumbag Diamond get away with his dirty tricks? How much you want to bet he never even mentioned cooperation to Briggs?"

"Mark thinks that if we convict Atari, we'll get a second bite at the apple."

"Screw Mark. I thought the bosses at DEA were idiots, but this guy takes the cake."

"I hear you."

"How long should we wait? Weeks? Months? Meanwhile a hundred million bucks a week in Afghan heroin is running free. Terrorism might not be my responsibility, but heroin is. I don't like sitting on my hands not acting on a tip like that."

"I know. For me, this is mainly about getting Lester Poe's killer, but you're right, the drugs need to be stopped. Could you get your boss to call Mark? Maybe pressure from him would help."

"No. The chain of command at DEA was told by the Justice Department to back off and let the FBI handle everything. My boss won't do anything."

"Maybe we should look for a way to reach out to Rick Lynch behind the scenes. He could probably use our help."

"You mean, go around the Chinese wall? That guy's got a stick up his ass the size of Montana. What are the chances he'd agree to something like that?"

"Let me work on it. I might be able to figure out an alternate route," she said, thinking of Dan O'Reilly. Dan had told her in so many words that he was overseas working for Rick Lynch. Of course she'd said he shouldn't call, but she had a hunch he wasn't going to listen anyway. Maybe she'd reconsider her moratorium on speaking to him—for business purposes only, of course.

"In the meantime," Melanie said, "we have to track down Vegas Bo. Think about it, Papo. Atari's former lieutenant, set up out west with a great new source of heroin. And Atari tight with a guy who just brokered the biggest heroin supply agreement in history. What does that tell you about who Bo's source is?"

"Gamal Abdullah is supplying heroin to Vegas Bo?" Papo asked.

"It makes sense, doesn't it?"

"You might be onto something. I'm with you. Let's find this guy Bo right away."

# 17

Melanie opened her eyes and stared at the ceiling, the darkened bedroom vibrating with bluish light. Since turning two, little Maya had been sleeping soundly, but that hadn't translated into better sleep for Melanie. First it was work keeping her awake. The previous fall, when Bernadette DeFelice got elevated to the bench and Susan Charlton became chief of Major Crimes, Melanie had been promoted to deputy chief. Her name and cell number went out to every supervisor in FBI, DEA, ATF, ICE, and all the other alphabet-soup agencies as somebody to call for authorization if they wanted to make an arrest. It was like having an infant again: she hadn't gotten a solid night's sleep for months. Then, in December, right before Christmas, Dan O'Reilly confessed that he'd come close to having sex with his ex-wife and that he needed time to sort out his feelings. The crushing insomnia that descended felt like, if not an old friend, at least a familiar foe.

Enough time had passed since Dan dropped that bombshell and ran away to his foreign assignment that Melanie had made some progress. She was over the worst of the heartbreak. On top of that,

March had been a slow month for arrests, and in the past couple of weeks, she'd finally started sleeping again. Then Lester Poe had gone and gotten blown up, and here she was looking at the ceiling just like before. No point in lying here. She knew she wouldn't get back to sleep, not for a while anyway.

In the kitchen, Melanie jiggled the mouse, and her computer sprang to life. The light it cast in the dark room soothed her. She'd been reading every obituary of Lester that she could get her hands on. Now that he was dead, she'd developed an insatiable curiosity about his life. She couldn't believe all the interesting things she'd never known about him, things she hadn't bothered to ask him and that he hadn't thought to tell her. There hadn't been time in their brief acquaintance. She'd learned that he'd clerked for Chief Justice Warren. That he'd lived in Alabama for nearly a decade and still owned a big farm there, in a town where the municipal courthouse was named after a man he'd defended who'd later been lynched. That he'd been married once before Brenda, to a beautiful French socialite named Gabrielle Bertin, and had a son with her who was not much older than Melanie. In a different frame of mind, Melanie might have taken these new facts as evidence of how little she'd known Lester, and been reminded to treat this like any other case. Instead, the more she learned, the more she wanted to know, the more emotionally invested she got, and the more determined to solve his murder she became, no matter what the consequences to herself or her career.

At least it was better than obsessing about Dan O'Reilly.

Melanie Googled Lester for the fifth time that day. All the results that popped up she'd already read. She clicked on one of them, a news story about his civil rights days that she remembered had a picture of him she really liked. It showed the Lester of thirty years before standing at a bank of microphones. He would have been about the age Melanie was now, and he'd been shockingly handsome—jet-black hair, powerful features, every inch the dashing crusader after justice.

As she gazed at Lester's picture, she reached into the pocket of her bathrobe and pulled out the Saint Jude's necklace that had belonged to him, letting it run through her fingers.

"Jesus, snap out of it, the guy is dead," she said aloud, dumping the necklace on the counter beside her computer.

The phone rang. She grabbed it.

"Hello?"

"Don't hang up, okay?" Dan said.

"Okay."

"Really?"

"Yes, really." She'd decided to talk to him—for her own purposes. This was her shot at an end run around the Chinese wall.

"Good, I'm glad. I'm at the Legat in the embassy in Madrid. I managed to find a phone in a private spot, and I thought maybe we could finally talk."

"Is the line secure?"

"As secure as anything gets."

"Meaning—"

"Whosever listening is one of ours."

"That's no good."

"What difference does it make? They don't care about you and me."

"We're not talking about you and me."

"No?"

"No. I told you, we're done. But I still need your help with something."

Dan went silent for a moment.

"You know I'll always help you," he said finally, "and maybe eventually I'll manage to change your mind. In the meantime, what do you need?"

Melanie hesitated, worrying that maybe somebody really did

monitor calls from the FBI's Legal Attaché Office, but what could she do? Her options were either talk to Dan or nothing.

"I'm concerned that certain details might not be reaching your colleagues," she said. "You know I'm working on the Briggs trial, and that I was an eyewitness to the car bombing. Because of all that, they've got me walled off from the investigation. Anything I want to say to Rick Lynch has to go through layers of bureaucracy."

"I talk to Rick five times a day."

"I figured you might."

"Whatever you want him to know, I can get it to him."

Melanie had missed that rough-and-ready quality about Dan. No preliminaries, no long-winded explanations, no bullshit. He did what needed to be done.

"Right before the bomb went off, I had a long talk with Lester about the cooperation," she began.

"Lester's the attorney? The one who died?"

"Yes. He told me something important, something that isn't getting enough attention."

"Tell me. I'll make sure it does."

"Lester was worried that his office phones had been compromised. Normally when somebody tells me their phones are bugged, I think paranoia. But Gamal Abdullah obviously found out that Atari was about to talk. It's possible he found out some other way, but maybe—"

"Maybe the lawyer's phones really were tapped."

"Right. And even if they weren't, maybe the leak still came from inside Lester's office. His partner, Evan Diamond, took over the case—"

"Diamond? Evan Diamond, you said?"

"Yes. Do you know him?"

"Yeah, I had him on a trial a few years back. Total dirtbag. We turn over our witness list, and bang, the next afternoon in Bogotá our star witness's mother gets whacked in a drive-by shooting on her way to mass. We could never prove anything, but the witness refused to testify and Diamond's client walked."

"That's exactly what I'm afraid of, Dan. Just that type of problem on the Briggs case. My office is treating Diamond with kid gloves because he's opposing counsel. Meanwhile we just turned over witness statements, and our trial is only a week away."

"I get the picture. This does sound important. Anything else you want Rick to know?"

"That's it. Look at Diamond."

"Look at Diamond. You got it. And you, watch your back. Watch your witnesses, too."

"Thanks. I appreciate it, Dan. Good night."

"Hey—"

She hung up before he could get another word out. Melanie's heart was well hardened against Dan O'Reilly, yet she knew that talking to him was still a dangerous enterprise. Even talking to him about work was dangerous. They were on different planets in so many ways, but on the job they'd always been in sync. On the job was where they'd fallen in love.

Melanie sighed and let her gaze wander back to the image of Lester on the computer screen. What would life be like now if he hadn't been murdered? She'd be proffering Atari Briggs, sitting across the negotiating table from Lester, anticipating their dinner date. She'd be moving forward instead of letting the past nip at her heels.

She clicked refresh, hoping maybe something new had been uploaded during the minutes she'd spent talking to Dan.

Success! A story she hadn't read yet.

Melanie scanned the headline. BOMBING VICTIM'S WIFE FOUND DEAD, it read, followed by the subhead, *Seventies Icon Brenda Gould ODs in Apparent Suicide.*

# 18

Saturday dawned with an iron-gray sky threatening snow and little Maya snuggled up, warm and cozy, next to Melanie. Maya was an early riser, and once she'd graduated from a crib to a toddler bed, she'd developed the habit of tiptoeing into Melanie's room and falling back to sleep beside her mommy. Melanie hadn't done a thing to stop her. It was extra time together, and cuddly, precious time at that.

But even the sight of her daughter's sleeping face couldn't quell the anxiety Melanie felt upon waking up this morning. After reading about Brenda Gould's suicide, she'd lain awake for hours, turning the meeting with Brenda over in her mind, searching for any clue that the woman had been planning to take her own life—and finding none. Admittedly, Melanie was no psychologist, and she had no experience determining whether a person was suicidal or not, especially a person she'd only just met. Still, if Brenda Gould had been planning to kill herself, she'd put on a pretty good front. She'd appeared sad rather than desperate, reflective rather than grief-stricken—in short, relatively calm for a woman who'd just lost her husband. Did that mean anything, or was it simply a mask Brenda had donned for the benefit of a stranger? Melanie reminded herself repeatedly that Brenda had a history of drug use, and that if the overdose death wasn't a suicide, it might be an accident. Yet Brenda had claimed to be clean, and she'd said it in a way that Melanie had completely believed.

It was this last factor that kept Melanie tossing and turning, remembering Brenda's warning that Evan Diamond was dangerous, playing with the Saint Jude's medal that Brenda had given her as a talisman against him. She spent hours kicking herself for not getting the details on Evan out of Brenda when she'd had the chance. But what could she do about that now? Was she supposed to start investigating Brenda Gould's death? She wasn't even allowed to investigate the car bombing because she'd been ordered to focus on the Briggs trial. She could only imagine what Mark Sonschein would say if she told him she wanted to spend her time figuring out whether Brenda Gould had committed suicide or not.

When she thought about explaining herself to Mark, she realized how far-fetched the whole idea sounded, and forced herself to get out of bed and get dressed for the office. It was Saturday, but it was also her ex-husband's weekend with Maya, which turned out to be a good thing for Melanie's schedule. The trial was bearing down on her so fast that she'd planned witness prep sessions for today. She had plenty of work to fill up Sunday, too, so if she'd had Maya all weekend, she would've been in trouble. As much as Melanie missed her daughter when she was with her daddy, she had to admit that the joint custody arrangement was a lifesaver sometimes.

Melanie woke Maya up, got her dressed, and made scrambled eggs and toast for breakfast. The buzzer rang just as she was cleaning up the dishes.

"Daddy," Maya said, lifting up her arms so Melanie could take her out of the booster seat.

"Yep. Hold on, sweetie."

Once free, Maya ran to the foyer and stopped short at the front door. For security reasons, Melanie had her well trained never to open it on her own. That was a grown-up's job. With Maya jumping up and down beside her, Melanie peered through the peephole and saw her ex, gorgeous as ever with his rugged blond looks and his casually expensive clothes. The second she opened it, Maya raced past her and leaped into her daddy's arms.

"Hey, precious."

"Daddy!" Maya looked into the hallway. "Where's Kate?"

Kate McCall was Steve's new girlfriend. The fact that her ex had started dating somebody seriously at the same time that Melanie had ended her relationship with Dan O'Reilly was one of the things that had made this winter seem so grim. When Melanie first met Kate, she'd envisioned all sorts of nightmare scenarios. Kate the Stepmonster convincing Steve to stop paying child support, talking him into moving far away so Maya would grow up not knowing her daddy, or worse yet, scheming to steal Maya's heart and replace Melanie in her daughter's affections. Not that she thought Steve would ever behave that way, but the presence of another woman in his life, and in Maya's, at just the wrong time made her panic.

Not only had none of those horrors come to pass, but things on the home front were actually better with Kate around. She was a responsible, intelligent, kind woman, a colleague of Steve's with an important job, who was excellent with Maya. Maybe Steve had grown up in the year and a half since Melanie had caught him cheating and thrown him out, or maybe Kate just tolerated less garbage than Melanie had. But having Kate in his life had settled Steve down. He was now handling joint custody in a mature, civilized way that made Maya's life better and Melanie's less complicated. Of course, Steve's new relationship meant that Melanie hadn't had her ex-husband to go crying to when she broke up with her boyfriend. But that was a good thing, right?

"Yeah," Melanie said. "Where's Kate?"

"I was out late last night. Client dinner. So I never ended up going over to her place. But we're meeting her later at Serendipity."

"Dipity!" Maya exclaimed. It was her favorite ice cream shop.

"Have a great time," Melanie said.

She found herself hoping for his girlfriend's sake that Steve wasn't backsliding to his old ways. But he wasn't her problem anymore, and that was a relief. Steve was a good father, and he was even a good ex. But he hadn't been terrific in the husband department.

Melanie saw Maya out the door with lots of hugs and kisses, feeling a pang at letting the little one go. But she looked on the bright side. She had the weekend free to work, which she really needed to do.

# 19

Melanie wasn't the only government employee who worked weekends for free out of dedication to the job. Across her desk—which was littered with graphic photos of a young black man lying on an autopsy slab—sat Deputy ME Gary Nussbaum. Gary had performed the autopsy on Damond Purcell ten years earlier. Damond, also known as Little D, was the gangsta that Vashon Clark had gunned down on the orders of Atari Briggs. Melanie counted herself one lucky prosecutor that the ME who'd autopsied her victim was still on the job a decade later and available to testify. But then, this case was blessed that way. The star witness, the wiretap tape, the cop who'd responded to the crime scene, the ME who'd done the autopsy—everybody and everything had fallen into place so beautifully that she kept waiting for the other shoe to drop.

Melanie had been working with the ME for hours already, and they'd made good progress. Even better, he was going to make an excellent witness, lending some gravitas to her lineup. Straightforward, smart, bespectacled, and unassuming, he came across as a man of science with no ax to grind. Melanie planned to keep Nussbaum's testimony streamlined and to the point. He'd taken fingerprints from Little D's corpse that had been used to make a positive identification. He'd photographed the body at various stages in the autopsy, and she wanted to introduce some of the photos. Getting the jury to understand the ugliness of death helped get them past the natural human reluctance to sit in judgment on another human being. She'd also ask Gary to testify about cause of death—gunshot wound to the head—and introduce into evidence the nine-millimeter bullet he'd removed from the decedent's brain. Another amazing stroke of luck, finding that bullet lodged inside Little D's head. A nine-millimeter was powerful enough that in many cases, all the ME had to work with to determine the caliber of the bullet was a gaping exit wound and rampant speculation. Here, they could prove the caliber and link the bullet back to that phone call where Atari had promised Vashon Clark a "clean nine." A nice, neat case. So why did she have such a bad feeling in the pit of her stomach?

She was in midquestion with the deputy ME when her phone rang.

"This should be our lunch," she said. They'd ordered sandwiches from the deli across the street half an hour ago.

"Great. I'm starving." Gary looked at his watch. "It's two o'clock already. I have to leave soon."

"We'll hurry," she said, and picked up the phone. "Melanie Vargas."

"You have a collect call from a correctional facility," the automated voice said. "Caller, state your name."

"Vashon Clark."

Melanie accepted the charges. "Vashon, what's up?"

"Yo, I'm glad you in the office. I got a real problem in here."

Melanie sat up straighter. "Somebody bothering you?"

"I heard some shit that don't sound good," he said, lowering his voice. "Somebody asking questions about why I'm going to court so much."

Just what she'd been afraid of. They'd handed Evan Diamond a witness list with Vashon Clark's name on it, and now Vashon was in danger.

"Who's asking questions?"

"Some asshole. I don't know his name, but I'm nervous."

"Have you been threatened?"

"Ms. Vargas, when you inside, and somebody suggests you a rat, that is a threat. Lotta guys in here would kill me for the rumor alone, even if they don't know me, even if I'm not telling on *them*. And they'd be heroes for doing it. It's open season on rats in here, you feel me?"

"Okay, well . . . let me think a minute. I can have you moved to a secure floor."

"Yeah, I know all about that. The rat floor. Once they take me out of general population, that's a confirmation for everybody to see. I might as well hang a sign around my neck."

"The only other option is WitSec. Witness Protection. When they do it on the inside, it's totally secure. A whole separate facility. But even an emergency application takes weeks to process. We couldn't do it in time for the trial. And while the application's pending, they put you in twenty-four-hour lockdown. I can't prep you like that, and you don't see the light of day. Not even an hour for exercise."

"Aw, man, that's fucked up. I can't handle lockdown."

They were silent for a moment. Melanie thought about what it would do to her case to lose this witness.

"Vashon?"

"Yeah."

"We have to go with option one. We can't leave you in general population with people starting to make noise about you snitching. We'll segregate you for now, put you on a floor with other coopera-tors. The only time you'll mix is when you're getting transported to court, but the transport vans are pretty secure. I'm less worried about somebody reaching out for you then than in the shower or the cafeteria or something."

"You're right. I'm vulnerable where I am now. I'm'a go with your recommendation."

"Good. I'll put in the separation request right away, but it won't go into effect until Monday morning. Watch yourself in the meantime."

Melanie hung up and turned to Gary Nussbaum. "Sorry, I had to take that. It was an incarcerated witness calling, and he's in danger."

Gary looked at his watch. "Unfortunately, we're running out of time. I need to leave in half an hour to pick up my kids from my ex-wife. She lives in Great Neck. I was supposed to have them all day, so I'm on thin ice already. I can't be late."

"Believe me, I know. My daughter's with my ex today so I can work."

"You're divorced, too?" Gary asked, looking interested. "I noticed you weren't wearing a ring, but I figured there must be a boyfriend or something in the picture?"

His question was clearly meant to start a more personal discussion, but Melanie didn't take the bait. Fortunately, the phone rang. This time, it was the food. Melanie went out to the elevator to get it.

As they ate their sandwiches, Melanie started typing Vashon's separation request on her computer screen.

"I'll just do this separation request quickly," she explained to Gary, "then we'll finish up and get you out of here. My witness is getting threats in the MCC, and I have to take them seriously. We had one murder on the case already."

"Right, the lawyer, Lester Poe. I've been following that on the news. A colleague of mine did the autopsy. Just bits and pieces left of the poor guy. Apparently—"

Melanie held up her hand. "Lester was a friend of mine."

"Oh, I'm sorry. Terrible thing. And now his wife, too. I was supposed to be on duty today. I would have caught her autopsy, but I had to come here to meet with you."

"Really? So who's doing it instead?" she asked, turning around in her seat to look at him.

"My friend Sandy Levine, who's subbing in for me."

Melanie thought about Brenda Gould. How calm she'd seemed, how unlikely to kill herself. On top of that, Melanie was fairly certain Brenda intended to give the FBI the goods on Evan Diamond, which seemed inconsistent with being suicidal. The fact was, Melanie could mull this over all day and not get anywhere. There was no need for further speculation. A man sat before her who could answer her questions with one phone call. Guilty as she felt about using sex appeal to get information, Melanie knew that Gary Nussbaum would be happy to give her a peek at the autopsy report. All she had to do was ask.

# 20

It was Sunday, and Melanie had witnesses lined up all day long like planes coming in to LaGuardia. But even though she was anxious to get to the office, and even though she wasn't interested in Gary Nussbaum—not like that, anyway—she couldn't bring herself to cut their breakfast short. That would be rude. The man was doing her a huge favor. Not only had he gotten a copy of the autopsy report on Brenda Gould, but he'd come out in the middle of what was turning into a major nor'easter to deliver them to her.

So she had a second cup of coffee, and a third. They chatted about their work, their backgrounds, and being single parents. In a moment when Gary was talking to the waitress, Melanie even studied his face and decided that he wasn't bad-looking if you put aside the mild eyes and soft hands and the fact that he cut up dead people for a living. Not her type, but not objectionable, either, or at least not hideous.

It occurred to her that this was what dating would be like. Right after her divorce, she'd fallen in a fast straight line into an incendiary love affair with Dan O'Reilly. She hadn't so much as stopped for breath, and with Dan in the picture, there hadn't been room to think of anyone else. Then Dan was gone, and there was a stretch of time when she lay curled on her bed unable to move. The second she began to emerge from her cocoon of mourning, Lester had walked onto the stage, larger than life and ready to play a starring role. For so long, nothing had been ordinary. Melanie hadn't considered the possibility of being—well, underwhelmed.

The idea was so depressing that it finally got her to consult her watch.

"Oh, my, look what time it is. I have a witness coming in. I'd better be on my way," she said, and pulled her wallet from her handbag.

"Here, let me get that," Gary said, pulling out his wallet as well.

"No, no. We'll go dutch. You're my witness. Neither of us should buy anything for the other."

He chuckled. "You're afraid the defense lawyer will cross-examine me about having breakfast with you?"

"Knowing Evan Diamond, he definitely will, and I'm not kidding. If I pay for your food, it looks like I'm trying to buy your testimony. If you pay for mine, it looks like we're on a date and you get accused of a different form of bias."

"I do suffer from that bias, Melanie. I was hoping we could see each other again."

"Oh."

"If that's okay."

"I'm flattered, and I had a lovely time this morning, but . . . I— I'm just not ready."

"I thought you'd been divorced for a while now."

"Well, to be perfectly frank . . ." She faltered here, because what woman was ever perfectly frank in giving the brush-off to a man she didn't find attractive? Melanie wasn't ruthless like that. "I'm seeing somebody," she said, and shut her mouth.

"If I were a lawyer, I'd say you just made inconsistent statements, but whatever. I hope you'll think about it and change your mind. I really enjoy your company."

"Thank you. I've enjoyed working with you, too."

He laid down his money and pulled a thick cardboard folder from beneath his coat.

"Can't forget this," he said, handing it across the table. "There's a copy of the report in here, as well as the autopsy photographs."

Melanie flipped open the front cover and gasped. The photos were on top. The first one was a close-up of Brenda lying naked on the autopsy slab. Her eyes were open, her skin inert and blue, and there was a huge syringe sticking out of her rigid, rail-thin left arm.

"Oh my God," she said.

"I would normally never do this," Gary said, looking concerned, "but seeing as you were friends with the family, and given that the husband was deliberately murdered, I wanted to put your mind to rest that there was no foul play."

"There wasn't? But look at this needle, left there like that. Isn't that strange? Don't you think somebody else could've—"

"Oh, no, this is common in OD situations. We see it all the time. It simply means she lost consciousness when the drugs hit her bloodstream and didn't have time to remove the needle. Given the massive dosage, that's to be expected."

"Massive dosage? But why would she intentionally—"

"Let me explain," Gary interrupted. "The preliminary tox screens, which are generally quite accurate, showed cause of death as acute opiate poisoning combined with a blood alcohol level of point two-seven. In plain English, she OD'd on a cocktail of booze and heroin."

"Heroin. I'm shocked."

"You must've been unaware that the decedent had a long history of heroin abuse. Overdose becomes increasingly likely as people continue to use into middle and old age. The body's tolerance changes. Users need more to get high, but at the same time they're less able to metabolize the drug. That's what happened here. In terms of the massive dosage, her blood alcohol level tells us she was drunk when she shot up. She made a mistake and her body couldn't handle it, simple as that. No evidence of foul play. No evidence of suicide."

"It was an accident?"

"That's what we believe. Though admittedly, it can be tough to sort out accident from suicide in a heroin overdose. Think about it. Gunshot, hanging, slitting the wrists, those are your clear-cut suicide methods. Even overdosing with barbiturates or aspirin is obvious, because you need to swallow a whole bottle to die, and that's tough to do by accident. But with heroin, the only way we can distinguish accident from suicide is if they leave a note."

"And she didn't?"

"No."

"And there was nothing unusual in the surroundings that suggested either suicide or . . . anything else?"

"A couple of minor finger marks on her wrists. Not nearly enough to amount to defensive wounds, but more like somebody took her hands too hard and she didn't resist. Other than that, zilch."

"It was an accident," Melanie repeated, shaking her head. "Oh, well. I guess it's time to put Brenda Gould out of my mind and concentrate on the trial."

# 21

For a place so far removed from the state of nature, New York City exposed its citizens to the elements like nowhere else. Melanie kept her head down and wrapped her arms tight around the autopsy report as she fought her way through the driving rain to the subway. The walk was several blocks, and when she reached the wide-open avenue, a savage wind nearly knocked her down. Today of all days, she'd forgotten her umbrella. Frigid water droplets rolled off her hair and down the neck of her good wool coat, which smelled like a wet dog. At moments such as this, she wondered how much longer she could stand to live in the city of her birth. She dreamed of a warm place, or at least a place where she could afford to keep a car.

Susan had stuck a yellow Post-it on Melanie's computer asking her to stop by as soon as she got to the office. Melanie dumped her stuff and hurried down the hall to the chief's suite. The legs of her jeans were so wet that they stuck to her skin with every step, and her supposedly waterproof boots made squishy sounds.

Susan, Papo, and Jennifer Lamont were all huddled around the conference table.

"You look like a drowned cat," Susan said.

"Gee, thanks. What's up?"

"Have a seat, Mel. Papo was telling me you two're looking for this guy Vegas Bo."

Melanie sat down across from Susan, frowning. Susan, while an easier personality to work for and a closer friend, was more hands-on than Bernadette had been as chief. Melanie preferred to make her own decisions on cases, and this trait in her new boss irritated her considerably.

"Yeah. So?" Melanie asked.

"My view is, it's too late in the game to start hunting down new witnesses."

Melanie's blood pressure began to rise. She hated when Susan questioned her tactics.

"I'm sorry, but we need him," she insisted. "Bo's our insurance policy. Didn't you listen to that voice mail I left you? Vashon Clark's been getting threats."

"Yeah, and you took care of it. You separated him. He should be fine now."

"What if he's not? Bo was right in the middle of the hit on Little D. He provided Vashon Clark with the gun he used to do the murder, on Atari's orders. It's all on the tape. If we find Bo and flip him, not only is he our safety net if something happens to Vashon, but he could really bolster our case. We both know the jury's gonna eat Atari up. Evan Diamond is smooth as they come. Did you see him on the six o'clock news? If we give him half a chance, he'll have the jury believing his First Amendment BS. Don't you want another witness?"

"Well—uh—I hear you," Susan said. "I'm just concerned you'll end up wasting a lot of time on this and not be able to find the guy."

"Vashon gave us a solid lead on Bo's whereabouts. Papo, give Susan the rundown."

"I got a couple of agents detailed out of DEA's Las Vegas office to set up surveillance at the location, and they spotted Bo right away. He's got a stash house and mill, but not in Vegas, in this for-shit little town out in the desert called Pahrump. Nothing for miles but whorehouses, meth labs, and tumbleweeds. Bo's running a sizable crew. Between ten and fifteen guys in and out of the location, mostly black males, some Hispanics. I told my boys to set up and take some photos, but the place is so sparsely populated that surveillance is tough. They can't stay put in one place long enough to snap a picture without risking getting made."

"Even so, that's terrific," Melanie said, turning to Susan. "They've already located him. We can move quickly on this. Not a problem."

"We-ell, there is a slight problem. I got a call from the DEA supervisor in Vegas. They want the collar, and they want to take their time and do it right. They don't want us burning the lead by popping Bo prematurely on some ten-year-old murder con-spiracy."

"Well, they can't have the collar," Melanie insisted. "It's our lead. It's our case."

"If we have to duke it out with them, we get dragged into a huge time suck, Mel."

"I'll take care of it. I'll handle the turf negotiations. I'm a deputy chief now. I have the juice. Now that we have Jennifer on board, she can take a few of my minor document witnesses. That should free up my time."

"I'd be happy to do that," Jennifer piped up, "or I could approach Mr. Diamond and ask him to stipulate to some of the testimony."

"We tried that," Melanie said, shaking her head. "He said no."

"Sometimes a new face helps," Jennifer said. "He did a trial before my judge when I was clerking, and we had good rapport."

"Either way," Melanie told Susan, "Jennifer buys me some time to track down Vegas Bo. I'm doing it, Susan. We need him as a witness. The case could hang in the balance."

# 22

Her boxes weren't yet unpacked or her diplomas hung to put the world on notice of her Ivy League education, but the telephone in Jennifer Lamont's office was now working. That was all she cared about as she slammed the door behind her and sank into her swivel chair. She had a phone, and she had an excuse to call Evan.

She knew exactly the tone she wanted to strike. Professional at first. Not too personal. But just personal enough to remind him of their . . . encounter on Friday night. She remembered the cold touch of his fingers on her hand, and her pulse started to race. Why, oh why, had she taken hers away just as his started to warm up, to feel like flesh? Nobody would have walked in. Since then, she'd imagined a hundred scenarios for what might've happened next if she hadn't been such a chicken.

Jennifer picked up the receiver, then lost her nerve and let it clatter back into the cradle. Finally, she took a deep breath and punched in the numbers. Her fingers were shaking, but in a delicious, butterflies sort of way.

Voice mail, after all that. Disappointment overwhelmed her, so much that the beep sounded before she was ready.

"Uh, hi, Evan, this is Jennifer Lamont from the U.S. Attorney's Office. I hope you've had a chance to review the discovery I gave you on Friday night. I need to speak to you regarding—"

A loud screech sounded on the line.

"Hey, Dixie."

"You're there."

"Sure I am. You think you're the only one with a trial to prepare for?"

"Well, I thought, you know, high-priced firm and all . . ."

Jennifer felt incoherent, but he picked up the ball and ran with it.

"What? That I have some hotshot associate doing all the heavy lifting? That I'm nothing but a mouthpiece?"

She loved the teasing tone in his voice, did her best to match it.

"I thought you were just another pretty face," she said.

"Look who's talking."

"Oh, come on now. You're a flatterer."

His voice was soft and insinuating as silk. "Don't play coy. You're beautiful, and you know it, too. Long auburn hair, big green eyes, the little freckles across your nose. Mmm, and your body in that nice, tight sweater you were wearing the other night. You're incredible."

Jennifer couldn't speak for a moment. No man had ever complimented her like that. She'd always thought of herself as ordinary-looking, even mousy. But in Evan's eyes, she was beautiful.

When she'd finally collected herself enough to speak, her voice came out all husky. "You . . . you shouldn't say those things."

"Why? Because you like it too much?"

She laughed. "No. Because this is business, and you're opposing counsel, and you're married."

"Damn, and here I thought you'd be happy to know how I felt. I thought you were calling because you missed me. I miss you, you know."

"Well, you shouldn't."

"Shouldn't seems to be your favorite word. I can see I'm going to have to work on eliminating it from your vocabulary."

"You're right, it is my favorite," Jennifer said, turning serious. "I'm very attached to it. It's the only way I keep from screwing up all the time. Otherwise . . ." She trailed off.

"Am I hearing right? Wholesome little Dixie, living life on the edge?"

"Yeah, that's me. I know it doesn't seem that way, but I really do."

"I'm happy for the company, then. That's where I live."

"I see that."

"Of course you do. It's why you like me so much."

She was struck dumb yet again. He saw right through her.

"Get over yourself," she said. "How do you even know I like you?"

Now it was his turn to laugh. "Go ahead, fight it. I like a good buildup. But you'll fall in the end. See, I know something about you that you don't even know about yourself."

"What's that?"

He lowered his voice till she felt like he was whispering right into her ear. "Somebody like you, who lives life on the edge, who feels the power of the dark side? What you really want . . ."

"Yes?"

"Is for me to pull you in."

# 23

Melanie and Papo were sitting in her office literally waiting for the phone to ring. They'd left word for the chief of Narcotics in the Las Vegas U.S. Attorney's Office to call them about Vegas Bo.

"I'm starting to think Susan was right," Papo said. "We're wasting our time. The guy's never gonna call us back today. It's Sunday."

"He's lazy."

"Either that, or we're stupid."

"If that damn phone company witness wasn't late, at least we'd have something to do while we wait," Melanie remarked.

Jennifer Lamont tapped on the office door. "Sorry to interrupt. Is it okay if I come in?"

"You're not interrupting," Melanie said.

"Take a load off," Papo said, removing his big feet in their scuffed motorcycle boots from the chair next to his.

Jennifer sat down. She cast her eyes downward, which made her look even younger than she was.

"Melanie, you said if I had questions, I should just ask. Hope you don't mind."

"Of course not."

"I'm trying to understand the facts better. Who's this new witness I heard you talking about in there?"

"His real name is Kevin Bonner, and he was one of Atari's lieutenants in the drug business. When Atari ordered Vashon to do the hit on Little D, he said Vegas Bo would give Vashon the gun."

"Do we know where he is?"

"Yes, he's in this town called Pahrump, out in the Nevada desert halfway between Las Vegas and Death Valley. The DEA is setting up on him even as we speak. We're just waiting for a call from the prosecutor to work out the politics."

"And Bo helps us because . . . ?"

"We could really use another witness with direct knowledge about the hit. When Atari told Bo to give Vashon the gun, he presumably told him why, what it was for. That's great testimony if we can get it. But the bigger issue is, we don't want to hang the whole case on one witness. Right now, we can only get the wiretap tape into evidence if Vashon testifies and the jury believes him. Evan Diamond doesn't know this, but the only other person besides Vashon who can authenticate that tape is the DEA agent who handled the tape recorder ten years ago, and he's in Iraq. My hope is, Bo would be able to authenticate the tape, too. I have a hunch that he was in the room listening when Atari and Vashon had that phone call."

"So if you lose Vashon, you lose the tape," Jennifer said.

"Yes, and we lose the whole case, unless we have Vegas Bo in pocket by then."

Melanie's phone rang. "Excuse me," she said.

"Melanie Vargas." Melanie gave Papo a thumbs-up. "Hi, Glen. I have the case agent here with me. I'm gonna put you on speaker."

"Who'm I talking to?" asked a gruff male voice from the speakerphone.

Melanie glanced at Jennifer and put her finger to her lips.

"Agent Paul West from DEA is here with me. We call him Papo. Papo, this is Glen Begley, chief of Narcotics in the Las Vegas U.S. Attorney's Office."

"Papo? What kind of criminalistic name is that?" Begley said with a big belly laugh.

Papo smiled. "I'll tell you, scares the bejesus out of the scumbags when they hear it."

"I'll bet it does. So what can I do for you fine folks on a Sunday that's important enough to interrupt eighteen holes for?"

"We're handling the case against Atari Briggs," Melanie said.

"Heard of it. I'd have to be living in a pit in the ground to miss that one."

"There's a witness we need, and we've got a lead on him. He's in your jurisdiction, and we'd like your assistance in placing him under arrest."

"This is Kevin Bonner you're talking about."

"Yes. So you know why I'm calling."

"I've been briefed by our local DEA. But from what they tell me, Bonner belongs to them. He's part of a major ongoing narcotics investigation."

"Ongoing for one day," Melanie said. She caught Papo's eye and pointed at the telephone like, *Do you believe this shit?* "Local DEA only knows about this operation because we told them. We gave them the address. They didn't have a clue about it before yesterday."

"That's not how they tell it. They claim to've had informant information on this Pahrump location going back months."

Melanie looked at Papo, who shook his head vigorously.

"No way," Papo said

"They did, son. They showed me the reports," Begley insisted.

"If they had something, they hadn'a done jack shit with it before yesterday. I know. I talked to Andre Ferris myself, and every word I said was news to him."

"What we got here is a failure to communicate," Begley said. "And I have to side with my agents. They're looking to make a case, maybe go up on a wiretap. I can't pull the rug out from under 'em with a premature arrest. I work with these boys every day of the week."

Melanie hit the mute button and caught Papo's eye.

"Is there any truth to what he's saying?"

"Total bull. Whether the DEA guys are feeding him a line and he's buying it, or whether he's in on it, I can't say. But they're trying to dick us over, plain and simple."

She took the phone off mute.

"Glen, I'm going to trial in a week. I'm not about to sit on my hands while you build probable cause to steal my target. I'll be faxing you an arrest warrant within an hour for Kevin Bonner, and if you don't execute it right away, I'll have Main Justice on your ass before you know what hit you."

Begley belly laughed again. "I love New York. Everybody plays hardball."

Melanie rolled her eyes at Papo. "Is that a yes?" she said into the phone.

"If you feel that strongly. But somebody's got to make it right with DEA. If those boys get mad at me, my business dries up."

"I'll take care of that," Papo said. Then under his breath, "I'll punch their fucking lights out is what I'll do."

"You get them on board, you have my blessing," Begley said. "All right with you folks if I go back to my golf game?"

"Sure thing," Melanie said. "Thanks for your time. We'll be in touch."

"Honey, I'm sure you will."

Melanie dropped the call. "Can you believe that guy?"

"I can't believe those agents," Papo said. "Fuckin' snakes, and they're supposed to be my brothers."

"We need to get an arrest warrant on Bonner right away, and fax it to Begley before he changes his mind. You have time to sit here and write up a complaint with me?"

"I'm fine, but what about you? Don't you have all those document witnesses coming in?" Papo asked.

"Oh, don't worry about them," Jennifer exclaimed. "I got Evan Diamond to agree to stipulations."

"Jennifer, that's amazing," Melanie said. "Good for you! How'd you manage it?"

"I called and asked him, and he just said yes," she said with a shrug.

It had really been that easy. He'd said he could never refuse her anything.

"He knows you clerked for Fox, right? And Fox hates it when attorneys won't stipulate. Maybe Diamond was afraid you'd tell your judge on him."

Jennifer smiled. "That must be it."

# 24

The separation order wasn't due to take effect until the next morning, and Vashon Clark was looking over his shoulder with every step. His cell mate was a Latin King, a Puerto Rican from Marcy Projects named Freddy Moreno who knew exactly how many trips Vashon had made to "court." Freddy didn't buy that the trips had been to argue an appeal. Freddy told Vashon you don't show up for your appeal, your lawyer does that shit on his own. He knew that for a fact, because he himself had three strikes, and three appeals to go along with them. When his lawyer lost the last one, Freddy got locked up for twenty years, and now he had nothing to do but watch TV and beat the shit out of whoever annoyed him. Rats annoyed him.

In the cafeteria for supper, Vashon sat down at his usual table. American chop suey tonight. It looked decent enough, but the burned crust of cheese on top smelled like puke. On the inside, you stuck with your own kind. Everybody at Vashon's table had black skin and was locked up for slinging dope in Bed-Stuy or East New York. The Bed-Stuy guys sat on one side of the table and the East

New York guys on the other. Vashon had known a few of 'em since he was four feet tall, but if they thought he was snitching, they'd shiv him in the back without a second thought and smile when they wiped off the blade.

A big motherfucker with a shaved head sat down next to him. He was called Eight Ball because he'd started in the cocaine trade before moving to heroin. Vashon didn't say a word, just looked at his plate and moved the food around.

Eight Ball started shoveling in big piles of the shit. "Word is you snitching," he said through a mouthful of macaroni.

Vashon pulled a face. "Who say that? Whosever talking shit about me, I'll pound 'em into the fucking concrete."

"It's comin' from a lotta places. I'm thinking you might could use some protection."

Vashon gave a clipped nod. They were talking out of the sides of their mouths, not making eye contact.

"Maybe that," he said, "if what you saying is true. What you gonna ask from me if I decide I want you to help me out?"

"Twenty large, payable like so. A grand in my commissary account and nineteen to my moms in the Louis Armstrong Houses."

"Fuck that. You think I got that kind of cash?"

Eight Ball glanced at him, cool indifference in his eyes. "Funny. The people who want you dead do."

"I got a bounty?"

Eight Ball had finished inhaling his food. He ignored the question, burped, and started walking away with his tray. Vashon thought he might throw up, which helped him see an opportunity.

The room was enormous, row after row of long tables filled with hundreds of inmates, and only a few COs scattered around the perimeter. Vashon saw that he would have to be loud to attract their attention.

He dropped to the floor, writhing and holding his stomach and moaning at top volume. Medical care was so bad here that inmates did everything they could to avoid the infirmary. It would be empty tonight, and safe.

"Motherfucker's a rat!" somebody shouted.

In an instant, he was surrounded. Inmates were issued slip-on canvas shoes with rubber bottoms because the Bureau of Prisons recognized hard soles for the deadly weapons they were. But if enough motherfuckers kicked and stomped on you with their soft shoes, you'd still die. As the first foot sailed toward his head, Vashon Clark pulled himself into a fetal position and screamed at the top of his lungs.

# 25

Melanie had enough to do on the trial that she knew she needed to put Brenda Gould's overdose death out of her mind. The autopsy report's conclusion that the death had been accidental definitely helped. Yet the photograph of the syringe protruding from Brenda's arm stood in such contrast to the cogent woman Melanie had met mere hours earlier, and the fact that the OD had stopped Brenda from snitching to the FBI about Evan Diamond was suspicious enough that a small, nagging doubt still persisted. Gary Nussbaum had told Melanie that Brenda Gould was a junkie of long standing. Maybe if she could find some evidence of that, Melanie could silence the alarm bells once and for all.

As Sunday afternoon drew to a close and she found herself with fifteen minutes to spare, Melanie logged onto Nexis, which archived news stories going further back in time than the Internet did, and searched Brenda's name. A vast panoply of information came up. As she systematically made her way through the articles, her mental image of Brenda—and by extension, of Lester—changed dramatically.

Melanie had imagined Brenda indulging in chic designer drugs, going a little too far, and winding up with a ladylike stint in rehab at a place like Betty Ford from which she would emerge fully recovered. All suitably jet-setty and within the boundaries tolerated by high society for its "creative" members. That was the impression Brenda had given her. But the reality was far uglier.

Brenda had suffered a truly public and dramatic breakdown over a period of years. She'd been arrested for possession of every substance under the sun—cocaine, heroin, methadone, painkillers, you name it. She'd also been found wandering, more than once—unwashed, disoriented, even naked. Some of these episodes had occurred during the period when Lester and Brenda were divorced. But others had happened while they were still together. Melanie spent some time matching up the decades, and discovered that Lester was just as likely to be in Cannes with some starlet as arguing before the Supreme Court during his wife's drug binges. Instead of looking like the hero for taking care of his befuddled wife after her collapse, Lester was starting to seem absent, neglectful, or worse.

As her research continued, the picture darkened further. Apparently Brenda's messy decline was not the worst scandal attached to Lester's name.

Debutante Found Dead at Lawyer's Hamptons Mansion, the first article read. The stories were from 1986, right before Brenda and Lester divorced, but the squalid phrases leaped out at Melanie as if they'd been written yesterday. *Suspicious circumstances. Girl's nude body discovered in swimming pool. Lawyer's son questioned. Famed civil rights lawyer questioned over girl's death. Lawyer's alleged affair with debutante.* With every story, there were photographs, grainy and blurred yet packing a punch. The girl—lovely, slim and blond, tawny-skinned, with an effervescent smile. Lester's son, whose name was Philippe, a skinny, brooding kid with a shock of black hair whose miseries went far beyond the average teen woes over girls and acne. And of course, Lester himself, gorgeous and commanding, yet, in these photos, closed somehow, even secretive, or was that just Melanie's imagination? Shouldn't she give him the benefit of the doubt, given that he wasn't here to defend himself?

Melanie devoured everything she could find about the case. Charity Bishop was the girl's name, and she came from a wealthy family that had made a stink over her death. The story stayed in the news for the better part of a year. But slowly, over time, the worm turned. The spin started to go Lester's way. Did Melanie detect the hand of a talented publicist at work?

Details emerged that cast doubt on the girl's character. Charity had been a regular at some of the seedier bars in Southampton. She'd had relations with lots of men that summer, including one known drug dealer and a few local blue-collar types with criminal records, some of whom couldn't account for their whereabouts on the night of her death. Earlier that night, she'd been pulled over by a town cop when her Triumph Spitfire had been spotted weaving on Montauk Highway. That encounter failed to produce any official action—no arrest, no ticket, not even a warning—and one news story came right out and said that Charity had bought off the cop with sexual favors.

After that story made the rounds, the authorities seemed considerably less enthusiastic about pursuing Lester Poe or his son. As Lester had been known to say, a strong offense was the best defense.

Besides, Lester and Philippe had alibis. Rather, they had *an* alibi, one that required the two of them to back each other up. They said they'd been at dinner together at a popular roadside burger joint in Southampton. There was no independent evidence to corroborate their claim, but given the nature of the restaurant, there wouldn't be. The place didn't take reservations, so there was no written record that they'd been there. And the restaurant was so swamped every night that when the college-kid waitresses couldn't remember seeing them, it didn't strike anybody as odd.

One thing that did strike Melanie as odd—why Charity Bishop had been swimming at their house when both Lester and Philippe were out—was never explained in anything she read.

Brenda Gould, however, admitted she'd been home at the hour when Charity Bishop was believed to have died, but claimed she hadn't seen or heard anything. When interviewed by the local police, Brenda said that she'd fallen asleep watching television in the media room and awoken to find that her husband and stepson had gone out. She'd gotten up to fix herself something to eat, and noticed that the patio lights were on, so she turned them off using the switch inside the kitchen, next to the sliding glass door leading to the patio. She certainly hadn't seen a body floating in the pool, or she would have called the police immediately. Instead, she finished her sandwich and went off to bed. She had no idea that Charity was in the swimming pool until the pool man discovered her body the next morning and raised the alarm. Brenda claimed not to have heard anything unusual that night. Indeed, she said she hadn't even known that Charity was at the house.

Shortly after Charity's death, Brenda disappeared into rehab again. She and Lester were divorced by the end of that year, and Brenda dropped from public view, spending most of her time in Big Sur.

As time went on, the scandal simply faded from the news. It didn't appear as if anybody had ever been charged. Lester kept quiet for a while, resurfacing a year or two later arguing cases, dating beautiful women, and bailing out his increasingly hopeless ex-wife, whose problems with drugs and the law grew ever worse.

Melanie had kept Lester's Saint Jude's medal with her since the afternoon Brenda gave it to her. Now she unzipped the internal compartment of her handbag and withdrew the chain, letting it swing between her fingers, catching the light, before dropping it into her desk drawer and slamming it shut.

That night, for the first time since the bomb had exploded, Lester's ghost left Melanie alone to enjoy a dreamless sleep.

# 26

Monday morning, Melanie arrived at her desk refreshed and ready for action, only to be met by the first in a series of major disasters. She'd just hung up her coat and turned on her computer when the phone rang, caller ID displaying a Bureau of Prisons exchange.

"Melanie Vargas."

"AUSA Vargas?"

"Yes."

"Roland Hughes from BOP. I'm looking at a separation request that came in over the weekend regarding inmate 463483–053, one Vashon Emilio Clark. You're the authorizing AUSA?"

"That's right."

"Bad news. When I plugged the number into the computer, I got that the inmate has been transferred to intensive care at Bellevue Hospital."

"Oh my God, what happened?"

"From what I gather, he was attacked in the cafeteria last night by a bunch of prisoners yelling 'rat.' Nearly caused a riot. If the COs hadn't intervened, he'd be dead now."

"Why the hell do you people have to be closed on the weekends?" Melanie cried.

"Don't blame me, ma'am," Hughes said calmly. "I don't know your case. Why didn't you put in your separation request sooner?"

"There hadn't been any direct threats."

"Well, we're not mind readers. If there were no threats, how are we supposed to know to separate your inmate?"

"Ugh, you're right. I'm sorry, Roland. I'm upset. He's in intensive care, you said?"

"Yes, ma'am, but he's gonna pull through. They'll be upgrading him from critical to serious condition shortly, the doctor said."

"What'll this do to my trial? He won't testify now."

"I can't help you there. But I do have information on where he's located, if you're interested."

"Yes, I want that. But what I really want is to figure out what happened and who's responsible. Do you have the names of the COs who were present during the incident? I'd like to interview them."

"I can give you the two guys who were closest to the action when the attack began."

Melanie scribbled down their names and took the information on how to find Vashon Clark.

"What kind of security do they have in the prison ward over at Bellevue?" she asked.

"It's all right, but if somebody wants your witness dead, it's not enough. If they can get him in the MCC, they can get him just the same in Bellevue. Easier, probably. I was you, I'd have one of your cops show up and stand by his door."

Roland Hughes's idea was a sound one, and Melanie hung up and immediately beeped Agent Papo West with a 911. Papo was on his way to Melanie's office to do trial prep. They agreed to meet at Bellevue instead.

Melanie caught a cab easily in front of the courthouse, since everybody else was on their way in for the morning calendar, and soon she was standing at Vashon Clark's bedside with her hands clenched into fists. She'd seen it many times, the ugly face of witness intimidation. Vashon's babyish features were swollen beyond all recognition, his limbs swathed in casts and bandages. The bad guys were so ruthless that Melanie was beginning to believe they'd win in the end. How could they not, when they were willing to do whatever it took to silence their accusers? They had no fear. Why should they? They got away with it. They shut people up, sometimes permanently. Vashon Clark was lucky. On past cases, witnesses had died. Looking down at his face, Melanie saw other faces. Rosario Sangrador, the brave housekeeper who'd agreed to testify against that madman Slice on the Benson case. "Fabulous Deon" Green, the flamboyant party promoter who'd taken on a drug-dealing nightclub owner on the schoolgirls case and paid the price for doing the right thing. Even David Harris, a wealthy lawyer living in a secure cocoon, who'd been an eyewitness to a murder, was tracked down by the killer. Vashon Clark was a murderous thug, and yet Melanie liked the kid. He was also somebody she'd believed could handle the pressure, navigate the system. Seeing him brought low made her wonder whether *anybody* could handle this kind of pressure, or whether she should be worrying about her own safety. Prosecutors loved to believe that just because a bad guy went after a witness didn't mean he'd look to hurt the people bringing the charges. It was one thing to reach out for your homeboy who'd betrayed you, but retaliating against the prosecution was a whole lot riskier and took a much more brazen character. It wasn't likely to happen. At least, that's what she told herself.

But who had done this to Vashon? Atari Briggs himself? Evan Diamond? Or was it simply the law of the street asserting itself? Criminals policing their own? She'd find out, but at the moment, with Vashon unconscious, there was little to be gained by standing here. Hopefully, when he woke up he'd remember the incident well enough to tell her who was behind it.

Melanie had had a frank discussion with the attending physician about Vashon's injuries. He had several broken ribs, a fractured femur, and numerous cuts and contusions. But the good news was, the attack had focused on his midsection, and he'd taken remarkably few blows to the head. He'd suffered a minor concussion, which wouldn't cause anything worse than a bad headache. There'd been no brain damage, and if Vashon had any remaining interest in testifying, he would have the mental capacity to do so. As to when he could appear in court—something she desperately needed to know—if he went in a wheelchair with his casts still on, it might be as soon as two weeks.

When Papo West showed up, Melanie filled him in. Her biggest concern was ensuring that no further harm came to Vashon.

"Don't worry," Papo said. "We'll have a guy on his door twenty-four/seven. Nothing else is gonna happen to this kid. We need him healthy for trial. How much extra time you think the judge is going to give us?"

"With Diamond yelling and screaming about speedy trial rights, I'm not convinced we'll get any postponement."

"How can that be? Diamond's got to be behind this. He can beat our witness and make it so he can't testify, and we have to go to trial anyway?"

"We need proof. Right now it sounds like this was a jailhouse smack-down that has nothing to do with Atari Briggs or his lawyer. If that's the case, Atari can't be penalized for it. It's *our* tough luck."

"Give me the names of those guards. I'll go interview 'em the second my boys show up to watch this door," Papo said.

"I'll come with you."

. . .

Overcrowded conditions meant that space was tight at the MCC. For their interviews with the two guards later that afternoon, Melanie and Papo were assigned a visiting room in the basement normally used by defense lawyers to meet with incarcerated clients. It consisted of a minuscule space with only one chair, separated by a reinforced glass barrier from an equally tiny space where the prisoner normally sat. They waited for about ten minutes before a knock came on the metal door behind them.

Corrections Officer Jack Quinn was in his fifties, paunchy and bald with a red face, and had been doing prison work for over thirty years. There were two ways to go when you spent your career in corrections—cynical and bitter, or cynical and amused—and Quinn had chosen the latter.

"Jeez, we're a bunch of sardines here. Mind if I keep the door open?" Quinn asked after they'd shaken hands.

They ended up doing the entire interview standing up, spilling out into the brightly lit acid-yellow hallway.

"These bozos, always up to something," Quinn said. "You can always count on the Bed-Stuy table for entertainment."

"Bed-Stuy table?" Melanie asked.

"Where your boy Vashon was sitting last night. They're a bunch of players who know each other from back in the hood, in Bed-Stuy and East New York. I was about thirty feet away along the north wall, but I had my eye on 'em because there are some known troublemakers in the bunch, and one in particular, a real mean mother they call Eight Ball. His real name's Bryce Timmons, and he's doing twenty-to-life for a drug-related homicide. Long story short, Timmons sat down next to Vashon last night, and right away I got the feeling something nasty was coming. They try to keep it on the down low, but I can always tell from the body language. So I'm watching, but then Timmons faked me out. He got up and walked away with his tray, and I'm thinking, problem resolved. Not so fast. Thirty seconds later, your boy Vashon's lying on the floor clutching his stomach and howling."

"Did Timmons hit him?" Melanie asked.

"I'd looked away, so I didn't see, but once Vashon was down on the floor, Eight Ball turned around and started shouting that Clark was a rat, and him and about ten other guys converged and started kicking the shit out of Clark. We had to get in there and really crack heads to pull the bozos off."

Other than telling them that a confrontation with Eight Ball had preceded the attack, Quinn had little of value to offer. None of the inmates involved had breathed a word to him about what set off the incident in the first place.

The second guard, a heavyset African-American guy whose name was Isaiah Carter, told a similar story. He hadn't noticed anything until the moment Vashon Clark dropped to the floor grabbing his stomach, but he seconded Quinn's statement that Eight Ball—Bryce Timmons—had been the one to start the attack by crying rat. But Carter seemed to have a better rapport with the inmates, and when Melanie asked whether he had any idea what had prompted the attack, he dropped a bombshell.

"Word on my cell block this morning," Carter said, "is Eight Ball was paid off —twenty large to organize an attack on Clark. A grand to his commissary, nineteen to his mother is what I heard. I got a few prisoners who I keep close to the vest, do 'em favors so they'll keep me in the loop. They're both saying it was well known that Atari Briggs's peoples put a bounty on Clark, because he was their rat."

"Can we talk to your informants?" Melanie asked.

"Given current circumstances, no, ma'am. I'm sorry, it would expose them to too great a risk of retaliation. Besides, they don't know anything firsthand. It's all just hearsay, gossip, what's the word in general population. The only one who's gonna know firsthand is Eight Ball himself. My feeling is, the offer came to him directly. He's an enforcer, see. He's somebody you'd turn to first if you wanted to bounty somebody."

"Will Eight Ball talk to us?" Melanie asked.

"Normally I'd say no," Carter replied. "He's not the cooperative type. On the other hand, he just got sixty days in the hole for this incident. That's twenty-three hour lockdown. Now, if anybody could eat that without cracking, Eight Ball can. On the other hand, it ain't no fun. You never know, maybe he could be incentivized."

"Reduce his punishment?" she asked.

"Yes. We'd need approval from the deputy warden."

The deputy warden was available and agreeable. Half an hour later, back in the basement interview room, Melanie and Papo watched as the door on the other side of the glass opened. Two COs escorted an enormous man with a shaved head into the prisoner area. He was shackled and covered in cuts and bruises, but he carried himself like he was the one running the show.

Papo slid open a small window in the glass, revealing a wire screen that made it easier for them to hear one another. Melanie pulled the single chair up to the window as Eight Ball was pushed down into the chair opposite.

"This is Bryce Timmons," one of the guards said.

"Who's she?" Eight Ball demanded of the guards, tossing his head back and refusing to make eye contact with Melanie.

"Mr. Timmons, I'm Melanie Vargas. I'm a prosecutor from the U.S. Attorney's Office, and I want to talk to you about the incident in the cafeteria last night."

"I know my rights. I don't have to talk to nobody."

"That's correct, you don't have to. But I'm prepared to offer you thirty days off your sixty-day sentence of isolation if you choose to. We know you were offered a bounty of twenty thousand dollars to attack Vashon Clark. We want to know who offered you that money."

In response, Eight Ball merely snorted and continued not to look at her. Melanie let thirty seconds go by. When it was apparent he didn't plan to speak, she said, "If you don't tell us, we go about our day, but you go back to the hole. Sixty days in there is a long time."

Finally, he looked at her. His eyes were cold and dead. They made her wonder how many men he'd killed.

"There wasn't no brawl last night," he said. "The COs are lying. They beat us all senseless for no reason, and they're lying to cover up. I'm gonna sue every last one of 'em."

Melanie saw that she'd never get through to Timmons. He was a hard case, past reaching now if he'd ever been reachable at all. Reluctantly, she told the guards to take him back to solitary.

Melanie and Papo were making their way slowly out through endless barred doors and holding areas when they were stopped and told that the deputy warden would like to speak to them. A squat female CO handed Melanie a greasy telephone.

"Ms. Vargas, Deputy Warden Tony Vasquez."

"Hi, Tony. No luck. He wouldn't talk. We got nothing."

"I'm glad I caught you, then. You'll want to hear this. Somebody just deposited a thousand dollars into Bryce Timmons's commissary account."

# 27

Following the money was never easy, especially when the parties to a transaction took pains to keep it secret. Melanie and Papo spent the next several hours chasing down records of the commissary deposit and learning what they could about Eight Ball's mother's finances, but ended up nowhere. They even brought in an assets expert from DEA's forfeiture unit to consult. By late afternoon they were back in Melanie's office, having succeeded in nothing beyond learning that the commissary deposit was made with an untraceable money order, and that there were no bank accounts in New York City held in the name of Eight Ball's mother.

"That doesn't mean she has no bank account," Papo said, leaning back with one boot braced against Melanie's desk. "It just means she has no account in her own name."

"Even if we could find her account," Melanie said, "we'd never see a nice, clean check coming in from Atari Briggs or Evan Diamond. Contract hits are a cash-only business. The best we'd do is a lot of cash, maybe a money-laundering charge."

"You're probably right about that."

"What if we were to look at the other end of this contract? Not the payment, but the offer. How did Eight Ball find out that Atari and his people would pay the twenty grand? A phone call? A visit? They must have conveyed it to him somehow."

"Not by telephone. Every inmate knows his calls are being recorded."

"Yes, but you'd be amazed what people still say," Melanie insisted. "I've had cases where inmates actually *did* discuss murders over prison phones. Seriously."

"If you want, I can send over a subpoena and get Eight Ball's recorded phone calls, as well as his visitor's log. But I'm warning you, it won't be done in time for trial. That kind of information takes weeks to get. Months, sometimes."

Melanie sighed. "We don't have that kind of time. I'd like to be able to go to Judge DeFelice now with evidence that the defense was behind the attack on our witness. Then she might at least grant us a postponement."

"To get the kind of proof you're talking about, if it even exists, won't happen until the trial's over."

"Then we'd better hope Vashon recovers quickly, and that he's still willing to testify."

"There is one other thing we can do," Papo said. "What you've been saying all along. Find another witness. Where the hell is Vegas Bo?"


But when they finally succeeded in getting Glen Begley on the phone, the news on Vegas Bo was as bad as it could be.

"Your boy Kevin Bonner is in the wind," he announced over the speakerphone with barely concealed glee.

"He's *gone*?" Melanie cried. "When were you planning on telling me this?"

"I'm telling you right now."

"But you knew exactly where he was. How did he get by you?"

"He knew where we were, too. He made the surveillance. DEA went to execute the warrant this morning, and the whole place'd been stripped and abandoned. Nothing left but a few empty glassines and a whole lot of garbage. We lifted some prints and got some heroin residue out of the sink, though."

"A lot of good that'll do me. I need him in the flesh!"

"What can I say? Shit happens."

"You screwed this up, and that's your response?"

"I was hoping this wouldn't degenerate into finger-pointing. I told you before, the location is difficult to surveil."

"Then you should've been sitting on it around the clock so he couldn't get away."

"This wasn't even our case. We were doing you a favor."

"That's funny, because just the other day you were saying it was your case, and that Bo was your target. And now he vanishes into thin air, presumably to resurface later under your indictment. Convenient, isn't it?"

"I don't like your implication."

"I'm not implying a thing. I'm saying it straight out. You blew the warrant on purpose to buy time to poach my target. Main Justice is going to hear about this."

Melanie slammed the phone down. "Can you believe that?"

"Let me call my people in Vegas and see what went wrong," Papo said, leaning across her desk and picking up the receiver.

"I'd better go tell Susan. Between Vashon and this, our case just fell apart. "

Melanie ran down the hall to Susan's office. Susan, Jennifer, and a young DEA colleague of Papo's were in the middle of a prep session with a cooperator named Michael Watkins, who'd been a night-shift manager at one of Atari Briggs's heroin spots. All four of them looked up as Melanie burst into the room.

"What's wrong?" Susan asked.

Melanie glanced at Watkins. It wasn't smart strategy to blurt out in front of one cooperator that another had just been nearly beaten to death.

"I need to talk to you outside. Now."

Susan's face suddenly looked as upset as Melanie felt. They hurried to the anteroom, pulling the door shut behind them.

"What? Tell me," Susan said.

"Vashon was badly beaten last night by some other inmates in the MCC cafeteria. He's in Bellevue in serious condition with multiple fractures. He'll recover, but he won't be available to testify by the trial date. It looks like Briggs was behind the attack. We have anecdotal evidence that the lead attacker was offered twenty thousand, but nothing we can prove."

"Shit. He's our main witness."

"That's not all, Susan. Our potential backup witness, Kevin Bonner, is gone, gone, gone. DEA in Nevada lost him. He packed up and shipped out. Nothing left at the location but some garbage and a few glassines. They have no clue where he is."

"All right. I need a minute to think."

"There's nothing to think about. Our case just fell apart. We need to call the judge and ask her to postpone the trial."

"After the stink Evan made about speedy trial, she'll never agree to that," Susan said.

"We beg if we have to. We have nothing left. If we can't get extra time, we might as well dismiss the charges right now and let Atari Briggs walk."

# 28

**M**elanie arrived early for the status conference, before the marshals had even set up a security checkpoint. Much to her surprise, the heavy wooden double doors to Judge DeFelice's courtroom were unlocked, which was normal around the courthouse, but not what she would've expected in a high-security case. Melanie poked her head in cautiously and saw that the cavernous space appeared deserted. She found herself tiptoeing down the center aisle, mesmerized by the silence. Some might find the institutional hush oppressive or even creepy—the buzzing of fluorescent lights bouncing off the dead gray-white marble of the walls under ceilings tall enough to dwarf the tallest human being. But to Melanie, who loved courtrooms, it was as peaceful as a church in here, and she was grateful for the chance to still her tumultuous thoughts.

At the opposite end of the courtroom, the door behind the judge's bench banged open and Tracey Montefiore stomped in, shattering the tranquil moment.

"Here you are," the blowsy courtroom deputy exclaimed. "I've been trying to get you on the phone forever. The judge wants to see you ASAP."

"Me? Now?"

"What did I just say?"

"Shouldn't I wait for Susan and Mr. Diamond?"

"Nope. She said just you, and make it snappy. Come through the back. Nobody's here to see."

Tracey unlocked the door she herself had just passed through. Melanie hustled to obey, but she wasn't happy. Whatever reason Bernadette had for wanting to see her alone, it couldn't be good.

The door led to a back hallway that Melanie had been admitted to once or twice before to drop off court papers after hours. Somehow she hadn't realized that the blank, unmarked doors across from each judge's chambers were the back entrances to their courtrooms. With one step across the narrow hallway, she stood at the door to Judge DeFelice's chambers and buzzed, turning her face up to the security camera as if to the sun.

Bernadette's secretary was on the phone but waved Melanie vigorously toward the inner sanctum. Melanie marched right in, surprising a federal judge in the process of fixing her makeup. Bernadette wore a red suit that Melanie recognized from days gone by, and seeing her in that familiar outfit felt like old times. So did the lump of fear in Melanie's throat. A similar lump had been her perpetual companion during her many visits to the chief's suite, back in the days when Bernadette had run Major Crimes.

Her former boss snapped her compact shut and nodded curtly at one of the chairs in front of her desk. Bernadette had a mobile and expressive face. On the rare occasion when she was happy, she was attractive, even beautiful. But when, as now, she wore an expression of anger, she looked plain, bitter, and old.

Bernadette skipped the preliminaries and went straight for the jugular.

"The last time you sat in that chair, I let you stonewall me, and a witness landed in the hospital. I'm done with the games, Melanie. I refuse to play the fool anymore. You tell me right now what's causing all the violence on this case, or I'll make big trouble for you. I can't say it any plainer than that."

"Your Honor, perhaps when Ms. Charlton—"

"Susan's not here, and I don't give a damn what she thinks anyway. I trained you. I trust you. You owe me. So spill it."

"I'd love to tell you what I really think, Your Honor. But I shouldn't be meeting with you alone, without the defense lawyer present."

"You want me to invite Evan Diamond? Isn't he the pond scum who had your witness attacked?"

Melanie didn't respond. She sat there and let her old boss, who knew her so well, read the answer in her eyes.

"Can you prove it?" Bernadette asked after a pause.

"No. We know who they gave the contract to. We can prove some money changed hands. It was done carefully. There's no obvious signature on it, and finding one could take a very long time. More time than we have."

"Unfortunately, with no evidence, there's not much I can do to help you."

"I understand."

"What about Poe's murder? What have you got on that so far?"

"Judge, other people are in charge of the investigation. They've got me focused on the trial—"

"You're walled off?" Bernadette demanded.

"Yes."

"That's idiotic. The threat is obviously coming from the trial. Who's in a better position than you to investigate?"

Melanie threw up her hands. "I know!"

"Tell me everything you've got and let's see if we can't make some progress here. *Idiots* running the office since I left."

"All right. On the day he died, Lester Poe approached me and told me that Atari Briggs wanted to cooperate against a target named Gamal Abdullah. You know who he is?"

"The terrorist."

"Yes, but the information Atari had was about narcotics activity. Abdullah supposedly brokered a high-level supply agreement. Afghan heroin delivered weekly to some of the biggest players in domestic narcotics, all over the U.S., to the tune of a hundred million bucks a month, with the proceeds going back to the warlords in Afghanistan."

Bernadette whistled. "Impressive. But why would Atari give you that? He'd be putting himself in danger, and for what benefit?"

"To get out from under the jail time, I guess."

"What jail time? Atari's in the catbird's seat and always has been. The press loves him. Jurors love him. All he ever needed to do was get rid of one witness, which he just did without breaking a sweat."

"Maybe Atari was in danger. Maybe he wanted to throw in his lot with the government so he could get Witness Protection."

"Why? Briggs can afford all the protection he needs."

"What can I say, Judge? I don't know why he came forward. Lester never told me, and now he's dead."

"And I assume you can't ask Briggs himself, because he's changed his mind about cooperating and refuses to talk to you."

"Yes. How'd you know that?"

"God, how do you manage without me? In twenty years of practice, Evan Diamond has never once cooperated a client. So it stands to reason that he wouldn't cooperate Atari Briggs now. Duh."

Bernadette sighed with irritation and leaned back in her chair. Melanie noticed her wedding photo in a silver frame on the credenza, just beyond Bernadette's right shoulder. She'd hoped, as many in the U.S. Attorney's Office had, that Bernadette's marriage the previous summer would make her easier to deal with. Her new husband,

Lieutenant Vito Albano of the NYPD, was a much-loved figure in the law enforcement community and roundly hailed as a good guy. Despite his balding pate and sloping shoulders, Bernadette twittered like a schoolgirl whenever his name was mentioned. But her happiness with Vito had failed to spill over into Bernadette's work life.

"Sorry, Judge," Melanie said.

"I don't want apologies. I want ideas. I want solutions!"

"I keep thinking this could all be worked out if only I could speak to Briggs without having Diamond involved. What about appointing shadow counsel?" Melanie asked.

"Hmm, I suppose that's a possibility."

"I've never actually done that in any of my cases. How does it work?"

"We need some real basis for believing that Diamond is standing in the way of Atari's cooperating."

"What I have is Lester Poe proffering the cooperation, then immediately getting blown up, and Diamond subsequently insisting that Atari had never said he'd cooperate."

"These are unusual and very difficult circumstances. I'd be willing to proceed if you made a record about that."

"Okay. So what do we do?"

"Atari appears before me, but without Diamond present. We can do it right here in chambers so the proceeding is kept secret. I get a court reporter in here and ask Briggs on the record whether he wants to cooperate but is being prevented from doing so, whether by threats or intimidation or whatever. If he says yes, I appoint a different lawyer and kick Evan off the case."

"How do we get Briggs to come here without Diamond?"

"We tell him to." She smiled. "I'm the judge, girlfriend. He has to listen. Why do you think I like this job?"

"Can I come to this proceeding?"

"Oh, yes. The government is present, along with a lawyer from

Legal Aid who'll act as Briggs's shadow counsel and give him neutral advice. Plus me and the court reporter. And Tracey, my courtroom deputy, because I like to have her at everything. She's a smart girl, Tracey. Don't underestimate her."

"What if Briggs says no? That he wasn't pressured and doesn't want to cooperate?"

"Then you lose big-time. We go to trial. I give you an extra week or two because your witness is in the hospital, but unless you can *prove* Briggs ordered your witness attacked—?" Bernadette raised her eyebrows.

"I can't. Not yet. We're investigating, but so far it looks like guys on his cell block pulling a vigilante stunt."

"Then a week is the best I can do give the speedy-trial issue. Diamond stays on the case. He screams dirty tricks because you tried to interfere with his relationship with his client, then beats the pants off you in court. The press hangs on his every word and reviles you by name. Not pretty. Don't you love this job?"

# 29

Susan caught Melanie's eye and motioned sticking her finger down her throat. They were at the government's table in the now-crowded courtroom, waiting for the status conference to begin. Jennifer Lamont sat between Susan and Melanie as they—along with everyone else from the press and courthouse staff who filled the spectator benches—watched Evan Diamond and Tracey Montefiore flirt shamelessly at the front of the courtroom. Evan was half perched on Tracey's narrow desk beneath the judge's bench, whispering something in the courtroom deputy's ear as she giggled wildly.

"Isn't that illegal?" Jennifer demanded.

"It's disgusting the way he sucks up to her," Susan whispered. "But what can we do? Tracey's a slut. The judge knows it, but she's wrapped around Tracey's little finger, so she doesn't control her."

"Somebody else should *control* her, then." Jennifer's face was flushed, her eyes narrow slits.

"Well, but it's not only her. Diamond's a slut, too. Look at him, the man-whore."

Susan laughed, but Jennifer appeared on the verge of exploding.

"Relax, kiddo," Susan said, patting her on the back. "That's the burden of being the government. Everybody else gets to misbehave, and we don't. The upside is, we win in the end, and we know we did it fair and square."

Melanie looked at her watch. "Half an hour late already."

"Hey, Evan," Susan called out. "Stop hitting on the courtroom deputy and get your ass over here. I have a question for you."

Diamond smiled and unfolded his long body from its perch on the table.

"What are you, angling to get the courtroom calendar early?" Susan asked when he reached them.

"We were just chatting."

Susan snorted. "Poor little Jennifer is getting disillusioned. So how about currying some favor with us prosecutor chicks instead and telling us when your famous client plans to show up."

"I called him twice. The last time was twenty minutes ago and he said he was five minutes away. I'm actually starting to get worried."

"Looks bad, Evan. Very bad."

"You're not kidding. I can only imagine the pleasant mood it's gonna put this judge in, in contrast to her normal sweet demeanor."

"You'll be lucky if she doesn't remand him. Atari in the clink. Imagine how they'll react in general population."

"It's got to happen eventually," Melanie joked.

"In your dreams," Diamond said, grinning.

"Miss Vargas?" Tracey Montefiore called, holding the Bat phone against her chest and giving Melanie a meaningful look. "Judge De-Felice's secretary would like you to stop by chambers now and pick up that paperwork from another case."

"Oh, the other case," Melanie said, leaping to her feet. "I'll be right back."

Susan and Evan Diamond were both savvy enough in the ways of the courthouse to shoot curious glances her way as she retreated down the center aisle.

In chambers, from the very beginning, things did not go as Melanie had hoped.

Bernadette sat in the same spot in the big chair behind her desk where she'd sat half an hour earlier, but this time she wore her black robe. One of the old-time court reporters, a guy with a magnificent head of hair known to everybody as Silver Max, balanced on a tiny stool beside the judge with his steno machine at the ready. Patty Atkins, a no-nonsense criminal defense lawyer whom Melanie knew well from other cases and had a lot of respect for, sat in one of the guest chairs with her hands folded in her lap. Meanwhile, Atari Briggs, resplendent in an Armani suit and diamond studs, regarded Patty with obvious disdain.

"Who is this chick? I never met her before. *My* lawyer's waiting for me in court, and he's already pissed that I'm late."

"Ah, Ms. Vargas," Bernadette said, looking up. "Have a seat and we'll go on the record."

"What's *she* doing here?" Briggs demanded, pointing at Melanie. "If she's here, why isn't my lawyer here?"

"Ms. Montefiore, call the case," Bernadette instructed Tracey, who had followed Melanie into the room.

"*United States of America against Atari Briggs,* number CR–08–2673-BAD"—Bernadette's middle name being Ann, all of her cases were marked with the initials BAD, which amused courthouse denizens to no end. "Parties, enter your appearances."

"Melanie Vargas for the government."

"Patty Atkins, present at the request of the court to consult with

Mr. Briggs. I note for the record that Mr. Briggs has retained other counsel, and that Mr. Briggs and I have not yet spoken."

"Mr. Briggs," the judge began, "I called you here today to advise you in greater detail than you have been advised previously about your right to counsel. Do you understand what is meant by the right to counsel?"

"Yeah. I got a right to a lawyer. That's what I'm saying. I already *have* a lawyer. I don't need this woman."

"Just listen," Bernadette said. "You have a right to counsel. You also have a right to what's known as *conflict-free* counsel. Do you understand what that means?"

"No."

"It means you have a right to a lawyer who represents your interests and your interests alone. Who gives you advice based only on what's best for *you,* not what's best for him, or what's best for a codefendant, or what's best for some member of the criminal underworld. Does that make sense?"

"The lawyer I got now, Evan Diamond, he's fine with me. He represents my interests. If I have no problems with him, I don't see why you do."

"The court has reason to believe that Mr. Diamond may be interfering with choices you want to make about your case. Ms. Vargas, please make a record of the facts regarding the cooperation."

"Yes, Your Honor. I spoke with the defendant's previous lawyer, Lester Poe, right before his death, and he told me that—"

"Whoa, whoa, whoa," Briggs said, shaking his head vigorously. "I know what she's gonna say, and it's a lie, a big lie."

"You'll get your turn, Mr. Briggs. Let her make the record. Ms. Vargas, proceed."

But Briggs's outburst made Melanie lose her train of thought. Was it possible that this man didn't want to cooperate, that he never had? That he'd planned all along to rely on his face and physique and charisma to sway a jury, or brute intimidation, rather than snitching on one of the most dangerous men in the world? The thought hit her with the bitter force of truth. She almost decided to back down and call this whole thing off, but how could she do that when everybody was sitting there waiting for her to speak?

"Ms. Vargas?" the judge prompted.

"Judge, Mr. Poe told me that the defendant had significant incriminating information against a target of great interest to the government, and that he would be willing to provide such information in return for a sentencing reduction—"

"Lies!" Briggs exclaimed.

"Let her talk, or we'll be here all afternoon," the judge said, but her annoyance level was building visibly.

"Mr. Poe indicated that the defendant wanted to postpone the trial and explore cooperation," Melanie continued. "A few minutes later, Mr. Poe attempted to enter his vehicle and was killed when the vehicle exploded. Mr. Diamond was subsequently retained to represent Mr. Briggs. The government approached Mr. Diamond about the cooperation. Mr. Diamond told us that Mr. Briggs had no interest in cooperating. Given that Mr. Poe had said the opposite a mere day before, and had then been killed, under those unusual circumstances, we were concerned that Mr. Briggs's sudden change of heart was the result of intimidation or the threat of force."

"Thank you," Bernadette said. "Mr. Briggs, those are the facts that caused me to be concerned for your welfare. I have called you here to make sure you know that if you're being threatened, we'll help you, and if your lawyer isn't serving your interests, we'll provide you with another lawyer. Do you understand?"

Atari's jaw stiffened and his eyes flashed. "Look at me. I'm worth fifty mil. You really think I need your help?"

Bernadette was taken aback. "Well, any defendant who—"

"You know what I understand? I understand that it's y'all trying to intimidate me, not my lawyer. You're trying to put out there that I'm a rat because you want to ruin my reputation and disgrace my name. I'm no rat. I never was. I never will be. Whosever saying I want to cooperate is full of shit. If Poe said it, he's a liar. Evan Diamond is the best lawyer I ever had. He's who I want. Now can I go find him, please?"

"Yes, in one moment," Bernadette said. She turned her hard eyes on Melanie; they were lit with fury. "For the record, I am fully satisfied that Mr. Briggs is happy with his representation. The government's concerns were overblown, possibly deceitful. I hereby order that a transcript of this proceeding be produced and provided to defense counsel, Evan Diamond, as well as to the chief of the Criminal Division in the U.S. Attorney's Office for consideration of any disciplinary action that might be warranted against Ms. Vargas. Ms. Vargas, I'll see you at the status conference five minutes from now, and I expect you to make a full explanation of your behavior in open court. Understood?"

"Yes, ma'am," Melanie said, her voice shaky.

Bernadette smacked the gavel on her desk. "Adjourned."

# 30

Had Lester Poe lied when he'd said that Atari Briggs wanted to cooperate? Melanie agonized over that question all the way back to the courtroom. She was about to face the firing squad because she'd believed Lester when he'd told her that Atari had the goods on Gamal Abdullah and planned to snitch. Well, of course she'd believed him. Lester was Atari's *lawyer*. It made sense that he'd approach her about cooperation, and he'd never lied to her before. She couldn't fathom why Lester would have lied this time, but Atari's denial in Bernadette's chambers had rung disturbingly true. Now she didn't know whom to believe. Her actions had been justified if what Lester had told her was true. But apparently, he'd lied, and the shadow counsel proceeding had gone south in a big way. Melanie was about to suffer the consequences. There wasn't much she could do about it, either, except think fast and try to contain the fallout.

Atari had arrived at the courtroom before her. He was sitting at the defense table, telling Evan Diamond what had happened in a loud, angry voice. Evan glared at Melanie as she walked down the center aisle of the courtroom, and so did Susan Charlton, who'd heard Atari's every word.

"What the hell is he talking about?" Susan demanded under her breath as Melanie sat down at the government's table. "You did a shadow counsel proceeding without me?"

"Look, it wasn't my idea," Melanie said. "The judge ordered me to come to chambers."

"Why would she do that? Out of the blue, she decides Atari needs shadow counsel? You must have said something to her."

"After she heard Vashon was attacked, she called me to her chambers and grilled me about the security posture of the whole case. I told her—"

"You went to her chambers by yourself?" Susan exclaimed, so angry she nearly spit.

Melanie gestured at Susan to keep her voice down. "You weren't here," she whispered, "and Tracey insisted. What could I do?"

"Call me on the fricking telephone. Don't run off and have some ex parte conversation with the judge."

"Bernadette didn't give me any choice. You would have done the same thing."

"No, I would not. Besides, when Tracey told you to go back to chambers the second time, I *was* here. I was sitting right next to you. I'm your goddamn trial partner, Melanie, and you didn't have the courtesy to tell me that you were running off to do a shadow counsel hearing?"

"Maybe you've forgotten, but Evan was here, too," Melanie said in a low tone. "How could I tell you in front of him?"

Even to her own ears, that sounded like a feeble excuse. Deep down, Melanie knew that the reason she hadn't told Susan was that she didn't want to be overruled. She'd been convinced that the shadow counsel proceeding would save their case. Well, it had been a catastrophe. Maybe it was Bernadette's idea originally, but Melanie would be taking the fall alone.

Tracey Montefiore sauntered through the back entrance, which meant that the judge wouldn't be far behind.

Melanie turned to Susan. "I'm sorry, I truly am," she said. "I thought this would solve our problems, and it backfired. I screwed up badly. But please, for the sake of the case, help me with damage control. Bernadette is about to come in here and make me put everything on the record."

"About the cooperation?" Susan asked. "You can't talk about Abdullah in open court."

"I understand that."

"Refuse to answer."

"She may not let me."

"If she holds you in contempt, then you suck it up and go to jail," Susan said.

That prospect seemed real enough that Melanie couldn't speak for a moment.

"It—it would help if you backed me." But it was clear from the expression on Susan's face that no help would be forthcoming.

"This is your mess," Susan said. "You made it. You fix it."


Evan Diamond came out swinging.

"Did the government think my client wouldn't fill me in?" he demanded of the judge once the case had been called. They stood before the bench, Diamond at one podium and Melanie at the other. Susan hadn't even come up with her.

"I heard all about this so-called shadow counsel proceeding, and it was a farce," Diamond said. "An outrageous violation of the attorney–client relationship. I demand that the indictment against my client be dismissed and all charges dropped."

Melanie had managed to make a few notes on a legal pad before the case got called. She'd known that Diamond would try to get the charges dismissed, but in the pressure of the moment, the phrases she'd jotted in response looked like chicken scratch to her. She opened her mouth but couldn't figure out where to start.

"Your motion is denied," the judge said calmly.

Melanie looked up in shock.

"You'll see when you get the transcript that Mr. Briggs was represented very ably by Patty Atkins," the judge said. "He was never asked about the facts of the murder case. He was only asked whether he wanted to cooperate and whether he was happy with you as his lawyer. There's plenty of precedent saying that's the right thing to do when the defendant may be being prevented from cooperating. Mr. Briggs reassured me that he was satisfied with your services, and the proceeding was stopped. His rights were not violated in any way."

"My client was never prevented from cooperating!" Diamond insisted. "I resent the implication that I would do such a thing. He never wanted to cooperate in the first place."

"Mr. Briggs already told me. Nobody's accusing you of anything, Mr. Diamond."

"It's not me I'm worried about. How does it look for him? This whole sideshow was designed to humiliate my client publicly and force him to plead guilty. I demand an investigation. I demand that the government attorneys be forced to testify under oath."

"That won't be necessary," the judge said, and Melanie could hardly believe her ears. Bernadette was coming to her rescue.

"I insisted that Ms. Vargas put the facts on the record during the shadow counsel proceeding. You'll get a copy of the transcript. I'm satisfied that she had a basis for requesting the proceeding. Now let's move on."

The rest of the status conference passed in a blur. Melanie described the attack on Vashon Clark and asked for a month's delay to make sure he'd be available to testify. The judge gave them two weeks, which wasn't enough, but she seemed to feel that she'd done Melanie enough favors for one day. They now had seventeen days to pull off a major miracle, or else lose the trial of Melanie's career and let a killer walk.

"The judge saved your butt," Susan said grudgingly when Melanie returned to the government's table.

"I wasn't expecting that," Melanie said. "She *was* the one who got me into this whole mess. Maybe she felt guilty."

Susan shrugged, gathered her files, and walked out of the courtroom without another word. Melanie might've escaped sanctions, but her relationship with her trial partner had taken a real hit. To redeem herself, she needed to produce a break in the case. A big break. Fortunately, she had an idea of where she might find one.

# 31

**Melanie had to stop** herself from gasping as Philippe Poe extended his hand, that's how much he looked like his father. They were at the reception following Lester's funeral, in the grand apartment, and Melanie hoped for a quiet moment to peek into Lester's office. In the meantime, she'd learn anything she could about Lester from his look-alike son. The moody boy in the old newspaper photos was unrecognizable in the dashing man standing before her. Philippe was smaller in stature than his father had been. His hair was still ink black, not yet silver. And he had the rough complexion of a man who'd had poor skin as an adolescent, whereas Lester's face had been smooth and tanned. Other than that, Melanie might've been looking at the dead man.

"You are?" he asked, taking her hand in both of his. The grand parlor was crowded with people, some of them famous, but he made her feel as if she had his complete attention. Another way in which he resembled Lester.

"Melanie Vargas. Pleased to meet you. The service was very moving."

"Yes. I always knew he did a lot of great things with his work, but the eulogies . . . so beautiful."

"Yes, they were."

"Did you know my father well?"

"I'm a prosecutor, and we had a case together. He was a remarkable man. Even though we were on opposite sides, we became great friends."

"I see," Philippe said, his eyes flicking up and down to take Melanie in more completely. Maybe it was the slight French cadence that lent a worldly air to his words, or maybe it was that knowing glance, but she suddenly understood what it had been like to have Lester for a father. There must've been a lot of women around.

"I'm very sorry for your loss," she said. "Especially with Brenda's death right afterward. That must be so difficult."

"Brenda was my stepmother. She wasn't exactly my favorite person." He paused. "That must have sounded callous, but she wrecked my parents' marriage."

"I didn't know that."

First the Charity Bishop scandal. Then the possibility that Lester Poe had lied about Atari Briggs wanting to cooperate. Now this. Melanie really hadn't known the man, and her view of him was rapidly tarnishing.

"She didn't exactly go around talking about it," Philippe said.

"I know how you must feel. My father has a second wife I've barely ever spoken to. If she died, I wouldn't shed a tear."

Philippe laughed. "That's the first natural thing anybody's said to me all day."

"It must've been hard for you."

"Oh, I was too young to know anything at the time. Brenda came on the scene right after I was born. And later, well, I was used to it."

"You live in France?" Melanie asked.

"Yes. Did my father tell you that?" Something in his voice seemed to hope that Lester had thought to mention him.

"No. I read it in one of the obituaries."

"My mother is French. She moved us there after the divorce and ended up remarrying. I consider Jacques my real father, but I spent summers with Lester in Sagaponack, and we were good friends. He was like a favorite uncle for me."

Sagaponack. Perhaps the most exclusive enclave in the Hamptons. The place where Charity Bishop had been found floating, naked and dead, in Lester Poe's swimming pool.

Melanie had come here in search of new evidence. She needed to find some, so she decided to take a shot in the dark.

"Funny," she said, looking Philippe smack in his gray eyes. "I had the distinct impression Lester didn't like to talk about Sagaponack, although I never quite understood why. Do you know?"

He turned bright red. An older woman in an elegant suit was gliding toward them.

"Excuse me, I must say hello to my aunt," Philippe said, his voice suddenly cold. "The host is expected to mingle. We have food in the dining room, so help yourself."

"Thank you."

From Philippe's reaction, Melanie concluded that Charity Bishop was still a sore spot for him thirty years after her death. Interesting, given that neither Lester nor Philippe had been charged with a thing. And obviously, no love had been lost between Philippe and Brenda, either, for whatever that was worth. It struck her that with Brenda out of the way, Philippe stood to inherit a lot of money. Melanie made a mental note to learn about Lester's will.

She moved into the dining room, which featured high ceilings, an enormous crystal chandelier, and shimmering floor-length drapes. A magnificent buffet table laden with delicacies called out to her, but she was merely passing through on her way to perform reconnaissance. She planned to slip into Lester's office, go through his desk, and find something—anything—that could shed light on Atari's aborted cooperation. She wasn't violating attorney–client privilege because Lester wasn't Atari's lawyer anymore. She wasn't violating the Fourth Amendment despite the lack of a search warrant because Lester was dead and his right to privacy had died with him. There was no legal impediment to her plan. If there were other objections—moral, practical—she refused to let them stand in the way of finding answers. Melanie wasn't born to be cautious. When she tried to be cautious—say, by not getting all the information she could have out of Brenda Gould the day they met—it never turned out well.

Melanie kept to the perimeter of the grand dining room and turned her face toward the art on the walls. Otherwise, in this law-heavy crowd, somebody would surely recognize her. She retraced her steps as best as she remembered from the morning she'd visited Brenda Gould. As she moved toward the back of the apartment, the buzz of conversation dropped away and she walked in silence, her steps muffled by the thick Persian carpet. The corridor was dark, and the occasional glimpses she caught into dim rooms revealed that all of the mirrors were covered with blankets. Her overheated mind thought *vampires* until she recalled that this was a Jewish mourning custom. But it set her on edge nonetheless.

At the very back of the house, she found the heavy wooden door that led to Lester's office. All her nerves were taut with anxiety as she reached for the antique glass doorknob. But it wouldn't turn. The door was locked. She got down on her knees and examined the mechanism. It had an old-fashioned keyhole, the type she imagined sticking a hairpin into, but who carried hairpins nowadays? She did have a Bic pen. She tried shimmying the long stem of the plastic pen cap around in the keyhole, but that accomplished nothing. She turned the doorknob, harder this time. Still locked. Melanie decided she'd better give up before she attracted attention, so she got to her feet and turned to go.

She let out a shriek. Evan Diamond was standing right on top of her, regarding her with a malignant grin.

# 32

He reached out and grabbed both her arms, hard. Melanie twisted around to try to get away from him. But Diamond was strong, and he had her in an iron grip.

"Let go of me!" she cried.

"What the hell do you think you're doing?" The calm in his voice sent a shiver through her.

"I was looking for the bathroom."

"You were not. You were trying to break into Lester's office. What did you think you'd find in there?"

She opened her mouth to scream and he slapped a hand over it, which left one of her arms free. She slammed the liberated elbow into his stomach and jerked the other arm down hard. He grunted and let go. She got a few steps down the hall before he caught her by her hair.

"Aaagh!"

She was just about to scream her head off when Bob Adelman came down the corridor toward them, his mouth slack with shock. Bob was a criminal defense lawyer who'd been a friend of Lester's.

He was also a decent guy, somebody who would help her if he could, though he was short and stocky and no match for Diamond in a fight.

"Bob!"

"What the . . . my God, what is *happening* here? I was on my way to the bathroom and I heard the commotion. What are you *doing*?"

Adelman's mere presence was enough to bring Diamond to his senses. He let go of her hair and stood there brushing imaginary dirt from the lapels of his perfect suit. He wasn't even mussed, whereas Melanie's knees were shaking and her breathing was coming in shallow heaves.

"You're crazy," she said. "I could have you disbarred."

"You have *me* disbarred?" Diamond snarled at Melanie. "I know what I saw. You were about to commit a crime. You just try to come after me and I'll have your license."

"Please, both of you, people will hear," Adelman said.

"Mind your fucking business, Bob. I know where you live, too. This isn't over."

Diamond stalked away. When he'd disappeared from sight, Adelman asked, "Are you all right?"

"I need to catch my breath."

"I can't believe he grabbed you like that. What was it about?"

"We're on the Briggs case together. We don't see eye to eye."

"Apparently not." He paused, as if waiting for her to say more. "Suit yourself, Melanie. You don't have to confide in me. But be warned. I know Evan Diamond well, and he's a dangerous man."

"Yes, I see that. Rumor's one thing, but now that he's grabbed me by the hair, I have a whole new perspective."

Melanie's breathing had calmed down. Adelman regarded her with open curiosity. He was pleasantly rumpled and had a trustworthy, hound-dog sort of face. Melanie had always had a good feeling about him.

"I'm just on my way out," Adelman said. "If you've paid your respects, maybe you should come along. I know a diner where we can get a cup of coffee and talk without fear of being overheard. I've learned some troubling things lately about Lester and Evan Diamond. Things that might interest you."

The diner that Adelman took her to on upper Madison was one she'd been to before. It was overpriced, a hangout for wealthy moms and their spoiled preschoolers, but the food was good. With everything happening on the case, Melanie figured she might not get dinner tonight, so she broke down and ordered a cheeseburger despite the extortionate price tag.

"Coffee and a black-and-white cookie," Adelman said. "The cookies are excellent here."

"I can't believe I had a physical fight with Evan Diamond," Melanie said.

"I guess you never practice in Brooklyn criminal court," Adelman said. "With what goes on there, I've seen distinguished members of the bar land in the hospital."

Melanie laughed.

"You know what *I* can't believe?" Adelman said. "I can't believe Lester's dead."

"You may not remember this, but you introduced me to him."

"I do remember. At Clyde Williams's fund-raiser at the Met, right? Les was very taken with you that night."

"Was he?" she asked wistfully.

"Very much so. He called me the next day and interrogated me about you."

Melanie blushed.

"Naturally I said a lot of nice things," Adelman continued. "I'm surprised he never asked you out."

"Oh, but he did," Melanie said. "He took me to dinner and tried to recruit me."

"Funny, I didn't get the sense that he was planning to offer you a job," Adelman said.

"Maybe not. But pretty soon after that, we ended up on opposite sides of the Briggs case, so a date was out of the question."

Adelman frowned. "Briggs. I need to talk to you about that case. There's some background you might not be aware of. But first, Melanie, do you know yet who killed Lester? Can you tell me? If I knew, it would explain a lot of things, and I might be able to connect some dots for you."

"I wish this could be a give-and-take," Melanie said, shaking her head. "I have a lot of respect for you, Bob, and I trust you as much as I've ever trusted anybody from the other side of the aisle. But to answer your question, I don't exactly know who killed Lester. You know the guy who detonated the bomb was found dead?"

"Sure, that was all over the news. An Algerian, right?"

"Yes."

"But no ties to terrorism."

"No *known* ties," she emphasized.

"From what I read, the guy was a small-time con. Credit-card scams, selling clone phones. Penny-ante stuff. And he'd been in the U.S. since he was a kid," Adelman said.

"That doesn't mean anything. He could've been a sleeper."

"He'd never been overseas. Unless you know something that's not in the paper?"

"Look, in all honesty, they've got me walled off from the bombing investigation because I'm trying the Briggs case. I don't know much more than what you've read, and what little I do know is confidential. I could lose my job if I told you anything."

The waitress slapped their food down in front of them. Melanie doused her burger with ketchup and took a bite.

"I don't want to put you in a bad position," Adelman said. "I'll tell you what I know, no strings attached. If it helps, great. If not, at least I got it off my chest."

She nodded.

"Okay, first of all, there was big trouble between Evan and Lester. Evan wanted out from under Lester's shadow, but he didn't want to give up any of the spoils. He was trying to muscle in and take over the firm," he said.

"Why would he think he could do that?" Melanie asked. "Lester's clients wouldn't abandon him for Diamond."

"They might if Les agreed to it."

"Why would Lester agree to be forced out of his own firm? He built it from the ground up. I've never understood why he shared an office with Diamond, or worked with him even as much as he did."

"Evan was blackmailing him, that's why."

"You know that for a fact?"

"I do."

"Over what?"

"Something that Lester was involved in that left him vulnerable. Something from a long time ago."

"You're talking about Charity Bishop."

"You know about that?" Adelman asked, looking astonished.

"I've been doing my homework. I probably shouldn't tell you this, but—well, what the hell, the bomber's dead. Bob, I was there when Lester was killed. I saw it all. We were talking one minute and the next Lester was"—she hesitated, and cleared her throat—"well, he was . . ."

Adelman squeezed Melanie's hand. "I know."

"Anyway, since then I've felt very . . . *connected* to Lester. The long and the short of it is, I need to find out why he died and who's responsible."

"I understand."

"So the blackmail *was* over Charity Bishop's death?"

"Yes."

"Did you know Lester back then, back when it happened?"

"Oh, yes. I've known him for a long time. We were classmates in law school. We've stayed very close over the years."

"Did you ever meet the girl?"

"Once. In the city, midtown, at lunchtime. This was, what, twenty years ago? More? I bumped into her and Lester on the street and he introduced me."

"They were having lunch together?"

"Apparently."

"They were alone?"

"Yes."

"Do you know, was he sleeping with her?"

"I don't know that for a fact, but from what I observed, I'd bet on it. You know she was Philippe's girlfriend, though, right?"

"No! No, I didn't know that."

"Philippe was very serious about her. Picking-out-the-ring serious even though he was very young at the time. It wasn't mutual, however. She wasn't the type of girl who wanted to settle down. After the fact, I did some digging into her lifestyle and found out that she was quite the wild child. Very promiscuous. Hardly the right woman for somebody like Philippe, who was awkward and quiet and had some fairly traditional views about life. She liked his money. And from what I could tell, she liked his father."

"You were the one who dug up the dirt on Charity, weren't you? The scandals that got covered in all the papers back then?"

"I represented Lester during the investigation, if that's what you mean. He was under a cloud of suspicion, quite unfairly in my view. There was no solid evidence that Charity had been murdered, but if she had, there were plenty of other suspects. I did what any competent lawyer would do for his client and brought that fact to the public's attention."

"Lester had an alibi, but as I recall, it wasn't a very persuasive one."

"What do you mean? He was out to dinner with his son."

"There was no evidence for that except the statements the two of them gave. Bob, tell me the truth. Did Lester kill Charity Bishop?"

"I'm not sure anybody killed her, but I'm positive that *Lester* didn't. Philippe? Maybe, who knows? Look, I saw the autopsy report. The Bishop girl had drugs and alcohol in her bloodstream, a contusion on the back of her head, and water in her lungs. Water in the lungs means she was breathing when she hit the swimming pool."

"But somebody knocked her on the head and pushed her in."

"Maybe. Or maybe she fell and knocked herself on the head."

"Did the autopsy reach a conclusion on that question?"

"The report concluded that the contusion came from a blow with a blunt object. But I could've found an expert to testify that it came from hitting her head on the side of the pool, no problem."

"What makes you so sure Lester didn't do it?"

Adelman shrugged. "What can I say? I know the guy for a lotta years. He wouldn't hurt a woman."

"But if Lester was innocent, how could Diamond blackmail him with Charity's death?"

"It wasn't *himself* that Les was protecting. He was innocent, but I'm not so sure about Philippe. Or frankly, Brenda."

*"Brenda?"*

"She was home, at the house in Sagaponack, at the time of the incident. You have to see this in context. Les had a long history of protecting Brenda, of saving her from herself. That's how they met. She was strung out on drugs, and he took care of her. Les always had to save the world, and saving Brenda was part of that. Besides, if something untoward happened here, it happened because of Les's relationship with Charity Bishop. The guilt alone would have been enough to motivate him to cover up."

Adelman took a swig of his coffee and grimaced.

"So Brenda's motive for hurting Charity would have been jealousy?"

"Sure, what else?"

"But didn't Brenda and Lester have an open relationship? She told me so herself, that she had lovers and so did he."

"That didn't mean she was happy about the situation, or that she never got jealous. In any event, they got divorced right after this happened, so draw your own conclusions."

Melanie thought about that for a minute, and new possibilities opened up. Brenda had pretended not to care about the other women in Lester's life. But obviously she'd cared. Enough to kill one of them?

"I suppose if Brenda had killed Charity and Lester had discovered that fact," Melanie said, "he might've divorced her for that reason."

"That's very likely. Les may have been a ladies' man, but he was honorable, Melanie. He would never have approved of murder."

"You're suggesting he helped cover one up."

"I'm suggesting he protected somebody he loved. That's Les, to a tee."

"If Diamond was blackmailing Lester over the Charity Bishop case," Melanie said thoughtfully, "could that blackmail have anything to do with Lester's death?"

"Les's death, I'm not sure." Adelman leaned forward, raising his bushy eyebrows. "But I'm convinced it had something to do with Brenda's. Melanie, Brenda Gould's death was no suicide."

"I didn't think so, either, but then I got a copy of the autopsy report. She died from an overdose of alcohol and heroin. They don't even think it was suicide. They ruled it accidental."

"No way," he said, shaking his head. "Brenda was clean, I'd bet on it. If she was going to fall off the wagon, she'd do it with booze. Not drugs."

"Tell me everything you know about the day Brenda died," Melanie said.

"She was about to be interviewed by the FBI. She'd called and asked me to come along with her when she talked to them. She planned to tell them everything about Les and Evan, including the fact that Evan had them under all sorts of illegal surveillance. Phone taps, bugs, you name it. Les was sweeping every week and there was always something new. I'm sure whatever was in there is gone by now. Evan's not stupid."

*Phone taps,* Melanie thought. *Maybe Atari's cooperation was real after all. Maybe Diamond overheard something and squealed to Abdullah.*

"I can't believe Lester tolerated this situation," she said.

"I told you, Evan had something on him about this Charity Bishop thing that had never come to light before. He was doing his best to get rid of the bugs, but he didn't want to go to the police about it. Anyway, I showed up at the town house Friday at three o'clock so Brenda and I could talk before the FBI arrived. The ambulance was already out front. I went into the foyer and talked to the cops. The guy told me Brenda OD'd, that the house was sealed off, and that the family had the situation under control. I'm thinking, family, what family? The only family Brenda had was Les. Then I'm standing downstairs in the hallway, and I hear Evan upstairs schmoozing the police."

They were both silent for a moment, thinking about the implications of that.

"None of this is proof, you know," Melanie said.

"I understand that. If it was, I would've come to you sooner."

"Diamond's office is downstairs, so there's an innocent explanation for his presence in the building at the time of the OD. As for family, maybe the police meant Philippe. Maybe he was here already for his father's funeral."

"No. I know it wasn't Philippe, because I picked him up myself at the airport the following morning."

"Diamond killed Brenda to shut her up?"

"That's what I think. But like you said, none of this is proof. Cookie?" he asked, pushing the plate toward her.

Melanie had finished her cheeseburger but she was still hungry. She could feel the lost pounds piling right back onto her hips, but she couldn't help herself. Life was too damn stressful.

"Thank you." She broke off a piece and munched on it.

"So what are you going to do with my information?" Adelman asked.

"Whatever I can. But given the lack of hard evidence, and the Briggs trial in two weeks, that might not be very much at the moment."

"Oh, right," Adelman said, nodding. *"Briggs."*

"You said you had some background on the case for me?"

"You may already know this, but Evan used to represent Atari Briggs."

"I didn't know. When?"

"Long time ago. Back in the early nineties, when Atari was on his way up in the drug business in East New York. I'm surprised this isn't institutional knowledge in the U.S. Attorney's Office. You people have too much turnover."

Melanie grabbed Adelman's sleeve. "Bob, this is important. What case did Diamond represent him on?"

"Oh, it wasn't just one case. Evan was house counsel to Atari's organization. They were thick as thieves."

# 33

Jennifer Lamont had a meeting scheduled with Evan Diamond at five o'clock to review stipulations, and all day it'd been the only thing on her mind. She'd been daydreaming about it continuously with a sappy smile on her face—that is, up until the moment she sat at counsel table and watched him nearly lick the ear of that fat, ugly courtroom deputy. Now she thought she'd spit on the floor if she ever saw the man again.

Jennifer was sitting in Susan's office, listening to Papo West on the speakerphone. They were talking about the need to send a team to Las Vegas immediately to track down Kevin Bonner, the possible backup witness in the case. Jennifer made a mental note of the name, thinking how much Evan would like to know it, and how he wasn't going to get a thing from her now.

"One of you guys needs to come with me, you know," Papo was saying. "We've got a turf problem. That's not an agent issue. Only a prosecutor can work out jurisdiction."

"Take Melanie. Jennifer's too junior, and as chief, I'm needed here."

"As chief, you can pull rank," Papo said.

Susan laughed. "You got me."

*"Prosecutors.* Who the hell runs away from a free trip to Vegas?"

"Turf wars make me crazy. I'd end up shooting somebody," Susan said.

"Out there it's legal to shoot anybody who pisses you off. That's the beauty of it."

"Melanie will handle this as well as I ever could. I'll let her know."

"All right."

They said their good-byes and hung up.

Jennifer looked at her watch. "I need to call Evan Diamond's office and cancel that meeting about the stipulations."

"Cancel? Why would you cancel?" Susan asked.

"Oh, well," Jennifer said, blushing, "with the trial postponed, I just assumed—"

"Don't assume. We need those stipulations signed. I'd be worried he'd change his mind. You call him right now and make sure it's still on."

When Evan Diamond showed up—forty minutes late—Jennifer went out to the guard's station to meet him. Looking into his opaque black eyes gave her a thrill that distracted her from her jealous fury. This was going to be tougher than she thought.

"Come in, Evan," she said coldly, squaring her shoulders.

She walked ahead of him back to her office. They didn't speak. She crossed the threshold first, leaving the door gaping open, and retreated behind her desk, gesturing for him to sit in the guest chair.

"I've prepared the stipulations we discussed," Jennifer said, keeping her voice impersonal. "I'll show them to you, and if you have any objections, please let me know. I'd like to resolve any disagreements and get everything signed now so we know what witnesses to call."

His face fell. "You're upset. You're upset at how I talked to the court-room deputy. Baby, I'm so sorry. Swear to God, that meant nothing."

Jennifer hadn't anticipated that he'd apologize, or that he'd even care, or that her coldness might have the power to hurt him. The look on his face weakened her defenses. *And* he'd called her baby. She loved that word.

"You practically had your tongue in her ear," she said, but her tone was pleading rather than angry.

"Believe me, I can't stand the sight of her, but I have to try a case in that courtroom. If you don't suck up to her, she punishes you. You gotta understand, I have a client to think about. This says nothing about my feelings for you."

Jennifer experienced a brief moment of sanity. Her door was open. "We shouldn't be talking like this."

"Not here. You're right." He leaned forward, dropping his voice to a near whisper. "Is anything else upsetting you? Did somebody say something against me?"

"Yes, somebody said something," she scolded. "They think you ordered the attack on Vashon Clark. They're investigating."

"They're investigating *me*?"

His eyes narrowed, and Jennifer saw the enormity of what she'd just done. She'd breached every rule of confidentiality. She'd told a target he was being investigated. She'd joined the enemy.

"Yes," she said.

His voice was low and urgent. "That's going to happen. They'll come after me because I'm a threat. And they'll tell you every sort of evil thing about me. I swear to you, Jennifer, none of it is true."

"No?"

"Of course not."

"You didn't have Vashon attacked? Because getting him out of the way certainly helps your case."

"Is he badly hurt?"

"Yes."

"Where is he now?"

She went hot all over. Was he just using her? "Uh, uh—I—"

"Never mind, don't answer that. I never want you to think that I'm using you. Listen, baby, attacks like that happen every day on the inside. It had nothing to do with me."

Jennifer didn't believe him. But to her astonishment, she found she didn't care.

"Let's get the stipulations signed," she said. "Then maybe we can figure out a way to talk alone."

# 34

Melanie was so tired that she could barely see, and though she managed to unlock the front door of her apartment with one hand while holding numerous legal folders and a big stack of mail with the other, she tripped over the threshold and dropped everything just inside the front door. She nearly burst into tears, that's how ragged her nerves were, but the light spilling from the living room cheered her up. Not only did she have a kid, she had a kid sister, and Linda had come by to babysit Maya tonight after Yolie left.

Melanie collected her things and went to see her sister in the living room. Linda was splayed out on the sofa, her legs in black tights up on the sofa back as she talked on the telephone. Always the fashion queen, she was wearing a Pucci minidress with lots of chains and bangles, so that she made a lovely tinkling sound every time she moved.

"*Hola, mami, dáme un besito,*" Linda said.

Melanie blew her a kiss. "How long you gonna be?"

Linda held her manicured thumb and forefinger an inch apart. Melanie took this as a signal to go lose the suit she'd been wearing since seven o'clock this morning. But first she needed to stop in Maya's room.

The light from the hallway shone on the little girl snuggled against the wall, surrounded by stuffed animals, her dark lashes lying against lustrous skin. Melanie reached out and stroked her daughter's hair, and Maya shifted and sighed in her sleep, her eyelids fluttering. The breathless pang of love and guilt was like a stitch in Melanie's side. Week after week and month after month, she couldn't find enough time for Maya. A few hours on a good night—what kind of life was that for a mother and child? She knew she needed to make some changes, but *which* changes exactly— well, that continued to elude her.

Back in the living room after donning her bathrobe, Melanie found Linda still on the phone.

"No way I'm paying that for some shit hole with no pool. I want to be in South Beach anyway." Linda caught sight of Melanie. "Teresa, let me call you in the morning. Mel's here, and I have to get the latest scoop on my lover boy, Atari. Ciao, baby." Linda swung her legs around and sat up.

"How's my hottie?" was the first thing she said.

"He's a drug dealer and a killer, just like the last time you asked."

Melanie plopped down on the sofa beside Linda.

"I try to care about that, Mel, but I just can't. Those eyes, that body, mmm, *mamacita, le amo.* Did you tell him I'm his fangirl?"

"That didn't come up."

"What about the interview? Did you ask him yet? I'm gonna wear my Versace. It takes a serious outfit to make a man like Atari Briggs sit up and take notice."

"I hate to break it to you, but given that I'm about to put him behind bars for the rest of his life, he's not likely to grant my sister an interview."

Linda was an entertainment correspondent for a local cable TV show.

"You know if you win that trial, every woman in America will hate you, right? Including me."

"If he's convicted, won't that tarnish his image?"

"Tarnish? It'll just give him street cred. We'll love him all the more, and be very mad at you."

"I try to care about that, Lin, but I just can't."

"*Loca!* Don't you love his music?"

"Honestly, I've never even heard it."

"That's foolish if you ask me. You know he raps about the life, right? I bet there's evidence for your case in there and you're totally ignorant of it."

Melanie looked at her sister with a spark of interest. "Seriously?"

"Hell, yeah. Every track on *Myrtle Avenue Mayhem* is a different murder. He raps about packing drugs, his money-counting machine, his favorite guns. What's your case about again, exactly?"

"A hit Atari ordered on a guy named Little D, who was selling his own product at Atari's spot."

"Hmm. There's a track on *Back in the Day* called "D Is for Dead" that sounds right. Let me see." She tapped out a beat on the coffee table with her fingernails. "It's like this. 'You take one real clean in the back of the head, your blood in the street, your brains on the concrete.' I'm blanking on the rest."

Melanie looked stunned. "You say that's called 'D Is for Dead'?"

"Mmm-hmm."

"Little D was shot in the back of the head and left to die in the street."

"See, there you go. Atari's music is so relevant."

"Do you own that CD?"

"I have all his stuff on my iPod. If you want, give me your MP3 and I'll download it for you."

"That would be great."

"I help you, you help me to get the interview," Linda said with an ingratiating smile.

"Ugh, you don't get it."

"C'mon, I'm kidding. You look tired, *chica*." She patted the sofa. "Put your feet up here."

Melanie swung her feet around, and Linda began massaging them.

"Oh, you are *such* a good sister," Melanie said, throwing her head back. "Tell me you're not leaving, puh-lease. Maybe you won't find an apartment. Then you'll have to stay."

Linda had just been offered a job as a weekend anchor at a network affiliate in Miami. It was a huge break, the one she'd been waiting for. But hard as Melanie tried to feel happy for her sister, she couldn't get past the fact that she was losing her best friend.

"Oh, I'll find a place," Linda said. "And I am leaving. Sorry."

"But it's only temporary, right?"

"Sweetie, it's for as long as it takes." Linda regarded Melanie steadily, then reached out and placed her hand on Melanie's. The gesture was so full of sympathy, of pity even, that Melanie immediately suspected something was up.

"What?" she demanded.

"I might as well tell you now, since we're on the subject. Mom has some news, but she's too chicken to tell you herself." Linda paused, grimacing.

"You're giving me a heart attack."

"Mel, she's getting older. She's ready to retire."

Melanie sat up instantly. "She's going with you?"

"I tried to talk her out of it. But remember last month when I went to interview and she came along for the weekend? She went crazy for the place."

"How could you do this to me?"

"Me? You think I *want* to move to Miami with a sexy new job and bring my mother? Please! She'll be so in my way. There was nothing I could do, honest."

Linda's news came at the worst possible moment. Dan leaving, Lester dying in front of her, the case falling apart, the trial bearing down on her, and now this. Melanie thought of Maya, lying so innocent under the covers in the back bedroom, completely unaware that her little world was about to change. Her grandma and her aunt were a big part of her life.

"You're not just leaving me, you're leaving Maya. How can you abandon her?"

"Don't get all dramatic on me. Maya has the best mommy in the world. And Yolie is a fantastic babysitter. You can come visit, and if that's not good enough, there's an obvious answer."

"What's that?"

"Move with us. I could totally see you there. It's a happening place, sis, and there's a real-estate bust on. You could pick up a great condo, cheap."

"I can't move."

"Why not? How bad do you complain about life up here, huh? Your job is killing you. You have no time for Maya. You hate the weather. You're miserable."

"I love my job. As for Maya, of course I want more time with her. But that wouldn't be any different in Miami. I'd have to work just as hard."

"You'd love it there."

"Lin, stop. There are so many reasons I can't move that I can barely count them all. Steve lives here and we have a custody agreement. I could go on and on. Anyway, I don't have time to discuss this any more right now."

"Why not?"

"I'm leaving for Las Vegas tomorrow on a case, and I have to pack. And since you and Mom are ruining *la pequeña*'s life by abandoning us, you can watch her for me at night till I get back."

Ten minutes after Linda left, as Melanie was in the middle of packing a suitcase, the phone rang.

"Hello?"

"Is she gone?" Dan asked.

"Is who gone?"

"Your sister."

"How'd you know she was here? Are you having me watched?"

"Christ, no. I called before, and she answered, that's all. She didn't tell you?"

"No, but don't take it personally. Linda doesn't do messages."

"Believe me, this was personal. She gave me an earful. Whatever you told her about me, she hates my fucking guts."

"I told her about you and Diane. And yes, that would make her hate your guts."

"Did you tell her I didn't go through with it? That I came straight to you and confessed, and—"

"Dan, I'm not interested enough in this topic to waste my breath discussing it with you. Is there something else you want to say? Otherwise this conversation is over."

The connection was good. She heard his aggrieved sigh loud and clear.

"I'm trying to pass along some information that might help you."

"Fine, I'm listening."

"The tip the dead lawyer gave you about Gamal Abdullah is not panning out."

"Meaning what?"

"Abdullah's not moving around Spain under the alias Sebastien Calais. We can't find any evidence of that alias ever being used or even associated with his organization. Abdullah's not in Spain as far as we can tell. He's not anywhere else in Europe, and hasn't been for some time. Our information is, he was in Pakistan for a while, and—get this—he's believed to've died in an explosion that went down in a bomb factory there several months ago."

"Gamal Abdullah is *dead*?"

"That's what we think, but keep it on the down low. Nobody knows we know he's dead. If they knew we knew, it would burn our source."

"Okay."

"What we're hearing is, Abdullah was with his technical guys in a bomb factory in the tribal regions about two months ago when somebody screwed up and connected the wrong wire. Place went up like a Roman candle, took a bunch of the scumbags out. We don't have bodies or DNA. The IDs are based on informant information alone, but this source is considered highly reliable."

Melanie rubbed her forehead. "I'm trying to think what this could mean," she said. "Atari Briggs claims he never offered to cooperate against Abdullah, that Lester Poe lied to me. But Lester was assassinated using the same plastic explosives that Abdullah was known to use, which suggests Abdullah killed him to stop the cooperation."

"Don't make too much of the fact that the explosives match. Anybody with underworld connections can buy those same explosives on the black market."

"The explosives aren't the only evidence. I had new information today confirming that Diamond bugged Poe's phones. That would explain how the news got to Abdullah that Briggs wanted to cooperate against him. Then, boom, Lester's killed and Evan Diamond takes over the case. The cooperation shuts down. It's a straight shot.

Evan Diamond blabs to Abdullah, then Abdullah orders the hit on Lester to stop the cooperation. Well?"

"I'm telling you, Abdullah was dead already. That lawyer was feeding you bullshit."

Melanie considered what she'd learned about Lester Poe in the course of the past few days. Brenda shooting up while he partied on. Charity Bishop dying in his swimming pool. Evan Diamond black-mailing him. She hadn't really known the man, had she?

"Anything's possible," she said.

"Under the circumstances, we're closing down over here and pounding leads closer to home. I'll be back stateside tomorrow."

Melanie didn't react to that news, and Dan's words hung in the air.

"Question for you," he said. "Any truth to the rumor you were sleeping with the lawyer?"

"Who told you that?"

"Never you mind. All the way in fucking Spain, I'm hearing this shit."

"Oh, it must be true, then. God, are you really stupid enough to listen to that BS?"

"How quickly they forget. Yeah, I'm pretty stupid."

"I'm not talking to you about who I do or don't sleep with, Dan. Now is there anything else?"

"Yes, although I don't know why I still care enough to say it. The leads are closer to home now. Watch your back."

# 36

On the plane to Vegas, Melanie was trapped in the window seat as the enormous Papo West snoozed beside her, his mouth hanging open. When the flight attendant gave the all clear to use electronic devices, Melanie reached into her bag for her iPod. She yanked on it, and it came out all tangled up with that Saint Jude's medal that had once belonged to Lester Poe, the one Brenda Gould had given her. She'd thrown the necklace in her handbag late last night while she was packing, on an impulse. Plenty of people brought lucky talismans to Vegas, but Melanie wasn't planning to gamble. She was just nervous about this trip. They needed a break on the case soon, or it would be too late, and crazy as it sounded, the Saint Jude's medal gave her confidence that she'd prevail.

Melanie untangled her iPod headphones and then scrolled to the Atari Briggs music that Linda had downloaded. Maybe listening to the hottest rapper on the planet wouldn't feel like work to some people, but it did to her. Other than the occasional old classic like Tupac, who had soul and something to say, Melanie didn't like rap. Too much glorification of the type of violence that destroyed lives, with too little artistry masking the depravity. But if Linda said there was solid information about Atari's crimes in these tracks, Melanie believed her. It wouldn't be the first time. Every narcotics defendant she'd ever locked up had a rap demo to promote, and they all drew material from their real-life experiences in the drug trade. Why should Atari be any different?

She went straight to the track called "D Is for Dead," the one that Linda had identified for her. Sure enough, it was like listening to Atari confess his role in whacking Little D. She listened to it several times to catch all the lyrics, and the track began to worm its way into her head. It was catchy—the sound harsh, with a hypnotic beat, Atari's voice rough and insinuating and sexy. Each time she listened she found another detail that lined up with the facts of the murder, just as each time she listened she felt a little more drawn to the artist. She couldn't deny it. The man had star quality.

> You steal from me.
> Son, I don't play.
> D is for dead at the end of the day.
> That's how I keep shit going my way.
> You mess with my name.
> You finish up dead.
> Take one real clean in the back of the head.
> Your blood in the street.
> Your brains on the concrete.
> Learn the lesson yet?
> D is for dead
> My shorty done the deed so I don't break a sweat.

She wondered if there was a video that went with this track, and if so, what it would reveal. She wondered whether Bernadette would allow a rap song into evidence. Even if the judge agreed to it, was that a smart thing to do? The press was on the DA's back already about prosecuting Atari for his music. A crafty ploy on Evan Diamond's part, making it politically dangerous for the prosecution to use this powerful evidence.

Melanie jotted down the lyrics of "D Is for Dead" in her notebook and moved on to some of the other songs. *Myrtle Avenue Mayhem* was Atari's breakout debut album, nearly ten years old now but still selling mad copies in download. Linda had told her that every track on the album described a different murder. If the lyrics were true, and not merely the posturing of an ambitious showman, then Atari Briggs had a lot of bodies on him. Eleven, to be exact, not counting Little D. When Papo woke up, she'd make him listen. Maybe they could match the tracks up with unsolved murders. That would be a new one—handing over an iPod full of tunes to Cold Case and telling them to go to town.

After a while, all the songs started to sound the same, and Melanie zoned out, lulled by the noise and vibration of the jet. Outside her window, far below, a sprinkling of snow clung to the frozen plains. The first couple of verses of "Cold Hard Flash" went right by her. It wasn't until halfway through the track that the allusions to the world's most precious gem caught her ear.

*You cut glass*
*But you can't cut me*
*Your bullets didn't touch me*
*Brothers dying in the rain you started*
*I call out their names*
*RT and Fro Joe and KP*
*Your hired guns missed me*
*They ain't never gonna hit me*
*My onetime friend, now my enemy*
*Cold hard flash*

*Like your name*
*Is all you are*
*It's all the same to me*
*You gonna see*
*Don't turn your back*
*Don't sleep at night*
*I'm'a get you*

She went back and listened to the track from the beginning. By the end, she was too excited to wait for Papo to wake up on his own.

"Hey," she said, shaking his shoulder.

He struggled to raise his eyelids. "What? Huh? We landing?"

"No, you have to listen to this."

She yanked off her earbuds and held them out to him.

"Naw," Papo said, waving her away. "I don't want music. I'm catching some z's."

"Papo, this is Atari I'm listening to. He did a song about the hit on Little D and another one on Evan Diamond. Atari and Diamond go back a long way. According to this, there was some kind of falling-out between them, some kind of war. People died because of it. Diamond might've tried to kill Briggs. Please, listen."

With obvious reluctance, Papo sat upright and put on the earbuds, and Melanie scrolled back to "Cold Hard Flash."

"Atari doesn't come right out and say Evan Diamond's name," she said, "but I'm convinced that's who he's talking about. Listen and tell me if I'm crazy."

From Papo's expression, Melanie expected to be told in short order that she *was* crazy. But then she rolled the track and watched him get drawn in.

"Play it again," he said.

Papo listened to "Cold Hard Flash" twice more before removing the headphones.

"Here's what I can tell you," he said. "KP is a pretty common street name because the initials stand for 'kingpin.' Could be any number of different guys. RT I never heard of. But Fro Joe was a real guy, a well-known player in Bed-Stuy in the nineties. Went down in a hail of bullets during a war with a rival faction. Whether that's the same guy Atari's talking about in this song, I don't know for sure, but probably."

"What about Diamond? Doesn't it sound like he was mixed up in the war, too? Like maybe even he tried to have Atari killed?"

"I don't see where you get Diamond off this song."

"'Cold hard flash like your name'? 'You can cut glass'? How obvious could it be?"

Papo looked at her with the dull eyes of someone who'd rather be sleeping. "You *are* crazy."

"But Fro Joe was real."

"He *was* real. So what? Every cop who worked narcotics in Brooklyn knew Fro Joe. All the little bangers like Atari Briggs knew him, too. So Atari put him in a song. It doesn't mean Atari slung junk with him, and it certainly doesn't mean Evan Diamond was in that drug war."

"I never said that."

But Melanie looked so disappointed that Papo patted her head. "Tell you what, kiddo. Once we're set up in Vegas, I'll call headquarters and get one of the old-timers on the phone. If there's something about Atari Briggs and Evan Diamond and a drug war, we'll find out."

# 36

When you're a New Yorker, you think you've seen it all, but Melanie had never seen anything like the MGM Grand. The green glass building on the Las Vegas strip was butt ugly, but so arresting in its garishness that she found it impossible to look away. A gold lion stood guard out front, so enormous that it might've beamed down from a planet full of giants. It seemed to shoot off alpha rays, but really it was reflecting the setting sun as the strip turned orange and cobalt and purple. Inside, the lobby was vast, with a polished checkerboard marble floor spreading out in all directions, punctuated by crystal chandeliers that packed enough candlepower to outshine the Rockefeller Center Christmas tree. And everywhere, the people were just as megawatt as their surroundings—white, black, Hispanic, and Asian, dripping jewelry, rocking the tight clothes, and showing plenty of skin. Melanie held her own in Manhattan, but here she felt like a hick.

"How'd you pick this hotel?" she asked Papo West as they stood in line at the registration desk.

"It's so big that we can blend into the crowd."

"You might. Not me. Not unless I take a pair of scissors to my clothes."

"You look fine."

"I look like a J.Crew ad that got lost and wound up in the Frederick's of Hollywood catalog."

Papo wasn't much for talking about personal style, and anyway, his Nextel was chirping. He took a call from one of the local DEA agents. Melanie continued to feast her eyes on the dazzling freak show all around her, her nose twitching at the unfamiliar aroma of cigarette smoke wafting through the air. Nowhere in New York did it smell like this anymore, like the inside of some old-time speakeasy. Her gaze meandered around the cavernous room until a familiar shape at the elevators arrested its progress, and, for an instant, seemed to stop the very beating of her heart.

Was it him? The height. The breadth of those shoulders. That dark hair falling in crisp waves against his neck. Could it possibly be—*Dan O'Reilly?* His back was to her. The jacket was different. Had he bought a new jacket? Would he have gotten here from Spain so quickly? And why would he come *here?* Had his investigation into the role of Gamal Abdullah in the car bombing led him to Las Vegas? That seemed too startling a coincidence. Could he be here to see her? But she'd made it so clear they were over. It couldn't be him.

But did any other man have that body?

In a daze, Melanie stepped out of line and took two halting steps toward the elevator before a large group of Japanese tourists flooded into the lobby and blocked her view. She got lost among them like a salmon swimming in the middle of a turbulent school. By the time they'd cleared, Dan, or the mirage of him, had disappeared.

"We're next!" Papo called.

Melanie went and checked in. But this business trip had just changed irrevocably for her. Even if the sighting of Dan had been a mere hallucination, a figment of her lingering passion, she wouldn't be able to forget it. She'd be searching every face in the crowd now, just to catch a single glimpse of his blue eyes.

When Melanie and Papo sat down with local DEA in person, around a conference table at DEA's bustling Las Vegas Boulevard district office, relations improved dramatically. Andre Ferris was the supervisor of the Las Vegas district office, with nearly fifty men under his command, but he'd taken time out of his day to meet with them and appeared to be trying to help. He was lean and sun-burnished, with black hair and a Wild West swagger about him. The two junior agents—Duvall Smithson and Alejandro Morales—were low-key and easier to read. Melanie and Papo quickly became convinced that the three of them were telling the truth about having independent information on Vegas Bo. They'd received a tip about the same stash location weeks before Papo had called to ask for assistance in making the arrest. They'd just been taking their sweet time acting on it.

"We appreciate you meeting with us so late in the day," Melanie said. "Beyond that, we owe you an apology. We really believed you fabricated that tip so you'd have an excuse to poach our target. We were wrong."

"I'm sorry, too," Papo said. "Especially since I called you guys every name in the book."

The DEA–6 report in question was lying on the table. It listed the very same address in the desert town of Pahrump, Nevada, that Melanie and Papo had originally heard about from Vashon Clark, except the report was dated three weeks before Vashon told them.

"All it took was one measly backdated report to get you people off our backs?" Ferris said.

After a second of awkward silence, Ferris winked, and everybody broke out laughing.

"A little humor to ease the mood," Ferris said. "No hard feelings.

This happens all the time. Two separate investigative teams zeroing in on one and the same target from opposite directions. To me, it says we're all on the right track."

"I couldn't agree more," Papo said. "Right target and right location. Now all we need to do is figure out where the dirtbag ran to."

"We have an informant who can help with that, but first I'll give you some background," Ferris said. "The tip on the stash location was part of a bigger investigation we started about six months ago. We heard that a bunch of serious players from back east were muscling in on our Mexican gangs. Previously, most of the heroin in Vegas was Mexican black tar. Cheap and plentiful, but the most godawful stepped-on shit you're ever gonna find. Suddenly we're seeing this beautiful pure product. It took off like wildfire. Users dropping like flies left and right, overdosing because they couldn't handle the purity."

"Have you seized any of the pure stuff?" Melanie asked Ferris.

"Haven't done rips yet because we were building our case brick by brick and didn't want to burn it. But we made a couple of small-scale buys. Your next question's gonna be did we send that heroin to Washington for chemical analysis. Answer's yes. They believe its Central Asian in origin, probably Afghan, and very similar to samples that have been turning up recently in Chicago and Atlanta and Detroit."

Just when Melanie was about to give up and decide that Gamal Abdullah was either a hoax or a phantom, along came new evidence that Vegas Bo and other big players were indeed being supplied by an Afghan source. Melanie threw Papo a meaningful look.

"Afghan. Fits with our terrorism angle," she said.

"Yup."

"Not only did the new heroin cause ODs," Ferris continued, "it caused bloodshed. Suddenly we had a gang war on our hands, because the Mexicans weren't going quietly into the night. They were giving the East Coast boys some push-back, and it was getting ugly.

We've had sixteen drug-related homicides so far this year. That's a big number for us. So if we can take this Vegas Bo down, we can solve a serious problem."

"What do you hear about these players from back east?" Melanie asked. "Who are they? What type of backgrounds do they come from? Criminal histories?"

"We believe they're blacks from New York."

"African-American?" Melanie asked. "American-born, as opposed to Caribbean or African immigrants or—?"

"Right. Americans, not foreigners. New Yorkers. My informants are very clear on that part. Seems to add an element of stress to the interaction." Ferris raised a bushy eyebrow humorously.

Melanie smiled. "What about their history in the trade?"

"Longtime players is what we're hearing. But we were just getting started with the identification process when the lot of 'em cut and run. Let me show you some surveillance pictures."

He slapped an eight-by-ten glossy down on the table.

"Here's the stash location in Pahrump," he said, pointing to a photograph of a mobile home mounted on a cinder-block foundation. The place appeared desolate in the extreme, mint-green paint peeling off in long strips and several broken windows taped over with plastic. The front yard was lumpy red dirt, barren of vegetation except for a few scraggly weeds and littered with garbage.

"The mobile home isn't on what you'd call a street per se," Ferris said. "It's more like a dirt path. Duvall'll drive you out there in the morning for a look-see so you can better understand. There's nothing around for a quarter mile in either direction except vacant lots and your occasional coyote. For these boys to sit on the place night and day just wasn't feasible."

"Yeah," Agent Smithson said. "As it was, we were as careful as we know how to be, and we still scared 'em off."

"I can't figure it at all," Agent Morales added. "We limited ourselves to drive-by surveillance. Different car every time. Never even slowed down when we took the pictures. And there *is* occasional traffic on that road, so the car alone wouldn't've hinked them up. Yet they made surveillance anyway."

"You do think that's what happened, right?" Melanie asked. "That they made you?"

"What else could it be?" Ferris asked.

"Somebody tipped them," she said, shrugging.

"It would have to be either somebody in our shop or somebody in yours. Who'd do that?"

"You're right. I don't think so, either," she said.

"Okay, when we did surveillance, before the targets hightailed it, we did get some decent pictures," Ferris said. "There was a lot of activity in and out of the location. Here you go, two nice clear ones with your boy Kevin Bonner."

Ferris laid out two more glossies. Vegas Bo looked just the same as he had in his mug shot taken a decade earlier—scary, with a big scar on his face and home-drawn gang tattoos scrolling down his neck. In one of the pictures, he was with somebody, and in context, standing next to another person, he was one huge dude. Mean, ugly, and nasty, not somebody you'd want to run across in a dark alley.

"He'll make a beautiful witness, won't he?" Papo joked, echoing Melanie's thoughts.

"Witness? Wait a minute, you're thinking of flipping this goon?" Ferris demanded.

"That's why we're here," Melanie said. "Didn't your U.S. Attorney's Office tell you? We have Bonner nailed on a hit from a decade ago. Atari Briggs ordered it. Bonner provided the gun. And a third guy, our cooperator, was the shooter. We're hoping Bonner's willing to fess up and finger Briggs for ordering the hit."

"Whoa, hold your horses. In our case, Bonner's the kingpin. He's the one running the show. If we let him flip and take his cooperation,

he ends up cooperating down the food chain against the lowly work-
ers. We don't do that in this office. Looks bad."

"I understand your discomfort, Andre, really," Melanie said. "But
Atari Briggs is a high-priority target according to Main Justice. We've
been told to move heaven and earth to bring him down. I'm sure
they'll take the same line with you."

"So I don't have anything to say about it, is what you're telling
me."

"Not really. But look on the bright side. If Bonner flips, he'll give
you a lot of people on your end. C'mon, who else've you got in those
surveillance photos? Maybe some of them are big fish."

Ferris looked disgruntled, but he handed over the folder with the
surveillance photos nonetheless. Melanie proceeded to lay out the
remaining ones on the table. There were five in all, each one showing a view of a different man entering or exiting the mobile home.
In several photographs, the subjects carried duffel bags, a sure sign of
narcotics activity inside the trailer.

"Three of these mopes have been ID'd by scanning their faces
into the mug-shot database. All three come up as previously arrested
in New York or New Jersey on narcotics or weapons charges. Duvall
can give you the details. The other two, we don't know who they
are."

Melanie and Papo were both studying the photos. Papo reached
out and placed a fingertip on one of them.

"Him?"

"Nope, not ID'd yet," Ferris said.

"I was looking at him, too," Melanie said thoughtfully.

The photograph was the only one of a white man, and he had a
distinctive appearance. Hulking of build, with the squashed-in face
of an ex-boxer, under a thatch of ginger hair that looked wrong for
him, like it belonged on the head of a smaller, gentler human being.

"When was this photo taken?" Papo asked.

"The day the boys did their big surveillance. What was that, Sunday?"

"Yes, boss," Smithson said.

"He looks familiar, doesn't he?" Papo asked Melanie, his brows knit.

"Yes. But from where?"

"Our hotel?" Papo asked.

"I don't think so."

"Yeah, I don't, either."

They looked at each other. She looked back down at the photograph, concentrating with all her might.

"I think it was back in New York," she said. "I think I saw him in court, at our status conference yesterday."

"That's it. You're right. I saw him, too."

"That status conference was closed to the public. He wasn't just a spectator. Either you had a press pass or some connection to the defense or the government. They didn't let civilians in because of the disruption the last time."

"So either he's a member of the press . . . ," Papo began.

"Or he's part of the defense team," Melanie finished.

# 37

Melanie and Papo had an hour to kill before their scheduled rendezvous with Andre Ferris's informant, so they hung around the DEA office and made phone calls back east. Melanie managed to catch Susan Charlton and Jennifer Lamont still in Susan's office despite the fact that it was nearly ten o'clock in New York. She gave them a full run-down of what she'd learned in the past twelve hours, including the fact that Evan Diamond had been house counsel to Briggs's drug organization back in the day and might have been involved in a drug war, and the possibility that the redheaded man surveilled meeting with Vegas Bo over the weekend at the stash location in Pahrump had been in court in New York the day before.

"The guy's face is clear as day in the surveillance photo," Melanie said. "I'm going to fax it to you."

Melanie sent the fax through, and within minutes Susan and Jennifer had the picture in their hands.

"Sorry, Mel," Susan said. "Neither of us recognizes him. I can ask around with the marshals if you want."

"Yes, good idea. And keep your eyes open for him. The status conference yesterday was closed to the public. So either he came in with the defense team—"

"Or he's press," Susan said.

"Right."

"Doesn't it make more sense that he'd be with the press?" Jennifer asked.

"What would a reporter be doing out in the middle of nowhere meeting with a drug dealer?" Melanie asked.

"Trying to get an interview?" Jennifer suggested.

"Who knows," Susan said. "Let's hope the Marshals' Service kept some kind of list so we can find out. But let's assume for a minute he *is* one of Atari's people."

"Or one of Diamond's," Melanie said.

"Either way, what does that mean for the case?"

"That there's ongoing contact between Vegas Bo and the defense," Melanie said. "That wouldn't be surprising, I suppose. Atari and Bo were close associates for years. But it's worth keeping in mind as we pursue Vegas Bo as a witness. Vashon Clark told us Bo has a grudge against Atari, but he may be more hostile than we think."

"If they're still working together, Bo won't cooperate," Susan said.

"Probably not."

"You know what we should do? We should pull phone records on Atari and Evan Diamond, both. See if they're calling any Nevada numbers," Susan said.

"Great idea," Melanie said, "but it could take a while. We have to jump through extra hoops to get lawyer phone records, don't we?"

"There is extra red tape involved," Susan said. "We have to get authorization from Main Justice before we issue any subpoenas for telephone records. It's never too early to learn how to massage the bureaucracy. What do you say, Jennifer? Are you up for taking charge of getting Evan Diamond's phone records?"

. . .

Next, Papo West dialed the home number of an agent named Eddie Carlucci, a longtime street narcotics agent who was on the verge of retirement.

"Eddie knows every back alley from East New York to Red Hook," Papo said as the rings sounded on the speakerphone. "If anybody can give us the history between Briggs and Diamond, he can."

They found Carlucci in a voluble mood, with the loose tongue of somebody who had a few too many beers in him.

"Atari Briggs . . . and Evan Diamond," he repeated aloud. "Oh, yeah. Two winners! Briggs was a young kid at the time, eighteen, twenty maybe, but he ran a bunch of spots in East New York. Diamond was a real flashy cartel lawyer. Dark hair, fancy suits. House counsel to Atari and his boys. There was a war, and a bunch of players went down. Fro Joe was the biggest to get hit in that incident."

"Exactly. I told Melanie you were the man to ask. We're doing the trial against Atari Briggs, and Diamond's representing him. We heard there was a history there."

"They're together again? That surprises me, because Diamond was in the thick of that war, and he was lined up against Briggs. It got ugly. Lotta bodies dropping."

Melanie and Papo exchanged glances.

"Keep going. This sounds right," Papo said.

"It went like this. Atari, if I remember right, had three lieutenants. Two Ton Tyrone, who was there for muscle, dumb as a rock. Shake and Bake, fucking psychopath, impossible to control. And Vegas Bo, who was a mean motherfucker but the only one of the three who was worth his salt. I mean Bo was a smart kid, and *cold*. Real kingpin material."

"That's all foursquare with what we're hearing," Papo said.

"Well, they were making money hand over fist, but Atari wasn't paying down the chain like he should have. He was keeping too much for himself, and people were unhappy. Meanwhile, he was all distracted with the rap bullshit, too. They'd have a problem down at the spot, and you couldn't find the guy because he was off in some goddamn recording studio. He wasn't keeping tabs on his own corners. Naturally, somebody of Vegas Bo's caliber, he saw an opportunity."

"He moved in to take over the candy store."

"Exx-actly. Thought he deserved it. And Diamond was in on it with him. They arranged a hit on Atari at this nightclub in Canarsie where they all hung out. It was supposed to go down when Atari was leaving, but see, not everybody was as fed up with Atari as Bo was. He still had his loyalists, and somebody tipped him off to what was coming. He pulled a team together at the last minute, and they ambushed the shooters. There was a big battle."

"You know, I'm remembering this," Papo said.

"It was all over the papers at the time. Five bodies dropped, including Fro Joe. Atari got away without a scratch. But he knew the game was up. After that, he took the money and ran. Shut down his spots. Went off to do his music."

"What happened to Vegas Bo and Diamond?" Papo asked.

"Nothing. The guys who could've substantiated their involvement died in the gun battle, and we couldn't prove anything."

"The smart ones always get away. Atari never struck back at Diamond?"

"No. He talked a big game, but never retaliated that I heard of. You ask me, Atari was scared of the lawyer."

"High time Evan Diamond got his comeuppance," Papo said.

"There's something I'd pay money to see. He pretends to be respectable, but he's worse than his clients. Here's an example for you. I had two cases where he sold phony paperwork."

"Paperwork? What, like fake IDs?"

"No, forged legal paperwork. For a while, every scumbag in Brooklyn knew that anything you needed to get along in the life, you could get from Evan Diamond for a price. If you wanted to rob drugs from your kingpin, he'd give you a phony search warrant and a seizure receipt documenting that the feds took the drugs. You hand that to the boss and say, hey, I got hit by the cops, and you don't get whacked. There were some big-time stash-house robberies that used Diamond's paperwork for cover until word got around and the bosses wised up. He was selling the package for ten grand a pop."

"No kidding."

"Yeah, I'm telling you, it happened on one of my cases. Oh, and here's another one. This is priceless. Diamond phonied up a sentencing reduction order for one of his scumbag clients and had the client mail it to the Bureau of Prisons in an envelope from the Clerk's Office to get released early. It almost worked, too. They caught it at the last minute. The client was charged with attempted escape. So he flipped and told me Diamond was behind the whole scheme, but the U.S. Attorney's Office wouldn't prosecute on the word of a drug dealer against a member of the bar. I tried to have the guy make a recorded call to Diamond."

"And?" Papo asked.

"Didn't work. Diamond's too smart, and he's too cautious. He recognizes that anybody he commits a crime with might turn on him, so he's very careful on the phone. We could never get him on tape. We dusted the forged paperwork, and the only prints we found were the client's. No way the guy could've managed the forgery with the supplies he had access to inside. It was too professional a job. We believed him that Diamond forged the documents, but we couldn't prove it. Diamond must've worn gloves. The point I'm trying to make is, you'll never get this guy. He's too damn careful."

# 38

Jennifer Lamont lived way the hell out in Carroll Gardens, the heart of brownstone Brooklyn, in a dark, cozy basement apartment with an old-fashioned marble mantel and original woodwork. She loved the apartment for its charm and affordability, but centrally located it was not. When she went out, which she did occasionally, she would meet her date or her friends, such as they were, in Manhattan, and so in the year plus she'd lived there, nobody had ever come to visit. This was why, as she stood at the kitchen counter in her sweatpants eating Cap'n Crunch for dinner, she failed to recognize the buzzer when it first sounded.

"Was that the . . . ?" she asked her cat.

It sounded again. "Oh my God, Snickers, it *was* the doorbell. It's after eleven. Who could it be?"

In her heart of hearts, Jennifer knew exactly who it was. So she stopped pretending for the benefit of the cat, and screamed, "Just a minute!" Then she rushed to her bedroom, tore off her sweatpants and ratty old Yale T-shirt, yanked on the only cute pj's she owned—

pink cotton with a camisole top, bought on sale at Victoria's Secret—and squirted on some perfume. She raced back to her front door and took a deep breath to compose herself.

"Who is it?"

"It's Evan. Open up."

She cracked the door wide enough to peek out. His face was so perfect that it dazzled her eyes, but she'd keep her distance. Just because she'd changed her clothes, just because she wanted to look nice in case she let him in, didn't mean she'd *decided* to let him in. She needed to figure out a way to stop herself from doing stuff with him. Doing something like what she was thinking about doing with a man like Evan Diamond was not only stupid and self-destructive, it was crazy.

"How—how'd you get my address?" she asked. "I'm unlisted."

"I'm not an amateur. It's cold out here. Let me in."

And he put his hand on the door and shoved past her. He was wearing an expensive-looking cashmere overcoat, and carrying a greasy brown paper bag that gave off an aroma of cilantro and garlic.

"What's in the bag?" she called after him.

But he'd already disappeared into the kitchen. A moment later, he emerged, threw his coat down on the sofa, and came over to where she stood at the open door.

"Close it already. You're letting the cold air in."

She remained silent, her eyes huge and fixed on his, which were impenetrable in their blackness.

"What are you, afraid of me or something?" He paused. "You are, aren't you?"

Evan smiled like the thought pleased him, then removed her hand from the door, shut and bolted it.

He was inside now; so much for her resolution. What next? Jennifer's heart was hammering so hard that the lace-trimmed edge of her camisole quivered with each beat. He was tall and gorgeous, and he smelled clean from the cold outside. But those things were merely the inert ingredients of his appeal; the magic was supplied by something else entirely. He was dangerous, so dangerous that she couldn't predict how far he'd go. With him, she was falling with no safety net, and it thrilled her to the core. *We're alone here,* she thought, and then: *He could do things to me and nobody would stop him.* She certainly wouldn't stop him herself.

Evan watched her chest heave up and down with a calm, scientific interest, then ran his fingertip along the lace and down the curve of her breast. Not only did she not slap his hand away; Jennifer instinctively threw her shoulders back and offered her body to him. But it wasn't clear he wanted it. He turned away and started taking off his tie.

"To answer your question from a minute ago, dinner's in the bag. Are you hungry?" he asked.

He tossed the tie onto the demi-lune table where she kept her mail. She tried to pay attention to his question, but the sliver of aqua-blue silk enthralled and distracted her. What could he mean by taking off his tie? What did he intend? Did he want to make love or was he merely getting ready to eat?

"No," she managed. "No, thank you. I just ate some cereal."

He turned back and twisted his finger in one of the straps of her camisole, pulling it off her shoulder. "Victoria's Secret, right?"

"Yes."

"You went and put them on for me?" he asked.

"Yes."

He grabbed her shoulders and pushed her against the wall so suddenly that her head banged. She gave a soft grunt, half pain, half desire.

"For future reference, if I want you to wear something in particular, I'll tell you," he said, looming over her. "Don't ever leave me standing in the cold again. Do you understand?"

And he took her gently by the throat with one powerful hand, pressing his thumb into her windpipe, not so hard that he cut off her air supply, but hard enough to show her that he could. She couldn't tell if this was a game or not, but she didn't care. She loved knowing that he was in control. She didn't have to decide anything anymore, not even whether to live or die. He would tell her what to do. Her only fear was that he wouldn't care enough to do so.

"Jennifer, do you understand?"

"Yes."

"Good girl."

He let go, and took her face ever so gently between his hands, giving her the tenderest, most loving kiss. His lips were still cold from outside, but his tongue was warm. She thought she might faint. She went limp, her body relaxing against his, impatient to feel his hands all over her. But he pulled away.

"Let's eat now," he said. "That food smells good."

"But . . . but can't that wait?" she pleaded.

He smiled sympathetically and caressed her cheek. "You'll get what you need, baby. But first I want my dinner. It's been a long day."

"Okay."

He went and sat down at the white laminate café table in the corner—an IKEA special that she never actually used, preferring as she did to eat standing up at the counter—and looked up at her like she was the waitress and he was the customer waiting for his food. It amazed her that he'd walked away from sex like that. She'd been so obviously willing, but Evan was unmoved. He'd rather eat his dinner. His indifference humiliated her. Jennifer wanted to yell at him, to scream at him to get out.

Instead, she went into the kitchen to get the food like he'd told her to. She moved as if in a dream, taking dishes from the cabinets and forgetting where she'd put them, pulling foil containers from the bag and staring at them like she couldn't understand what they were. All she could think about was what he'd promised, the words he'd used. *You'll get what you need.* What did that mean? Did he plan to hurt her? To rip off her clothes and ravish her? To make love to her tenderly? She needed all of those things. She felt dizzy thinking about his voice saying the words, about the possibilities. Her legs were trembling. She grabbed the counter to hold herself up.

"Poor Dixie. You're in a bad way, aren't you?" he said from the doorway.

She closed her eyes tight and didn't say anything. Coming up behind her, he ran his hands lightly over the bare skin of her arms, and leaned down, his lips against her ear, pressing her tight against the counter with his body. Relief flooded through her at the thought that he wanted her.

"You don't need to be afraid," he whispered, his breath warm against her hair.

She began rocking back and forth against him in slow motion.

"I don't?"

"No. I'll take good care of you."

Tears began to leak from her eyes. "You will?"

"Of course, baby. Daddy loves you. You want me to show you how much?"

"Yes," she whispered, "please."

"Are you a good girl?" he said into her ear. "Do you deserve it?"

"You mean will I bring you your food?"

Without warning, he twisted her arm sharply behind her back and pressed against her. That's when she knew that this would be the most exquisite sex she'd ever experienced, the first time a man had truly possessed her. Until now she'd only been with stupid boys.

"Not the food," he said. "What do you know that I should know? Don't you care about my problems?"

"Yes. Yes, I know a lot. I know everything."

"All right, then. I need details, and then you'll get what you want."

# 39

The hotel casino where Melanie and Papo were meeting the informant was tricked out to look like the deck of the starship *Enterprise*. Klingon cocktail waitresses in full space regalia cruised the floor taking drink orders. Melanie felt like a space alien herself tonight. They'd stopped at their hotel, and she'd made a quick visit to the boutique in the lobby, looking for an outfit that said "Vegas" instead of "Fed." She'd been successful, and now she was in disguise, wearing a skimpy, spaghetti-strapped top covered with big silver spangles, blue jeans and high heels. Every time she moved, the paillettes on her chest shimmied and clicked. With Papo posing as her biker honey, Melanie blended right into the scenery.

They found seats at the far end of the bar, which was crowded. Papo opened his wallet and sneaked a peek at the informant's mug shot, then scanned the room methodically.

Nothing.

"Duvall says this dude's always late anyway," Papo said.

"Where are Duvall and Alejandro now?"

"Duvall's on a buy. Alejandro should be here. But I got a feeling this meet is more important to us than it is to them. Might as well order a drink. Could be a while."

Papo ordered a Jack Daniel's, Melanie a glass of Chardonnay.

"If I were you, I'd watch out for the wine in a place like this," Papo said with a grimace.

"Really?"

"Well, as long as you don't mind it coming from a carton."

Their drinks arrived. They sat for a while, Papo's eyes restlessly searching the floor of the crowded casino. The place reeked of cigarettes. For the first thirty minutes she'd been in Vegas, Melanie had found the all-pervasive smell of smoke decadent, almost glamorous. Now it just gave her a headache. She wished she had a Tylenol. Instead, Papo pulled a crumpled pack of Marlboros from the pocket of his black leather jacket and offered her one.

"No thanks, I don't smoke. I'm surprised you do."

"Who, me?" he said, holding the cigarette between his thumb and forefinger, dragging deeply and watching the smoke curl into the air with narrowed eyes. He was relishing every second. "I don't smoke, either. Anyway, if my wife asks, that's what you say."

Melanie laughed.

"What happens in Vegas stays in Vegas, right?" Papo said. "Hey, I think that's him. Wait here."

Melanie didn't exactly see who Papo was talking about. He crossed the casino floor and vanished from sight behind a tall neon-and-metal flange that was meant to look like part of the spaceship. She kept her eyes trained on the spot where he'd disappeared until it became apparent he wasn't coming back right away.

After five more minutes passed, Melanie was beginning to get nervous. Enough things had gone wrong on this case, enough people had been hurt, that she wasn't entirely comfortable about her own safety. Or Papo's for that matter, and he had a wife and two kids at home. To distract herself, and also so she didn't look quite so much like a hooker trawling for johns at the bar, Melanie whipped out her phone and checked her e-mail.

There was nothing terribly interesting. A few notices from judges' chambers about scheduling matters, an e-mail from Jennifer that the stipulations had been signed and photocopied, a notice of a retirement party for someone in Business Crimes whom she didn't know.

A minute later, Melanie became aware of somebody standing beside her, in front of the seat Papo had vacated, but she was still reading and didn't look up.

"The goon in the leather jacket, is he coming back?" a familiar voice asked.

Melanie lowered the phone and stared straight into Dan O'Reilly's blue eyes. The sight of them was enough to put her months of hard work getting over him in immediate jeopardy, so she looked away, out at the casino floor.

"He'll be back any minute now," she said, trying to sound nonchalant.

"Mind if I sit here in the meantime?" he asked. His tone was light and flirtatious, as if they were meeting for the first time, as if he'd never broken her heart.

"It's a free country," she said.

Dan took a seat.

"You come here often?" he asked.

She couldn't help smiling at the pickup line. "No. I'm here on business."

"Me, too. Any luck?"

"Possibly, but I don't like to talk about it sitting in a crowded bar," she said.

"Discreet. I like that in a woman."

Unable to fight her curiosity any longer, she looked at him. Big mistake. It was all still there. The thick dark hair—she remembered the feel of it passing like silk through her fingers. That football-hero body, neatly attired in pressed khakis and a denim shirt. That face, those eyes. She could handle it, barely, as long as she acted like she was some random woman in a bar and he was a stranger hitting on her. She decided to pretend she was her sister. Linda could handle any man in any bar anytime, even one she'd loved and lost.

"Can I buy you a drink?" he asked, staring back at her.

"Thanks, but I'll stick to my Chardonnay."

"Suit yourself."

She didn't say anything. She couldn't; she was too busy trying—and failing—to break the spell of his glance.

"You know," he said, "you remind me of this girl I used to know. She was beautiful, like you, and she wouldn't fall for my lines. either."

"Smart girl."

"Yeah, very smart. Smart enough to break up with me."

She forced herself to look away. "So you admit she had her reasons?"

"Oh, definitely. I've thought about it a lot, and now I understand she had good reasons. The problem is, I'm still hung up on her."

*Channel Linda, channel Linda,* Melanie told herself. The best way to deal with him was to act like this was all a big joke. She refused to let him back into her heart. It was too late to make things right.

"That's probably not something you want to confide to a woman when you first meet her," she said, tossing her head. "That you're still hung up on somebody else, I mean."

He laughed. "Thanks for the tip. I'll work on my technique."

Melanie's phone rang.

"Excuse me," she said, flipping it open. "Hello?"

"Who's that guy you're talking to?" Papo asked.

Melanie looked Dan in the eye. "Just some guy at the bar who's trying to pick me up."

"I finally found our friend," Papo said. "Look up. See us at the slots?"

Melanie looked across the casino floor to where the slot machines were blinking and flashing, and spotted them sitting together at one. "Yes. I'll be right there."

She hung up. "Sorry, I have to work now. Enjoy your stay in Las Vegas. Be careful who you hit on, though. Not everybody's as nice as me."

And she walked away feeling not that she'd won, but that she'd been lucky to make a narrow escape.

Melanie walked over to the slot machine next to the one where Papo and the informant were sitting, put a chip in the slot, and pushed the button. The clanging noises that emerged were distraction enough to cover up anything they had to say. The informant was short and beefy, with slicked-back hair, dressed all in black, and he went by Gordo el Tercero. That wasn't a name; it just meant he was the third fat guy to join his crew. Either Gordo was really nervous or else he'd done a few lines of coke before the meet—or both—because his body jiggled incessantly as they spoke.

"Ms. Vargas is the prosecutor," Papo said by way of introduction. "Tell her what you just told me about Vegas Bo."

"Like I'm saying to your friend here," Gordo began, "Bo show up in Vegas six months ago. He got a major connect and he tell everybody he gonna bring in killer product. Nobody want to deal with him, though. *Los mexicanos* got their own sources. They don't want to give Bo a piece of their action. So he move in real shakedownlike, try to take over all the spots."

"Now, how do you know this?" Melanie asked.

"How I know?"

"Yes. Were you part of a crew that had dealings with him? Is this a rumor you heard on the street? I need to be able to evaluate the information."

Gordo looked at them with disdain.

"Alejandro tell me I don't have to go into none of my own shit wi' you. That I don't need to give myself up on nothing. I don't know you people from nobody. I'm just here because Alejandro say show up."

Papo held up his hands placatingly. "Yeah, yeah, we're cool, Gordo. Keep going."

"Uh, no we're not. Wait a minute," Melanie said.

Melanie pulled Papo aside.

"I need to hear his answer," she said.

"I don't think he's gonna tell us. It sounds like Alejandro limited the deal to just the 411 on Vegas Bo's location."

"Where *is* Alejandro?" Melanie asked Papo. "He limits my debriefing of the informant and doesn't show up to deal with the consequences?"

"I don't know where he is, but Gordo belongs to him. He's doing us a favor by allowing us talk to the guy at all. So let's just get the information and get the hell out of here."

"How can we tell if there's anything to what Gordo's saying if we don't know the first thing about him? Do you have the first clue what his criminal history is?"

Papo grinned. "I'm confident it's substantial. Alejandro thinks he's reliable. Besides, from the looks of the guy, he's not gonna stick around much longer. Either we go with the flow or we let the tip walk. I say take the information."

"What's up with how antsy he is?"

Papo shrugged.

"All right," Melanie said with a sigh. "We take the information."

They went back to the slot machine.

"Gordo, we're willing to let the questions about your background slide," Melanie said. "Just tell us what you know about Vegas Bo."

"Like I said, he was muscling in. The bullets start to fly. The heat come down. What I hear, he got a tip he gonna be raided and he change up his location."

"He knew he was being watched?" Melanie repeated.

"Yes, ma'am."

"Was that just because he saw the surveillance vehicles?"

"No. What I heard, he tipped off."

"Huh, really. So, do you know where he went?"

"Yes, ma'am. A different trailer in Pahrump. I got the addy right here in my phone. If you go there now, maybe you can get the jump on him."

# 40

By six A.M. the next day, Melanie and Papo were in a G-car heading out of town on the main drag, Agents Smithson and Morales following close behind. The emerging sun was beginning to soften the neon that had carried the graffiti'd strip malls and gas stations equipped with twenty-four-hour slot machines through another rough night. They were driving toward the west, where the mountains glistened salmon pink and promised a fresh start.

Melanie rubbed the sleep from her eyes and reached for the venti Starbucks in her cup holder.

"If you were tired, you should've slept in," Papo said from behind the wheel. "This is just a drive-by to do some reconnaissance on that scumbag informant's tip. It could be a bust. We may not find Bo at all. You could've grabbed some downtime."

"And sit by the pool on the government's dime?"

He smiled. "You're such a stickler. How much overtime have you pulled this month without pay?"

"I'd rather get it done, Papo. Who knows, maybe Bo will be there, and maybe he's ready to talk. He'll be much more likely to flip if the prosecutor comes along to explain the benefits of cooperation."

"Your call."

They stopped at a red light. Some bikers in black leather pulled up beside them, gunning their engines. Papo looked over and motioned like he was tipping his hat. The light turned green and the bikers took off zooming. It was written plain on Papo's face that he wished he was riding off with them instead of going out to some godforsaken desert town to check out a dead end.

"Did Alejandro say why he never showed up to the meet last night?" Melanie asked.

Papo shrugged, his hands on the wheel. "*Negocios.* Something came up on another case, I think. These guys are good, though, really. Now that I've met 'em, I take back everything I ever said against 'em."

"Yeah, I agree."

They fell silent, and Melanie took another swig of coffee. Caffeine always helped.

"Hey, you know last night when Gordo told us Vegas Bo got tipped off?" Melanie asked.

"Yeah?"

"Do you think he was telling the truth?" she asked.

"I believe that Bo said it. Was Bo telling the truth or just yapping, though? Hard to say. Making surveillance is one thing. Tells people you're not dumb. But having an insider who can tip you off is a whole different level. Sometimes guys'll say that to up their street cred."

"Hmm."

They were winding through brick-red mountains now, and Melanie got distracted by the scenery. Strange vegetation spotted the landscape. The plants weren't exactly what you'd call cactus, more like malformed little stumps and burned embers masquerading as trees.

The color of the earth was unlike anything she'd imagined existed outside the planet Mars. Spectacular, yet it had an eerie quality. She couldn't help wondering what would happen to someone who got lost out here alone.

Papo's phone, sitting on the console between them, began to vibrate. He picked it up and looked at the display.

"The wife," he said, flipping it open. "Hey, babe, what's up?"

He talked to her for several minutes about something having to do with one of his kids and school.

"Sorry about that," he said, hanging up.

"Not a problem. Everything okay?"

He waved her off. "No biggie, just teenagers. You have no idea what you're in for. How old's yours again?" Papo asked.

"Two. She's a riot."

"Enjoy it. Once puberty hits, you'd think they got captured by pod people. I deserve it, though. All the grief I gave my mother when I was that age."

"Yet look at you now."

"Yeah, living life on the straight and narrow." Papo looked out at the landscape and smiled. "I can't complain."

# 41

For a long time, despite the clear air and the dead flat landscape making for perfect visibility, the town they were driving toward didn't seem to be there. It was nothing but outskirts. An occasional gas station. Lots of billboards advertising brothels. As AMERICAN AS FREE SPEECH AND APPLE PIE, one read, sporting a photo of a buxom blonde reclining on a bed wearing a Stars and Stripes bustier.

By the time they found the sign advertising homemade beef jerky that was to serve as their landmark, the town center had come into view in the distance. There were fast food places and casinos and even a traffic light, all of it shimmering in the dust kicked up by the big rigs and pickups, and baking in the desert sun. Melanie felt the heat even inside the air-conditioned car. Outside, according to the dashboard thermometer, it was ninety-seven degrees and getting hotter.

Papo picked up the radio mike. "Alejandro, you read me? Over."

"Loud and clear, bro," came the response crackling over the speaker. "This looks like the turn. Over."

"Yup. Traffic's pretty light this early. Hang back a little so we don't come in too close together and hink anybody up, okay? I'll do the first pass. Over."

"Roger that. We'll give you a five-minute lead. Maintain radio contact. Over."

Melanie and Papo turned at the beef jerky sign while the other car pulled over to the side of the road. Papo took a map from between the seats and spread it out against the steering wheel. He made several turns in quick succession. They drove for a while. He looked at the map, frowning.

"Something wrong?" Melanie asked.

"The directions we have don't add up with what I'm seeing here."

"You're driving. Let me take a look."

Papo handed Melanie the map along with the instructions from the informant about how to find the location. Eventually they figured out that they'd made a wrong turn, retraced their steps, and found their way back to the route.

As they bumped along the dirt track in the American-made two-wheel drive, the car's undercarriage scraped the tops of the rocks lodged in the clay, making a sound that set Melanie's teeth on edge. A sharp pebble flew up and cracked against the windshield like a bullet.

"Shit," Papo said. "Look at that. Chipped the goddamn thing. Now I'll have to fill out paperwork."

The dirt road seemed to go on forever, leading nowhere. They passed a couple of trucks heading in the opposite direction, and at one point an old Camaro passed them, doing at least sixty and throwing up a spray of red dirt. There were a few habitable-looking houses, but most of the structures along the route were either tumbledown shacks or abandoned trailers. Melanie understood now why places like this were so hard to surveil without arousing suspicion. Driving by was one thing, but you'd have no credible reason to stop. There was nothing to stop *for*.

"That's it up ahead," Papo said, slowing down and inclining his head.

They were still about a thousand feet from the trailer, but the decrepitude was so apparent you could smell it. Instead of being properly mounted on a concrete foundation like the trailer in the surveillance photo yesterday, this one sagged atop cinder blocks that appeared to crumble away under its weight. The metal siding had faded and was covered with rust. One long strand of siding curled away from the trailer like flypaper, and the front yard was covered in garbage. There was no sign of human habitation.

"Looks abandoned," Melanie commented.

"I want to go in for a better look," Papo said. "Get down on the floor."

"Why?"

"Because I'm responsible for your safety, that's why. Jeez, you prosecutors. Always gotta give the case agent lip," he said, smiling.

"Oh, all right."

There wasn't room in the sedan's footwell to kneel facing forward, so Melanie turned toward the back of the car, resting her chin on the passenger seat.

"This is torture," she said.

"Yeah, now you know what agents go through."

Papo slowed to a crawl and peered out the windshield as he drew closer to the trailer.

"No vehicles present," he said, "unless they're parked behind the thing. The glass is busted out of the windows, but they're covered over with paper, so I can't see in. It doesn't appear any lights are on, though. Nothing moving. Ah, shit, the place is definitely abandoned. We wasted our morning."

He sped up, having passed the trailer, and Melanie started to unfold herself from the footwell.

"Stay there," Papo commanded. "I'm gonna go down the road a ways, turn around, and take a second pass. Once I'm a hundred percent sure, I'll go in and see what I see. You never know. Maybe there's evidence inside."

As he drove, he grabbed the radio mike.

"Yo, you read me, boys? Over?"

"Roger," Agent Morales responded. "You find the place?"

"Yup."

"Any signs of life? Over."

"No, looks abandoned. I'm gonna go in to look for evidence of recent habitation. Where are you? Can you come back me up, over?"

"Yeah. We got lost for a while, but I think we figured it out now."

"They must've taken the same wrong turn we did," Papo said to Melanie. "How much longer you think you'll be, over?" he said into the mike.

"Hopefully just a few minutes, so hang tight. Over and out."

Papo turned around in an empty gravel lot and headed back in the direction they'd just come from. Shortly before they got to the trailer, he pulled to the side of the road, rolled both windows down, and turned off the engine to listen. They sat that way for a while. A scratching sound came from the direction of the trailer.

"What's that?" Melanie whispered.

"Just the loose siding blowing in the wind," Papo said. But he sat absolutely still for a while longer, straining his ears.

"That informant was full of it," he said finally. "There's nobody in there."

Melanie returned to her seat and stretched out her tingling legs. She looked at her watch. The morning was nearly gone. "Where the hell are those guys?" she asked.

"Still lost, I guess, but I'm getting antsy waiting on 'em," Papo said.

She nodded her agreement. They had so much work to do, and besides, it was hot in the car with the air conditioning off.

Slowly, Papo opened his door and stepped out, pausing for a moment behind it to draw his Glock nine-millimeter. The gun was black and angular, deadly-looking. With the door open, dust blew into the car. Melanie felt it in her eyes and throat. Papo was taking nothing for granted. He scanned every inch of the trailer. Melanie had always been impressed with his thoroughness, and it gave her comfort to see it now. He closed the door with a soft click. She watched in silence as he walked toward the trailer.

He was halfway across the trash-strewn front yard when the shot rang out, followed by his agonized cry.

# 42

Melanie dropped to the floor and reached for the radio, her blood pounding in her ears.

"Alejandro? Duvall? Do you read me?" she whispered frantically.

"Roger, Melanie. Everything okay?" Agent Morales replied.

She slapped her hand over the radio as if she could stop its sound. It was so damn loud. Had the shooter heard?

"Papo's been shot. Call an ambulance," she said, her voice low and urgent.

"Jesus Christ! Duvall, call it in. Melanie, where are you? Are you safe?"

"No. I'm in the car outside the trailer. Where the hell are you?"

"Jesus, I'm sorry. We're more lost than we thought—"

She switched the radio off in a fury. They *weren't* two minutes away. Help *wasn't* coming. What was the point of talking on the radio? All she'd do was give up her own location to the shooter.

Through the open car windows came the sound of a car engine sputtering to life. It sounded like the vehicle was behind the trailer. Tires were crunching over dirt, beginning to accelerate. Beating back the urge to stick her head up to see better, Melanie instead pushed herself as far down into the footwell as her body would go. The vehicle was coming her way, and damn fast from the sound of it. Did he plan to ram her on purpose? Tucking herself into a ball, she braced for the impact, praying that the air bags wouldn't inflate and suffocate her. But it never came. The shooter sped past her down the dirt road. Melanie jumped up and threw herself into the backseat, straining to see out the back windshield. She committed the visual image to memory: American-made car, old, big, a faded shade of gold. Nevada plates, starting with the letter *D*. And the driver—she couldn't be sure, but maybe he had red hair.

She crawled back into the front seat and flipped the switch on the radio.

"Alejandro, can you hear me? The shooter took off in a gold sedan!" Melanie said.

"Which way did he go?"

"Down the dirt road I'm sitting on, but in the opposite direction from where we came in."

"Describe the car."

"American-made. Big, probably four doors. Old, from the eighties maybe. Faded gold in color. Nevada plates, starting with *D*. Driver is a white male, I think, with red hair."

"I'll put the description out to all units. Sit tight. We're on our way."

The radio cut off. Melanie stared at the mike in her hand, momentarily paralyzed. She needed to go to Papo, to do what she could for him until the ambulance arrived, but she was afraid of what she knew she'd find. She couldn't bear seeing him dead. But even less could she bear the thought of her stalwart case agent left to die alone.

She got out of the car with shaking legs and a heavy heart. Papo was lying in the dirt, his long frame spare and straight, dressed all in black. She went up beside him and knelt down. There was a hole in his throat. Dark blood pumped out of it, making a sucking, bubbling sound. She heard a mewling sound, too, and it was coming from him, the large man making tiny sounds of agony.

His eyes were open and cognizant. He was still alive. She reached for his hand. In the broiling afternoon it was cold as ice. The earth beneath him was dark with his blood. His gun lay on the ground beside him, useless, unfired.

"Papo, it's me, Melanie. An ambulance is on the way. Hang in there, okay? It'll be here any minute."

As if on cue, a siren howled in the distance. She looked into his face. He was fading fast. She reached into her pocket, pulled out the Saint Jude's medal that had belonged to Lester Poe, and closed his fingers around it. His eyes flickered in response, and she took heart.

"Did you hear that? The ambulance is coming. It'll be here any second. Just hold on a little longer, and everything will be okay. For your wife. For your kids. You can do it."

The siren grew louder and louder. She leaped to her feet and ran out to the road, flapping her arms to show them where to stop, tears streaming down her cheeks. Within a minute, they had their stretcher out, and she led them back to where Papo lay. Melanie dropped to her knees again, crying out in disbelief. The Saint Jude's medal had given him comfort in his dying moments, but it hadn't been enough to save his life. Papo's eyes were still open, but something in them had changed. The light had fled from them. He was gone.

# 43

That evening, Melanie was sitting alone at a bar in the Las Vegas air-port waiting to board the last flight back to New York when Dan O'Reilly walked in and took the empty bar stool beside her.

"Déjà vu all over again," she said, looking at him with desolate eyes. She didn't question his presence there—why he'd come or how he'd found her. In her grief, she was simply glad not to be alone.

"This time, you have to let me buy you a drink," he said, his voice solemn. "That coffee you're nursing isn't strong enough for what you've been through."

She nodded. He ordered a pint of Guinness for himself and a glass of white wine for her. The drinks came, and they each took a sip.

"I'm going back to New York tonight, too," he explained. "I was hoping I might run into you here. I was worried, Melanie. Are you all right?"

Melanie had to look up at the ceiling to stop the tears from coming. "No, I'm not," she whispered. "I still don't believe it. He died right in front of me. He . . ."

Her chin quivered. Dan reached out and grasped her hand.

"He was *such* a good man," she said. "He had kids, Dan."

"I am *so* sorry, sweetheart."

Melanie had been holding back her tears, but the sight of Dan's beautiful face, so close to hers and so full of empathy, and the touch of his hand, so warm and alive, unleashed them. She started to cry openly, oblivious to the other travelers sitting nearby. The tears streamed down her cheeks, and she fumbled in her handbag for a Kleenex. But the more she wiped them away, the harder the tears flowed, until she didn't know if she was crying for the loss of Papo West, or the death of her love affair with Dan, or all of the crazy, terrible things that happen to people who deserve better.

"Shhh," Dan said, when she couldn't seem to stop. He reached out and stroked her hair soothingly. "I know, I know. It's gonna be okay, sweetheart."

"No, it's not. Papo's *dead*. It's not fair. Why do the good people die?"

"Shhh. C'mere."

Dan stood up and pulled her to her feet. His hands found the curve of her waist, and he drew her toward him, cradling her against his broad chest as if she was a child. As she cried, he leaned down to kiss her, first on her forehead, then on her closed eyes, then gently on her lips. Dan's kiss, so familiar and so long-missed, was too much for her despite the warning bells going off in her head. Her lips parted, and she gave herself up to it. In the breathless, dizzying moment that followed, she blotted out the pain of Papo's death, but she also reminded herself of the power of her feelings for Dan, something she simply couldn't afford to do.

"Stop!" she cried, pushing him away. "We're in a public place."

"In a bar in the Las Vegas airport? Sweetheart, nobody's even looking."

But they both understood that that wasn't her real objection.

"I have to go to the gate," she said, and turned to run.

Dan threw some money down on the bar and followed. "Wait, I'll come with you," he called out, matching her stride. "You're on the last flight, right? It's gate seventeen."

They flew over the moving walkway and through the terminal. The whole way, though Dan was right beside her, Melanie wouldn't meet his eyes. When they got to the gate, she headed for the far corner of the gate area away from any people. Melanie sat down and wiped her eyes with a tissue. Dan dropped into the seat beside her.

"Please, I'd rather be alone right now," she said.

"Look, I'm sorry. I shouldn't have kissed you. That was wrong."

"It *was* wrong. I never would've let you if it weren't for Papo dying. You took advantage of me."

"I didn't mean to. But how could I watch you cry and not reach out for you? You know I still—"

"Don't say it," she warned, raising her hands as if to push him away. "Please, leave me alone."

"I picked the wrong way to help you deal with being upset, that's all. I should've talked to you about the case instead. The new developments."

Damn Dan O'Reilly. He always knew how to get past her defenses.

Melanie glanced around. Nobody was within earshot. "What developments?" she asked, lowering her voice.

"Just so you know where I'm coming from, talking shop at a time like this, I've lost guys before in the line of duty. Guys on my squad who I cared about. To me, the way to honor them is to carry on with the work. You still feel the pain, but you don't stop to mourn, not right then. You finish the job. When the job's done, that's when you have the luxury to fall apart."

She looked into his clear blue eyes and saw the wisdom of his words. "You're right. So spit it out. What can you tell me?"

"I was here in Vegas for the same reason you were. To hunt for

Kevin Bonner. Vegas Bo. And I found him. He's been holed up in a hotel suite on the strip."

"Which hotel?"

"That information, I've been instructed to keep confidential."

"C'mon, Dan. We're on the same team."

"I understand that you're the prosecutor. But you're working with DEA, and this is an FBI gag order I'm talking about. We're sharing information with them. Just not every single detail yet."

"Papo West was shot while investigating a location believed to be in use by Vegas Bo's crew. Now do you see how critical information about Bo's whereabouts could be to solving Papo's murder?"

"Kevin Bonner didn't kill your case agent. I can tell you that much. At least, not by his own hand. I had him under surveillance all day today, until after I heard about the murder, and he never left his hotel suite."

"If Bonner didn't kill Papo personally, maybe he ordered the hit," Melanie said.

"That trailer was not in use as a drug stash. It was abandoned. All DEA has to say different is the word of one skanky informant."

"Even if the trailer wasn't in use, the tip could have been a setup," Melanie persisted. "I didn't like the looks of that informant, I can tell you that much."

"Or the shooting could be unrelated. It could've been some crankhead drifter who got interrupted at the wrong moment. The car you saw flee the location was found abandoned on a side street in town. It'd been reported stolen yesterday from a gas station near the Utah border."

"I know. I heard that already. So what? The fact that the car was stolen doesn't mean that the shooting was random. No skilled killer is going to flee the scene in his own ride. Dan, I saw the shooter from behind. He had red hair—"

"Even more likely it's unrelated, then. Vegas Bo's organization is all African-Americans."

"No, wait, let me finish. DEA canvassed all up and down that dirt road. They found an elderly woman who'd been crossing the road and almost got run down by the gold sedan. She got a clear look at the guy and gave a detailed description. Then DEA showed her some photos. She's pretty sure the driver was the same guy who showed up in some surveillance photos going to meet with Bonner himself. The same redheaded guy whom I'd seen in court in New York. We haven't been able to identify him yet, but I'm convinced he's connected to Atari Briggs or the defense team somehow."

Dan studied Melanie's face.

"Well?" she demanded.

"You always did know how to work an investigation," he said, that movie-star grin teasing at the corners of his mouth.

"Dan, will you tell me where to find Vegas Bo?"

"I'm sorry, sweetheart, I can't. It's not the right move now. We need to leave him out there and keep watching him."

She paused to check again that nobody was close enough to overhear, and leaned toward Dan, dropping her voice.

"Because you suspect he had some involvement with the car bombing, right?"

"It's possible. Certain things have been ruled out by now. Gamal Abdullah himself wasn't behind it. He couldn't've been; he was dead before it was ever in the planning stages. The explosives used were purchased on the black market by an individual with ties to the drug trade and no, repeat, *no* ties to Abdullah. We're on the trail of this individual now, which is what led us to Bonner."

"This individual, he works for Bonner?"

"Works? Not exactly. But they're connected."

"You're telling me Vegas Bo is responsible for the car bombing?"

"It's not that simple. I'm still figuring it out. Maybe not. Maybe he just made a connection for somebody."

"What about Gamal Abdullah supplying Afghan heroin to Vegas Bo's organization? Did that ever happen, or not?"

"Not that I can substantiate, no."

Melanie propped her chin on her hand and stared off into space. Dan sat there and watched her think.

"Well?" he asked.

"I'm remembering how Lester told me Atari wanted to cooperate against Gamal Abdullah, and then five minutes later Lester got blown up using the same type of explosives Abdullah used."

"I already told you, Abdullah was dead by then. The explosives were a coincidence."

"Maybe the explosives weren't a coincidence," Melanie said. "Maybe they were a neatly packaged explanation. They sent you off in search of a dead man, didn't they? Somebody who the real killer probably already knew was dead. And now all the evidence is pointing back toward Briggs and Vegas Bo and the drug trade."

"But it was the dead lawyer who told you his client wanted to cooperate against Abdullah in the first place. Why would he set up an explanation for his own death?"

Melanie shrugged like it was obvious. "Because he believed it."

"I don't get it."

"Atari told Lester he wanted to cooperate against Abdullah. Lester believed him. He relayed the message to me. The cooperation was phony. It was a setup, and then Lester was killed. The real question is, why did Atari Briggs want Lester Poe dead?"

# 44

A tari Briggs was in his suite in the Drayton Hotel working with his fashion stylist on his trial wardrobe when his bodyguard buzzed to say that his lawyer would like an audience with him.

"Sure, let him in. I always got time for my lawyer," Atari said.

"He has a guy with him I don't like the looks of," the bodyguard said, speaking quietly.

"What's the dude's name?"

"Alexei Grinkov."

"Yeah, Alexei can come, too, but he's strapping for sure. Check him everywhere. He carries a lot of weird Bruce Lee–type shit, not just heaters."

The stylist was kneeling at his feet, adjusting the cuff on his trousers. She was a petite bleached blonde in tight jeans and platform shoes, more accustomed to styling starlets and designing handbags. But she'd learned to be flexible when opportunity knocked, and dressing Atari Briggs for his trial was a publicity boondoggle to rival any other.

"This one is perfect for opening statements," she said. "It has a solid banker vibe to it, yet with an edge that says hip-hop. But if you're not satisfied, Brioni sent over some gorgeous things—"

Atari pulled his money clip out and peeled off a few bills.

"Baby, go get yourself a cappuccino for a while, would you? I got some business to transact."

The stylist, who was used to being treated like a diva rather than a servant, turned crimson and opened her mouth to tell Atari where he could put his money. But the next minute, the double doors swung inward to reveal one of the enormous business-suited bodyguards from the hallway, and beside him, Evan Diamond and Diamond's driver. Alexei Grinkov was as big as the bodyguard but scarier to look at. It was plain to see from his smashed-in face that he'd survived a thousand blows. The coldness of his eyes suggested that he'd given worse than he'd gotten, which meant all those other guys must be—*dead*. After one look at Grinkov, the stylist plucked the money from Atari's hand and beat a hasty retreat.

"Owen, stay," Atari instructed the bodyguard, who took up a position by the door.

Briggs, Diamond, and Grinkov sat down around the coffee table on massive leather sofas. Briggs poured them each a scotch from a decanter.

"To your health," Diamond said, taking his glass and raising it to Atari.

"What's the word?" Atari asked. His face was impassive, his tone impatient.

"Alexei was out there over the weekend. He did what needed to be done to get the Mexicans off our backs. So we're in good shape, except for one small problem. My source in the U.S. Attorney's Office tells me DEA is close on Bo's heels. They're not letting up."

"We knew that. Bo already moved the stash, so why is this a problem?"

"They figured out he moved it, *and* they're looking for the new stash, *and* they're still looking to pop him. That's why. Some people might consider going after that girl in the USAO who's driving the investigation, Melanie Vargas. But that's very risky. It would be an amateurish move. Especially since the case agent got taken out, it would rain a shit storm down on us."

"Even if that wasn't us?" Atari searched Diamond's face with narrowed eyes, trying to figure out how much he knew that he wasn't letting on.

"It heats us up anyway. The best option is for Bo to drop from sight for a few weeks. Just till after your trial is done. From what I understand, the only reason they want him is to flip him on you. Once you're acquitted at trial, you're bulletproof because of double jeopardy, so they won't need him anymore. Then we're out of the woods, see?"

"Isn't double jeopardy just for what I'm charged with now? They could still come after him to get me on some other shit that ain't charged in this case."

"What are you, a lawyer now?" Diamond said.

"I'm just saying, I don't see where it helps for him to take himself out of play at this exact moment. Whack the bitch instead. This is a *sensitive* moment. I want to be in regular contact with him to monitor business during the critical phase, you feel me? Now is not a good time for him to drop from sight."

"Atari, leave this to me, and focus on what you're good at, okay? Are you working out enough? Do you need a facial? Because I want you to look good for the cameras. I've got something up my sleeve, I promise. This trial is when we take the Atari Briggs legend to the next level."

# 45

At five-thirty the following afternoon, a bitter March wind was rattling the window's in Susan Charlton's corner office. The shadows were growing long, but encroaching gloom fit the mood of the occupants so well that neither of them moved to turn on the light. Susan sat in her swivel chair, tugging anxiously at her short red hair. Melanie sat in a guest chair, staring at the papers spread across Susan's desk, kneading her aching forehead with her fingertips.

"I'm having trouble understanding what this means," she said. "I'm just . . . I think I'm so depressed about Papo that I can't think straight."

"If it's not leaping out at you, then maybe I'm wrong. I *want* to be wrong."

"Unfortunately, if there's one thing I'm sure of, it's that you're not wrong."

"You don't think I'm being paranoid? Too many years in this goddamn job can make you paranoid."

"No," Melanie said, shaking her head, "you're not paranoid. Somebody falsified one of these subpoena responses, Susan. No question in my mind, you're right about that. I've looked at this pile," she said, laying her hand on a stack on the left side of Susan's desk, "and I've looked at this pile," she said of the stack on the right, "and I've compared them, and they're different. At least half the phone numbers called are different, even though the two piles are for the same phones and the same time period."

"But how can that be?" Susan asked.

"Take me through it again, exactly what happened."

"Okay, you and I had a conversation a day or two ago where you told me about the surveillance photo of that redheaded guy who met with Vegas Bo, right?"

"Right. He's critical. He may be involved in Papo's death."

"Unfortunately, we haven't been able to ID him yet. But in that conversation, we said maybe he was part of the defense team, and that we should go after Evan Diamond's phone records."

"Yes. I remember."

"I had you on the speakerphone. Jennifer was sitting right where you're sitting now. I assigned that task to her. After we hung up, I gave her a complete tutorial on what to do, because, since Evan's a lawyer on a pending case, we need approval from the front office and also from Main Justice down in Washington to subpoena his phone records. She took notes. There's no way she didn't know how to go about it, because I told her myself. As far as she told me, she was pursuing that paperwork."

"Okay."

"Meanwhile, we heard about Papo. *Everybody* heard about Papo, including the FBI. It turned out Rick Lynch and his team had pulled Diamond's phone records a while back, right after the bombing."

Melanie nodded, remembering how she'd asked Dan O'Reilly to ask his boss to take a closer look at Evan Diamond.

"Well, Diamond's phone records show numerous calls to various cell phones and landlines in the Las Vegas area in the past three weeks."

"Huh."

"Interesting, right? Rick Lynch gave me this pile," Susan said, pointing to the one on the left, "and told me that I—or somebody at DEA—should look at the phone numbers Diamond was talking to in Vegas to see if they could come up with any suspects in Papo's murder."

"Okay. What about the other pile?"

"An hour ago, Jennifer walked into my office and handed me this second pile. I believe her exact words were, 'I've got Mr. Diamond's phone records for you.'"

Melanie frowned. "Seems kind of quick, doesn't it?"

"Exactly! I said, 'Jeez, kid, you're a red tape wiz.' I mean, never in the history of mankind had anybody, to my knowledge, gotten such quick turnaround on any Main Justice paperwork."

"What did she say?"

"She didn't really *say* anything, but she looked kind of funny. I noticed it at the time. She looked uncomfortable. And of course, once I discovered that the records Jennifer gave me were so different from the ones I got from the FBI, I called down to Washington."

"You called Main Justice?"

"Yes. I spoke to the chief of the section that reviews requests to obtain defense lawyers' telephone records. He told me that Jennifer had never applied to them for permission."

"She never contacted them?"

"No," Susan said. "I don't know how or where she got these phone records, but it wasn't by following procedure."

"Couldn't she have gone straight to the phone company? Maybe somebody there screwed up, and gave her the phone records without the required approval from the Justice Department."

"No. I checked that, and they hadn't received any request from Jennifer, either, with or without the approval. I'm stumped about where she got them, but as for what the records say . . . In each pile, we have records for Evan Diamond's cell phone, records for his home phone, and records for his office phone. I've compared the two piles and verified that we're talking about the same phone numbers and the same time period, which is the last three weeks. And when you go page by page, the call details are just . . . well, they're just completely different, Mel. Different numbers for the outgoing calls. Different numbers for the incoming calls. Different times of day. Just, *different.*"

"Some are the same, though," Melanie said, squinting at the pages.

"Yes, some are the same. Like, Evan's cell phone calls his home phone. A call like that might appear identical in both sets, but the calls before and after it are altered."

"His cell calling his home shows up in both piles?"

"Yes."

"Susan, that's significant."

"Why is that significant?"

"Because that's a completely innocent call. He calls home to ask his wife if he should stop for a carton of milk. Nobody could draw any sort of incriminating inference from a man calling his own house."

Susan went white. "You're saying maybe it was only incriminating calls that were altered. Innocent calls were left alone."

"Yes. Isn't that what you were thinking?"

"No. God, no. I feel sick."

"What were you thinking?"

"I was thinking this was a case of neglect. We get those every once in a while. There was an AUSA when I was in General Crimes, went through a divorce, had some mental problems. He got behind on his cases, and instead of asking for help, he started doing some messed-up shit to cover up. My boss found out one day because a defense lawyer came to her and complained that his client had been in jail for eight months without an indictment ever being issued."

"Oh my God."

"Yeah. Like, unlawful detention, gulag-type shit."

"What happened?"

"That was the tip of the iceberg. There was a huge mess to clean up. But he was allowed to resign voluntarily and it was all hushed up."

"That's sick."

"That's life in the big city, babe. How much do you wanna bet that whatever shit's going on here'll get hushed up by the front office, too. Anyway, I was thinking that Jennifer couldn't hack the paperwork on these phone records. She was too scared to tell me, so she phonied them up and hoped I wouldn't know the difference. What you're suggesting is much worse."

"Maybe we're jumping to conclusions," Melanie said. "Maybe there's an innocent explanation. I can't for the life of me comprehend why Jennifer Lamont would falsify records to cover for Evan Diamond."

"She's sleeping with him, that's why."

"Do you know that for a fact?"

"No, but why else would she cover for him?"

"Isn't that kind of circular thinking?"

"I have her personnel folder here. I was going through it when you walked in."

Susan's phone rang. As she reached for it with one hand, she thrust the green manila folder at Melanie with the other.

"Take a look. You'll see what I mean," she said, and her expression spoke volumes about the horrors within.

Melanie opened the folder. Anybody's background check is bound to rattle a few skeletons. The process is too damn thorough. But Jennifer Lamont's file revealed things so hair-raising that Melanie would never have suspected them in a thousand years. The seemingly polished Jennifer hailed from a backwater town in rural Tennessee. Her mother had worked intermittently at menial jobs, and for much of Jennifer's early life, her father was in jail. Unfortunately for her, when she was seven, he got out. After that, the file was thick with police reports of domestic disturbances at the Lamont house. When Jennifer was ten, her three-year-old brother went missing, and the police were called. Both parents claimed the child had a tendency to run off, but a search party soon discovered the little boy's battered corpse in a shallow grave in the woods behind their trailer. His skull had been crushed with a blunt object, and the autopsy revealed the multiple healed fractures that spoke eloquently of recurring abuse.

Jennifer was sent to foster care and never saw any of her family again. She bounced around for a couple of years, changing foster homes and schools several times. At one point, a placement was terminated because the caseworker suspected that Jennifer was being molested by somebody in the household, although Jennifer herself denied it. At age twelve, she was finally placed with a childless couple in Chattanooga who seemed to give her love and attention. They sent her to a Catholic high school, where her teachers took an interest in her, and Jennifer blossomed. She made straight A's, became the captain of the debate team and treasurer of the student council, and got into Yale. Despite all the upheaval in her early life, Jennifer's background check showed no counseling or psychotherapy. Ironically, the lack of therapy on her record was read as lack of trouble, and probably helped her get clearance.

Susan hung up the phone. "Well?"

"Harrowing stuff," Melanie said, "but it says nothing about whether she's sleeping with Diamond, and nothing about whether she falsified his phone records."

"Well, how do you propose—"

"Wait a minute, I just thought of something completely obvious that we haven't done yet," Melanie exclaimed, flipping open the personnel file. "Okay, this is Jennifer's home number, so remember it. 718–555–6239."

"Got it."

"What did I say—6239?" she asked.

"Yes," Susan said.

Melanie picked up the pile of phone records Rick Lynch had provided and began scanning them, moving her finger over the entries as her eyes ran down each page.

"That's it," she said, smacking the papers with the back of her hand. "They're talking to each other. A lot."

# 46

Melanie and Susan were seasoned enough prosecutors to understand that the mere placing of a phone call, without proof of its contents, could always be explained away. Jennifer Lamont and Evan Diamond were two lawyers working on a contentious criminal trial together. They had legitimate reason to speak. Perhaps not as often as they had, or as late at night. But what looked like a smoking gun to suspicious minds could be recast as innocent in the hands of a skilled lawyer. They were going to need better evidence if they wanted to take action against Jennifer to stop any leaking that was going on.

"We need a wiretap," Melanie said. "We need to know what they're actually saying, not just that they're talking."

"We'll never get one," Susan insisted. "We don't have enough proof. No judge would sign off on a wiretap just based on these phone records."

"You think they're sleeping together. Can we prove that? Are they meeting in hotels? Is he visiting her apartment late at night?"

"One way to find out," Susan said, reaching for the phone.

The wheels of justice kept spinning even in the face of profound loss, and DEA had already assigned a new case agent to the Briggs case to replace Papo West. Susan got Tommy Yee on the phone, explained the situation, and told him to come right over. Twenty minutes later, Tommy sat beside Melanie, his hardened eyes blazing like they'd burn holes into the phone records.

"The thought that an AUSA tipped off a piece of shit like Diamond," he said, shaking his head. "It makes me sick. She could be responsible for Papo's death."

Melanie had written warrants for Tommy Yee in the past, and seen him in action enough to get a feel for his character. He was smart and skilled, but he had an unpredictable streak that needed to be reined in. Too many tours of duty in the Golden Triangle could turn a good agent wild.

"We're not sure Jennifer is tipping off Diamond," she cautioned. "It's just a suspicion. We have to proceed cautiously."

"Oh, I'll be cautious. She won't see me coming. You can bet your ass I'm gonna find out what's going on. I know what Diamond looks like. Do you have a picture of the girl?"

Susan passed Tommy the copy of Jennifer's temporary ID with her picture on it.

"Innocent-looking thing, isn't she?" he said. "You never can tell."

"That has her address and phone number listed also," Susan pointed out.

"You have an address for Diamond?"

"Office address, yes. The home address I need to get from court records," Susan said.

"What about motor vehicle?" Tommy asked.

"No."

"No problem. I can get that for both of them." He stood up. "All right, any last instructions?"

"Don't hurt anybody, and don't get hurt," Melanie said.

Tommy smiled. "Don't worry. I've calmed down a lot."

# 47

Steve had Maya until the next morning, and Melanie dreaded coming home to an empty apartment tonight. The early spring weather was ugly, bitter gusts of wind laced with a chill rain. To make matters worse, her favorite doorman, Hector, had the night off, and the new guy, Vladik, was working in his place. Vladik was condescending and a little hostile. When she said hello to him on the way to the mailboxes, he barely responded. She unlocked her box only to find a thick stack of bills.

Upstairs, she unlocked the door and walked into the foyer expecting the welcome of home, only to find the apartment looking small and in need of a thorough cleaning. Had it always been this small? Sometimes the four walls felt like they were closing in, and she longed to live in a house. That would be nicer for Maya, but how could she afford it? Melanie was starving, and she dumped the mail and marched to the kitchen without stopping to take off her coat. There was almost nothing in the refrigerator—some milk and yogurt, and some turkey meatballs Yolie had made for Maya that Melanie wouldn't dip into. She'd have to get groceries tomorrow.

In the pantry, she found a couple of cans of tuna fish and a few Top Ramens. Nothing appealed, so she ate a yogurt standing at the open refrigerator door to take the edge off her hunger.

While she was licking the last bit from the spoon, the intercom rang.

"Yes?"

"Mr. O'Reilly here to see you," Vladik said.

"I'm not expecting him," Melanie said, taken aback.

"I should send him up—yes or no?"

If Hector had been on duty, she would've trusted him to tell Dan that Melanie couldn't see him right now. After what had happened between them in the airport, surely Dan would understand. And yet, precisely because of what had happened, Melanie didn't want to leave the delicate task to somebody as insensitive as Vladik, who was sure to screw it up. She'd have to convey her message herself.

"All right, send him up," she said.

By the time she'd thrown the yogurt container away and hung up her coat, the doorbell was ringing. She stopped to peer through the peephole. In her line of work, you couldn't be too careful. Though with the way her heart turned over at the sight of Dan's face, opening the door to him had dangers of its own.

She opened it only a crack. "Why are you here?"

"Sorry to stop by unannounced. I figured if I called first, you'd say no for sure. So I took a shot." He smiled, but there was no laughter in his eyes, only anxiety.

"Is this about the case?"

"No, I . . . I've been thinking about that kiss. I can't *stop* thinking about it. I just needed to see you, is all."

"It's not a good idea, Dan."

Melanie moved to shut the door, but Dan got his foot in there. "Please. I won't take a lot of your time. You know, I just went to pick up my dog from my brother's house. Guinness. You remember him?"

"Of course I remember your dog."

"I'm gone three months, and all of a sudden he got old. I don't know how it happened. He's moving so slow, and there's this white patch under his chin that wasn't there before. It made me sad. It made me need to see you."

The yearning in his eyes was hard to contemplate. She looked down at his shoe again, wedged in the door.

"I'm sure it was difficult for him that you went away," she said. "Why don't you go home now, and be with him? That's the best thing. I just can't see you. I'm sorry."

Dan looked like he'd been punched in the gut, but nodded in resignation and moved his foot. Melanie shut the door, but she couldn't make herself walk back to the kitchen like she knew she should. She just stood there leaning her head against it.

"Are you still there?" he asked, after a moment.

She sighed. "Yeah."

"If you let me in, I promise I won't talk about old times. I won't try to win you back, nothing. I'll only talk about work. Even if it's ten minutes, that's okay. I came home for the first time in months, and everything felt so different. Then I thought about how it felt to hold you . . . If I could just see your face, Melanie, hear your voice, I know things would start to seem normal again. It doesn't have to be more than that."

She didn't say anything.

"I don't mean to spook you. I'm not gonna go all stalker on you or anything."

Melanie was still quiet.

"Are you there?" he asked.

"Yes. This is a mistake. You should go away." Her hands were shaking with how much she missed him. This was bad for her.

"Did you eat?" he asked. "If you didn't eat yet, maybe we could grab a bite. Maybe I shouldn't ask to come in your apartment. Would it be better if we went somewhere else?"

His acknowledgment of that boundary gave her the justification she needed to say yes.

"All right. But quick."

"Sure."

"Let me get my coat," she said.


She was careful to take him to a place they'd never gone to together in the past, a Thai restaurant that did mostly a take-out business. She didn't need the memories of their usual haunts. With the weather, and the fact that it was after nine o'clock and midweek, most of the tables were empty. It turned out that Dan had never eaten Thai food before, so she ordered for both of them, and got them bottles of Singha beer.

Dan took a swig of the beer and nodded. "Not as bad as I expected," he said.

The familiarity of his face was almost too much for Melanie to handle. She was letting an old obsession take root again, just when she'd nearly succeeded in beating it. A voice in her head kept telling her to get up and leave, but she couldn't.

"You look different," he said. "It's hard to believe you could look better than you used to look, but—"

"*Dan*. Either we keep this about work, or—"

"Okay, I'm sorry."

The waitress came by with their spring rolls and chicken satay.

"You'll like these," Melanie said, pushing the satay toward him. "Dip them in the peanut sauce."

She remembered how she loved to watch him eat. He was a big man with a big appetite, yet he remained neat.

"There's been a development in the bombing investigation," he said.

"Can you tell me what it is?"

"Yeah, I can. You and the rest of the trial team are gonna be informed tomorrow anyway, because it relates to what you're doing. The bomber's body was transported to New York, and the ME's office finally identified him. Yusef Hosseini. A Yemeni guy from Detroit with a long sheet. Drugs, but weapons, too. Small arms, even. Just finished up a federal bid for dealing in hand grenades. He's the same one who purchased the explosives."

"It makes sense, doesn't it, that the guy who purchased the explosives would also detonate the bomb. He probably built it, too."

"But wait, there's more, and this is the interesting part. Remember how I said the guy who bought the explosives had ties to Vegas Bo, and that's how I ended up in Vegas at the same time you did?"

"Yes."

"Well, it was this guy, Hosseini. Hosseini and Vegas Bo were cell mates in Leavenworth. They both got out within the last year."

Melanie was holding her beer. She set the bottle down with a hard thunk of glass.

"I can't believe that."

"It's no coincidence," Dan said.

"I don't think so, either. Vegas Bo hired the bomber."

"Either that, or made the introduction for somebody else."

"Who would Bo have made the introduction for? Atari? Or Evan Diamond?"

"I guess it all depends on who wanted your boyfriend dead."

"My boyfriend?"

He took a pull on his beer, watching her. "Yeah, Poe."

"He wasn't my boyfriend."

"No?"

The relief on his face simultaneously touched her heart and made her want to hurt him, the way he'd hurt her with Diane. Why shouldn't she have a new boyfriend, when he still had feelings for his ex-wife?

"He was very attractive, though," she blurted, and she saw from Dan's expression that she'd managed to land a blow. Somehow it didn't make her feel any better.

"But . . . he was old enough to be your father."

"He was rich, powerful, handsome, charming. It's easy to excuse age in a man when he has those qualities. There was a bigger problem, though. Lester wasn't who I thought he was. Since he died, I've learned some things about him that have disappointed me. On the other hand, he was persuasive enough to make you forget the bad."

"What exactly happened between the two of you?"

She shook her head. "I swore I wouldn't talk to you about this sort of thing."

"I need to know."

"We don't have that kind of relationship anymore."

His words came in a rush. "I used to think about it all the time when I was over there. Is she with somebody? Were you? I wasn't. Not since we broke up."

Just then the waitress appeared and slapped down fragrant platters of pad thai and panang curry. Melanie noticed that Dan hadn't eaten much of the appetizers.

"You don't like the food?" she asked.

"No, it's just . . . seeing you again. It's hitting me in the gut. I can't believe I lost you. I look back and I don't understand how it happened. I know you were upset that I was feeling this connection to Diane, but what I really needed was some time to get my head straight. I never thought you wouldn't give me that. I knew I would come back to you in the end, that it was a question of making that break with my past, of knowing in my heart that it was the right thing. But I guess you didn't know I'd come back. You didn't trust in my good faith. Maybe I asked for too much."

Their eyes met and held, and the confusion in Dan's, the loss—those feelings were too powerful for Melanie to see. She was getting sucked into the vortex where she couldn't afford to go.

"I'm not ready to talk about this," she said. "I'm still really hurt, and you're too good at making me forget my objections. Maybe I'll always feel this way. Maybe it's too late for us. I'm not sure. But I do know that now is not the time to discuss it, not when I'm still reeling from watching Papo West die. Look at what already happened between us in the airport, Dan. I refuse to fall back into a relationship with you by accident, or because I'm upset. That would be wrong for both of us."

"I understand."

"So either we keep away from talking about our feelings, and act like two colleagues having dinner, or else I have to go."

"You can't leave."

"Then don't get personal like that."

"I'll lay off. I promise. But stay. Just look at all this food. You need to eat, and I need you to tell me what it is because I don't have a clue."

# 48

Jennifer Lamont was sitting in a hotel bar sipping a cosmopolitan and feeling very grown-up. The space was light and airy, high-ceilinged, the walls and floors covered in a matte white limestone, the chocolate leather bar stools and cozy little tables occupied by chic young New Yorkers. A tinkle of glasses and the occasional peal of laughter could be heard above the constant buzz of conversation. She savored the moment: it was rare that she felt part of the glamorous city whose heart beat all around her. She'd come to New York well after 9/11, when all that grim, unpleasant danger was a thing of the past and a feeling of golden age, of boomtown, had settled back over the city. Yet Jennifer had never been able to enjoy it. By instinct, she held herself apart. She didn't know how to live in the moment. But tonight, waiting for Evan to show up, with a little alcohol in her, she felt liberated and happy for the first time in as long as she could remember.

She caught sight of him over at the hostess's station. The hostess had long dark hair and a fabulous ass, and Evan seemed more focused on her than on searching the bar for Jennifer. The hostess handed him something, then turned to greet a group that had come in behind him. Only then did Evan head in her direction.

He stepped up to the bar several seats down from her and ordered a drink. They'd agreed to pretend that they were meeting by accident just in case anybody was watching. The ruse added a level of excitement that made Jennifer squirm in her seat.

Evan downed whatever was in his shot glass and asked for another. Only then, his gaze wandering idly around the bar, did he appear to notice her.

"Jennifer?" he called.

"Oh! Hi, Mr. Diamond."

He picked up his glass and carried it over to where she sat. They shook hands formally.

"Nice to see you," he said. "Am I interrupting? Are you meeting somebody?"

"I was, but my friend just called to say she has to work late."

"I'll keep you company for a few minutes, then. I'm early for a client dinner. Can I refill that for you?"

"Um, isn't there a rule against that?"

"One drink? I think it's de minimis, although I applaud your diligence in following the ethics rules. Bartender," he called, gesturing toward Jennifer's glass.

Jennifer leaned toward him. "That girl. What did she give you?"

"What girl?" he asked under his breath.

"The hostess. She gave you something."

Annoyance flitted across his face. "Oh. She saw me on TV. She wants an autographed picture of Atari, so I took her address to mail her one."

For the next fifteen minutes, they made small talk about the case, while the cosmopolitans went to Jennifer's head. She was dizzy with lust, looking into Evan's black eyes, imagining what he would do to her when they got upstairs. The bruises from the other night were just turning green and purple. They were the marks of his desire for her, and she wanted more to add to her collection.

"Look at the time," he said, consulting his watch. "I'm meeting a client in the restaurant. It was nice running into you."

"Same here," she said.

"See you in court."

"You bet."

"That's courtroom 1802."

Her eyes followed him as he strode out of the bar, the long, lean physique, the broad shoulders in the expensive suit. When he was gone, she lifted up her napkin, found the card key there, and smiled.

# 49

As she arrived at her office the next morning, Melanie got off the elevator to find an unexpected guest waiting for her in the seating area near the guard's station.

"Melanie," Bob Adelman said, rising to his feet, briefcase in hand.

"Bob?"

"The guard told me to wait. I was hoping you could spare me fifteen minutes or so."

"Oh, I thought you were waiting for someone else." She looked at her watch. "I have a meeting, but it's not till ten. Come on in."

"Thank you."

A few minutes later, she was behind her desk with Adelman sitting across from her.

"Something strange happened, and I wanted to bring you into the loop on it right away," he began. "It relates to Brenda Gould's death."

Melanie was booting up her computer and changing into her work shoes. "Please, go ahead," she said.

"I learned that a friend of mine, a former client who's a mover and shaker in the real-estate business, had lunch with Philippe Poe in New York. This lunch happened the day *before* I picked Philippe up from the airport."

"I don't get it. So what?" she said, turning to face him, shoes on.

"Let me start again. Friday—which was the day Brenda died—my friend Judith Wells of Wells Fine Properties had lunch with Philippe. The purpose of the lunch was to discuss Judith's taking on selling Les's town house. At that moment, as far as Philippe knew, Brenda was still alive, and the town house was going to Brenda under Les's will. The next morning, I drove out to JFK to meet Philippe when he arrived from Paris. That arrival was a fake, staged for my benefit. He'd actually arrived the day before."

Melanie stared at Adelman. "You're sure about this timing?"

"Positive. Do you see the logic? If I thought Philippe had arrived on Saturday, after his stepmother was already dead, I would never suspect him of any foul play. Nobody would. Meanwhile, he was already making arrangements to dispose of property that was rightfully Brenda's."

"But why would he be so stupid? To have lunch with your friend the day before he asked you to pick him up? Didn't he realize that you'd find out?"

"Judith is a legendary real-estate broker, one of the few who can be trusted to properly handle a commission of this magnitude, and it was the only time she could fit him into her schedule. Besides, Philippe has no idea that she and I know one another. It was mere happenstance that she mentioned it to me. I might very well never have found out."

"Are you certain Philippe knew the town house was going to Brenda when he met with Judith Wells about selling it? After all, Lester had already died. Maybe he thought it would be coming to him."

"I'm absolutely certain that Philippe knew what the will said. Les's will was rewritten ten years ago when he and Brenda got back together. I know because I handled the drafting. Both Philippe and Brenda were informed of the terms. Les told me he'd informed Philippe and Philippe's mother, Les's ex-wife, both."

"Could Philippe have been, perhaps, trying to help his stepmother out? He knew she was distraught. Maybe he wanted to take care of the details for her?"

"If you knew Philippe's relationship with Brenda, you'd know that 'helping her out' was not a possibility for him."

Remembering the remark Philippe had made about Brenda at the shiva after Lester's funeral, Melanie saw that Adelman was probably right.

"Was Philippe cut out of Lester's will entirely?" she asked.

"No. He got a healthy bequest, but the bulk of the real estate, and thus the assets, went to Brenda. Brenda had that kind of hold over Les, and I can tell you, Philippe wasn't happy about it."

"What did Philippe get under the new will?"

"Philippe had a big trust fund during his childhood that got discharged to him in full when he turned twenty-one. That was a couple million Lester had already given him. On top of it, Les still bequeathed him about a million dollars in stocks and other assets under the new will. Les felt that was plenty. You have to understand, Philippe and Les had a troubled relationship. Philippe's mother turned him against Les early on, and it showed in Philippe's behavior. He resented his father, he despised his stepmother, and he took no pains to hide any of that. Besides, Philippe's stepfather is a wealthy guy, and there are no other children in that family. He stands to inherit there. Contrast that to Les's feelings about Brenda, who he viewed as helpless and dependent and deserving of his protection."

"How much was Brenda supposed to get?" Melanie asked.

"Between the town house, the estate in Sagaponack, which is dazzling, and the villa on St. Bart's, we're talking almost twenty million in equity."

"That's a motive. No denying it," Melanie said. But then she frowned. "*If* the real estate goes to Philippe after Brenda's death. Lester died before Brenda. Wouldn't the property that Lester bequeathed to her go to her heirs, rather than to Phillippe?"

"Lester's will provides that the properties go to Brenda, but only if she's alive at the time that his will is probated. If she's not, they go to Philippe."

"When is the probate?"

"Three weeks from now."

# 50

Melanie was still mulling the news Bob Adelman had given her when she got a call summoning her to an emergency meeting in Susan's office. They had a team meeting scheduled for ten, at which Mark Sonschein would presumably report that Vegas Bo and the car bomber had been cell mates at Leavenworth. But something had come up in the interim that couldn't wait the half hour till then. As to what it was, Susan had been vague on the phone.

Susan and Tommy Yee were huddled together at the conference table when Melanie walked in. They had a pile of surveillance photographs in front of them. Susan's complexion looked disturbingly green.

"What is it?" Melanie asked.

"It's bad, Mel. Mark's on his way down here right now, then Tommy'll walk us through the shots from last night."

"Here I am," Mark said, striding in. "This better be some damn good proof, because otherwise I refuse to believe what I'm hearing."

"It's as good as you're gonna get without me being inside the hotel room," Tommy said. "I felt like some sleazy PI working a matrimonial case following this little slut around."

"Save the pejorative language and calm down, would you?" Susan said.

"Calm down?" Tommy demanded. "This *is* calm. Little bitch could be responsible for the death of a brother agent. Tell me to calm down. Jeez."

"You're undermining your credibility here, Tom," Mark said.

"These pictures are for real, buddy. I don't know what you're implying, but—"

"We all believe they're for real," Melanie said, putting her hand on his shoulder. "Just show them to us, and let us draw our own conclusions about the evidence."

Tommy nodded, appeased.

Everybody gathered round, and he proceeded to rearrange the photographs into a different order on the table.

"Yesterday at approximately eight-thirty P.M., I was stationed outside this building when I observed the female subject, Jennifer Lamont, emerge and get in a yellow cab. Here she is getting into the cab," he said, touching the photograph that sat in the upper left-hand slot on the table, which showed Jennifer's shapely leg and her head as she folded herself into the backseat.

"I followed her to Fifty-seventh and Fifth, where she proceeded to the bar at the Four Seasons hotel. She sat down at the bar and ordered a drink, which I later learned from the bartender was a cosmopolitan. Here she is sitting alone at the bar." He tapped the next photo. In it, Jennifer Lamont sat on a bar stool with her legs crossed, sipping a cocktail, wearing a short skirt, a tight sweater, and slingback heels.

"Is that what she wore to work yesterday?" Melanie asked.

"No, I remember she was wearing pants," Susan said.

"She must've changed in the bathroom before she left the office," Melanie said. "Which strongly suggests to me that she had plans to meet a man."

"That doesn't mean she had a date with Diamond," Mark pointed out. "Maybe she was going to that bar to pick somebody up. That may show a lack of judgment, but it's not illegal."

"Just wait, you'll see," Tommy Yee said. "Okay, subject remained alone at the bar for approximately twenty-two minutes, at which time the male subject, Evan Diamond, was observed entering the bar area. Male subject proceeded to the bar and did not initially sit down next to the female subject. Within a period of three minutes, however, he moved over to where she was sitting, as you see in this photo." He tapped the next one, in which Evan Diamond stood over Jennifer. Because of the angle, their faces were not visible.

"So they ran into each other by chance!" Mark exclaimed.

"What are you, this girl's bitch?" Tommy demanded.

"Mark is chief of the Criminal Division," Susan said. "You have to understand, he doesn't want to believe the worst of one of his line assistants."

"Doesn't want the scandal is what you mean."

"You're both wrong," Mark said. "I'm merely reacting to the proof as presented so far. What Tom has shown me indicates two individuals meeting by chance."

"That's not it," Tommy said. "They're wise to the fact that they might be followed. Consciousness of guilt is what we got here. After you hear the rest of my report, I know you'll agree with me. Okay, so the two subjects remained at the bar and spoke for approximately nineteen minutes more. These next six photographs were taken during that time period."

In the photographs, Diamond was sitting next to Jennifer, and they faced each other. None of the pictures showed them touching, yet the lust was palpable on their faces and in their body language.

Her flirtatious gestures, the way their eyes stayed glued together, the way he stroked her glass when she set it down on the bar—all spoke of what would come next.

"This ain't no business meeting," Susan said. "You can see how much they're into each other."

Even Mark couldn't disagree.

There were no more pictures on the table. Tommy's outrage had to be based on more than what he'd shown them so far. Melanie saw that he was clutching a manila folder.

"Is there more?" she asked, gesturing at the folder, and Tommy's triumphant expression told her she was right on the money.

"There is, and it's some damn good surveillance photography if I do say so myself. Now, you all know I'm a narcotics agent, right?"

"Yeah," Susan said.

"I'm skilled at observing hand-to-hands. That's my specialty. How many times have I been stationed in a crowded bar and tasked with knowing when an exchange is going down? A million times, right? And normally, the bad guys are palming the dope and the cash and trying to make sure nobody sees. They're trying to make my life hard, right?"

"What's your point?" Mark demanded.

Tommy opened the folder and laid out a series of four additional photographs, his face breaking into a Cheshire-cat grin.

"I see Diamond reach into his jacket pocket so," Tommy said, pointing to the first photograph, which showed exactly that. "He palms something. I can't see what it is, but here's his hand moving in a way that I recognize from hand-to-hands. I know he's transferring something. You see?"

In the second photograph, Diamond's right hand was indeed cupped strangely, as if it concealed an object.

"And here, he puts it on the bar. Then here—and this is after he leaves—she picks it up."

It was the fourth photograph that sank Jennifer. The object she'd removed from under the napkin was in plain view for the lens to capture.

"A key card," Mark Sonschein said.

"Yup."

"All right, you've convinced me," Mark said, turning away toward the window with a look of disgust.

"Wait a minute, I'm just getting to the good part," Tommy said.

"There's more?"

"This was the foreplay, man. Now for the main event. So, Jennifer never met me before, right, but Diamond did. I was the case agent on Fred Ruggerio, remember, that Mob cocaine case about seven, eight years back?"

"Diamond had a defendant on that?" Mark asked.

"Yeah, Little Freddy, the main guy's nephew. Ended up taking a plea. Anyway, I didn't follow Diamond out of the bar because I knew he'd make me. But with Jennifer, I followed her right onto the elevator. Got in there right with her, and let me tell you, the girl was horny as hell. She could barely stand still. The heat was coming off her in waves."

"Could you save the commentary, please?" Susan said. "I'm grossed out enough as it is without watching you drooling over this."

"Believe me, I'm as disgusted as the next person by whorish behavior in somebody who's sworn to preserve, protect, and defend. I'm just saying, nobody was twisting this girl's arm. She's mad into this guy."

"Just the facts, Tom," Mark said. "What happened next?"

"She pushes the button for eighteen. I just look at her and nod because I'm going wherever she's going. The doors open. I say, 'After you, miss.' She gets out and goes one way. I go the other. Then I turn around and follow at a safe distance. Catch up in time to see her enter room 1802, which I subsequently determined from hotel records that Diamond rented in his own name."

"Sloppy," Susan said.

"His wife may not look at his Amex bills, but I sure as hell do," Tommy said. "And I kept a copy for the prosecution. Anyway, once the hotel-room door closed behind the female subject and I heard it lock, I sidled up to it with my catlike prowl, placed my trusty amplification device against it, and listened."

"Pervert," Susan said.

"I was just executing my sworn duty as an agent, ma'am."

"So? What happened?" Mark asked, raising an eyebrow.

"He tied her up and whacked her around something good. From the sound of it, it hurt. You want more proof, check her for contusions."

"Are you serious?" Mark asked.

"Yes I am, and it was voluntary on her part. Otherwise I would've gone in and rescued her, but she was begging for more. If you don't believe me, I got that on tape."

Melanie hadn't been distracted by Tommy's overheated account. She kept her eye on what mattered.

"But did they talk any business?" she asked.

"Of course, what am I saying? I'm leaving out the most important part. She gave him a—sorry, I can't resist—a *blow-by-blow* of everything that happened in the office yesterday. Including the fact that she's getting sent to the library to do research and isn't going to be directly involved in witness prep. That pissed Diamond off to no end, and he told her unless she can keep getting witness information for him like she's been doing, she's not useful to him anymore."

Susan dropped her head into her hands. "Ugh, I feel sick."

# 51

The law library in the U.S. Attorney's Office felt like a vestige from the past, likely to fade sooner rather than later to a mere memory, its place taken by an attorney gym or some such innovation. It held paper books that were virtually never consulted by the current generation of line assistants, who'd grown up doing their legal research on computers.

Jennifer Lamont was something of an anachronism herself. She liked quiet, and she liked the heft of a book in her hand. The old *Federal Reporters* had stiff, gold-embossed bindings that seemed to impart the majesty of the law to her through her fingertips. But since she was one of the few who felt this way, Jennifer was alone in the deserted library this morning with only her tumultuous thoughts for company. When the door banged opened, she therefore understood that the people who entered had come for the purpose of finding her. And since she was not a person with a high opinion of herself, or one who expected to be sought out by her superiors for happy reasons, she immediately feared the worst.

Mark led the group over to the table where she sat, surrounded by piles of books, stray sheets of yellow legal paper, and the remnants of her Starbucks breakfast.

"Jennifer, I'm glad we found you." He turned to the man beside him. "Check and make sure the place is empty. Then lock the door. I don't need anybody overhearing this."

When Jennifer looked at the man Mark had spoken to and recognized him from the hotel elevator last night, her mind went dark. She knew that in a minute she'd be asked to explain herself, but she was as blank as an actress hit with a numbing case of stage fright just as the curtain rises. The long table at which she sat had many chairs. Mark took the one directly across from her, so she knew he would be the chief inquisitor. Melanie and Susan sat down in chairs that were off to the side, out of the line of fire. From this, she gleaned that they would not defend her, and that she would be left to fend for herself.

The chair beside Mark had been left empty for the returning man.

"We're cool, boss," he said, taking his seat.

He had a folder with him, and a small device that Jennifer thought must play audio. His eyes were full of eagerness, and of something that looked disturbingly like hatred.

"Jennifer," Mark said, "this is Special Agent Tommy Yee of DEA. Agent Yee has replaced Agent West on the Briggs case. We need to ask you some questions. Extremely disturbing information has come to light suggesting that you have been passing sensitive information to the defense. We need to hear from you right now on exactly what you've done."

Jennifer went hot and cold at the same time, and lost all control over her actions. All she could think of was escape. Before she was even aware of forming a clear intention, she'd leaped up, sent her chair crashing over behind her, and bolted for the door. Agent Yee was out of his chair in the blink of an eye. He tackled her, bringing her down with a hard crash onto the cheap industrial carpeting. It smelled of dust and mold. His bulk on top of her squashed all the air out of her lungs. She was choking, her face pressed to the floor, her arms shooting pain as he twisted them around behind her back. She heard the metallic ratcheting noise before she felt the cuffs go on.

"Don't act like you don't like it," he whispered in her ear. She regretted that her wailing—which she heard coming from somewhere outside her own body—prevented the others from hearing his outrageous insult.

He hauled her to her feet and dragged her back to the table, undoing the handcuffs and locking one end of them to the chair before thrusting her down into the seat. Jennifer was crying, the noise like soft, strangled coughs. She looked at the faces around her for reassurance, but Melanie and Susan looked stricken and embarrassed, while Mark only looked disgusted.

The agent sat beside her this time, ready to grab her if she tried to get up. His heavy breathing sounded like violence and arousal rather than exertion, and Jennifer had enough experience of those reactions from men to recognize the difference.

"We have probable cause to arrest. Read her her rights," Mark commanded.

"Before I do that, this is for my own protection," Tommy said, still panting as he reached for Jennifer's free hand and yanked it up onto the table, displaying the red mark that ran all around her wrist. "This is a rope burn from last night. I didn't do this to her. I didn't bust her up, either, so if she has bruises they're not from me. You were all here. You're my witnesses. A devious sneak like her is gonna cry brutality the first chance she gets. "

"We all saw what happened," Mark said, nodding crisply. "You used necessary force and nothing more. Now read the Miranda."

Tommy pulled a plastic card from his wallet and recited from it. "You have the right to remain silent. Anything you say can and will be used against you in a court of law. You have the right to consult an attorney or have one present during questioning. If you cannot afford an attorney, one will be assigned to you free of charge. Do you choose to waive these rights and talk to us now?"

They all looked at Jennifer. Her chest was heaving, and tears were leaking from her eyes. Humiliation overwhelmed her so completely she couldn't speak. She couldn't imagine speaking ever again.

"I've given this speech a thousand times," Mark said. "I never thought I'd have to give it to one of my own. Jennifer, we have strong evidence against you. The evidence includes telephone records, surveillance photographs, and a tape of an encounter you had with Evan Diamond last night which not only involved sexual contact, but during which you passed him confidential information. We can charge you with obstruction of justice. We can charge you with conspiracy to commit witness intimidation and witness tampering. We can possibly charge you with conspiracy to commit murder and leaking classified information. You're facing substantial jail time. Nobody at this table has any sympathy for you, and I can assure you no judge or jury will, either.

"Now, having said all that, you're a lucky girl, because I'm here to offer you one last chance to redeem yourself. If you provide us with a full confession, and agree to cooperate and help us make a case against Evan Diamond, we will allow you to plead guilty to reduced charges, and we will provide you with a letter at the time of your sentencing that will release the judge from any mandatory minimum sentences that may apply. I know you understand what I just said because you're a trained attorney. What is your answer?"

There was a long silence. Somewhere, the heat kicked on, and water flowed through a pipe, making a clanging noise that reverberated to Jennifer's bones. She looked back over the long haul of her bitter life and realized that she'd never been happy—never, not for an instant—except for the few brief hours she'd spent in Evan Diamond's company. But she also saw that she meant nothing to him.

She cleared her throat. When she found her voice, it came out small. "Will I be disbarred?"

"Yes. That's certain."

To lose what she'd worked so hard for, what she'd hung her slim self-worth on, suddenly that seemed like a bigger tragedy to Jennifer than anything else she'd suffered. She wailed, looking up at the ceiling as if to high heaven. "Oh, God! Please! I . . . want . . . to . . . die!"

Mark waited for her sobbing to quiet down before speaking again. "Tom, make a note that suicidal intent was expressed and convey that to the COs when she's brought to MCC. Look here, Jennifer, there's no easy way out of this. You're young, and you're not going to die for a long time. Once you're remanded, the MCC will keep you under special observation to make sure of that."

"Remanded!"

"Of course." He had to speak loudly to be heard over her sobbing. "We're not playing games here. Haven't you heard what I've been saying? You're going to jail if you don't cooperate, and you're going *today*. So either do as we ask, or it's time to stop worrying about getting disbarred and start worrying about basic survival. Whining and excuses won't get you anything on the inside. Now what's your answer?"

"What—what would I have to do . . . against Evan?" she said, wiping her hand across her wet face and quieting.

"Wear a wire. Get him to admit to planning attacks on our witnesses."

She shook her head, looking down at the table as tears dripped down her nose. "What happens if I can't?"

"Can't or won't?"

"Can't. For whatever reason. I freak out or make a mistake or something."

"If you come back with nothing, that's a problem," Mark said.

"Cooperation is judged by results, not by intentions. Otherwise we'd have no basis for determining whether you really tried. People in your position have been known to act with something less than good faith. But I have great confidence in you, Jennifer. You're smarter than you give yourself credit for, or at least, smarter than you pretend to be. We've all seen it in your work, as well as in your ability to deceive us."

"I'm sorry," she said, pleading with her eyes as she looked around the table at them. "Please believe me. I got in over my head. I never wanted to hurt anyone. Evan treated me better than any man had in a long time, and I got fooled by that. My judgment was off."

"That's the understatement of the year," Mark said. "I'm sure you have your reasons, Jennifer. Save them for the judge on sentencing day. As for us, we judge you by your actions, not your words. We don't want to hear excuses. To set things right in our eyes, you need to take action. Now, what's your answer?"

Jennifer saw that Mark was serious. If she didn't agree here and now to cooperate, she was going to jail. Her mind was muddled with shock, and she couldn't think straight. There was too much pressure. She needed time and space to sort this out. But one thing stood out clearly in the confusion. It wouldn't be fair for Evan to get away with no punishment. If not for him, none of this would be happening to her.

"I guess so. I'll try."

# 52

The recording Tommy Yee had made at the hotel the previous night was a good starting point, but it wasn't the kind of slam-dunk proof they needed to go to the judge. It said too much about the secrets Jennifer *hadn't* managed to leak to Diamond, and not enough about the ones that she had. Ideally, they'd get Diamond on tape discussing their witnesses by name and—in the best-case scenario—admitting to his role in planning the attacks. The entire team agreed Diamond was probably too smart to let himself get caught on tape. Yet, they felt they had to try.

Melanie, along with the rest of the team, headed to the big conference room that had been reserved for the 10 A.M. meeting. Getting there from the library required taking the elevator up several floors and walking down a long, busy corridor. Tommy Yee removed Jennifer's handcuffs for the journey. A cooperator was useful only so long as the target didn't suspect that she'd turned. Jennifer in handcuffs in her demure business suit would be a shocking sight, certain to stir a tidal wave of gossip that might reach Evan Diamond's ears. Without the handcuffs, she looked like the same eager junior team member she'd been the day before. Even with the traces of tears still visible on her face, nobody would suspect. Only Melanie and the other team members knew the truth—that they'd unmasked a traitor in their midst. In the conference room, there was no time to dwell on how they'd all been fooled. Melanie shut the door, Tommy replaced the handcuffs on Jennifer's wrists, and they set about brainstorming ideas for the undercover operation.

"Do we try a phone call or an in-person meeting?" Mark asked from his seat at the head of the table.

"Why not both?" Melanie said. "Isn't that normally what you'd do with an undercover drug buy, Tommy?"

"Yeah, first we get the target on the phone setting up the meeting. We arrange the meeting for a location we can access ahead of time so it can be rigged with hidden cameras. Then we film it and, if we get good stuff on film, give the arrest signal and move in for the bust."

They hashed out the details and decided that Jennifer should attempt to place a monitored, recorded telephone call to Diamond right away, setting up an assignation for later that night. If he fell for it, she should arrange to meet him at her apartment rather than at a hotel. DEA would go into her apartment ahead of time and set up hidden cameras in every room. Tommy and a few other agents would monitor the meeting from an undercover van parked near Jennifer's apartment. When they had enough evidence on tape, they'd move in and make the arrest.

"Here's something we need to know," Tommy said, turning to Jennifer. "Does Diamond carry? Should we expect him to be armed?"

But she didn't answer. Conflict was written on her face so starkly that every person in the room had to doubt whether she had the resolve to carry out the plan.

"Jennifer, answer the question *now,*" Mark snapped.

Jennifer started to cry again, tears and makeup running down her splotchy face.

"I've seen illiterate peasants fresh off the boat make better coop-erators than her," Mark said. "I'm getting fed up."

"You want me to take her to court and get her remanded, boss?" Tommy asked.

Jennifer wailed louder.

"No!" Melanie exclaimed. "If Jennifer doesn't make these tapes, what happens? We go to trial on Briggs like nothing ever happened, and let Diamond get away with witness tampering and possible in-volvement in killing a federal agent?"

"I don't like it, either, but look at her." Mark threw his hands up toward Jennifer, who continued to sob.

Mark had been playing the hard-ass bad cop all morning. Look-ing at Jennifer's decimated face, Melanie decided she could use a dose of good cop. A renegade AUSA was virtually unheard of, and everybody in the room felt personally betrayed by Jennifer. Nobody had reached out to build rapport—the most basic interrogation tech-nique. Despite what she knew about Jennifer's troubled past, Mela-nie didn't have an ounce of sympathy in her heart for a woman who would pony up government witnesses to her lover to be killed. But if it would help the case, she could fake it.

"Let me talk to her," Melanie said.

"What?"

"Tommy can stand guard outside the door. Leave us alone and let me talk to her."

Jennifer was intrigued enough by this suggestion to look up and nod.

"All right," Mark said, standing up. "I suppose you can't make matters any worse."

The others filed out of the room, leaving Melanie and Jennifer alone. A box of tissues sat on the credenza. Melanie retrieved it and came to sit beside Jennifer, handing her one.

"I can't even imagine what it feels like to be you right now," she said gently as Jennifer wiped her eyes. "I thought I should get Mark out of the room. You looked like you needed a chance to clear your head."

"He's putting so much pressure on me," Jennifer said, still sniffling.

"I see that."

"I screwed up. I know that. It was wrong to sleep with a defense lawyer."

"That's not the problem here. You know that, right? You gave him information that was probably used in planning attacks on government witnesses. You passed forged phone records to Susan—"

"You know about that?"

"Yes. That seems the least of it now, but it is a solid obstruction-of-justice charge with devastating proof. Based on the phone records alone, you'll be fired, disbarred, prosecuted, and you could do jail time."

"Oh, God!"

"You didn't screw up by yourself, Jen. You had a lot of help. Diamond lured you into it."

"It's not true."

"Are you in love with him? Is that why you wouldn't tell Tommy whether he carries a gun?"

Jennifer looked down at the crumpled Kleenex in her hand. "He hates Evan. I could tell from the way he talked about him. He'll say he saw a gun and use it as an excuse to start shooting."

"*Does* Evan carry a gun?"

"Yes. A revolver. He wears it in an ankle holster."

Melanie put her hand on the girl's. "Jennifer, you need to face reality. Your average defense lawyer does *not* walk around with a gun strapped to his ankle."

"All the agents have guns."

"They're law enforcement."

"I thought it was sexy."

Melanie wanted to slap her, but she'd keep her eye on the ball.

"Diamond's ruining your life. He's gotten you in terrible trouble. Can't you see that, Jen?"

"Sometimes. But then I think that if I go through with this, he could get shot. I could never forgive myself."

"What about the people he's hurt? Don't you care about them?"

"If I believed it was true. You could be wrong. You don't know for sure."

Jennifer's eyes welled up again. Melanie needed to make her see that Diamond didn't deserve her loyalty. There was one surefire way to accomplish that. She'd used it in cases where girlfriends had key testimony to offer but were too attached to their men to speak out against them. Show the woman that her lover was untrue, and suddenly her resistance to testifying melted away. Luckily, in this case, Melanie had proof at her fingertips.

"Do you think Diamond really cares about you, or is he just using you?" Melanie asked.

"I understand it must look that way to you. But we have a connection that I've never felt with anyone else. He feels it, too, I know he does," Jennifer insisted, but there was enough desperation in her voice that she didn't seem to believe her own words.

"He has other women," Melanie said. "Don't you know that? And I don't mean his wife."

Jennifer didn't answer, but the stubborn set of her jaw suggested she didn't want to know.

"We've analyzed his phone records, Jen," Melanie went on. "Not the fakes he gave you to pass along to us, but the real ones. He was calling other women besides you. For example, last night after the two of you left the hotel, he placed a call to a woman who Tommy Yee later identified as the hostess from the bar where he met you. And he went and met her for a drink. *After* the two of you had sex."

Jennifer's eyes widened like she'd been hit in the gut. "How do you know?"

"Tommy followed him, and we have the phone records. Do you want to see them?"

Jennifer looked away. "No."

"Because you need to know that this is true."

"I saw him get her number. I believe you."

"I'm sorry to have to be the one to tell you that," Melanie said.

Jennifer said nothing.

"Diamond deserves what he gets. Not only for the way he's used you, but because of all the other people he's hurt as well. I'm certain that he ordered the attack on Vashon Clark. Right before the attack, Vashon was told there was a twenty-thousand-dollar bounty on his head. The word inside the MCC is that that came from Atari's camp."

"That doesn't mean Evan was involved."

"Jennifer, open your eyes."

"I don't believe it."

"Well, you should. There's good evidence. And not only that, but we have reason to believe Diamond was involved in the murder of Papo West. Do you see what the stakes are here? You could be charged with conspiracy to murder a federal agent."

"You're making this up."

"No, I'm not."

Melanie saw that they'd reached an impasse, and that it would take something dramatic to shake Jennifer from her self-imposed blindness. She got up and flung open the door.

"Tommy, do you have that file with all the surveillance photographs? I need it."

Tommy Yee handed Melanie the file. She brought it back to the table. Jennifer watched with tremendous concentration as Melanie shuffled through the folder.

She placed the surveillance photo of the redheaded man with the boxer's face on the table facing Jennifer and locked eyes with the girl.

"This is the man who we believe murdered Papo West. Tell me who he is."

Jennifer looked at the picture and went so pale that Melanie thought she might faint.

"You know him, Jennifer. That much is obvious. Things will go much better for you if you tell me. Who is he?"

"His name is Alexei. I don't know his last name. He's Evan's driver."

# 53

After seeing the photograph of Diamond's driver, Jennifer seemed to come around. She agreed to place a monitored phone call. An agent from Tommy Yee's squad brought over recording equipment. It was important to get the details right. The call needed to originate from Jennifer's office so her extension number would show up on Diamond's caller ID. Diamond was smart and cautious. Something as simple as Jennifer placing the call from the conference room might be enough to put him on his guard. Jennifer asked that Melanie accompany her when she went back to her office with Tommy to make the recorded call. The others would wait in the conference room. Too many people in a small space could create background noise and tip Diamond off.

In Jennifer's office, Tommy slipped behind her desk and went to work attaching the recording equipment to the telephone. Jennifer sat down in her swivel chair, looking nervous enough that Melanie decided to go over again what they'd agreed that she should say on the phone. The problem was not with Jennifer understanding. The girl was plenty bright, and she would've made a good investigator if things had gone differently. Whether she was emotionally capable of following through was another matter.

"You still don't seem ready," Melanie said. "Shall we go over the plan again?"

"That might be a good idea," Jennifer said with a faraway look in her eyes.

"The point is, Diamond knows how the game is played," Melanie said. "He lives with enough duplicity that he's always on high alert. Even from you, he'll be expecting treachery, so you have to go the extra mile to allay his fears. You need to fake him out. Suggest there's a big problem, but don't come right out and say it openly or he might get suspicious. Act like *you're* the one who's worried about saying incriminating things over the telephone. If he seems like he's falling for it, and you can draw him out and get him talking, great. If not, just make a date to meet him tonight at your apartment. He'll feel safe there. Then we can get him on tape for sure. Got it?"

Jennifer hesitated.

"What's the matter?" Melanie asked, not unkindly.

"I've never set up somebody I cared about before. I'm not sure how you prepare for that. The only way I can feel okay about it is to tell myself I'm only doing this to clear Evan's name."

"Whatever it takes," Melanie snapped, frustrated. "Are you ready?"

Jennifer nodded. "Let's get this over with."

Tommy handed Melanie a set of padded headphones that would enable her to hear both sides of the conversation, and began to dial. Even as Melanie watched him punch in the number, she didn't know whether Jennifer would do what was required to get Diamond on tape. The line was ringing. Melanie held her breath. A pulse beat in Jennifer's temple, and her eyes were clouded and troubled.

"Poe and Diamond," the receptionist answered.

"This is Jennifer Lamont from the U.S. Attorney's Office. I need to speak with Mr. Diamond."

"One moment, please."

They waited.

"Hello?"

"Hi, Evan. It's Jennifer."

Diamond paused a second too long, as if weighing his response.

"Jennifer. What can I do for you?"

The tone was businesslike, impersonal. Melanie had a bad feeling already. There was a yellow legal pad on the desk. She grabbed it, scrawled TAKE IT SLOW, and held it up at Jennifer.

"There's something I need to discuss with you," Jennifer said.

"Go ahead. You have my complete attention."

"No, it's better if we don't talk over the phone."

"Is this about the Briggs case?" Diamond asked.

"Sort of."

"Is everything all right?"

"Not exactly. But I probably shouldn't go into it now. Can we meet somewhere?"

Melanie nodded her approval. Jennifer was doing a good job of throwing him off.

But apparently not good enough.

"Why do we need to meet?" Diamond asked. "If you have something to say, just say it. This is a busy time for me, with trial preparation and all."

"If you want me to say it, I will," Jennifer said, panicking. "We're in trouble, Evan. Susan Charlton suspects."

Melanie was shaking her head, and waving her hands at Jennifer, but it was too late. The words were out.

A pause again, longer this time.

"Suspects?" Diamond said eventually. "I can't imagine what you're referring to. This is a very odd conversation."

BACKTRACK! Melanie wrote on the legal pad.

"Uh, I'm—I'm sorry. I didn't mean to come out and say that," Jennifer blurted. "I'm under a lot of stress. Can you please meet me later, so I can explain in person? Can you come to my apartment tonight?".

"Your apartment? Miss Lamont, I'm flattered, but that's really inappropriate. I'm sure your supervisors would be very upset if they knew you were coming on to me like that."

TELL HIM 7 AND HANG UP, Melanie wrote.

"Seven o'clock," Jennifer said. "Please come. I'll be waiting."

Jennifer put her head down on her arms and started to sob. Melanie and Tommy Yee exchanged glances over her head. It had not gone well.

"Don't feel bad, Jennifer," Melanie said. "You did your best. He's a hardened target."

"I totally blew it," Jennifer said between sobs. "He hates me."

"Not necessarily," Melanie said. "Diamond was being careful over the phone, but I'm not convinced he won't come to your apartment tonight. In fact, I think he probably will."

Jennifer sat up, looking hopeful. "You think so?"

"I think so," Tommy Yee with a cynical twinkle in his eye. "Now Diamond suspects you're cooperating. He'll come by just to whack you."

# 54

The weather had turned yet again, and it felt like spring instead of winter. The sun was warm and high in the sky, shimmering against the squat buildings of the downtown skyline as Melanie glanced out the back window of Tommy Yee's G-car. She used to love this view from the Brooklyn Bridge, the Gothic stone arches ahead contrasting with the sleek twin towers behind. But now the view was diminished by the absence of the towers, so that she couldn't look at it without remembering the history. She couldn't enjoy it anymore; it would take future generations to do that. She was glad Maya would escape the burden of that difficult context. It was happier to be ignorant sometimes, and she wanted happiness for her daughter.

The block where Jennifer Lamont lived in Carroll Gardens was something out of the past rather than the future. The row of flat-fronted brownstones each had a tiny front lawn enclosed by a cast-iron gate. A few of the patches of grass displayed the religious statuary that hinted of an elderly Italian lady still residing within, some held trash cans, but many others had the over-the-top landscaping of the freshly gentrified. In front of every house, the snow had melted, and the crocuses and dandelions had begun to bloom. The flowering trees were just coming into bud, promising a glorious profusion within a matter of days. It occurred to Melanie that maybe the answer to improving her own situation was forsaking Manhattan for a small patch of Brooklyn. To have a garden where Maya could play. That could be lovely, and the private schools out here might be less expensive, or at least more low-key.

As she got out of the car, the velvety air and the smell of wet earth made their errand seem less urgent and dangerous. Jennifer was docile now. Her handcuffs were off, and as she unlatched the gate and led them to the basement door, it was almost possible to imagine that she'd invited Tommy and Melanie for a social visit.

Inside, the apartment was dark and smelled of the litter box. A tabby cat with luminous green eyes rubbed up against Jennifer's legs, meowing. The girl picked the cat up and hugged it to her chest. Three other agents who'd driven over in the surveillance van and parked in the alley behind Jennifer's apartment filed in the back door carrying equipment in cardboard boxes. Evan Diamond might be too smart to show up, or he might be too curious not to. Maybe he'd come to Jennifer's apartment simply to retaliate. Whatever he did, they'd be ready. Jennifer opened the blinds and turned on lights, and Tommy began inspecting the apartment for the best spots to hide video cameras.

"Is there a place where I can sit to do some paperwork and make some phone calls?" Melanie asked Jennifer.

She'd come along so she could take part in planning the evening's surveillance, and also to hold Jennifer's hand and make sure she didn't buckle under the weight of her disgrace. But Melanie had time to kill while the equipment got installed, and lots of other work to do.

"The table is best," Jennifer said. "I don't have a desk. No space for it."

Melanie sat down at a white table in the corner of the living room and took a manila folder from her shoulder bag. When she'd come back to her office after the disappointing phone call to Evan Diamond, she'd found a fax waiting for her. It had come in response to a subpoena she issued after talking with Bob Adelman about Philippe Poe's suspicious travel arrangements, and it contained Air France Flight manifests showing flights from Charles de Gaulle to JFK on the dates surrounding Lester's funeral. Quickly, Melanie scanned the fax and found exactly what she'd been looking for. What Bob had told her was true. Philippe Poe had bought his ticket in his own name, and had traveled to New York two days prior to the day when Bob picked him up from the airport. Philippe had arrived in the evening—the night before his stepmother Brenda Gould's overdose death.

Now that she knew Philippe Poe's itinerary, Melanie became convinced something was fishy. Philippe had been in town when Brenda died, but had taken great pains to lie about it to Bob Adelman. He'd had lunch with a broker to discuss selling a property that wouldn't belong to him until the death of his stepmother several hours later. Melanie made a note to interview that real-estate broker: if she backed up Bob Adelman's report, that would be damning evidence indeed.

But if Philippe had been involved in his stepmother's death, had he acted alone? He hadn't arrived in New York from France until the night before. What were the chances that he'd managed to step off an airplane and gather the tools he'd need to murder his stepmother while making it look like a drug overdose? Brenda's death had required a syringe and some highly pure heroin, things Philippe couldn't have carried with him on the flight. Would a foreigner have managed to sniff out a good spot to buy heroin after one night in New York City? Maybe—if he'd had help.

In the depths of Melanie's manila folder was a lab report suggesting that he had. It contained a detailed analysis of the syringe that had been found sticking out of Brenda Gould's arm. The syringe held the residue of a highly pure batch of heroin, South Asian in origin, which matched samples of the product that Kevin Bonner was selling exactly. And there was something else telling about the syringe. It had no fingerprints on it—none, not even Brenda's, which made Melanie think that somebody had wiped it clean after plunging it into Brenda's vein.

Next, Melanie turned to the more complicated task of analyzing Evan Diamond's telephone records. Agents from Tommy's group at DEA had completed the painstaking work of getting subscriber information on each and every number that had called or been called by any one of Diamond's telephones. They'd written the subscriber name and address in the margins of the records, and despite sometimes sloppy handwriting, Melanie had no trouble zeroing in on the target. There it was over and over again, in the days before and after the deaths of Lester and Brenda. Repeated telephone contact between Philippe Poe and Evan Diamond. There was even a series of calls, two days before Brenda died, where Philippe and Diamond spoke, and then Diamond hung up and immediately dialed a Las Vegas number. Requesting a delivery of the heroin that would be used to murder Brenda Gould? Melanie would be willing to bet on it.

Lost in thought, imagining how the murder might have gone down, Melanie realized that she'd missed something important. She'd been relying all along on the autopsy report's recitation of the condition of the room in which Brenda's body was found. The facts in the autopsy report presumably came from the deputy ME who'd investigated the scene. But the police would have responded as well, and might have noticed things that the deputy ME hadn't. Melanie had never seen the police report.

She spent the next twenty minutes on the telephone, bouncing around the Nineteenth Precinct, until she landed with Officer Millie Nuñez, who'd been called to the scene of Brenda Gould's death. Officer Nuñez had an excellent memory and the inclination to help.

"I thought it was sad," she said. "Big empty house, and the lady had been looking at old home movies while she shot up. She must've been so lonely. I thought for sure the ruling would come back suicide, especially since her husband had just died."

"The neighbor downstairs was there while you were in the apartment?" Melanie asked.

"Yeah, I remember he said he was the business partner of the dead husband."

"Evan Diamond, right?"

"Yeah. Good-looking guy. A lawyer. You know he's Atari Briggs's lawyer."

"Yes, I know."

"I live for Atari."

"A lot of people feel that way. It surprises me coming from a cop, though. He's a stone-cold killer."

"I know, but he gets it right. Life on the streets is really like that."

"Now, Millie, was Diamond already there when you first got to the scene?" Melanie asked.

"Yes, Mr. Diamond let me and my partner in. He had a key. He was actually the one who'd discovered the body and called 911 in the first place."

"What was Diamond doing in the apartment that led him to discover the body? He works in the office on the first two floors of the building, you know. The apartment is on the top three floors, and it's a completely separate unit. Did you find out why he was there?"

"Yes, I asked him that. We always get a statement for the report about the circumstances of the discovery. What I remember, he said he went upstairs to get some paperwork. The guy who'd died, the business partner—"

"Lester Poe."

"Right, the one who got blown up downtown last week. Poe kept an office in his house. Diamond was on his way to that office to get some papers when he discovered the body."

"What room was Brenda's body found in?"

"The media room on the fourth floor."

"But isn't the office on the third floor at the back of the house?"

"Uh—you know, we never established where the office was. I had no reason to question this guy's account, because what happened to the woman, it looked voluntary. He said he was on his way to the office, so I guess we assumed the office must've been near the media room. We were just taking a statement, not looking for inconsistencies. And then we got called away with a robbery in progress."

"I suppose there was nobody else there to contradict Diamond. Nobody alive, anyway."

"No, the only other individual we had any contact with was not involved in discovering the body."

"Who was that?"

"When we arrived, another man was standing with Mr. Diamond waiting for us in the hallway. He left and went back in Mr. Diamond's office, and Mr. Diamond escorted us upstairs alone. We were told he was a client of Diamond's and hadn't been present and didn't know anything about the body."

"This other man, did you get his name?"

"No. Like I said, he was just a client. Mr. Diamond assured us he hadn't been inside the premises where the body was found, so he wasn't relevant for us."

"What did he look like?"

"Um, let's see. Late thirties, maybe. Black hair. Not bad-looking except he had kind of a bad complexion. But I'm sure he wasn't involved. He's not even from here. He was visiting from France."

"France?"

"Yes."

"Do you think you'd recognize this man if I showed you a photo of him?" Melanie asked.

"The French guy? Sure." Millie paused. "I'm getting the sense you think this might've been a homicide."

"I'm looking into the possibility."

"Do you have any basis for that? Because I really didn't think so."

"My questions are based on concerns that the victim's lawyer raised with me, things that he knew were going on in her life that suggest someone was trying to get to her money."

"From what I observed at the scene, if anything, I'd say this was a suicide. Like I said, she was watching home movies when she shot up."

"Home movies?"

"Yeah. We found a whole stack of 'em on the side table, and one in the DVD player. We didn't have time to review them, but I bagged them up as evidence just for this reason. I thought they might help establish the victim's state of mind."

"You took all of them?"

"Yes. The ones from the table and the one that was still in the player. The one from the player I'm sure she was watching when she died, because the power on the machine was still on. That one, I remember, we couldn't find the jewel case for it, which struck me as strange since all the others had them."

"Where are these DVDs now?"

"They went to the ME's Office along with her clothing and some other effects found in the immediate vicinity of the body. The OCME retains personal effects for what, six months I think, so they should still be there. Go take a look at the one she was watching when she shot up. I bet it's something really touching, you know? Some special memory. It might set your mind at ease that this was a suicide."

# 55

With Jennifer saying she was doing all right, and Diamond—if he decided to show up at all—not expected until seven, Melanie decided she had time to pay a call on her friend Gary Nussbaum at the Medical Examiner's Office. It wasn't quite four o'clock, and she was fortunate to catch a lift from one of the agents returning to DEA headquarters. The agent, a clean-cut kid originally from Virginia who'd been on the job only a couple of years, insisted on dropping Melanie at the front door of the OCME on First Avenue, despite the fact that it was on the opposite end of Manhattan Island from DEA headquarters in Chelsea.

Melanie had called ahead, so Gary Nussbaum was expecting her. He greeted her at the guard's desk with such eagerness that Melanie felt guilty for getting the poor guy's hopes up. But she'd had no choice: she needed to see this evidence.

"I signed the DVDs out from our evidence vault and I've taken the liberty of examining them so I could speak to you intelligently on this issue," Gary said as he led her down a long, grimy corridor.

"I'm most interested in the one that was in the DVD player at the time of Brenda's death."

"Yes. That one was different from all the others."

"Different how?"

"Come on in. I'll show you."

Gary's office was smaller than hers, a cubicle with a big plate-glass window looking onto the corridor but no window to the outside. He sat down behind his desk, which was the modular type that stuck out from the wall, and pulled over a second chair so she could sit beside him. He snapped on a pair of disposable rubber gloves, then held the carton out to her.

"You need to wear gloves if you want to handle the evidence," he said.

"Thanks," she said, taking some and pulling them on.

Gary lifted an armful of clear plastic evidence envelopes from a cardboard box that sat beside his desk and began sorting through them.

"Nineteen DVDs were recovered in total," Gary said, passing the envelopes to her one at a time so she could examine them. "Eighteen of them were seized by Officer Millie Nuñez from a table in the media room where Brenda Gould's body was found. All of those eighteen look identical to one another. They all appear to be home movies that were transferred from video to DVD format by a company called Tech Support Network, Inc."

"A company recorded them?"

"I'm saying that Brenda Gould paid somebody to have her home videos put on DVD, that's all. This is very common now, since nobody uses VCRs anymore. So the eighteen DVDs from the table were all identical, but the DVD found inside the player was different. The ones transferred by Tech Support were burned onto blank Hewlett-Packard DVDs, and they all came inside these white plastic jewel cases, you see?"

Melanie nodded.

"The one from inside the DVD player was burned onto a Sony DVD rather than Hewlett-Packard. Also, from what I can tell, there wasn't any jewel case seized to go with it."

"Officer Nuñez told me she couldn't find one at the scene. She thought that was odd."

"It is odd. Especially since Brenda Gould appears to have been careful to keep the others in their original cases. For us, the effect of that is, no label to tell us where the DVD in the player came from. All we know is that it's different."

"Can you play it now?"

"Certainly."

Gary removed the DVD from the evidence envelope, holding it gingerly between gloved fingers, and fed it into the drive. An old-fashioned date readout popped up on the screen, glowing luminous green against a black background. It read *July 28, 1986 21:49.*

"Oh my God," Melanie said, clutching Gary's arm. "July twenty-eighth, 1986."

He clicked his mouse to pause the image. "Presumably, that's when the original video was recorded."

"That's the date of Charity Bishop's death."

"Who's Charity Bishop?" Gary asked.

"A girl who died at Brenda Gould's house in Sagaponack. Gary, play the film."

"Died how?"

"She was found floating naked in the swimming pool. She had water in her lungs and a contusion on the back of her head. But the evidence was inconclusive, and no charges were ever filed. Play it, come on."

Gary clicked again, and the recording continued to play. It showed a grainy image of a brick patio adjoining a large swimming pool. The pool was lit from within and glowed aqua blue in the dim light.

Spotlights mounted on the shingle-style house created stark stripes of light and darkness on the patio. The film had been shot without the benefit of lighting, and it faded out to gray wherever the spotlights from the house didn't reach. In the background, voices could be heard arguing, but no people were yet visible on the screen.

"Turn up the volume," Melanie said.

Even with the volume louder, the sound was still muddy—the words unintelligible, only the hysteria in the voices clear. Two women moved into view, and from the way the lens focused on them, it was obvious that the cameraman had been waiting for exactly this moment.

*"Let me get dressed, you crazy bitch!"*

The young woman backed toward the camera, hunching over like she was trying to cover herself. Blond hair cascaded down her back, leaving her naked butt and thighs exposed.

"That's Charity Bishop," Melanie said, breathless, her eyes glued to the screen.

Charity turned sideways, bringing the other woman into clear focus. Older, darker, smaller. It was Brenda Gould all right, and she was brandishing some sort of club, threatening Charity with it.

"What's that in her hand? A golf club?" Melanie asked.

"Or a polo mallet," Gary said. "That's Brenda Gould, right?"

"Yes."

*"What were you doing in his bed?"* Brenda shrieked.

*"I was taking a nap. He's not even home. For Chrissakes, put that thing down."* Charity was slurring her words. She sounded drunk, or drugged. Melanie remembered that the autopsy report had shown a high blood alcohol level.

*"You're fucking him, aren't you?"*

*"You're really starting to piss me off, Brenda!"*

*"I know you are. Philippe told me he saw you together."*

Charity lunged for the mallet, but her reflexes were off. Brenda was faster and more coordinated, and brought the mallet down on Charity's outstretched hand with perfect aim.

*"Aagh! You hurt me!"*

Charity charged at Brenda, but she was unsteady on her feet. She tripped and pitched forward face-first into the grass bordering the brick patio. Brenda raised the mallet so fast that it whizzed by in a blur, making a dull squashing sound when it connected with the back of Charity's head.

Brenda stood there breathing hard. Whoever was holding the camera chose not to reveal himself and made no attempt to help the unconscious girl. After a moment Brenda walked over to the edge of the pool and dipped the head of the mallet in, swishing it around, then lifted it out and wiped it off in the grass.

"Who's the creep with the camera?" Gary asked. "He's not doing anything about this! He's *filming* it."

Brenda was once again standing beside Charity's inert form. She leaned over, grabbed her by the arms, and dragged her across the brick patio toward the pool. When she got to the edge, Brenda stopped for a second to catch her breath, then planted a foot firmly on Charity's nude backside and gave a spirited push. The body hit the water with a splash. Melanie and Gary both gasped.

"Did you see that?" Gary said.

"I can't believe it. Brenda Gould murdered that girl in cold blood. She looked like she was sober when she did it, too."

"What I want to know is who made this film? Who would stand by and watch somebody get murdered and do nothing to stop it? It's sickening." Gary paused. "I'm right, aren't I? He didn't call the police?"

"No. The body was discovered by the pool man the next morning."

"Then whoever made the film is an accessory to murder. Do you think it was Brenda's husband?"

"No, I think it was her stepson, Philippe, Lester's son. He spent summers at that house, so he had the access. And he was the one with the motivation. Charity was his girlfriend, and she betrayed him by sleeping with his father. He was every bit as enraged as Brenda was."

"He let her be killed? And he never went to the police?"

"This film was never turned over to any authority, as far as I know."

"How did it get into Brenda's DVD player?"

"Good question. Let's assume Philippe kept the tape and wanted to use it as leverage. But maybe he wasn't savvy enough to figure out how to do that on his own, so he reached out for help, to somebody who he knew was corrupt. Evan Diamond. We have evidence that twenty years later, Evan Diamond was blackmailing Lester Poe with damaging evidence concerning Charity Bishop's murder. This tape was the smoking gun. Diamond got it from Philippe. Philippe and Diamond were working together. At first, they were trying to get money from Lester. But after Lester died, they went after Brenda instead. They played the tape to pressure her, but something went wrong. Maybe she wouldn't go along with it. Maybe she threatened to call the police. I know the autopsy concluded that Brenda died from an accidental overdose, but, Gary, I don't believe that. Officer Nuñez told me that when she arrived at the apartment, Diamond and Philippe Poe were waiting for the police together. I think they murdered Brenda Gould."

# 56

Jennifer Lamont was curled up in the corner of the sofa with the cat on her lap, watching a bunch of strangers install devices in her closets and wire things to her telephone. She was grateful to the cat for sticking close by her. The warm vibration of his body against her stomach was her only comfort. Snickers was not a sociable animal and didn't normally like being held. He obviously sensed Jennifer's pain today. Pain wasn't the word—despondency. When she wasn't watching the DEA poke around in her private possessions, Jennifer was busy reviewing the tools she had on hand for killing herself.

On the kitchen counter, a brand-new set of Henckels chef's knives gleamed in the knife block. She'd bought them with the first paycheck from her clerkship. She could just cry, thinking of the hope she'd felt when she'd moved into this place. Her dreams seemed idiotic now, the prattlings of a stupid girl. She pitied her younger self, overreaching by such a wide margin, imagining that she might find a boyfriend, might watch the Food Network and learn how to cook for him. Of course the boyfriend never materialized. Who did she think she was—somebody other than her pathetic loser self? Cook-

ing for one person had been a waste. She ate cereal instead, and used
the knives for slicing bananas. All for the best, it turned out. They
waited in the knife block now, razor sharp and ready to slit her wrists.
What would it feel like, that first slice? Crisp and fresh, like snapping
a celery stalk? Mushy? Tougher and more sinewy? Would she be able
to make the cut, or would she chicken out, squeamish little coward
that she was? Hanging might be easier. One leap into the void, and
the ordeal would be over. Jennifer thought she could handle that.
These DEA guys were leaving a lot of cables around. Maybe she
could use one of them to do the job. Besides, she liked the drama of
the discovery. The girl swinging slowly, her feet dangling just inches
off the ground, her skin pale and tinged with blue. Tragic. She wondered who would find her body.

Tommy Yee came over to her.

"You holding up okay? Need something to eat?" he asked.

"No thanks. I'm not hungry."

She stared at him, trying to read what he was like inside. He'd
treated her so much nicer since she'd made that phone call to Evan.
He must be the type of man who believed in a black-and-white world.
Jennifer was his enemy or else she was his ally; nothing in between.
When she'd been feeding information to Evan, she was a worm, deserving to get squashed. If she'd been alone with Tommy Yee then, no
telling what he might have done. Rape, torture, humiliation—he'd
hated her enough to be capable of anything. She'd felt the hot blast
of that hatred when he'd grabbed her in the library. There weren't any
borders to it; it was infinite like the universe. But now everything
was different. This morning was another lifetime: now Jennifer was
Tommy's friend, his ally. More than that, she was his informant, and
he would care for her tenderly. Jennifer didn't find that strange at all.
She understood a code like that.

"You sure you're okay?" Tommy asked. "Your eyes look glazed
over."

"It's been a difficult morning."

"It has. That's why you need to keep your strength up. You have to stay focused. Diamond might actually show up, you know. If he does, it's your job to match wits with him, to get him to say stuff on tape. You have to be sharp."

Snickers meowed and leaped from Jennifer's lap.

"Can I ask you something?" she said to Tommy.

"Of course."

"Who'll take my cat if I die?"

He put his hand on her knee and squeezed. There was nothing lascivious in the gesture. In fact, Jennifer found it so reassuring and so comforting that she faltered for a second in her determination to commit suicide. She wondered whether Tommy Yee had a girlfriend. He seemed old and worn-out. Maybe he needed somebody young. Maybe he needed Jennifer enough that he'd be willing to overlook her shameful past.

"Don't worry, kiddo. I've been doing this a long time. I won't let anything happen to you," he said.

It wasn't dying in the cross fire that Jennifer worried about. Chances were, she wouldn't become Tommy Yee's girlfriend. She wouldn't find any miraculous relief from her problems. She'd get disbarred, face jail, and probably wind up killing herself.

"Just in case," she persisted. "Would you maybe take him? He's very easy. He cleans himself, and he doesn't need to go out. The cat food is less than ten dollars a week, even with a premium brand."

Tommy laughed. "Relax. Everything will be fine."

"But—"

"Yes, all right. If you die, I'll take your cat."

"Thank you."

The telephone rang.

"Are you expecting a call?" Tommy asked.

"No."

"Go ahead, answer it. We've got the equipment set up."

Jennifer reached for the telephone on the side table. Tommy crossed the room in two steps and put on his headset, nodding at her to pick up.

"Hello?"

"Jennifer?"

It was him.

"Evan."

"What are you doing at home? I called the office, and they said you'd left."

"I didn't feel well."

"Are you sick?"

"Weren't you listening before? Susan knows what we did. I'm going to lose my job. I'm so upset, I had to come home. Will you please just come here so we can talk about it?"

"Are you alone?"

Tommy nodded vigorously.

"Of course I'm alone," Jennifer said.

"Call you back," Diamond said, and hung up.

Tommy peeled off the headphones. "What was that?"

Jennifer shrugged. She was listless; a simple gesture felt like an effort.

"You know what I think it was?" Tommy said. "He was checking to see if you were alone. We need to get set up for a visitor."

"What kind of visitor?"

But Tommy had already started rallying the other agents, snapping out orders, gathering up equipment. The entire apartment was in motion—people throwing stuff in boxes, picking up debris, removing any sign that they'd been there. Within minutes, the other three agents had disappeared out the back. Jennifer's apartment had a door that opened out to the back garden, underneath the big wooden deck that her landlady used for barbecues in the nice weather. The garden was surrounded by a high wall that had a door of its own onto an alley where the trash cans were kept. The surveillance van was parked just beyond that alley. The other agents would monitor the video feeds from there and move in for the takedown when Tommy gave the arrest signal.

Tommy tested the back door to make sure it was unlocked so they'd be able to come in without alerting Diamond.

"What about you?" Jennifer asked. "Will you stay?"

"I'll be in the closet in your bedroom the whole time. You won't be alone. Do your best to draw him out, but if it doesn't work, or if you fear for your safety, don't take any chances. Holler, and I'll come running."

# 57

The midtown restaurant had recently received a third star from Michelin and was normally impossible to get into, but Evan Diamond had called ahead. He'd been tipping the maître d' for years with a heavy hand, but that wasn't what got him the primo table, one of the nice round ones along the windows that faced onto Fifty-first Street. All he had to do was mention Atari's name. Goddamn thug could get any table he wanted in any restaurant in the entire goddamn city. But what was he thinking—Atari was his friend now, his meal ticket.

The paparazzi were three deep outside when Alexei pulled the Mercedes up to the curb.

"Crap, look at this," Diamond said. "He expects Bo to walk into this shit? Bo's gonna turn around and run in the opposite direction."

As usual, Alexei said nothing, and only looked at him steadily in the rearview mirror.

"You have everything you need?" Diamond asked.

An inclining of the head, barely a nod.

"Just make sure it's permanent. A lot of people are gonna come looking for her. She needs to stay gone."

"Will not be problem," Alexei said. His voice, on the rare occasions when he spoke, was low and hoarse, rusty from lack of use.

"No?" Evan asked.

"She is bent. Cops know this. They are happier when she is dead because a problem disappears."

"Very astute analysis. I hope you're right. You'll remember to park this car where we agreed and use that one Bo got us. It's waiting for you in Brooklyn where I showed you on the map."

"Of course," Alexei said, annoyed.

Diamond looked in the rearview mirror and straightened his tie. Time for the close-up. Alexei was efficient and experienced and didn't want any instruction beyond what he'd already been given. He was also somebody who could be trusted to keep his mouth shut, as Diamond well knew. This wouldn't be the first time he'd entrusted Alexei with this type of sensitive task.

Diamond nodded crisply at Alexei as he pushed open the car door. Outside, he gave a jaunty wave to the paparazzi, relishing the sizzle and pop of the cameras as he plowed toward the door of the restaurant. With a crowd like this lingering, Atari must already be inside. Reporters shouted questions at him, but all the words ran together into a roar. Diamond was anxious about keeping Atari waiting. Their truce was fragile; he understood that, and the thug was used to star treatment. No sense in screwing up over a matter of formalities.

"We're feeling strong," he shouted, clasping his hands together in a victory sign. He didn't intend to stop for long enough to give a statement, but a mousy woman with glasses got right up in his face.

"Mr. Diamond, any truth to the allegation that Atari Briggs had a DEA agent killed to stymie the case against him?"

He should have ignored her. That would have been the smarter thing to do. But the question got under his skin, and something smug in her expression set him off. Instead of backing away or going around her, he grabbed her by the front of her shirt. The shocked look on her face egged him on.

"You people just make this shit up, don't you? With no concern for the consequences."

"I'm not making it up. Let me go!"

The cameras were clicking all around. Diamond was dying to punch the self-righteous bitch in the face, but that would have consequences, whereas what'd he'd done so far would not. He released her, turning toward the cameras, trying to rearrange his face into a normal expression so he didn't come across as a raving lunatic.

"This is what I'm talking about, the kind of vicious mudslinging that Atari Briggs has had to put up with since the government decided it was gonna string him up and make an example of him. What DEA agent? What killing? We never heard a word about this, and suddenly Atari is a cop killer? You people ought to be more careful about slurping up the filth the government puts in your bowls every morning. They plant a story and you think that gives you the right to ask the question. We deny it, but you slap a headline on it and call it journalism anyway. The reputation of an honorable man, an artist, a fine human being, is dragged through the mud, and meanwhile everybody throws up their hands and says, 'Who, me? It's not my fault.' Wise up, people, you're being used. If you're not part of the solution, you're part of the problem."

He turned and marched into the restaurant, feeling pleased with himself over that pithy little diatribe. He wasn't surprised that the story about the murdered agent was starting to circulate, although he wasn't thrilled about it, either. He'd expected it, and he'd take it in stride. A visit from the FBI would be more troubling, but if that happened, he'd take that in stride, too. His ducks were in a row, he was prepared, he was confident. He hadn't been anywhere near that trailer in the wasteland and neither had Atari. Just like they weren't anywhere near Carroll Gardens tonight. And if Alexei Grinkov had been, or was, well, Alexei Grinkov was a figment. Alexei Grinkov did not exist, not on paper anyway.

His gaze passed over Atari's bodyguards sitting at the bar, but his brain registered them.

At the table, the client was hardly suffering in solitude. The woman fawning on him was a TV personality with an instantly recognizable face. They were drinking champagne and gazing into each other's eyes. Atari knew how to work his assets, and Diamond admired his willingness to use them. He slid into the seat beside Atari and introduced himself to the woman.

"Yes, we were watching your impromptu press conference through the window," she said. Up close, she was Botoxed all to hell. Amazing what they could do with makeup to keep somebody looking fresh on camera.

"You missed your chance," he joked.

"I was lucky to be in here instead of out there with the riffraff," she said. "Atari just promised me the first interview after the trial, win or lose."

"I'm sure he didn't say that," Diamond exclaimed.

Atari smiled. His teeth gleamed brighter than the pearls around the woman's neck. "You're right. I said win. There is no lose."

"Silly me," the woman said. "Can you forgive me?"

"You're forgiven. But if you excuse me now, I got to consult with my lawyer."

"Thank you, Atari. I'm so excited. You're adorable, and I'm a huge fan. Best of luck with the trial. I'm sending positive thoughts your way."

"Thank you, and thank you as well for the champagne."

She left them alone. An open bottle of Cristal stood in a silver ice bucket beside the table. Diamond signaled the waiter to pour him a glass.

"Where's Bo?" Atari demanded. "I agree to a face-to-face and you keep me waiting?"

"Maybe he got spooked by all the paparazzi. I don't know why you had to do it here."

"Because I like roast monkfish. What the fuck you think? I'm about to go on trial. I need to project some confidence or the press is gonna turn on me."

"Fine, but it may have a price. You really think Bo's gonna run the gauntlet out there?"

"What's the problem? He's off probation. He can consort with whoever he wants. Thought I was doing the man a favor. All these years, I been hearing how he resents my lifestyle. I figure I buy him a nice dinner to seal the truce, and he goes and disrespects me."

"Relax, he'll show."

"A second ago you said he wouldn't."

"Let me borrow your phone. I'll call."

"What, so yours can't be traced? Use your own."

Atari was trying his patience. Diamond had to remind himself how much he was getting out of this gig. Not only the publicity, but all of the connections that Atari brought to the table for Diamond's operation with Bo.

Diamond sighed and pulled out his phone, but just at that moment, Bo walked into the restaurant. The hostess looked nervous at first as she took in his scar and his tattoos, but then she nodded her understanding and led him toward their table. All eyes followed Bo, though in a different way than they had Atari. Atari Briggs looked like a superstar. Kevin Bonner just looked like a criminal.

Atari was standing up, reaching out. Bo tried to get by with a gangland handshake, but Atari grabbed him and pulled him into a bear hug.

"Yo, my brother, it's been too many years." Tears stood out in Atari's famous brown eyes. "Too many misunderstandings. Too much trouble."

Diamond had never seen Bo express emotion, and the man did not break character now. He extricated himself from Atari's embrace, sat down, and looked around the restaurant.

"What the fuck," he said.

"Have some champagne and chill out," Diamond said, filling Bo's glass. "Atari's trying to do a nice thing to celebrate our new partnership before the meeting tonight."

Bo gave Diamond a killing look, one that said he'd just crossed a well-established line.

"What?" Diamond protested. "So I said the word *meeting*, big fucking deal. I didn't say who with. The tables in here are not wired for sound, I promise you."

"The lawyer's right," Atari said. "Relax and enjoy yourself. We'll have a nice meal. We'll do the meet. Then you come back to my hotel with me and I'll hook you up with some Russian girls. We got as many as you want. They all had their teeth fixed, and the passports say they're eighteen, so we ain't got no R. Kelly problems, you feel me?"

Bo had a drink, they ordered some appetizers, and everybody started to unwind. This would be a big step tonight, introducing Atari to the supplier. Once an associate met your supplier, he could go around you. He could cut you out. Time was, Diamond wouldn't have trusted Atari that far, but times could change. Atari wasn't their enemy anymore. Lester's getting whacked had turned into a bonanza, bringing them back together after so many years. God bless the prick who'd done it, whoever he was. Diamond was amazed at how easily Atari had come back to the fold, but catch a man at a vulnerable moment, solve his problems for him, and naturally he was going to be grateful. Atari was ready to put his celebrity at their disposal. A worldwide narcotics operation with the purest product, backed by that kind of glamour, protected by the umbrella of Atari's fame. Every cartel in the world would come calling, begging for a piece of the action. The money would come rolling in, and Evan Diamond would be as rich as he'd dreamed.

It felt good, having the old team back together like this. Diamond looked at his watch and saw that Alexei would be in Brooklyn by now, which kicked his mood up yet another notch. As soon as that unpleasant little business was settled, everything would be going his way.

# 58

It was just beginning to get dark when Melanie exited the Carroll Street subway station on her way to Jennifer Lamont's apartment. She'd gotten a call summoning her back from the Medical Examiner's Office because Evan Diamond had made contact with Jennifer by telephone. It was beginning to look like the savvy lawyer had fallen for their ploy, and actually planned to rendezvous with Jennifer tonight. It was twenty to seven already. Melanie planned to give the girl a final pep talk before Diamond arrived, then cram into the surveillance van with the agents. Participating in undercover operations was not in her job description, but this was an unusual situation, requiring skills no DEA agent could provide. Their normal cooperator was a hardened gangsta from Bushwick or a slick killer from Cali who merely needed to be told where to stand and what to say, not a fragile and barely functional Assistant U.S. Attorney who needed her hand held. Giving Jennifer emotional support could end up making the difference between success and failure on this mission.

Melanie turned on to Jennifer's block. The streetlights were coming on, and the perfume of simmering tomato sauce floated out toward Melanie from somebody's kitchen. She'd bet that the people on this block knew their neighbors. The idea of moving to Brooklyn was really beginning to grow on her. Melanie's building in Manhattan was mostly singles and professionals with few families. She'd love to have neighbors with kids who would invite her and Maya over for dinner. The air smelled fresh here, and it almost felt like the country compared to where she lived. Maybe that was the answer—find a place with a little backyard, and investigate preschools for Maya. A change of scene would do them good, and this was a lot less drastic than moving to Miami.

She saw Jennifer's apartment up ahead and slowed her pace. The street was deserted. It was about fifteen minutes before Diamond was expected to arrive, and she'd agreed with Tommy Yee that she'd make contact to check whether there'd been any unexpected developments before she approached the apartment. He'd told her to call his Nextel. If he answered and gave her an all clear, she'd go in. If not, she was to go around the back and wait in the surveillance van.

Melanie was scrolling through her directory looking for Tommy's number when she felt something hard poke her in the back. She didn't have to turn around to understand that there was a man standing behind her, and she didn't need to see the object to know that it was a gun.

"I recognize you. You are prosecutor," he said quietly.

He spoke with a heavy Russian accent, and from the direction of the sound, she could tell that he was tall. Somehow the image of the redheaded man from the surveillance photo, the one with the battered face, popped into her head.

"My wallet is in the bag. Please, just take it and don't hurt me."

"Why you are here? You visit your friend, no?"

He had to be the man from the picture. There was no other explanation. He worked for Diamond. He'd murdered Papo. And now he'd come for Jennifer.

He dug the gun in harder. It took Melanie's breath away.

"Answer me or I kill you."

She thought about lying, but it was no use. He knew who she was.

"Yes, I'm visiting a friend who lives on this block," she said.

"Take me to her apartment. Now."

# 59

The meet, which was held in a warehouse in Greenpoint that belonged to a client of Diamond's, went better than he could have hoped. The connect was no peasant. He was a worldly and sophisticated Pakistani who'd spent years cultivating relationships with the warlords in Afghanistan who controlled the poppy fields. He'd been educated in California and in Western Europe, which gave him a taste for American music and a desire to hang with the beautiful people. Meeting Atari was a huge kick for him, and pretty soon they had a commitment to up the weekly shipment by such a significant amount that Diamond and Bo were already figuring on hiring ten new shift managers and fifty street pitchers in Vegas alone. Beyond that, they'd reach out to kingpins in other cities who were interested in taking product on consignment.

At one point, when the connect and some of his people were working out shipping arrangements with Bo, Diamond leaned over and whispered in Atari's ear.

"I'm gonna invite him back to the hotel to party with the Russian girls."

"No, don't."

"Why not?"

"Because I don't feel like it."

"Normally in a business deal you offer hospitality like that."

"I just stroked the shit out of this motherfucker like you asked, and I don't want to see his face no more. If he needs to get laid, let him look in the phone book."

Diamond reflected that it was just as well if Atari and the connect didn't become bosom friends.

"Suit yourself," he said.

After the meet, Diamond gave Bo a lift in the Mercedes, and Atari and his bodyguards went in Atari's Bentley. They were planning to meet back at the hotel.

"You're gonna love this place, and the girls Atari has are prime merchandise," Diamond said.

Bo stared out at the traffic, looking sullen and dangerous.

"What's your problem?" Diamond asked.

He shrugged. "This shit don't feel right to me. The beef Atari got with us is too big to drop."

"The kid is all about the money, Bo. That's why he's trucing with us, because he smells the green. Besides, his lawyer got killed, and I stepped in to help him out. I made the lead witness and the case agent go away. The government's got to fold now, you watch. Atari is grateful to me, and he's demonstrating his gratitude. Lester's death brought us together."

"What do you know about that?"

"What, about Lester's murder?" Diamond glanced at Bo, who nodded. "Not much, but the man had a lot of enemies. He had his fingers in a lot of pies. I did ask Atari if he whacked Lester, if that's what you're thinking."

"Yeah. What'd he say?"

"He said no. I mean, obviously he wasn't gonna say yes."

"Obviously."

The traffic on the BQE was heavy tonight. Diamond concentrated on driving for a few minutes.

"I did think about it," he said eventually. "The thought crossed my mind briefly. But then I said to myself, Why would Atari whack his own lawyer?"

"To get to you."

"But why go through that? Why not just call me up and hire me? I'm in the yellow pages."

"That would be too obvious. If he came at you straight, he'd raise you up, wouldn't he?"

Diamond was silent again, thinking.

"Bo, I hear you, and I appreciate your sense of caution, but it's unwarranted in this situation. What happened between us and Atari was fifteen years ago. And okay, I understand that he vowed revenge, and he wrote some stupid tune about how he's gonna get me, but look at how much he has to lose now. All that money and all that fame. Who'd give that up over some ancient beef?"

"It ain't just any beef. Fro Joe was a brother to him. I think he's been waiting to set us up good, till he feels like he can get away with it. And there's something else, too, something that's been bothering me."

"What's that?"

"Normally I keep my ear to the ground, but being out in Vegas, information can take some time to reach me. I didn't hear this until yesterday, or else I would've been more on top of the situation."

"Yeah, what?"

"I had a shorty down in Leavenworth. We was cell mates for about a year or so. A Muslim brother from Detroit. Talented with weapons, especially explosives."

Diamond looked over with greater interest now. "Yeah?"

"He knew I'd been with Atari back in the day. He used to listen to the man's music all the time. Well, my shorty got out before me, and when we was going our separate ways, he asked me for an introduction. He had this crazy idea like he'd get a job working security for Atari and score mad benjamins and pussy. I said, look, Atari and me ain't exactly on good terms, but maybe I can figure a way to hook you with him. I sent him to Ninth Floor Pete in the Houses, with instructions not to mention that the connection came through me, because then Atari wouldn't take the introduction."

"Ninth Floor Pete. That *would* get him to Atari."

"They found the shorty's body upstate two days after your lawyer got blown up, bullet in the back of his head. He was the one who made the bomb."

# 60

Diamond would normally valet-park the Mercedes and give the attendant an extra fifty along with the car keys to make sure it came
back without so much as a speck of dust on it. But that routine
wouldn't be smart right now. They needed to avoid attracting attention, for the simple reason that they didn't know what would happen
once they went upstairs.

Diamond took Bo through a side entrance so they could get to
the elevator without walking through the main part of the lobby.

"You're wrong about this, I'm telling you," Diamond said as they
waited for the elevator to come.

"Let's hope so. I don't want to screw up this gig any more than
you do. But I won't be stupid, either."

"We agree that you're not planning to start a war for no reason,
right? I want no part of that."

"I ain't no pussy. I ain't giving up my weapons to his boys without
a fight, that's for sure."

A fortyish woman in a Chanel suit had come up behind them.

She heard that remark, took one look at Bo, and decided she didn't need to use the elevator right then.

The doors slid open and Diamond and Bo got on.

"See what you did?" Diamond said. "Now we've been noticed."

"What does it matter? If this is all in my imagination, then nothing's gonna happen, who gives a shit who saw us?"

"I'm just saying, why force a confrontation? That's not how I work. I'm about brains, not muscle. If I sense hostility, I walk away calmly and figure out how to squash the enemy at my leisure. That way, I keep my nose clean and stay out of jail. You could take a lesson from me there, Bo."

"Fine words, son, but they don't mean shit if somebody's gunning for you. If Atari wants us dead, I'll know as soon as I walk in the room, and when he makes his move, I'll take him out first. Nobody gets the jump on me. You think you can play it any other way, you're too stupid for me to deal with. Either you follow my lead, or you walk away now."

The doors opened on Atari's floor. The bodyguards were not in the hallway as Diamond was expecting. Instead, there was a cute little maid there, a Spanish girl, pushing a big laundry cart. Diamond smiled at her. She looked away in alarm, abandoning the laundry cart by the entrance to Atari's suite and taking off down the service staircase.

Bo was already knocking on the door.

"See?" Diamond said. "His boys aren't even here to take our guns."

"Yeah, where are they, then?"

Diamond didn't answer.

"You coming?" Bo demanded as the door opened.

Diamond stepped up behind Bo. Bo held his hands loose at his sides like some gunslinger from the Wild West, but it was just Atari alone, wearing a silk bathrobe.

"Hey, here you are. Right on time," Atari said, backing into the room. "I sent my muscle downstairs to bring up some of the girls. They'll be back any minute."

They stepped inside, and Atari closed the door. Diamond tried to catch Bo's eye to say, *"See?"* but Bo was concentrating all his attention on Atari, who'd moved past them into the room. Atari stood in front of the sleek leather sofa, smiling his celebrated smile, his hand moving toward the waistband of his pajamas. Beyond him, the two bodyguards sprang up from their hiding places behind the tall back of the sofa. The extra-long silhouettes of their guns told Diamond they'd been fitted with silencers.

Diamond had had a concealed carry for twenty years, and he practiced every weekend at the range, but he'd never been in a gunfight. For a split second everything came to a dead halt as he stared down the barrels of three big guns, until the first pops from the silencers spurred him to action. He bent down, going for his ankle holster, and the wall behind him exploded into a million fragments. He looked up and saw Atari's chest erupt into a volcano of blood. The top flew off one of the bodyguard's heads. The other took a bullet in the left arm but got off a round at Diamond with the right. Diamond felt his knees buckle before he'd made the conscious decision to drop and roll. On the way down, everything was in slow motion. *Drop and roll, drop and roll.* It was a drumbeat in his head, and he was pleased with himself for having such quick reflexes. It wasn't until he saw the bright red stain spreading on his snowy shirtfront that he understood he'd been hit.

# 61

Melanie reached out and pushed the doorbell. The man, who she'd decided was definitely the driver Alexei, was standing off to the side so Jennifer wouldn't see him through the peephole. Melanie's mind was blank with fear. She was terrified that the driver would decide to shoot them on the spot, right in the entry hall. That he'd pull out his gun, put it to their temples, and blow them away one after the other, *boom-boom*. If that was his plan, all the high-tech surveillance equipment in the world wouldn't save them, and Steve would be raising their beautiful little girl alone. Or else with Kate, or even with somebody Melanie had never met. She didn't want to die. She didn't want any other woman raising her daughter.

A darkening at the peephole revealed that Jennifer was behind the door.

"Melanie, go away," Jennifer said.

*Shit.*

"Hi, Jen," Melanie said in a perkier tone than she normally used. "I heard you were sick today, so I thought I'd come by on my way home and see if you needed anything."

*"What?"*

"What is going on?" the driver demanded in an urgent whisper.

"She's sick. She says she doesn't want any visitors," Melanie said, loudly enough that Jennifer would be sure to hear and alert the DEA agents who, Melanie hoped with all her might, were still inside.

The driver was beside her in a second. He pushed her head in front of the peephole with one hand and held his gun to it with the other.

"Open the door right now or I kill your friend," he said to Jennifer.

To Jennifer's credit, she yanked the door open right away. The driver shoved Melanie through and slammed the door shut behind them.

"Both of you, against the wall, turn around!" he yelled.

Melanie turned and faced the wall. The wallpaper was strange—a mustard-yellow toile with a repeat pattern of a squirrel chasing a nut. The driver pulled a roll of electrical tape from his jacket pocket and expertly bound both of their hands behind their backs. The tape pulled on Melanie's skin but she resisted crying out. That could set him off; people like this got pissed off easily. She was amazed that they weren't dead by now. Why hadn't he killed them immediately? After all, the prudent thing to do was to get it over with. Only in that way could he be sure of avoiding complications. He must want something from them.

The driver slapped a strip of tape over Melanie's mouth and kicked her feet out from under her so fast that she didn't have time to react. She came crashing down on her right side, hitting her ear hard against the wood floor. Her grunt of pain emerged guttural and harsh through the tape. For a few seconds the world faded to black. When it came back into focus, he'd dragged Jennifer over, shoved her down on the sofa, and was half kneeling on her stomach with his gun to her head.

"Where is the tape?" he demanded.

Jennifer trembled so hard that her words came out in a stutter. "Wh-what tape?"

He raised his gun overhead as if to strike her with it. "My boss think you were making tape of him when he talk to you on telephone. I want it now!"

"I—I d-don't have any tape!"

He beat her viciously about the head and face with the pistol, up and down three times in quick succession with all his might, and Jennifer screamed hysterically.

"Shut up, bitch, or I shoot now!"

Suddenly men burst out from every direction. Several came crashing through the front door and tripped over Melanie. Somebody's hard shoe caught her in the back and she cried out in pain.

"Get her out of here!" somebody shouted, but nobody took the time to do that, and Melanie huddled on the floor, afraid that she'd be hit if she moved so much as a finger. The air filled up with the reports of pistol shots and the smell of gunpowder. Jennifer screamed on and on. A man yelled in agony. The sounds and smells felt like being in hell.

Then, suddenly, silence fell.

"He's dead?" Tommy Yee's voice asked.

"Yeah."

"Definitely."

"Who else is hit?"

"Spinelli's hit, get an ambulance."

"Shit, is he okay?"

"Yeah, it's just a flesh wound."

"What about Jarrett over there?"

"I'm fine!"

Within seconds, they heard sirens. One of the agents came and sat on the floor beside Melanie, the same kid from Virginia who'd given her a lift to the OCME earlier that afternoon. It felt like years since she'd seen him.

"You okay?" he asked, but she still had tape over her mouth.

"Oops, hold on," he said with a grin, picking at the edge of the tape. "I'll do this quick, like a Band-Aid."

He yanked it off.

"Oww!"

"Sorry, that's got to hurt. You're all right, though?"

Melanie nodded. He took out a Swiss Army knife, cut the tape from her hands, and helped her to her feet.

"Thanks."

Blood gushed from Jennifer's forehead. Tommy Yee came back from the kitchen with a roll of paper towels. He tore off a generous piece and pressed it to her cuts to catch the blood that was pouring into her eyes.

"Head wounds bleed a lot. You're gonna be fine," he said.

The tan sofa was stained deep red, and Jennifer's clothes were soaked, too. The sight and smell of all the blood turned Melanie's stomach. She shifted her eyes away so she wouldn't have to look at the paper towel, which was rapidly turning crimson. Only then did she notice the man's legs protruding from behind the sofa. The pool of blood was widening by the second, and soon it would reach her shoes. She sidestepped it, and in doing so, brought the corpse into full view. She couldn't not look. The man's chest was a pulverized mass of blood and tissue. His eyes were open and staring at the ceiling. Two small, neat bullet holes in his forehead explained the red puddle spreading beneath his head. This was the first time she'd gotten a straight-on look at his face. Red hair and battered features. It was indeed the man from the surveillance photo, and he was definitely dead.

# 62

The nearest emergency room was at Long Island College Hospital in Brooklyn Heights. Melanie caught a ride there with Tommy Yee, arriving in time to wait with Jennifer for what seemed like forever until the triage nurse got around to admitting her. This was Brooklyn, and the nurse gave them to understand that a little pistol-whipping was hardly her most serious problem tonight.

When Jennifer was finally admitted, Melanie was instructed to stay behind in the waiting room. No room inside for visitors, the nurse said. Tommy Yee had been allowed in to pace around while the agents who'd been shot went to surgery, but apparently Tommy's shield was a more persuasive admission ticket than Melanie's creds. Either that or the nurse had just taken a personal dislike to her. Melanie sat down in an uncomfortable plastic chair and contemplated the madness—people bleeding, moaning, screaming in pain, while others read newspapers or made phone calls like nothing unusual was going on. She thought she heard somebody mention Atari Briggs's name but then decided that it had been her imagination.

She was nodding off, her head throbbing, when the sliding-glass doors parted and Mark Sonschein strode in. His somber eyes and grim mouth gave an even more alarming appearance than usual under the harsh fluorescent lights.

"What are you doing here?" Melanie asked.

The answer to the question was so obvious that Mark didn't bother replying.

"How's Jennifer?" he asked instead.

"She was pistol-whipped pretty badly, but no lasting damage. How is she otherwise? Not great."

Mark shook his head. "That girl needs help."

"I know. I can't believe nobody picked that up on that during the application process, especially with her history. We should review our screening process."

"She graduated cum laude from Yale Law School and had a glowing reference from Judge Fox. What were we supposed to do, not hire her because she was abused as a child? That hardly seems fair."

"You're right. Well, maybe she can get psychiatric care as part of her sentence."

"There won't be any sentence."

Melanie looked at him in astonishment.

"I've made an executive decision not to prosecute," Mark said. "There's nobody left for her to cooperate against with the driver and Diamond both dead and—"

"Diamond's dead?"

"Yes, didn't Tommy tell you?"

"No, he's been inside for over an hour. What happened?"

"Oh, it's bigger than that. Did you know the Bureau had Kevin Bonner under surveillance?"

"Yes. But in Las Vegas, right?"

"Uh-uh, here. He landed at LaGuardia last night. FBI and DEA did a joint operation. They fielded big teams and had an eyeball on him every step of the way. Around six-thirty this evening, Bonner met up with Diamond and Atari Briggs. They had dinner in an expensive restaurant, then went to a meeting at a warehouse in Greenpoint with a major Pakistani heroin supplier. When the meeting ended, they split up. DEA nabbed the supplier, and he gave them all the details about the drug deal. Diamond and Bonner eventually met back up with Atari at his hotel in Soho."

Mark stopped.

"And?" Melanie demanded.

"You're not gonna believe this."

She smacked him on the arm. "Tell me."

"There was a shoot-out. Diamond's dead. Atari Briggs is dead, too, and one of his bodyguards. Bonner and another bodyguard are in custody."

"*Atari's* dead? You're right, I don't believe it. You know what this means, don't you?" she asked.

"Yes. After all that work, you don't get to try your big case."

"We were gonna lose, anyway."

"Look on the bright side. This protects your win–loss record. Susan is very relieved."

"So, what happened? I mean, they're meeting about some big drug deal, everything is hunky-dory, and then—?"

"The Bureau believes it was an ambush," Mark said. "Apparently one of the bodyguards asked a hotel maid to find him a pushcart, you know, like they use for laundry? He gave her a hundred bucks to bring it to Atari's room and then disappear."

"A laundry cart? Why?"

"To remove the bodies. Atari had it all planned, to get back at Diamond and Bonner for trying to hit him years ago. It just didn't play out quite like he hoped."

"Amazing." Melanie shook her head.

"Oh, one other thing."

"Yes?"

"I was over at the hotel. I took a look at the crime scene. We have jurisdiction over these murders if you want to work on them. Anyway, your friend Dan O'Reilly was there."

"Is he all right?"

"Fine. He just asked that you call him, that's all."

# 63

Mark intended to wait for Jennifer Lamont to be released and give her the official news that she wouldn't be prosecuted. Not much would happen to Jennifer, in fact. Apparently, after consulting with Main Justice, Mark had decided that the best course was to allow her to resign voluntarily and tell prospective employers that she'd had difficulty dealing with stress on the job. She wouldn't even be referred for disciplinary proceedings with the state bar. If Melanie hadn't known the girl, she would have viewed this as a wrist slap bordering on unacceptable whitewash. But under the circumstances, she understood. She certainly hoped Jennifer would appreciate the narrow escape and benefit from it, though she was cynical enough these days to fear otherwise.

Philippe Poe would be dealt with more harshly. Melanie had detailed to Mark everything she'd learned about Philippe's involvement in blackmailing and murdering his stepmother. They'd contacted the DA's Office, and a warrant was being drawn up for Philippe's arrest. The NYPD would execute it as soon as the ink was dry in order to be certain he didn't flee the country.

Released from the need to wait for Jennifer, Melanie was free to go. Maybe it was the fact that she'd come close to death that night, or that others had come even closer and she'd gotten a good look at the results. But Melanie found that she couldn't ignore Dan's message, and before she knew it, she was on the phone with him, agreeing to meet him for a drink at a bar in Soho not far from the hotel where Atari Briggs and Evan Diamond had died.

Melanie got there first, and ended up waiting at a table in the corner sipping a scotch and soda—not her usual, but Chardonnay wasn't enough to get the things she'd seen that day out of her head. She saw Dan before he saw her, and the sight of him took her breath away. The height, the sheer massive power of the man. And that face, those eyes, that hair. Whatever happened in her life from now on, she wasn't likely to be with a man as gorgeous as him again.

He saw her and came right over, not stopping to order a drink.

"Sorry I'm late," he said, sliding into the chair across from her.

"It's okay. Just one drink, though."

"That's all I'm asking. I heard what happened tonight. Are you okay?"

"I'll make it. But this stuff with people dying, it's getting a little old."

He grinned—that high-wattage, movie-star smile of his, crinkling up the corners of his blue eyes.

"Maybe we should quit and move to a tropical island somewhere," he said. "Open up a little burger shack on the beach. Not to brag, but I'm an ace at flipping burgers."

She shook her head. "It's hard to hear you say things like that. There is no 'we' now."

"Well." Dan looked down at his hands, then up at her again, and she could tell that it cost him an effort to have to ask. "I was hoping you'd give me another chance. That's the real reason I wanted to see you tonight. To ask you for that."

"I'm sorry. I can't do that. I need to be by myself. I need it to be just me and Maya for a while. I need to sort things out."

"For how long?"

But Melanie merely shook her head. She stood up and laid some money on the table. She wouldn't let him pay for her drink. But Dan grabbed her hand, and the feel of his powerful fingers on hers brought back memories that seemed to linger somewhere under her skin.

"How long?" he asked again.

"I don't know. I wish I could tell you. Maybe a long time. It's not like I'm planning to be with anybody else, but I can't be with you right now, either. So don't wait."

He got to his feet, towering over her, and took her face gently in his two hands.

"You know me. You can tell me not to wait, but I'll wait anyway. I'm like a dog that way. Be safe getting home, okay?"

And he leaned down and brushed his lips across her forehead.